Broken DREAMS

BOOK TWO IN THE BROKEN SERIES

NEW YORK TIMES BESTSELLING AUTHOR

Kelly Elliott

Cover Designer: Angie Fields, i love it design studio

Editor and Interior Designer: Jovana Shirley, Unforeseen Editing, www.unforeseenediting.com

Photography by Jay Fuertez

Visit my website at http://www.kellyelliottauthor.com

ISBN-13: 978-0-9913096-5-8

Other books by Kelly Elliott

Wanted Series

WANTED

Saved

faithful

Believe
a novella

Cherished

Full-length novels in the WANTED series
are also available in audio.

Broken Series

BROKEN

Broken DREAMS

DEDICATION

This book is dedicated to
my amazing husband, Darrin,
and my beautiful daughter, Lauren.
Thank you so much for your support.

CONTENTS

High School: Sophomore Year

"He is so dreamy. God, Court, I can't believe he asked you!"

I rolled my eyes as my best friend, Whitley, jumped up and down with excitement. I knew I should have waited until later and told her on the phone.

"Jesus, Squeak, keep it down. I don't want the whole world knowing," I said in a hushed voice as I pulled her into the girls' restroom.

"Lollipop, Noah Wylie just asked you to the prom. *The prom!* Your brother's best friend, who you have lusted over for the last…how many years? The prom!" she yelled out as she began jumping up and down again.

I couldn't help but giggle. It was true. I'd been lusting after him ever since I could remember. I loved that dark hair of his and those deep green eyes that felt like they pierced my soul. He'd finally noticed me, and my brother was going to freak when he found out, which made this all the sweeter.

"Court, what did you say?" Whitley asked as she clapped her hands.

I shrugged my shoulders. "I told him I'd think about it."

"What?" Whit yelled out.

I lost it, laughing, from the expression on her face. "I'm totally kidding, Squeak. I said yes, but I told him if he thought he was going to be getting a piece of ass, he had another thing coming."

Whitley's mouth dropped open, and she leaned against the sink, shaking her head. "Court, he would never expect you to sleep with him. I mean, my God, he's your brother's best friend, and Tyler would kill him."

I shrugged my shoulders again. "I hope so. When I said it, I was kidding, but he got a funny look in his eyes. It did something weird to my stomach, like…I think I got turned-on by it."

"Shit, Court. You wouldn't…sleep with him, would you?" Whitley asked with wide eyes.

I gave her a wicked smile. "He's so perfect, Whitley, and he's everything I've ever dreamed of, but I don't think I could do that. I'm only sixteen, and he's almost eighteen and getting ready to leave for college. I want my perfect moment, ya know? I want the whole thing with Prince Charming sweeping me off my feet. I want the romance. I am wondering though why he asked me to prom. I mean, he's never given me a second glance, and he's always treated me like…well, like I'm his best friend's little sister."

Whitley gave me a big smile. "Maybe he's liked you this whole time, and he is just now getting the nerve to ask you out."

I smiled back. "Maybe! I hope so. Anyway, we need to go shopping for a dress this weekend. I know we have a few more months before the prom, but a girl can never start looking too early for a dress!"

Whit started with the whole damn jumping thing again. "Yes! Oh, this is going to be so much fun! It's your first real date and with the guy you have dreamed of going out with. It couldn't be any more perfect, Lollipop!"

I giggled as we made our way out of the restroom. "I know. And his parents are out of town this weekend, so I get to see him at my house for four whole days!"

We headed out to the parking lot to go to Whit's house. As we both laughed and talked about the prom on the way to my car, I glanced over toward my brother's Jeep. Noah was leaning against it, looking sexy as hell. He smiled at me, and I smiled back.

Yep, this is going to be perfect. My Prince Charming finally noticed me.

Twelve Hours Later

I heard my bedroom door open and then quietly shut. I opened my eyes and saw it was almost three thirty in the morning. I turned around to see Noah standing over my bed, looking down at me. I smiled, but he didn't smile back.

I sat up and tilted my head. "Noah? Is everything okay?"

"Do you know how many times I've come in here and watched you sleep, Courtney?"

My heart started pounding. "Um…really? Why?"

He smiled slightly and shook his head. "It's taken everything out of me to wait until you were older."

My stomach dropped, and I couldn't figure out what he was saying. "Noah, I'm confused. What are you talking about?"

He put his finger up to his lips and smiled bigger. "Lie down, Courtney. I've waited long enough."

Oh. My. God. Please…no… "Um…Noah, I think you should probably leave my room. If my dad or brother find you in here, they're gonna—"

The next thing I knew, his hand was covering my mouth, and he was forcing me down. I tried to scream and push his hands away.

He put his lips right next to my ear, and at first, his hot breath calmed me, but then he started talking. "I swear to God, Courtney, if you scream or tell anyone about what we are about to do, I will hurt your brother so badly that he can say good-bye to his football scholarship."

My eyes widened, and I felt the tears building.

"Are you going to make any noise, Courtney?" he asked as he looked me in the eyes.

Those eyes that used to hold me captive now only made me sick to my stomach.

What is he planning on doing to me?

"Courtney, answer me," he whispered as he lifted his hand off my mouth.

I slowly shook my head and said, "I won't make a sound."

He smiled. "Good girl. I've been waiting for you, Courtney. You're going to be mine."

I tried to keep in the sob, but it escaped. "Noah…why? Why are you doing this?"

He slowly started pulling off his boxer shorts, exposing himself to me. I felt like I was going to throw up.

No! No, this is not how my first time is supposed to be! He's supposed to make it special. He's supposed to make me feel like I am his everything.

Oh God, please don't let this happen.

This is not how it happens in my dreams! He is supposed to love me. I'm supposed to love him.

God, please no.

The moment his hands touched me, I jumped and let out a gasp.

He put his hand over my mouth again. "If you can't be quiet, I'm going to have to do something I don't want to do."

I quickly nodded my head, terrified of what he was talking about.

He started pulling up my T-shirt, and he looked my body up and down. When he began sliding off my panties, I grabbed his hands.

"Noah, please…oh God, please don't do this."

"You want this, Courtney. I see how you look at me. You want me just as much as I want you."

I thrashed my head back and forth as I cried, "No! I don't. I don't want this."

"Yes. You. Do."

"No, I don't. Stop! I don't care what you do to my brother. I just want you to stop."

He pulled back and looked at me. "Maybe Sissy wants me."

I threw my hand up to mouth. "No…" I whispered.

Sissy was my fourteen-year-old sister.

"You keep pissing me off, Courtney. Stop pissing me off. If you even think of telling anyone, I'll not only hurt your brother, but your parents might end up in a car accident caused by faulty brakes, and your little sister might get her cherry popped a little early." He began putting on a condom as his eyes locked on to mine.

I felt the tears pouring down my face as I closed my eyes. I totally relaxed my body and tried to just disappear. I needed to be anywhere but where I was.

"That's it, baby. Let me give you what you've been wanting."

As I felt him up against me, I cried harder, but I held my hand over my mouth to muffle out my cries of pain. With each time he pushed himself in, I grabbed the sheets and tried to hold it all in. He just kept moaning and telling me how good it felt.

I just want to disappear. This isn't happening.

Nothing had ever hurt me so badly in my life.

"Does it feel good, baby?"

I squeezed my eyes closed tighter and thought of my favorite book. I began saying my favorite quotes over and over in my head as I tried to block out the nightmare that was happening.

Once he was done, he stood up, took off the condom, and smiled at me. He tossed it in the trash and told me to get rid of it first thing in the morning.

"Soak in a hot bath, Courtney. It will feel better next time, I promise. The first time always hurts."

Next time? Oh God…no. "No! I don't ever want to do that again, Noah…ever!"

He bent down and grabbed my face as he said very slowly, "Yes. You. Will. If I don't get it from you, I'll get it from the next best thing. You remember what I said about what would happen if you told anyone? I mean, anyone, Courtney. This stays our secret."

I slowly nodded my head.

"Say it. *Now.*"

"It's our…it's our…" I was sobbing as I tried to get it out. "It's our secret."

He stood up and smiled at me. "Good girl."

He turned and walked toward my bedroom door. He unlocked the door and gave me one more look before he stepped out and closed it. I quickly got up and ran into my bathroom. I turned on my shower as hot as I could stand, and I stayed in there for at least an hour, trying to wash his scent away.

I sank to the shower floor. "That was not how my first time was supposed to happen," I cried out over and over.

Reed and I walked Whitley's parents and Stacey out to the car.

"Are you sure you have the directions down, Mr. Reynolds?" Reed asked as he held the car door open for Whitley's mother.

"Yes, son, I've got this. Now, be sure to take care of things while they are gone."

"I will," Reed and I both said at the same time.

We quickly glanced at each other, and I rolled my eyes as he looked away. I was house-sitting and puppy-sitting for Layton and Whitley while they were on their three-week honeymoon. I had no idea what in the hell the plant pussy was still doing here.

I thought back to last night when Reed had told me he wanted to make love to me. I instantly felt my cheeks turning red. I looked over at him, and he was staring at me. I put my hands up to my cheeks and closed my eyes as I imagined his breath against my neck.

Shit! Stop it, Courtney!

"Court?" Stacey said as she touched my arm.

I jumped and quickly snapped out of my daydream. "Sorry," I whispered.

"Honey, are you okay? Are you getting sick? You look flush." She put her hand up to my forehead.

I pushed her hand away and laughed. "I'm fine. I'm just tired."

I glanced over toward Reed, and he was giving me a concerned look.

"Well, take a nap, okay? You busted your ass yesterday and last night. Just think, at least you don't have to clean up since Layton hired someone to come in and take care of it," she said with a smile.

I smiled as Reed walked up and stood next to me. I could practically feel the heat coming from his body.

Shit. Why didn't I just tell him the truth last night?

"Courtney? Are you even listening to me? My God, you are a million miles away this morning," Stacey said with a laugh.

I let out a fake laugh. "Sorry. I guess I'm just thinking about Whitley and everything. Have a safe trip back, and don't stay away for so long, okay? Oh! And think about moving here, bitch."

When Stacey gave Reed a good-bye kiss on the cheek, my hands balled up into fists before I quickly shook them loose.

"Bye, you all!" Stacey said with a giggle.

I rolled my eyes at her lame attempt to sound country as I shut her door. Reed and I stood there and watched them drive away. Once they were out of sight, Reed and I both turned and faced each other.

"You can leave now," we said at the same time.

"I'm house-sitting," we said together again.

"What?" I yelled. "No, you're not. I'm house-sitting and dog-sitting."

Reed smiled and shook his head. "Um…I think you are mistaken. I'm house-sitting and…um…um…cow-sitting." He made a funny face when he realized how goofy that had sounded.

I tried so hard not to laugh, and I had to bite my cheek to keep from smiling.

"Cow-sitting? Really? Really, Reed?" I turned and made my way back up the stairs.

It didn't take me long to figure out what Layton and Whitley had done. They had arranged this whole thing.

"Well, I've got this covered, so you can head on home, Reed."

I silently prayed that he wouldn't argue with me for once, and he'd just leave. I needed to be alone for a bit, so I could try to figure out how I was going to kill Mitch while plotting my revenge on that bitch, Karen.

"Uh…sorry, Court, but I took three weeks of vacation, and I really don't think you can help Mitch take care of shit around the ranch."

I threw open the door before making my way through the house and into the kitchen. "Please, how hard can it be? I think I've got this covered. Really, you can leave the…cow-sitting to me," I said with a wink.

He gave me a smirk and turned to pour himself a cup of coffee. My cell phone rang, and I pulled it out of my back pocket.

Whitley. Oh God, I need to talk to her. "Whitley!" I shouted.

"Hey, Lollipop! How's it going this morning?"

I tried so hard not to start crying, but the moment I heard her voice, I lost it. I walked out onto the back porch and tried to calm down.

"Courtney, no! Oh, please, no. Layton and I thought it would do you and Reed some good to spend time together. Oh, please don't cry!"

I shook my head. *She must think I'm upset about Reed.* "No, Whit, it's not that. Oh God, Whitley…he's been cheating on me!" I blurted out.

"What? Who?"

I quickly wiped my tears away. "Santa Claus. Who in the fuck do you think I'm talking about?"

"Mitch?"

"Yes, Mitch, Whitley. He called me by accident last night, and I heard him talking to that bitch he had been with all night at the wedding, his ex. Then, I heard…I heard…" I couldn't even get it out.

I could overhear Whitley telling Layton what was happening.

"Court, take a deep breath, sweetheart. What did you hear?"

"I heard him fucking her, Whitley! Oh my God, I sat there, like an idiot, and listened to them having sex while she called out his name."

I collapsed into the rocking chair and began crying. I was trying to be quiet, so Reed wouldn't hear me. I could hear Whitley talking to Layton, but I wasn't paying attention.

"Oh God, Whitley, I knew he wasn't the one. I knew it! I mean, we've barely even slept together in the year we've been seeing each other. I knew he wasn't the one. He just proved it to me, and I sat there, like a fool, and listened."

"Courtney, honey, I'm so sorry I'm not there," Whitley said as she let out a sob.

"Oh, for Pete's sake, Whitley, I'm so sorry! I shouldn't have told you before you left for your honeymoon today. I wasn't going to tell you, but I heard your voice, and—"

Just then, Reed came flying out the back door. "Motherfucking son of a bitch. I'm going to kill him!" he yelled as he made his way to the ranch truck.

I jumped up and wiped the tears away. "Whit, did Layton tell Reed?" I asked as I saw Reed picking up the pace when he started jogging to the ranch truck. I took off after him.

"Um…"

"Whit!"

"Okay, well, he called Reed and told him to go fire Mitch," Whitley said in a panicked voice.

"What? Oh my God! Okay…well, listen, sweetheart, everything will be fine here! Enjoy your honeymoon."

"Wait! What? You can't just end a call like that, Courtney."

After running and catching up, I stood in front of the ranch truck. "Yeah, I can. I've got to go. Reed seems really pissed."

I hung up the phone and ran around to the passenger side of the truck. I jumped in, and Reed hit the gas, throwing me back into the seat.

"Jesus, Reed. Where in the hell are you going?" I asked as I desperately tried to get the seat belt on.

I glanced at Reed while he was mumbling something about killing Mitch for hurting me.

"Uh…Reed, can you put on your seat belt?" I asked.

He snapped his head over to me. "What?" He shook his head and pushed down on the gas.

I sat back and closed my eyes. *Shit, shit, shit! I shouldn't have said anything. How stupid of me to think that Layton wouldn't tell* Reed.

Layton had been looking for an excuse to get rid of Mitch ever since he found out that Mitch had been in contact with Layton's father all those years and never told him.

By the time we pulled up to Mitch's place, my heart was beating a mile a minute. There was a Nissan parked next to Mitch's truck.

That must be her car.

"Fucking son of a bitch," Reed said.

I grabbed his arm. "Reed, please don't do this."

He turned to look at me, and his eyes were filled with tears. I sucked in a breath of air and let go of his arm.

"He hurt you, Courtney. I really wish you had told me last night. Now, stay in the truck, Court."

He jumped out and took off. Before he made it onto the porch, Mitch came out.

"Oh shit," I whispered.

Mitch smiled at Reed and then looked at me in the truck. "You get what you wished for last night?" Mitch asked.

Wait, what in the hell does he mean by that?

"You motherfucker," Reed said as he walked up to Mitch and punched the hell out of him.

I screamed and jumped out of the truck. By the time I made it to the porch, Reed was on top of Mitch, beating the shit out of him. Karen came running out, yelling for Reed to stop. She came to a halt when she saw me. She put her hand up to her mouth and then looked back at Reed on top of Mitch. I couldn't move. A part of me wanted Reed to beat the hell out of Mitch, and the other part wanted him to stop.

"For Christ's sake, Courtney, stop your crazy-ass friend!" Karen screamed.

I slowly looked at Reed and finally snapped out of my daze. I ran over and started pulling on him. "Reed! Please just stop. He's not even worth it. Please, for me, stop!" I yelled out.

Reed instantly stopped and looked at me. The look in his eyes gave me a chill, and I quickly stepped back.

Reed stood up and looked at Mitch. "Pack up your shit, and get off the ranch. You have an hour to leave before I call the cops and have you removed."

"What?" Mitch, Karen, and I all said at the same time.

Mitch stood up and wiped the blood away from his mouth and nose. "Fuck you, Reed. You can't tell me what to do," Mitch said. Then, he looked over at me. "Did you fuck him last night, Court? I know how much you've been wanting to."

I sucked in a breath of air. *Who is this person standing in front of me?* He wasn't the same person I had been dating for the last year. *Men are all the same. They're all lying, deceiving fakes.*

"You better shut the hell up, Mitch. So help me God, I'll kill you if you say another word to her," Reed said as he took a step closer to Mitch.

I stepped in between them and put my hands up to stop Reed. I turned around and faced Mitch. "I heard you."

He looked confused and shook his head. "What in the hell are you talking about, Courtney? You heard me what?"

I took a deep breath and closed my eyes before opening them again. I looked straight into his eyes. "You accidentally called me last night. I heard everything you said to her, and then I heard y'all…I heard…" I couldn't even get it out.

Mitch closed his eyes and dropped his head. "Damn it, Courtney. I didn't want you to find out like that. It's just…"

I felt the anger building up inside of me, but when Reed put his hands on my shoulders, I instantly calmed down just from his touch.

"How long, Mitch? How long have you been cheating on me?" I asked as I tried to hold back the tears.

"Does it matter, Court? I mean, it doesn't really matter. You've been in love with Reed ever since we've been together. Don't deny it. You have a very bad habit of talking in your sleep, sweetheart," Mitch said. He glanced at Reed and then back at me.

"What?" I whispered.

Shit…what have I been saying about Reed in my sleep? I shook my head to clear my thoughts.

"So, you're blaming this on me? I've never been unfaithful to you, and you…" I took another breath. "Just tell me, how long have you been screwing your ex?"

"I think you should just leave now," Karen said as she smirked at me.

I wasn't sure what came over me, but I walked over to her, reached back, and punched the shit out of her.

"Courtney! Holy shit!" Mitch yelled as he grabbed Karen and looked at her mouth. "Baby, are you all right?"

Mitch looked at me and screamed, "Six months, Courtney! I've been with Karen for six months now. I thought for sure you'd find your way to the asshole behind you, but you just wouldn't leave. Even when we stopped having sex so many months ago, you still held on to a fucking dream that was never going to happen. I don't love you, and you don't love me. I never loved you, Courtney."

I took a step back and shook my head. "But all those things you said. You told me…"

Mitch helped Karen up and looked back at me. "I told you what you wanted to hear, Courtney. The only reason I went after you is because I knew Reed wanted you."

"Motherfucker," Reed said as he lunged at Mitch again.

Reed got two or maybe three good punches in before I pulled him back and away from Mitch.

"Leave. Now!" Reed shouted.

"Fuck off, Reed. You can't tell me what to do," Mitch said as he helped Karen into his house.

Reed grabbed Mitch and pushed him up against the house before getting right into his face. This time, I took a few steps back. I didn't even care if Reed killed Mitch at this point.

"I can, asshole. I'm fifty percent in partnership with Layton now, so I'm your boss, motherfucker, and I just fired your ass. Layton also told me to deliver a message to you as soon as possible."

Mitch smirked and was about to say something, but Reed hit him in the stomach. Mitch doubled over.

"That's from Layton. You have an hour to get the hell out of here and off this ranch."

Reed turned around, grabbed my hand, and practically pulled me back to the ranch truck. He opened the door for me, and when I jumped in, he leaned in and smiled.

"That was some punch, Rocky." He winked and shut the door.

My face got hot, and I couldn't help but smile. I'd never in my life hit anyone.

Reed jumped in the truck, started it and began driving. "Let's go into town and get some breakfast."

I glanced over at him and let out a gasp. "Oh my God! You're bleeding. You have blood all over you!"

Reed looked down at his shirt and smiled. Then, he glanced at me before turning back to the road. "That's his blood, not mine."

I shook my head. "No! You're bleeding above your eye, Reed."

He looked in the rearview mirror. "It's just a small cut. I'll wash it up, and then we'll head into town."

We drove back to Layton and Whitley's house in silence.

I kept replaying the whole thing in my head. *Mitch was only with me to keep Reed away from me? Mitch never loved me. He never really wanted to be with me. Six months…*

When we pulled up, I just sat there, frozen. Reed opened the passenger door and held out his hand, but I couldn't move.

"He never even wanted to be with me. He never…" I slowly turned, and the moment my eyes met Reed's, I began crying.

He reached in and picked me up. He carried me into the house as I buried my face into his shoulder, and I just cried. I felt like such a fool. In Layton and Whitley's room, Reed gently put me down onto the bed. He reached down and began taking off my sneakers. The feel of his hands just touching my body was driving me insane.

I'd given up a year of searching for something that didn't exist with someone who I'd thought could possibly be my Prince Charming. I should have listened to my initial instincts. From the first time he'd kissed me, I'd known that he wasn't the one. My heart had screamed it, but my head had denied it.

Reed pulled the covers over me, and I never took my eyes off of him as he looked into my eyes and smiled. He pushed a piece of my hair away from my eyes as he bent over and then kissed me on the forehead.

"I'll make us something to eat in a bit, but I have to take care of something first, okay?"

I nodded my head and closed my eyes. I couldn't look at him another second longer, or I would beg him to kiss me, and that was the last thing I wanted.

Why does my Prince Charming keep turning out to be nothing but a monster?

I felt myself drifting off into sleep. I prayed that the nightmares wouldn't return, and I fought like hell not to fall asleep.

The last thing I heard was a voice whispering next to my ear, "Sleep for a bit, angel. I won't let anyone hurt you ever again."

Reed…

TWO

REED

"I promise, Whitley, she's fine. Yes, I kicked his ass and fired him like Layton said. Yes, I promise I won't argue with her or instigate anything. Whitley! Will you just go on your honeymoon and stop stressing? Courtney will be fine. I swear to you, I won't do anything to hurt her any more, and I will spoil the hell out of her. I'm even making her lunch."

I rolled my eyes as I listened to Whitley give me another one of her cute little threats.

"I swear to you, Reed Moore, if you do anything to cause her stress, I will kick your ass."

"Whitley, can I talk to Layton now?"

"Fine. Love you, Reed!" she said in a chipper voice.

I heard her say something to Layton as she handed the phone to him.

"Is he gone?" Layton asked.

"Yeah, he stopped at the house and gave me all his keys and a few other items. Fucker even had the nerve to ask to talk to Courtney, and I told him to go jump off a bridge."

Layton let out a long sigh. "Shit, Reed, you're going to have your hands full for three weeks."

I laughed. "Nah, I already called Kevin. Now that he's home for good, he's looking for a job, so he said he could help out around here."

"Damn, I owe him one. Tell him thanks for me. And, Reed?"

"Yeah?"

"I don't know what's going on with Courtney, but I think something pretty big happened to her when she was younger. That night you, uh…well, when you were drunk and said all that shit, she got drunk and mumbled something to me that has bothered me ever since."

My heart started pounding. "What was it?"

Layton took a deep breath and said in a whispered voice, "She looked at me with tears in her eyes and said that she'd begged him to stop, but he wouldn't. At first, I thought she was talking about you until I really thought about it. I think she was talking about someone from her past."

I felt my heart drop to my stomach. "Who did she beg to stop? And what did he do?" I whispered back.

"I don't know. I've wanted to ask Whit so many times, but I don't think she really knows either. She has mentioned that something happened to Court in high school and that she changed. For a few years, she hated all guys and wouldn't date."

I shook my head, thinking back to the conversation Whitley and I'd had in the hotel. "Yeah, Whitley said the same thing to me once."

"Reed, just don't do anything to push Courtney, or you know, piss her off."

I let out a laugh. "I already promised Whit. I'll take care of everything, Layton. Just enjoy your honeymoon."

"Thanks, dude. Listen, they are announcing our flight. Have a fun three weeks," Layton said with a laugh.

Bastard. I still couldn't believe he and Whitley had set up Courtney and me like that. I hit End on my phone and put my head in my hands. I tried to figure out what in the hell I was going to do for the next three weeks. I was going to be alone with the only girl I'd ever loved, the only girl I'd ever wanted to be with, and the only girl who scared the fuck out of me.

I sat back in the chair and ran my hands down my face as I let out a long, drawn-out sigh. I flashed back to my mother sitting at the kitchen table, crying. I had begged her to stop crying, and she wouldn't.

She'd just kept rocking back and forth, saying, *He left us. He left us. He never loved us.*

I'd vowed right then at the age of ten that I would never fall in love and risk hurting anyone like my father had hurt my mother.

Love sucks and does nothing but bring heartache.

Then, I'd met Courtney. She'd changed everything, and all I'd found myself doing was fighting the urge not to fall in love with her. The more I'd fought it, the more I'd fallen deeper in love with her. Now, all I wanted to do was take away the pain that everyone else had caused her. I prayed to God that I would never, ever be the cause of any of her pain.

I stood up and walked over to the elk stew heating up on the stove when I heard something. Both dogs jumped up and ran out of the kitchen. I turned and walked into the living room. The next thing I knew, Courtney let out a bloodcurdling scream. I quickly ran down the hall with the dogs leading the way. I threw the bedroom door open to see Courtney thrashing around on the bed.

Courtney was crying out, "Stop! Please stop! No…please, God, no. Please don't do this again, Noah. Please stop!"

I ran over to her and tried waking her up. "Court…baby, wake up! Courtney…"

I gently started shaking her. Her eyes flew open, and she screamed.

"Courtney, it's me! It's Reed, angel. It's just me. You were having a bad dream."

She looked around, confused, and then looked back at me. The moment I saw the first tear fall, my whole world stopped. She began shaking her head and threw herself into my arms.

"No! They started again! The dreams started again," she said in between sobs.

My heart was breaking, and I wanted so badly to ask her who in the fuck Noah was.

"Shh…it's okay, Courtney. It's okay. Everything is going to be okay."

She began crying harder. "He wouldn't stop, Reed. He never stopped, even when I begged him."

What in the fuck is going on? What is she talking about? "It's over now, Courtney. No one will ever hurt you again, baby, I promise you." I tried to hold back the tears I was fighting to control.

"Reed…" she whispered.

I squeezed my eyes shut and just held her until her crying stopped and her breathing evened out. It was then that I realized she had fallen back asleep. I slowly moved her body down as I held her close to me. I laid her back down on the bed, and I removed her death grip from around my neck before placing her arms down along her sides.

I couldn't pull my eyes away from her beautiful face. She looked so peaceful, but not more than ten minutes ago, I'd never seen such fear on a person's face as I'd seen on her innocent face.

I sat up and watched her sleep for a few minutes. I was going to do everything in my power to figure out who in the hell this Noah was, and once I did, I would hunt his ass down and kill him.

I stood up and looked at the two dogs lying near the side of the bed. "Y'all stay with her and watch over her," I whispered. I turned and made my way out of the room. This time, I kept the door open.

By the time I got back to the kitchen, I was sweating, and my hands were shaking. "What in the hell is going on?" I leaned against the counter and tried to calm my beating heart. It felt like it was going to pound right out of my chest.

I stood there for a few minutes, trying to work it out in my head. *What in the hell was Courtney talking about?* I pushed away from the counter and turned the flame down on the stew. I stepped outside onto the back porch, and I pulled out my phone before hitting my mother's name.

"Reed, darling! To what do I owe this honor? I just saw you last night at the wedding. Miss me already?" my mother said with a chuckle.

I smiled and let out a small laugh. Just the sound of my mother's voice calmed me down, and my heart finally felt like it was starting to beat normally again.

"Just wanted to hear your voice."

She let out a small sigh. "What's wrong? I hear it in your voice. Is everyone okay?"

I slowly took in a deep breath and let it out. "Yeah, Mom, everyone is fine. Just been a long morning."

"I ran into Anna this morning, and she was not very happy. I wasn't really sure what to say when she told me my son was a son of a bitch who had led her on and wasted her time because he'd been in love with another woman the whole time. Care to explain?"

I sank down onto the wood chair and looked out over the west pasture. *How in the fuck am I going to explain this?* "Mom, can we maybe talk about that another time?" I asked, hoping she would just let it go.

"Reed Nickolas Moore, did you lead that girl on? She said you'd asked her to move in with you, and y'all had been talking marriage, and then you just broke up with her last night."

I sat up straight, and I was pretty sure my mouth was hanging open. "What in the fuck?" I practically shouted.

"Excuse me? I don't think so. I don't care how old you are. You do not talk that way to me."

I rolled my eyes and pushed my hand through my hair. "Mom, I didn't ask her to move in. She was pressuring me to move in with her, and I had no intentions whatsoever to ask her to marry me. I mean, I really liked her, but I didn't love her, and she was just jealous of—" I quickly stopped talking and held my breath, hoping that my mom had missed that last part.

"Jealous of Courtney?" she asked quietly.

I felt the heat building in my whole body. If Anna had talked about Courtney to my mother, I wasn't sure what I would do to Anna. "What did Anna tell you about Courtney?"

"Nothing."

"Mom, what did she tell you?" I asked very slowly, trying to keep calm.

"Reed, she just said you'd told her that it wasn't fair to her that you were in love with another woman and that you thought it was best if y'all broke up. I'm proud of you by the way. I appreciate the fact that you didn't lead her on any more than you already had."

What? What in the hell does that mean? "Wait, what does that mean, Mom? What do you mean, lead her on any more?"

She let out a sigh and then chuckled. "Honestly, Reed, anyone can see you're head over heels in love with Courtney. I noticed it months ago when you couldn't keep your eyes off of her while your girlfriend was standing next to you. I noticed it last night when the two of you were dancing. You could practically see how smitten the both of you were with each other. Now, stop being so damn stubborn, and for once in your life, take a chance on love."

"Um…" I didn't even know what to say. *If my own mother can see how much I'm in love with Courtney, then why can't Court see it?*

I heard the back door open, and I glanced up to see Courtney standing there. She looked absolutely breathtaking. Her blonde hair was up in a messy ponytail, and she had on yoga pants with a Texas A&M T-shirt. I couldn't help but smile as she gave me a weak smile.

"Hey, Mom, I've got to let you go."

"Oh, sure, the talk gets heavy, and you need to what? Go feed the dogs?"

I let out a laugh and shook my head. "I'm cow-sitting, Mom. I need to go feed the cows. I love you. Talk to you later." I hit End before she could say anything else.

Courtney walked up and sat down next to me. She had her ever-present Kindle in her hand, and she leaned her head back and took in a deep breath. "God, I must have needed that sleep," she said as she dropped her head and looked out over the pasture.

I sat there, waiting to see if she would say anything about her dream. *Does she even remember it? Does she remember being in my arms, terrified and shaking?* I cleared my throat. "How did you sleep, angel?"

She turned her head, and her smile faded for a brief second before she flashed that beautiful smile of hers. "So, I earned a nickname from you, huh?" she said with a wink. "I think I slept okay. Were you in the room at one point? I thought you were, but I think I was dreaming. And don't get all smart-ass with me. It wasn't a sex dream."

She doesn't remember. I smiled as I stood up and winked at her. "Baby, you wish you were having sex dreams about me."

I turned and walked into the house while she sat there in a laughing fit.

I walked up to the stove and held out my shaking hand. *She'll tell me when she's ready to tell me. Don't push her, Reed. Just don't push her away.*

I made up two bowls of stew and took them outside. She was buried deep into a book, and the smile on her face was so damn cute.

"Hungry? I've got some stew here."

She looked up and nodded her head as she reached out for the stew. She balanced her Kindle on her knees and went back to reading as she blew on the stew and then took a bite.

"So, what has you smiling like that? What are you reading?" I asked before taking a bite of the stew.

She closed her eyes and then opened them. "It's just a love story that's making me swoon."

"Swoon?" I asked.

She looked at me, scrunching up her nose, and I about died. It was the cutest thing I'd ever seen, and I just wanted to grab her and make love to her right here on the back porch.

"Swoon, Reed. You know…swoon!" she said with a giggle.

"Uh…doesn't swoon mean to faint from extreme emotion?" I asked.

She turned a little bit more and smiled bigger. "Yes, so swooning is like being in a state of ecstasy."

"Okay…so, it's turning you on?" I asked.

She rolled her eyes. "No! It's romantic. The guy is being utterly romantic, and it gives me butterflies in my stomach." She turned back and began reading again.

"What's he doing?"

She peeked over and looked at me. "You really want to know?" She slightly tilted her head. "Is there a reason you're being so nice?"

My heart hurt a little when she asked that. "I really want to know. I'm interested in knowing what makes you swoon," I said with a wink.

She sat back and took another bite of stew. After a few seconds of chewing, she began talking. "Well, it's one of my favorite books ever. It's called *The Marriage Bargain*, and the guy just realized he loves the girl. It was just a really sweet moment, and those always have the same effect on me every time."

I nodded and then asked, "How many times have you read it?"

She shrugged. "I don't know. Maybe nine or ten times."

I choked on my stew and sat up. "Ten times! You've read the same book ten times?"

She bit down on her lower lip and whispered, "Okay, maybe fifteen…give or take one or two."

Then, I really started choking.

"Are you okay, Reed?" she asked before she started laughing.

"Holy shit, Court. I'm going to die on elk stew here."

"What? What did you just say?"

"I said, I'm going to die from choking on the stew. Fifteen times?"

"No! You said, *elk* stew. Oh God! Oh God! Am I eating elk?" She began flailing her free arm all around.

"Um…yeah, I got it from Layton's freezer and heated it up."

"Eww-uh! Oh Christ!" She jumped up, leaned over the rail, and started spitting.

Lulu, the chocolate lab, came running over to check out what was going on. I almost fell out of my seat when I saw Courtney put the bowl down, and the dog started eating the stew.

"No, Lulu! No! Bad dog," I said.

I went to get up and grab the bowl when Midnight came running over to get his piece of the pie, and he knocked me off-balance. I stumbled and tried to grab a hold of the rail. Courtney screamed and reached out for me.

Oh hell, this is going to hurt. I tumbled over the rail and landed on my side with a thud. I was pretty sure that if I hadn't broken a rib, I sure as hell bruised it.

"Reed! Oh my God!" Courtney yelled as she came running down the steps and up to me.

I held up my bowl of stew and smiled. "Look, I didn't even spill any!" I said.

She busted out laughing and then stood there with her hands on her hips. "Jesus, you idiot! You scared the hell out of me." She turned and started to make her way back up the stairs. "For the next three weeks, I'm in charge of all meals. No more elk or deer or rabbit or whatever the hell you Texas boys eat." She reached down and picked up her bowl but not before scratching Lulu and Midnight behind their ears and kissing them both.

I watched as she started to walk into the house with both dogs following her.

"I'm fine! Really, I don't need any help!" I yelled out.

She waved her hand and disappeared.

Yep, the next three weeks are going to be either pure heaven or pure hell.

THREE

The last four days had been pure heaven. Reed would work around the ranch during most of the day. By the time he'd come back, I would have dinner cooked, and he'd take a shower, eat, and then head to bed because he was so exhausted. I'd fought the urge to head up to his room on more than one occasion.

Stupid good-looking cowboy in his stupid Wranglers and stupid tight-ass T-shirt, coming in all sweaty and hot-looking.

Whenever he'd taken off his cowboy hat, I'd swear I could have an orgasm just from looking at his messy brown hair.

Ugh. I closed my eyes and shook the image from my head. *Stop this, Courtney. You don't need a man in your life. The last one turned out to be no different than all the others ones, and Reed Moore has been nothing but trouble. He's certainly not your Prince Charming. Nope.*

Liar. He is so my Prince Charming.

I looked back down at my computer screen and tried to concentrate on the book I was editing. *Fuck this shit. I need a break.* I saved my work and closed my laptop, and then I reached for my Kindle. I opened up the book I was currently reading, and I slowly began to lose myself in the story as the sound of the pool water relaxed me even more.

I heard someone clear his throat, and I looked up to see Mitch standing in front of me.

I quickly stood up and said, "What are you doing here? If Reed sees you here—"

"I came to get a few things I'd forgotten at the foreman's cabin because I left in such a hurry."

I sat back down and looked away. "Oh. Well, I don't know where Reed put the keys, and I have no idea where he is or when he will be back."

He let out a laugh. "It's all right, Court. I can jimmy the door open and get in."

I shrugged my shoulders and went back to reading. I really didn't want to see him right now.

"Courtney?" he asked in almost a whisper.

"What?" I said, trying to sound unaffected by his presence.

I wasn't even sure why I was feeling upset. I was glad we were over.

During the last few days of spending time with Reed, I'd realized that I had just used Mitch to hide my true feelings for Reed. Although, right now, I was not anywhere near ready to admit those feelings to myself, let alone to Reed.

"I'm really sorry for what I did to you. I didn't mean to hurt you."

I sat up and looked him in the eyes. "Really? You admitted that you'd only dated me to keep me away from Reed, and you fucked around with your ex for six months. And you're sorry? Well, go take your sorry and shove it up your cheating ass."

I sat back and acted like I was reading. He turned and walked away. I let out the breath I had been holding, and I quickly wiped away the tear rolling down my cheek.

I hate all men. I hate them.

I was sitting in the little nook in Layton and Whitley's room, reading *The Marriage Bargain* for about the twentieth—plus ten—time. There was no way I would ever let Reed know how many times I'd actually read this book.

When I heard a knock on the bedroom door, I called out, "Come in."

I smiled when I saw Reed walking in. Every time he entered a room, the hairs on my arms would stand up, and I'd get the silliest feeling in my stomach.

"Court, you've either been reading, or you've been on your computer for the last week. You need to get out. Want to go for a ride with me?"

I set my Kindle down and pulled my knees up to my chest. "Where are you going?"

He smiled the biggest, goofiest smile I'd ever seen, and I couldn't help but giggle.

"My place, up the road," he said.

The look in his eyes held me captive for a few seconds.

Reed had bought the fifty acres Whit had wanted when she first moved here. At the time, neither one of them had known that they were bidding against each other. Reed had won out, and it was for the best because Whitley would have just ended up selling it.

I jumped up and said, "I'd love to see your place."

We drove in silence for fifteen minutes on the way to his property.

Reed looked over at me and asked, "What were you reading?"

I shrugged my shoulders and lied, "*The Lost Soul.* I just finished editing it and was reading it on my Kindle."

He laughed as if he knew I was not telling him the truth, and he shook his head. "Really? 'Cause you have that same goofy smile you had on your face the other day."

I looked out the window and smirked. "Well, you know, more than one book can make a girl swoon."

"I see." He pulled up to a gravel driveway and punched in a code to open the gate.

We drove for just a bit before he turned a corner, and I saw the house. I let out a gasp and put my hand over my mouth.

"Holy shit! A log cabin?" I asked as I turned and looked at him.

He had the biggest smile on his face. "Yep! I needed to come by and check things out since I haven't been here in a week."

He parked the truck, jumped out, and ran around to my side. I'd quickly learned that Texas boys liked opening doors for girls. I had to admit that I loved it. I loved it even more when Reed did it because he would always hold his hand out and help me down. I was afraid that one of these days, I was going to launch myself at him and kiss him because it turned me on so damn much.

"Let me show you around the place, angel."

Oh yeah, and the fact that he was calling me angel turned me on, too. It didn't help that I hadn't had sex in over six months, and I hadn't packed a single vibrator from home.

As we walked up to the log home, I couldn't believe how charming it was. I'd always wanted to live in a log home. My parents had a log cabin in Maine where we would spend the summers, and I loved it there. Granted, this one could fit in my parents' cabin five times over, but it had the same appeal, and just from the first glance, I loved this one, too.

"I pretty much only have to put the finish on the cabinets and a few other things, and then it'll be done," he said with a smile as he unlocked the front door.

"Wait, you built this yourself?" I asked, shocked, as I looked all around.

He let out a small laugh. "Yep! Layton and a few of the guys helped me, but I pretty much did it all on my own. It's been a dream of mine to live in a log cabin."

I spun around and looked at him. My heart dropped, and I was pretty sure I had just fallen in love with him a little more. "Really? Mine, too," I said out loud, regretting it the moment I did.

He gave me that crooked-ass grin of his and nodded his head. He grabbed my hand and began giving me a tour of the house. We walked into the living room that contained a huge rock fireplace. From there, we went through three bedrooms, two and a half bathrooms, and a huge laundry room. The house was big enough for a family of four or even five.

The living room, dining room, and kitchen were all open to each other. When we walked into the kitchen, I let out a gasp. It was huge. I glanced down at the island, and the first thing I thought of was Reed making love to me on it. I put my hands up to my face to cool my hot cheeks.

"You okay, Court?" Reed asked. "I know it's hot in here and all. I don't have the AC on."

I gave him a weak smile. *Oh, if he only knew the dirty thoughts running around in my head right now.*

As I walked by the island, I ran my hand over the cool granite. "I love granite," I whispered.

Reed leaned down and put his lips up against my ear. "I love this island," he whispered back.

He quickly turned and walked away before I could even say anything.

Holy shit. Did he know what I was thinking? Was he thinking the same thing?

After I got my wits about me, I followed him down a hall. "How many square feet is the house, Reed?"

"It's just about three thousand. Not nearly as big as Layton's place, but it's way more space than I need. I love it."

I nodded my head even though I was still behind him, so I knew he couldn't see me. "So do I. I grew up in a huge house, and I always wanted something smaller, cozier, if that makes sense."

He turned and walked backward as he smiled. "Yep. To me, this is huge. I grew up in a small house, single mom and all."

He turned back around and opened up a door, and we walked into the huge master bedroom. In the corner was a fireplace, and next to that was a huge bay window with—*oh God.* It was the window seat of my dreams. On each side of the window was a built-in bookcase. The bookcases went from floor to ceiling, and I about let out a moan while thinking of all the books I could put on those shelves to fill them up.

I followed Reed as he opened up another door. I noticed a huge walk-in closet that I was pretty sure was bigger than my bedroom in my current house. I had bought Whitley's house in Llano from her parents after she got engaged and moved in with Layton.

"Holy moly! This closet is huge!" I said.

Reed grabbed my hand and led me into the master bathroom. It was amazing.

"Oh, Reed…" I turned and looked at him.

He was grinning from ear to ear.

"Did you design all of this yourself?"

He let out a laugh. "Hell no! My sister said a woman needed to design the bathroom, so I let her make all the decisions in here."

I stopped and looked at him. "You didn't have Anna make any decisions?"

His smile faded, and he looked down at the floor. "Um…nah. I never brought Anna out here."

I tried really hard not to smile, but the fact that Anna had never set foot in this house made me want to hug myself.

The jet tub in the corner was flanked by two giant windows. It almost looked like the tub was sitting outside. The light in the bathroom was amazing. I walked up to the shower and stepped inside. There was a rain showerhead, a few other heads—I had no idea what they did—and a pretty decent-sized bench. I was stunned by how big the shower actually was. Two people could easily fit inside. I closed my eyes and pictured Reed making love to me in here with the water falling down on us. I didn't mean to, but I let out a small moan. The next thing I knew, I felt him behind me. I was almost afraid to open my eyes.

"Pretty amazing shower, huh?" he asked.

I slowly turned and looked up into his eyes. *Kiss me. Oh God, Reed, please kiss me.* "It's, um…it's beautiful."

He slowly backed up and stepped out of the shower, and I instantly felt like a young child who had just gotten her favorite toy taken away. As I stepped out of the shower, he took my hand again and asked how I liked the house. It was almost like he was looking for…my approval.

No, that is just silly, Courtney. Why would he need your approval?

We walked around the property for a bit, and I listened to a very excited Reed talk about his plans for the place. He wanted to build a shop, and he had the perfect place to make a garden. I couldn't help but feel just as excited as I listened to him talk about his future. I desperately wanted to ask him who he saw sharing this all with, but I just kept my mouth shut.

"I could totally see a giant tree house in that oak," I said as I pointed to a beautiful oak tree.

He smiled and nodded his head. "Yeah, I could, too."

"I always wanted a tree house. I begged my parents to build me one, but my mother said it was too dangerous." I smiled as I thought back to how I had begged and pleaded with them. "My kids will have a tree house," I whispered.

He took my hand and kissed the back of it, and the thousands of needles now pricking my hand caused me to suck in a breath of air.

Shit. Anytime he touches me, my body reacts.

"How would you like to go out with me tonight?" he asked with a sly grin.

I raised my eyebrow. "What do you have in mind?"

"Austin? Dinner with maybe a little bit of dancing at a club?" Reed said.

I bit down on my lower lip and nodded. "I think that sounds like fun!"

Before I knew it, we were heading back and getting ready to go out for the evening. I couldn't help but feel like an excited teenager going out on her first date.

I wanted so desperately to believe that Reed would be different. Maybe he really was different. He had been nothing but a gentleman all week. It was almost like he had done a one-eighty from the Reed I'd known—or at least, the one I thought I'd known.

Or maybe he just feels sorry for me?

Whatever the reason, I was going to enjoy myself. I still had a little over two weeks of this, and I intended on making it the best two weeks of my life.

FOUR

REED

I sat on the bed, grinning like an idiot. *She loved the cabin. I knew she would.* Every thought and detail I'd put into that house, I'd thought about Courtney and if she would like it or not.

As soon as we had gotten back to Layton's place, she hopped in the shower, and I pulled out a piece of paper and began working on my next project. When I was finished, I couldn't help but smile as I looked it over. It was perfect, and I was sure she would love it.

I heard a knock on the door, and I put the paper with the design facing down on the side table. I stood up and headed over to the door. I opened the door, and I just about dropped to my knees.

"Wow," was all I could get out.

Courtney was standing there in a black cocktail dress and silver high heels with her hair pulled up and a few curls hanging down.

"I'm going to guess I look pretty good since your mouth is practically hanging down to your knees, Moore. Could you eye-fuck me any more?" she asked with a wink.

"Yes, actually, I could. Court, you look beautiful. Is that your dress or Whitley's?"

She looked down and then back up at me, giving me a funny look. "It's mine! A girl can *never* be overpacked. I always tell Whitley to pack for anything and everything."

I found myself daydreaming about peeling that dress off of her and slowly making love to her. I shook my wayward thoughts away as I turned and grabbed my keys, wallet, and watch.

"Ready?" I asked with a smile.

She nodded with the enthusiasm of a small child and held her arm out for me to take. "So ready!"

"Let's go then."

After we ate, we grabbed a cup of coffee at Mozart's, and then we headed to the club for some dancing. I had to smile at how much Courtney loved to dance. She had more energy than the damn Energizer Bunny.

We walked up to the bar to get a drink when "Walking on Air" by Katy Perry started playing.

Courtney jumped up and down and then grabbed my hand. "I love this song!"

The next thing I knew, we were back out on the dance floor, dancing. She certainly could dance, and throughout the song, three different guys tried to cut in. With one go-to-hell look, they each quickly left.

By the time we left the club, Courtney finally seemed happy. This last week, she had buried herself in work and reading, and she'd hardly spoken two words to me. Now, she was going on and on, and I couldn't get a word in. I hadn't laughed so much in my life as I did on the ride home from Austin.

When we walked into the house, we were greeted by Midnight and Lulu. We both looked at each other and said, "Oh shit!"

"You didn't crate them!" Courtney said in a panicked voice.

Wait, what? "Me? I'm cow-sitting. You're the one who's dog-sitting," I said as I held up my hands and quickly looked around the house. *Oh fuck. If they chewed up anything, Layton will have our asses.*

"You check upstairs. I'll check down here," Courtney said as she took off her shoes. She started running around with Lulu right behind her.

"Gotcha!" I said as I made my way upstairs.

Every door had been shut, except for the second master bedroom where I was staying. I let out the girliest shriek when I walked in and saw one of my cowboy boots had been chewed up. Midnight ran in and went right for the boot. He picked it up and practically threw it at me, wanting to play fetch.

I grabbed on to the door to hold myself up. *My boots…oh God…he chewed up my boot.*

"What? What was that noise? It sounded like you stepped on a cat's tail or something!" Courtney said as she skidded to a stop and ran into me.

I pointed to my boot. "My…my…my boot. That bastard ate my boot…my favorite boots." I put my hands on my knees and took in a few deep breaths.

Court let out a gasp. "Oh…oh, Midnight, you bad boy. You didn't. That is unforgivable. You got his boots. Oh. My. God! My shoes!" With that, she took off running back downstairs, screaming, "I left the bedroom door open," over and over again.

When I heard her bloodcurdling scream, I knew it must have been bad. Midnight ducked and ran out of the room. When Court didn't stop screaming, I got worried. I ran downstairs and into Layton's room. I stopped on a dime when I saw her with a gun.

"Where in the hell did you get a gun?" I asked, confused as hell.

"Whit told me where one was. I'm going to kill them both. Get out of my way."

I looked around the room and didn't see any signs of torn up shoes. "Court, wait. The dogs? You're gonna kill the dogs? Why?" I tried to take the gun from her.

She shook her head, and I swore I could see steam coming from her ears.

"Reed, just tell me that this thing is loaded because I'm going to kill both those motherfuckers."

When she extended her hand with the gun, I grabbed it. "Jesus, Courtney. You never, ever handle a gun if you don't know what you are doing or if it's loaded." I checked the chamber, and it wasn't loaded. *Thank God.*

She pushed me out of the way and started screaming, "Lulu! I know it was you! You were so jealous of it."

"What? Courtney, stop and tell me why you are so pissed."

She spun around and looked at me. "I'm pissed because those animals…those beasts…those stinky, nasty, shit-eating dogs…ate my Kindle!"

Oh hell. Those poor dogs.

"I'm. Going. To. Kill. Them." She turned and started screaming each dog's name as she headed out of the room.

I was pretty sure they were hiding—or at least, I was hoping they were hiding.

"There you are!" she shouted.

I put the gun down and ran out after her. Lulu was sitting in the den, wagging her tail, as Courtney walked over and picked up a bat that Layton had leaning against the wall, and then she headed over to Lulu. I ran up, grabbed the bat, and spun her around. She began pushing me away while arguing that she needed her payback. I started laughing, and that just made her all the more mad.

I pushed her up against the wall and tried to get her to settle down. "For Christ's sake, Court, I will buy you a new Kindle. Just calm down."

Her eyes lit up for a brief second. "Are you admitting that you forgot to put them in their kennels?"

"What? No."

She began trying to get out of my grip, so I pushed my body into her.

"Fine! I admit it. Now, will you please stop trying to kill my best friend's beloved labs?"

"I want a Kindle Fire HD," she said with a smirk.

I looked at her, confused. "I don't even know what that is."

"Just say you will buy me a new Kindle Fire HD, and I will stop trying to kill the mutts."

I rolled my eyes and nodded my head. "Fine, Kindle Fire HD. Can we all play nice again?"

She smiled, but then something in her eyes changed, and she began breathing heavily as her eyes moved down to my lips. She licked her lips, and I tried like hell to back away from her, but I was frozen. I dropped the bat that I'd been holding in my hand, and I placed my hand on the side of her face.

"If I haven't told you yet, you look beautiful tonight," I said softly.

Her eyes were darting back and forth between my eyes and my lips.

I bent down and brushed my lips against hers as I whispered, "May I kiss you, Courtney?"

"Yes," she whispered back.

I teased her lips with mine for a few seconds before I deepened the kiss, and she opened her mouth to let my tongue explore hers for the first time. The moan she let out flowed through my body like nothing I'd ever experienced before. I put my other hand on her face and poured as much feeling into the kiss as I could. When I pulled back slightly, she still had her eyes closed. The feelings moving through my body confused me.

She opened her eyes and looked into mine. I stepped away from her and smiled as she smiled back at me.

"Good night, Court," I said.

She smiled bigger. "Good night, Reed."

I reached down and picked up the bat. "I'll just hang on to this for now."

She let out a giggle. "Probably a good idea."

I turned around and made my way over to the stairs. With each step, my heart was beating harder in my chest. When I got to my room, I sat down on my bed and threw my body back.

Holy shit. That was the most incredible kiss I've ever experienced. I wasn't sure how long I lay there, thinking about the kiss.

Oh yeah, everything has changed now. I was no longer going to sit and wait for her. *I'm going to fight for her love even if I have to fight for it for the rest of my life.*

FIVE

When I got back to my room, I shut the door and leaned against it, trying to calm my beating heart. I put my fingertips up to my lips that still felt like they were on fire.

"Oh my…" I whispered as I dropped my head against the door.

I'd never in my life experienced such a kiss. It felt like my whole body was still tingling. I closed my eyes and replayed the whole scene in my head.

May I kiss you, Courtney?

Swoon the hell out of me, why don't you, Reed Moore?

I slowly pushed myself away from the door and made my way into the bathroom. I stripped out of my dress and washed my face. I looked in the mirror, and I couldn't wipe the damn grin off my face.

I slipped into my comfy Victoria's Secret pajamas and crawled into bed. I heard something scratching at the door, and I realized that the dogs were still roaming the house. I got up and let them outside to go to the bathroom really quickly, and then I brought them back into the bedroom with me.

After I reached into my bag and took out my emergency Kindle, I looked at them both and pointed at them. "You both lie right there. Don't even think about moving."

I crawled into the giant king-sized bed and pulled the covers up. I tried to read, but I couldn't stop thinking about the kiss.

May I kiss you, Courtney?

Oh, dear God. How I want you to do more than kiss me, Reed.

Shit! Shit! Shit! Courtney, stop this right now!

Again, I tried to read, but clearly, I was consumed by the kiss, and every time I read something, all I could think about was Reed asking if he could kiss me. After staring at the same passage for thirty minutes, I finally gave up. I reached over and turned off the light. It didn't take long before I felt the bed move twice, and then I felt something flop down next to me…twice.

I smiled as I reached out and called Lulu to come closer to me. As I snuggled her, I whispered, "You tell anyone, and I will kill you."

I drifted off to sleep and dreamed of a certain cabin, shower, and Reed making love to me on his kitchen island.

"Yes, Whitley. Lulu and Midnight are fine, and the cows and horses are all still living, too. It's really amazing to see that Reed knows what he is doing. I've actually learned a few new things about plants, too."

Whitley laughed and said, "So, the last two weeks have been pretty good?"

I smiled as I thought about how much fun I'd been having with Reed. "Yeah, they've been okay," I said, trying to sound nonchalant about it all.

"Just okay?" Whitley asked with a giggle.

"Yep, just okay. Reed did buy me a new Kindle though."

"Why?"

Oh shit. Open mouth, insert foot, Courtney. "Oh…well, um…he kind of broke my other one."

"Oh damn, that sucks, but at least you got a new Kindle out of it! Hey, listen, I've got to run. I miss you so much, and I can't wait to see you and tell you how incredible this honeymoon has been!"

I smiled and said, "Okay, honey. Have fun and kiss Layton for me."

"Will do! Later, girl," Whitley said as she started to giggle before hanging up.

I set my phone down on the kitchen counter and smiled. I was so happy for her. She finally had her happily ever after, and no one deserved it more than she did.

I opened up the music app on my phone and looked for the perfect song to cook to. I was making tacos for dinner tonight.

"Oh, yes! This is the perfect song, Lulu!" I said as I looked down at my new best friend.

I had been sneaking the dogs into bed with me each night, and the nightmares had seemed to stop when they slept with me.

"Oops! I Did It Again" by Britney Spears started to play, and I began dancing and singing along. As I cooked the hamburger meat, I shook my ass to the music and sang as loud as I could. I turned around and saw Reed leaning against the doorjamb, smiling at me. I made my way over to him and grabbed his hands. We began dancing together, and we both started laughing when he busted out singing. Before I knew it, he was picking me up and spinning me around. When the song ended, he put me down and pushed a stray piece of my hair back. I willed him to kiss me, and when he began moving toward me, my heart started pounding in my chest.

Then, my cell phone rang.

Fuck me.

He smiled and shook his head as he walked away. "I'm going to go shower really quick."

"K," was all I could get out.

I looked at my phone to see that it was my brother, Tyler, calling.

"Hey, Ty. What's up?" I said, trying to sound chipper.

"Hey, baby sister. How is Texas treating you?" he asked, practically shouting.

I put my finger up to my other ear, so I could hear him better. "Tyler, I can barely hear you. Where are you?"

He laughed and said, "Hold on. Let me go outside."

"Okay, hurry though. I'm trying to cook dinner." I put the taco shells in the oven, and then I walked over to the refrigerator and took out the salsa.

"Are you sitting down, Court? I've got some huge news for you."

"I'm not sitting down, but I'm sure I can take whatever you've got for me while I'm standing."

He started laughing. "Okay, here I go…I'm getting married."

I stopped in my tracks. "No way! Tyler, that is wonderful news, sweetheart! I'm so happy for you."

He laughed again, but this time, it was harder. "That's not the only news I have for you. I'm in San Antonio for a meeting, and I want my baby sister to come see me! I looked it up, and you're only a few hours away."

I started jumping up and down. "No way! Why didn't you tell me you were coming to Texas?"

"I wanted to surprise you. Hey, guess who came with me?"

I reached up for a bowl to pour the salsa into as I smiled. I was hoping it was our parents. "Who?"

"Noah. He can't wait to see you."

My smile instantly faded as the salsa bottle slipped from my hand and hit the floor. I couldn't move. *No. Please, God, no.*

"Courtney? Are you still there? Court, what was that noise? It sounds like something just broke. Court?"

"Um…yeah, I'm still here. Sorry, I thought you said Noah was with you."

"Yeah, I did. Once he found out I was coming to Texas and I might be able to sneak in a visit with you, he asked if he could tag along. Ya know, Court, you broke his heart when you decided not to go to the prom with him. He really liked you, I think."

I'm going to be sick.

"So, when do you think you can come see me, sis? We just flew in, and I'll only be here for three days. We're heading up to Austin, so Meg can go to some wedding dress shops there. She's been in a pissy mood this whole trip."

I tried to talk, but my voice cracked. I cleared my throat and asked, "Meg is with you?"

"Yeah. So, when do you think you can come down this way?"

"I, um…well, I don't know 'cause I think I'm getting…I think I'm getting the flu. Maybe I shouldn't go out. I'd hate to get y'all sick."

Tyler let out a chuckle. "The flu, Court? Really? Do you just not like Meg?"

What? "What? No. Of course I do. I adore Meg. Listen, Tyler…I actually feel like I'm about to get sick. I'm sorry I can't meet up with you, but can I call you back later?"

"Sure. You don't sound so good, sis. Go take care of yourself, sweetie. Just call me later, and let me know how you're feeling, okay?"

I nodded my head and fought like hell to hold in the tears. "Okay." I quickly hit End and broke down crying.

Reed came walking into the kitchen as he said, "Hey, Court, I had a great idea—" He took one look at me and then down at the mess on the floor. "What happened? Are you hurt?" He ran over and picked me up before carrying me away from the broken glass and spilled salsa.

"The dogs! Oh, Reed, don't let them eat it. There's broken glass everywhere."

"Lulu, Midnight, kennels!" he yelled.

Both dogs ran out of the kitchen and to their kennels.

For a few brief moments, I felt so peaceful in Reed's arms before he put me down in the living room.

When he returned from locking up the dogs, he asked, "Angel, what happened? Why are you crying? Did you get cut or something?"

Noah is in Texas. He wants to see me. Why does he want to see me?

I flashed back to the last night he'd come into my bedroom.

The moment I felt the bed move, I knew it was Noah. For the last three months, he had been staying at our house more and more, and his nightly visits seemed to last longer and longer. I reached under my pillow and felt the cold metal. I opened my eyes and sat up.

"Get undressed, Courtney. We're going to try something a little different, princess."

I reached over and turned on my lamp.

"Turn off the light, Courtney. No one needs to know you're awake," he whispered as he took off his shirt.

After reaching back under the pillow, I pulled out the gun and stood up. I pointed it at him, and he jumped up.

"What the fuck? Where in the hell did you get a fucking gun, Courtney? Put it down before you hurt yourself."

"Fuck off, Noah. I'm done being treated as your rag doll. This little game you've been playing is over. I don't care if I spend the rest of my life in jail. You will never touch me again. If you so much as think of getting anywhere near my sister, I'll make sure you pay for it. Your time with me is over, motherfucker."

He stood there, looking at me, stunned. "Courtney, you know you wanted this as much as I did. I saw it in your eyes."

I wanted to scream, but I stayed calm. I shook my head and whispered, "No, I didn't. I wanted my first time to be with someone who loved me. I wanted my Prince Charming, and all I got was a monster who treated me like I was nothing but a piece of meat for him to do with as he pleased. You're not my Prince Charming. You're my worst nightmare."

He smirked at me and put his hands up. "Then, shoot me. I don't think you have it in you."

I slowly smiled and watched as his smile dropped from his face.

"You don't know me very well, Noah. How about I give you a warning?" I pointed the gun down to his thigh, and I was just about to pull the trigger when he jumped back.

"Stop! Courtney, stop! I get it, okay? You're serious. Just please put the gun down, okay? Just please put the gun down."

"Get out of my room. If you ever set foot in my room again, I swear to God, I will kill you."

He quickly put his shirt back on and went to leave. "I take it you're not going to the prom with me?"

My mouth dropped open, and I just looked at him. "I suggest you stop staying over. If I have to sit outside my sister's bedroom door with this gun, I will. And as far as prom goes, no, Noah. I never want to even talk to you again."

He grabbed the door handle and quietly opened the door before shutting it.

I dropped the gun onto my bed and broke down crying. I wasn't sure how long I sat on my bed, rocking back and forth, as I whispered over and over again, "Please, God…please…let that be the end. Please let that be the end."

"Courtney? Hello? Earth to Court?" Reed waved his hand in front of my face.

I pushed his hand away and took a step back. "Stay away from me."

He looked at me, confused. "What?"

"I don't need your goddamn help. I just dropped the jar. You don't need to come rushing in like you're my knight in shining armor or like I'm a child who can't take care of myself."

I felt my heart beating a mile a minute, and the hurt in Reed's eyes about killed me.

"Wait, I walked in, and you were crying. I thought…I thought you were hurt and—"

"I'm not. I just…I don't know why I started crying. It's just stupid hormones or something. I don't know. I just…I just need you to leave me alone."

I turned to walk back into the kitchen, and he grabbed my arm.

"Courtney, wait a minute. What in the hell happened? You were fine a few minutes ago. Now, you're pissed at me because I tried to help you?"

I spun around and jerked my arm from his grip. "I. Don't. Need. Your. Help. You're all the same, all of you. You're always wanting something, and you don't care who you use to get it." I stood there and fought like hell to hold in my tears.

He looked at me, and I saw the anger in his eyes.

"Who are you talking to, Courtney? Me or someone else?"

"What?"

He took a step closer to me. "Are you mad at me? Or are you pissed at some other asshole who hurt you, and you're taking it out on me?"

I swallowed and stepped away from him. "I don't…I don't want to be with you, Reed. You'll just end up hurting me like…like…"

"Like who? Mitch? Because if you even think you're going to compare me to Mitch, then you don't know me at all, Courtney."

I put my hands on my hips and straightened out my shoulders. "Does it matter? I know you've used women before, Reed. I know you've slept with other women, and it was meaningless. You're no different than the rest of them."

I turned to walk away, and he grabbed me again, spinning me around.

"Don't act all innocent, like you've only ever slept with Mitch, Courtney. What? You're a twenty-five-year-old girl who lost her virginity to Mitch? Is that what you're saying? So, if you want to judge me, let's hear all your dirty little secrets."

I tried pulling out of his grip, but my body started to tremble. "Don't say that," I whispered.

"Don't say what? You accused me of being an asshole who sleeps around. Why can we talk about my sex life but not yours?"

An image of Noah popped into my head—him on top of me, telling me how good I felt. I started to feel sick to my stomach.

I let a sob escape from my mouth, and I whispered, "Please let me go, Reed. Please let me go."

He took one look into my eyes and instantly let me go. "Courtney, I'm so sorry. I didn't mean to…"

I put my hand up to my mouth and fought to hold in my tears. I walked into the kitchen and grabbed the paper towels before making my way over to the mess on the floor.

Reed stepped in front of me. "I'll clean it up."

I looked up at him and sucked in a breath of air. He had tears in his eyes.

I slowly nodded my head and said, "I didn't mean to say all of that. I just…"

A small smile spread across his face. "It's okay. I crossed a line, and I'm sorry. I know you're not a child, and I need to stop treating you like one. I'm sorry."

He took the paper towels from my hand and bent down. As he began cleaning up the mess, I reached over and turned off the oven and stove before walking out of the kitchen.

I headed straight for the shower where I spent the next hour crying until I had no tears left to cry and scrubbing my body until the smell of Noah was gone.

SIX

REED

Kevin had stopped by earlier and helped me with some things that needed to be done around the ranch, and now, I was finally able to sit down and relax. I glanced around, looking for any signs of Courtney.

The last few days, she had been going over to Mimi and Frank's, the neighbors on the ranch next to Layton's. I was sure she'd been spending time talking about books with Mimi. She'd even bought Mimi a Kindle Fire HD after receiving the one I'd bought her since the dogs destroyed her original Kindle.

"Mr. Moore?" Johnny called out.

Johnny was the high school kid I'd ended up hiring last week to help out for a bit until Layton got back from his honeymoon. Johnny was friends with Ryan, the kid Layton had hired last summer.

I stood up and walked over to the gate. "Hey, Johnny. You get everything done?"

He nodded and smiled. "Yes, sir. Miss Will took Tink out for a ride a little bit ago. Should I stay and help her with the horse when she gets back?"

"Nah. Courtney is a big girl. She can handle it. Thanks, dude. I'll see you tomorrow after church, right? Mr. Morris will be back in the afternoon, and then you can officially meet him."

He reached out and shook my hand. "Sounds like a plan, sir."

He turned and headed off to his old Chevy truck, and I headed back to the chair I had been sitting in. It was so damn hot out, and all I wanted to do was jump in the pool, but damn Courtney had me sneaking around, reading this stupid book of hers. I wouldn't dare tell her I'd bought myself a Kindle, and I had loaded her favorite book on it. I had to know what it was that had always made her want to read it.

It didn't take me long before I was completely engrossed in Nick and Alexa's world. I thought I heard a noise, but I couldn't pull my eyes away from the Kindle. Nick was just about to—

"Whatcha doin' there?" Courtney whispered into my ear, scaring the shit out of me.

I jumped up so fast that it caused me to lose my balance. I stumbled backward and went right into the pool, Kindle and all.

Courtney started screaming, "No! My Kindle! You asshole, you ruined my brand-new Kindle."

I looked up at her as she began stomping her feet with her hands flying everywhere, and I couldn't help but smile.

I quickly removed the smile and started getting out of the pool. "Nice. You're worried about a stupid-ass Kindle. No, really, I'm fine, Courtney. I didn't just fall into a pool where I could have possibly hurt myself."

She stopped jumping around and looked at me. "It's not like you fell off a building, for Christ's sake. You fell into a pool…with *my* Kindle!"

She reached for the Kindle, and I swore she wiped a tear away. I shook my head and then pulled my shirt up and over my head. Then, I began unbuttoning my jeans.

"Whoa there, cowboy. Giving me a free strip show isn't going to make up for the fact that this is the second Kindle that has been destroyed while…"

I pulled my jeans down, and she stopped talking while she moved her eyes up and down my body. The moment she bit down on her lower lip and let out a small moan, I felt my dick jump.

This girl is going to kill me.

"Don't worry, Court. I'm not stripping. I don't want to walk through the house while I'm soaking wet." I started to walk away but not before I grabbed the Kindle. "By the way, this isn't your Kindle."

She picked up my wet shirt and jeans and followed me. "Wait, what? If it's not my Kindle, then whose Kindle is it? And why…" Then, she started laughing. "Oh. My. God. Reed Moore, were you…reading?"

I stopped, spun around, and looked down into her beautiful blue eyes while I gave her the best panty-melting smile I could muster up.

"Yes, Courtney Will, I was reading. Now, if you'll excuse me, I'm going to go take a shower and get dressed to go out."

Her smile dropped, and her mouth opened just a bit. "You're going out? Where?"

I turned and walked away from her, making my way into the house. I didn't want to tell her that after she had pushed me away the other day, I'd called up Melissa from work and asked her out for dinner. It was a dick move on my part, and ever since then, I had been trying to think of reasons to get out of it.

"Reed?" Courtney said in a soft voice.

I stopped at the edge of the stairs and looked back at her. "What?"

"I didn't mean it the other day when I said I didn't want to be with you."

With that, she turned and headed through the kitchen. I heard the back door shut, and a few seconds later, the sounds of her truck starting and pulling down the driveway filled my head. I just stood there, stunned.

I sat down on the stairs and put my head in my hands. For the first time in my life, I felt like I was going to cry over a girl. She had me all tied up in knots, not knowing which way was up or down.

I ran upstairs, took a quick shower, and then grabbed my cell phone. I was thanking God that I had left it on the dresser and not shoved in my back pocket when I'd gone into the pool. I hit Melissa's number and took a deep breath.

"Hey, handsome," she purred through the phone.

"Oh, hey. Listen, something has come up, and I'm going to have to cancel dinner."

"No. Oh no, Reed. I was really looking forward to dinner and maybe a little storage room fun again."

I closed my eyes and shook my head. "Yeah, that's probably not going to happen again, Melissa. I'm sorry. I, um…I've kind of…well, I'm sort of, like…"

She let out a laugh. "Reed Moore, you sound like you've fallen for someone."

I smiled and said, "Yeah, Melissa, I have. I don't want to hurt her or you, so I can't have dinner with you tonight. I hope you understand. I'm trying to figure things out with this, um…this girl, and…well, I'm doing a piss-poor job of it."

She let out another chuckle. "Reed, thank you for being honest with me. Hey, what we did was fun, and I'm not going to lie and say I wouldn't want to do it again. Can I offer you a bit of advice though?"

This is awkward in a way, but what the hell? "Sure."

"If you love her, go after her, Reed. Don't let her push you away, and don't you push her away because you're afraid of your feelings. Fight for it."

I dropped my head and let out a sigh. "Thanks, Melissa. You have no idea how much I needed to hear that."

"Go get her. I'll see ya when you get back to work. Enjoy the last few days of your vacation."

I thanked her again and said good-bye.

I hadn't had the heart to tell her that I had no intentions of going back to work. Once I'd decided to become a partner with Layton, I'd made the choice to quit my job and focus on the ranch, so I had given my notice the other day.

I got dressed and headed downstairs. I looked around the kitchen and decided I was going to make spaghetti and homemade meat sauce. I had no idea where Courtney had gone, but I was banking on her being back for dinner. I pulled out my phone and sent her a text message.

Reed: Dinner plans were canceled. I'm cooking dinner. Will be ready at six.

I sat there, staring at the candles that were almost halfway burned down. I glanced at the clock. It was seven thirty, and I had heard nothing from Courtney. I hadn't even eaten anything. The food was sitting in the middle of the table, cold and no longer looking good. Lulu and Midnight had been waiting in position for the last hour.

I glanced down and shrugged my shoulders. "I guess she's not showing up for dinner, y'all."

I heard the back door open, and both dogs jumped up and ran into the kitchen. I was hoping she would just walk right by the formal dining room and not see me waiting for her like a fool.

I was sitting with my back facing the entrance of the dining room, so I couldn't see her, but I felt her the moment she walked in. The whole energy in the room changed. She walked up behind me and leaned in close as she set a new Kindle Fire HD down on the table. I couldn't help but smile and let out a chuckle. Then, I felt her hot breath against my neck as she moved her lips up to my ear.

"I even put *The Marriage Bargain* on there along with some other books to help with your…swooning research."

It felt like a bolt of lightning went through my whole body when her lips were against my skin. I got up and stood in front of her. The smile on her face about dropped me to my knees. She slowly began backing up until she hit the wall. I walked up to her and bent down, putting my lips up against her ear. I could hear her breathing, and I swore I could tell what she was thinking with the sound of her breaths.

"I really love that fucking book," I whispered.

She let out a laugh as she put her hand up onto my chest. I pulled back and captured her eyes with mine.

She smirked and asked, "Did you swoon?"

I smiled bigger. "I don't think I'm ready to share that with you just yet."

"Reed?" she asked.

"Yeah, angel?"

"I'm scared," she said as a tear rolled down her face.

That single tear stopped my breathing as I used my thumb to wipe it away. "I am, too, Courtney. I am, too."

I put my forehead against hers, and we just stood there in silence for a few minutes.

"Want to go two-stepping?" I asked as I pulled back and looked at her.

She busted out laughing. She looked up into my eyes and nodded her head. I leaned down and captured her lips with mine. As I gently kissed her, I tried to pour as much love into that kiss as I could, but the last thing I was going to do was push her into anything.

I pulled my lips away and whispered, "Court, I'll wait forever for you. I'll wait forever."

SEVEN

I'd never had so much fun in my life as I was having with Reed tonight at Luckenbach dance hall. We'd been dancing for hours, and we'd laughed so much that I'd almost pissed my pants a time or two. The few times he'd kissed me, I'd thought I was going to need someone to tie my hands up to keep me from ripping off his clothes. No one had ever made me feel the way I felt when I was with Reed.

I was standing in the restroom, looking in the mirror, and I couldn't help but laugh, thinking about how Reed had bought a Kindle and had been reading my favorite book. I shook my head as I pulled my hair up into a ponytail.

A dark-haired girl walked up next to me and smiled. "I have to tell you, you and your husband must be very much in love."

I glanced at her with a confused look on my face. "My husband?"

She laughed. "Yeah. I asked your hubby to dance, and he told me he was too madly in love with his wife to dance with anyone but her. I thought it was so sweet. I wish I had a guy who looked at me the way he looks at you. All night, my friends and I have been jealous while watching y'all." She winked and walked away.

I stood there, stunned. *Wife?*

I giggled and made my way back out to my *husband*. The thought of being married to Reed did weird things to my body, and I had to put my hand on my stomach to calm my nerves. The moment I saw him, he smiled, and the song "Cyclone" by Baby Bash began playing.

"Time to show you exactly how I feel about you, Reed Moore."

I walked up and immediately began dancing against him. He grabbed on to my hips and started moving right along with me. Then, he let out a moan, and I couldn't help myself. I smiled as I turned my back to him and moved closer. I could feel how much he wanted me, and it was driving me insane. I leaned against him as he moved his hands up and down my body. He pressed his lips against my neck, kissing me, until he moved to bite on my earlobe.

"Oh God, Reed," I said.

"Courtney, you drive me crazy." He turned me around and pulled me closer to him.

We continued to dance like we couldn't get close enough to each other. The song stopped, and another song began. We both just stood there until I finally smiled.

"Do you know what I want to do next?" I asked.

He laughed. "Probably not what I want to do next."

I swallowed. I wanted to tell him I did want to do what he wanted to do, more than anything, but instead, I grinned and shook my head. "I want to drive down a country road with all the windows down while I sing along to a country song, just feeling free!"

He nodded, and the next thing I knew, we were back in his truck. The windows were down, and my favorite Keith Urban song, "We Were Us," was blasting over the speakers.

I yelled at Reed, "How did you know I love this song?"

He winked and said, "I make it my business to know what you love, Courtney."

Shit. There went that feeling in my stomach again. It wasn't butterflies. It was ten times more powerful than that.

Reed drove around, and I swore he played every one of my favorite songs.

By the time we got back to the ranch, it was well past one in the morning. Instead of parking at the house, he kept driving down the road, and then he parked in a pasture that had cows everywhere.

"Wow, you really take your cow-sitting job seriously," I said.

He started laughing and turned to look at me. "You ready, sweetheart?"

My heart was pounding. "Are we going to make out?"

He smiled and let out a small laugh. "Oh no, baby. We're going to do something much more fun. We're going cow-tipping." He jumped out of his truck and ran around to my door.

"Wait! What? I'm not tipping over a cow. Are you insane?" I said as he grabbed my hand and pulled me out of the truck.

He started laughing. "Baby, you can't really tip them over. Besides, cows don't sleep standing up."

I stopped walking and let go of his hand. "Then, what are we doing in a field with cows in the middle of the night?"

"We're going to play tag," he said with such a serious look on his face.

"Huh?" I said with a chuckle.

"Tag. You said one of your favorite things to do is play tag in a field of cows. So, we're playing tag"—he looked around and pointed to the cows—"in a field of cows."

I busted out laughing. "Oh my God, Reed. I was kidding with y'all when I said that."

He smirked and hit me on the shoulder. "Tag! You're it!" he yelled before he took off running.

"Reed! It's dark, and I can barely see!" I shouted.

"That makes it all the more fun. The moon is out. I can see perfectly."

I put my hands on my hips and said, "First off, you're a cowboy, so you should be able to see." I tilted my head and rolled my eyes. That even sounded stupid to me. "And second, I'm in my good pair of boots and jeans."

He stepped out from behind a cow. "Are you afraid you can't catch me?"

Oh no, he didn't. "Pesh, I can catch you. I happen to be very skilled in playing tag."

He slowly walked up to me, bent down, and kissed me. "I think we could have fun with the many different ways we could play tag together."

I sucked in a breath of air. I had never been romanced like this, and what he was doing to me was both thrilling and annoying.

He hit me on the shoulder again. "You're still it!"

He went to turn and run away, but he slipped in something. I couldn't help but start laughing as it looked like he was slipping on ice. The next thing I knew, he was down on the ground, yelling out every curse word known to man. I put my hands over my mouth to try to hold in my laughter.

"Motherfucking son of a bitch! Fucking cows and your damn shit!" Reed yelled out as he tried to stand up, but he slipped again.

"Jesus, are you slipping in cow shit?" I was laughing my ass off.

He looked at me, and I froze.

"Oh no! No, Reed…you wouldn't. Reed…" I started backing up as Reed stood. "Reed…if you touch me with cow shit anywhere on your clothes, I swear, any chance of having sex with me is out the door."

The next thing I knew, he began taking off his clothes. I kept walking backward until I bumped into a cow. The damn thing didn't even move. Reed walked up and put his hands on the cow, placing them on either side of me. I glanced down at his naked body as I licked my lips, and I swore I could feel my panties getting wetter by the second. I swallowed hard and looked up into his eyes.

"I, um…I'm seriously thinking I could make love to your stinky ass and not even care," I whispered.

Moving in, he was about to kiss me, but then he said, "Don't touch me anywhere, angel."

He kissed me, and as our tongues began exploring each other, I let out a long, soft moan. The idea of not being able to touch him was turning me on even more.

"Reed…" I whispered against his lips as he slowly pulled away.

He smiled and said, "I'm going to jump into the back of my truck. Will you drive us up to the house?"

"Okay." My chest was heaving up and down as I tried desperately to catch my breath.

He pushed off the cow and started walking to his truck.

"What about your clothes?" I asked.

Motherfucker. He had the nicest ass I'd ever seen.

"Stop staring at my ass."

I scrunched up my nose and tried to hide my giggle. "But it's such a cute ass!" I said as I began skipping over to the truck. I was totally on cloud nine.

I watched as Reed carefully picked up his clothes and threw them in the bed of his truck.

I couldn't wait to tell Whitley that I'd seen Reed naked—with cow shit on him!

I pulled up and parked Reed's truck. I sat and watched as Reed strutted his naked ass over to the water hose before he rinsed off.

"God, please don't let this night end…or be a dream," I whispered.

I bit down on my bottom lip as I let myself daydream about what he would feel like inside me. I squeezed my legs together to stop the throbbing I'd been feeling all night.

I jumped out of his truck and yelled, "Do you want me to get a towel?"

I couldn't see his expression, but I was pretty sure he was smiling. I turned and started to make my way to the house. I screamed when I felt Reed picking me up. He began running with me, and the moment I saw him heading toward the pool, I knew what he was going to do.

"No! My boots!" I screamed.

He threw me into the pool and then jumped in. When I came up to the surface, I was cussing like a sailor.

"Reed…Reed…oh shit! What in the hell is your middle name? Why don't I know your middle name? Damn it!"

He moved over to me, laughing. When he got closer, he pulled me to him. "Nickolas."

Oh, son of a bitch…I love that name. "Reed Nickolas Moore…" I couldn't even be mad anymore. All I wanted to do was wrap my legs around him and kiss him.

"Yes, Courtney Marie Will?"

I let out a gasp. "How do you know my middle name?" I asked.

He put his hand on the side of my face and whispered, "I told you, I make it my business to know everything about you, to know everything you love, and to try to make you feel safe and happy."

I looked down at his mouth. "You didn't tell me all of that."

"I didn't?" he whispered.

I shook my head and smiled at him as I looked into his beautiful eyes. I couldn't tell what color they were in the dark. Sometimes, they were green, and sometimes, they were blue.

"Reed…I…I…" I barely got out any words as my voice cracked.

"Talk to me, Courtney."

I closed my eyes as I took a deep breath in and slowly let it out. I opened my eyes and wrapped my legs around him. "I love you, Reed. I've loved you for so long, and I'm tired of being afraid of that love."

He closed his eyes and put his forehead against mine. "You totally just made me the happiest man on earth." He pulled away, opened his eyes, and smiled. "Courtney, I've loved you since the first moment I saw you. I'll love you for the rest of my life."

I slammed my lips to his and kissed him. It felt like we couldn't get close enough to each other as the kiss grew more passionate. I wanted to crawl inside his body and just stay there.

"Courtney, I want to show you what real love feels like. I want to take you completely. I don't want to just make you mine. I want to know you inside and out, baby. I want to make love to you like it's your first time."

I began crying. "It will be my first time, Reed. I want to forget about ever being with anyone else because…because I've never felt like this before, and my first time was…"

I started crying harder, and he held on to me tighter. I wanted to tell him the truth, but I didn't want to ruin this moment. As we stood there in the pool and held on to each other, I remembered his ass was completely naked.

"I know what I want to do next," I said with a smile as I looked into his eyes.

He pushed my hair away and smiled so sweetly at me. "Anything…you name it, Court."

"Please make love to me, Reed. Please…just love me."

I watched as his eyes filled with tears, and he smiled.

"Court…" he whispered as he began walking us out of the pool. "I have to take a shower first though."

He scrunched up his nose in the cutest damn way, and the butterflies went nuts in my stomach.

Oh God…I've totally given Reed Nickolas Moore my heart and soul.

I let out a giggle. "Yes, please take a shower first."

He gave me his beautiful crooked smile and said, "Oh no, baby, not just me. You're taking one with me."

My heart dropped, and I couldn't help but smile. I'd never done anything like that before. Mitch was the only guy I'd ever had a somewhat normal relationship with, and he had been a wham-bam-thank-you-ma'am kind of lover. He'd never done anything other than typical lovemaking, and even that had sucked. He certainly hadn't been my Prince Charming in the lovemaking area.

Reed set me down, ran over and grabbed a towel that had been left on a table since the other day when we had been sitting out by the pool. He wrapped it around his waist and turned to look at me.

I looked his body up and down as he stood there in the moonlight, looking all hot and shit. His body was amazing. He would go running every morning, and I swore, he'd work out every day in some way or another.

He had a tattoo on his back of a Texas longhorn with the colors of the Texas flag, and on the side of the bull's face, next to his eye, was an outline of the Texas star. On his chest, he had another tattoo of a Latin phrase. Ever since I'd first seen it, I'd wanted so badly to ask him why he had *cor meum*, which meant *my heart*, tattooed on his chest, but I had been scared to death that it was for someone else, so I'd decided that I would rather not know. I knew it was his most recent tattoo. I remembered a few months back when Layton had asked Reed how he liked his new Latin tattoo. He also had a small tribal tattoo on the other side of his chest. It was a circular pattern, and the shading on it was amazing. I had stared at it the other day, wanting nothing more than to run my tongue all along the design. I hardly ever saw the few tattoos he had because he always kept them covered up with a T-shirt. I knew he couldn't have any showing because of his job.

"You ready, Court?" he asked, snapping me out of my thoughts.

I glanced up and nodded my head as I pulled off my boots. I didn't want to walk through the house while I was soaking wet. I knew Layton would kick my ass if I got his wood floors wet, and plus, my clothes felt like they weighed a ton. I reached down, lifted my shirt up, and pulled it over my head. Afterward, I never took my eyes off of Reed's face. I wanted to watch him as I slowly slipped out of my wet clothes. I tossed my shirt onto a chair, and I decided to leave my bra on. I was silently thanking God that I had put on my light pink lace push-up bra with matching panties. The panties were my favorite lace-trim cheeky panties, and they always made me feel so sexy.

I unbuttoned my jeans and began to push them down. All thoughts of being sexy went right out the door when the bitches got stuck right below my ass, and I started hopping up and down, trying to get them off.

"Motherfucker! *Really*?" I yelled as I tried to pull the jeans off. I felt myself losing my balance, and I closed my eyes, preparing to go back into the pool.

I felt a jolt of electricity run through my body as Reed grabbed a hold of me to keep me from falling in.

"Only you could make all of that look sexy as hell, Courtney," he said in a low voice.

Wait, what? He thought that was sexy? Oh hell, he's going to be easy to please!

"Sit down on the chair, baby," Reed said.

He knelt in front of me and began working my jeans off. He finally got the soaking wet jeans off my legs and stood up. He reached down for my hand and gently pulled me up. His eyes moved up and down my body, like he was trying to memorize every inch of me. I'd never been so turned-on in my life.

"You're so beautiful, Courtney. You take my breath away. You're so damn beautiful," he whispered.

Oh God. I wanted him to touch me so badly that it hurt. I'd loved him and wanted him for so long. I was afraid if I moved, I would wake up from a dream. I stood there, not really sure what to say or do.

He placed his hands on my face and gently began kissing me. When he pulled away, he took my bottom lip and sucked on it, and I let out a soft moan.

"Reed…" I whispered against his lips.

He reached down and picked me up, and then he started walking toward the house. He was just about to open the back door when he practically walked us into it. The door was locked. He stood there for a few seconds, just staring at the door.

"Um…your truck keys are still in your truck. I left them in there," I said, thinking he needed them to unlock the door.

He looked at me and started laughing. "I don't have Layton's key on my key ring. I had it on another set of keys…that I left in the house. I was so excited about tonight that I left them sitting on the kitchen island."

I smiled and shook my head. "I have a set in my purse that's still in your truck."

He slowly began putting me down, and then he quickly kissed me on the lips. "Don't move!" he said before running over to his truck.

The only thing I could think was, *How is the gravel driveway not hurting his bare feet?*

By the time he ran his way back with nothing but a towel wrapped around him while cursing for forgetting the keys, I was so turned-on that I could hardly stand it. I wanted to reach my hand in my panties and ease the throbbing.

He ran up, unlocked the door, reached in to turn off the alarm, and then flipped on the kitchen lights. Following him inside, I held my breath and waited for the dogs to come running. I thought Reed was doing the same thing because we both just stood there, listening. Once we heard Lulu barking from her kennel, we looked at each other and smiled.

"Thank God," we both said and laughed.

"I'll go let the dogs out. You go upstairs and start the shower in my bathroom," Reed said.

I nodded my head, and I was about to head off to go upstairs when he grabbed my hand and pulled me to him. He looked into my eyes, and then his eyes drifted down to my lips. I purposely licked them, and he let out a moan.

"Jesus," he whispered.

He glanced down to my chest that was now heaving up and down from the excitement of the way he was looking at me. He took his finger and ran it along the edge of my bra. My whole body shuddered under his touch.

"Are you cold?" he asked me in a whispered voice.

I slowly shook my head. "No," I whispered back.

His eyes snapped up and met mine. I wanted him to know that it was his touch causing my body to react this way. He gently moved his finger down to my stomach. I'd never in my life felt the way I was feeling right at this moment. I needed him to touch me before I combusted right then and there.

"Reed…" I said as I placed my hands on his chest.

He barely slid his finger along the edge of my panties, and I let out a moan that I'd tried so desperately to hold in. The next thing I knew, he was down on his knees, slipping my panties off. My breathing was getting faster and faster as I willed him to kiss me down there. When he kissed my belly button, I threw my hands into his hair and dropped my head back.

I've dreamed of this moment for so long.

"I have, too, Courtney," Reed said.

I snapped my head down and looked at him. "What?"

He looked up and smiled at me. "I've dreamed of this moment for so long, too."

Holy shit! I hadn't realized that I'd said that out loud.

He lifted up my leg and put it over his shoulder as I reached back and held on to the kitchen island.

Yes! Oh God, yes!

When I felt his hot breath on me, I wanted to yell out, but I bit down on my lower lip. Then, his tongue swiped across my clit, and my whole body jerked.

"Oh God, Reed."

"Courtney, I want to make love to you first before—"

I grabbed on to his hair and pulled it. "Please, Reed. I'm going to die if you don't do this. Do you want me to die?" I pleaded, sounding so desperate, but I didn't even care at this point.

He let out a laugh. "Well, that would really suck if you died on me right now."

"I know, right?" I panted out.

Then, he buried his face into me, and I let out a moan. He sucked on my clit as I screamed out his name. The moment he slid his fingers inside me and moaned, I lost it. I began calling out his name as one of the most intense orgasms of my life ripped through my body.

Holy shit. "Oh my God. Oh…Reed…I can't…oh God." *Holy hell, I can't even form the words to say how incredible this feels.*

I could practically feel myself squeezing his fingers. Once I was finally coming down from my orgasm, I felt my leg giving out on me. Reed was up so fast, and before I even knew what was happening, he was carrying me toward the stairs.

I got my wits about me and said, "Reed, the dogs."

He let out a sigh, turned, and quickly headed their way.

"These fucking dogs are going to be the death of me!" he yelled out.

I laughed as he reached one hand down and let the dogs out of their kennels. They immediately began running and jumping.

"Oh, they want to play," I said with a giggle.

Reed looked at me and said, "So do I! To hell with them. They can come and go out the dog door. I can't wait another minute to be inside you."

"Oh," was all I could get out. I was still on the high from my orgasm.

Reed held me tighter in his arms as he carried me while he quickly walked back through the kitchen and opened the dog door for the dogs to go in and out of the house.

I buried my face into his bare chest as he ran up the stairs. I was nervous as hell but so incredibly excited.

"So strong, Mr. Moore," I said with a chuckle.

He laughed as he pushed open the bedroom door. Reed was staying in the second master bedroom that was almost as amazing as Layton and Whitley's bedroom. He walked over to the sitting area and sat me down on one of the oversized chairs. He reached for a blanket and put it over me.

"I don't want you getting sick. Give me two seconds to get the shower going." He kissed me on the nose and took off toward the bathroom.

I watched as he walked away, wishing I had pulled off his towel before he turned away from me. I threw my head back against the chair and tried to calm my beating heart.

Oh my God, what he just did to me with his mouth was amazing. The way he's treating me like a princess…please, God, please don't let this be a dream.

I heard the shower start up, and I slowly smiled. *I'm about to take a shower with Reed.* My stomach did all kinds of weird dips and dives, and I threw my hands up to my mouth to keep the scream buried inside. *Oh. My. God. I'm about to take a shower with Reed!* With excitement, I started moving my legs up and down so fast that I was sure if Reed were to walk in right now, he would think I was having a seizure. I closed my eyes and quickly said a prayer that I wouldn't fuck this up.

I didn't hear when Reed walked back up, but I could feel him, smell him. He always smelled so damn good, and it drove me insane when he got too close to me. Then, I felt his lips on my neck, and I let out a small moan.

"Reed…I'm so afraid I'm dreaming right now, and if I am, I don't want to wake up," I whispered.

"Oh, baby, trust me, you're not dreaming," he whispered back as he moved away from me.

I quickly opened my eyes, wanting to plead with him to keep kissing me. He held out his hand, and I pushed the blanket off of me as I took his hand. He helped me up and started walking backward toward the bathroom.

"Let me prove to you that you're not dreaming." He used his other hand and pulled off his towel.

I could finally look at him in the light and take it all in. I looked at his perfectly toned body and licked my lips. I tried pulling my eyes away to look back up into his eyes, but I couldn't.

Oh, for Christ's sake, Courtney, stop staring at his dick! It's not like you've never seen one before!

Right then, he sneezed, and I snapped my eyes back up to his.

He whispered, "Damn dogs."

I smiled. "I'd say God bless you, but"—I looked down at his dick again and then back up at him—"it appears he already has."

The smile that spread across his face caused me to giggle. He pulled me to him and slammed his lips against mine as he quickly began undoing my bra. I hardly even remembered that I was still in my bra.

When he pulled away, he looked right into my eyes. "My God, I love you, Courtney. I love your smart attitude, your sense of humor, and your breathtaking blue eyes that captured my heart the first time I ever looked into them."

He stepped back and let my bra fall away. His eyes traveled up and down my body in a greedy way, and I felt the blush hit my cheeks. I'd never had anyone look at me the way he was, and I felt embarrassed and so sexy at the same time.

He took both my hands and walked us into the shower. He grabbed the soap and the washcloth and started to soap it up. He began washing his body as I stood under the hot water. I took the soap and washcloth from him and took over cleaning his body. He closed his eyes, and I bit down on my lip as I moved my hand down to his dick before I began stroking it.

"Shit, Court, don't do that, or I won't be able to make love to you."

I quickly stopped and smiled. He still had his eyes closed, and I wanted to jump up and down from knowing how I was making him feel. I internally hugged myself before my eyes landed on the tattoo on his chest. I used my finger and traced it.

"My heart," I said.

His eyes quickly opened, and he whispered, "Yes."

I chewed on my lower lip, trying to get the courage to ask him about it.

"When I finally realized who my heart would always belong to, I got this tattoo. I've never told anyone what it meant, except for Layton. I didn't know you knew Latin," he said with a smile.

I nodded my head. *Who does his heart belong to?* I remembered he had been with Anna when he got this done, and I instantly began feeling sick.

"I, um…grew up Catholic, and my parents insisted I learn Latin, so I began studying it when I was twelve."

He let out a small laugh. Then, he took his finger and placed it on my chin. He lifted my head up until I was looking into his eyes. They were so beautiful and blue right now.

"You're my heart, Courtney. My heart will always belong to you. Always."

I sucked in a breath of air. "But…" I shook my head. "But you were with Anna when you got this, and—"

He moved his finger up to my lips. "I never loved Anna like I love you. I cared about her, but I never loved her. I never saw my future with her in it. I only ever saw you. I only ever wanted you in my future, Courtney."

I couldn't hold back my tears anymore. *I must be dreaming. I have to be dreaming.* I started to panic. *He has to know I've always loved him. I've always wanted him and dreamed about him, too.*

"Reed…I've always loved you. I'm so sorry for being so stupid and picking Mitch over you. It's just…it's just that I've never in my life felt this way. When I first saw you…the way my heart felt…the sound of your voice…how it all affected me…I was so scared. And then…oh my God, your damn name!"

Reed let out a laugh as he threw his head back.

"I wanted you so much that it frightened me. I was so scared that you'd hurt me. You were my dream, Reed, and I didn't want my dream to turn into my nightmare."

He looked into my eyes as he stopped laughing, and his smile faded. "I was scared, too, Court…more than you know. When I look back at how stupid we both acted…" He shook his head. "The last thing I ever want to do is hurt you, and I feel like I've hurt you so much already. I hate that I've hurt you."

I was stunned when I saw a tear slide down his face. If he had been standing under the water, I would have never seen it. My heart slammed in my chest, and I let out a sob.

"Reed…I need to move out of this darkness I've been living in. I need your love to help me do that. I don't want to be scared anymore," I said as I began crying harder.

"Courtney…" he whispered.

He picked me up and began kissing me. I wrapped my legs around him, and with each second that passed, I felt myself finally being led out of the dark.

"I'm going to make love to you, baby," he said against my lips.

Shower sex! Oh, hell yes! This just keeps getting better!

He turned around and pushed me against the back of the shower.

I wanted to scream out, *I'm about to have wall sex in a fucking shower and with the man of my dreams!*

I pulled on his hair as I brushed my lips against his and whispered, "Yes."

The moment I felt him inside me, I began crying again.

"Am I hurting you, Court?" he asked as he looked into my eyes.

I quickly shook my head. "No. Oh God, no, Reed. It feels like heaven."

With the way he was moving in and out of me so slowly and passionately, I could feel his love pouring into my body, washing away every bad memory. I never wanted this moment to end.

Just when I thought it couldn't get any better, I looked into his eyes and said, "Reed…I'm going to come."

The second I began calling out his name, Reed began to move faster. I felt myself squeezing him, and when he looked into my eyes, I knew this was real. This wasn't a dream, and I knew he would never turn this into a nightmare.

He started gasping for a breath, and the look in his eyes turned to fear. "I'm not wearing a condom, Court."

I smiled. "It's okay…on the pill. Please…I need all of you, Reed."

With that, he began calling out my name, and I felt his warm liquid enter my body. I threw my head back against the shower wall and closed my eyes. Nothing had ever felt so perfect to me.

He held me for the longest time, neither one of us saying a word.

When he pulled back and his eyes pierced mine, he whispered, “I love you.”

Then, he began kissing me, and we each whispered our names against each other’s lips.

EIGHT

REED

While I caught my breath and tried to keep my knees from giving out on me, I leaned one arm up against the shower wall as I held Courtney with the other. I'd never in my life experienced what I just had while making love to her. Every fear I'd ever had about hurting the one person I loved so much had seemed to vanish as she whispered out my name. I slowly slid her down, and then I put my hands on the shower wall on either side of her as I tried to catch my breath.

I just made love to Courtney. I just made love to the only girl I've ever loved. I shook my head and tried to keep myself from crying like a pussy. *God, I hope I made that special for her.* I closed my eyes and took in a deep breath.

When I felt her hands on my face, I opened my eyes to see her beautiful smile. Her blue eyes seemed to be shining, and I wasn't sure if it was from the lights or not.

"Courtney, I…I've never felt this way before," I whispered. "God, I hope that I didn't ruin things for you because I couldn't wait. I wanted to be inside you so bad. I'm so sorry—"

This time, she moved her fingers to my lips to stop me from talking. "Reed, that was so incredible. Even if I tried to tell you every day for the rest of our lives, you will never know how unbelievable that was for me. It couldn't have been any more perfect."

I let out the breath I'd been holding and pulled her to me. "I love you, Courtney. God, I love you so much."

"I love you, too, Reed, so very much."

I wasn't sure how long we stood there before she let out a giggle.

"What's so funny?" I asked.

She pulled back and made an adorable face, and it just about dropped me to my knees.

"I know what I want to do next."

"Um…" I looked down at my dick, and when it jumped, I felt pretty confident that I could make love to her again very soon. "I think he's ready!" I said.

She busted out laughing. "Oh, believe me, I want to do that again, too, but next, I want to go horseback riding. I've always wanted to ride during a full moon."

I looked at her and smiled. There wasn't anything I wouldn't do for this girl. I let out a small laugh and said, "If my baby wants to go horseback riding in the middle of the damn night, then we'll go horseback riding in the middle of the damn night."

She jumped up and down and hugged herself. It took everything I had not to push her against the wall and make love to her again. I reached around and turned off the water, and then I grabbed two towels. I wrapped her up in one towel, and then I quickly wrapped the other one around my waist. We stepped out of the giant walk-in shower, and I turned her around slowly before I began drying her off. I watched as she stood there with her eyes closed.

Why do I get the feeling that Mitch never treated her with the adoration she deserves? I was going to make her feel this way every day for the rest of my life.

As I moved the towel up and down each leg, I looked up to see her touching her breasts.

Holy shit.

I put my hand on the inside of her leg, and I slowly moved it up. She let out a soft moan and pinched one of her nipples.

Fuck the horseback riding. I stood up, scooped her up, and took her out to the bedroom where I gently laid her down on the bed. I quickly dried off in record time, and then I moved myself over her body.

"Reed…oh God…what are you doing to me?" she said.

I began kissing her nipples as I moved my hand down her body. The second I slipped two fingers in, we both let out a moan.

"Damn, Court, you're so wet, baby." I moved my lips up her chest and along her neck.

"Please…oh God…Reed, please make love to me again."

That was all I needed. I began teasing her entrance with my tip, and she thrashed her head back and forth on the pillow. I quickly rose up and looked her body up and down. I couldn't believe this was happening.

"Reed…you're killing me. *Please stop teasing me*," she begged.

I continued to barely slip my dick in and out.

"Reed! Damn it! Just fuck me already!" she yelled out.

Motherfucker. I've died and gone to heaven.

I didn't want to hurt her, but her telling me to fuck her pushed me over the edge, and I slammed my dick inside her. After a few pumps, she began calling out my name, and I tried to hold off for as long as I could, but she was driving me insane.

"Yes! Reed…harder! Faster! Reed…yes, I'm coming," she began crying out.

Holy shit. "Courtney…I'm gonna come." I began kissing her, capturing her screams of pleasure.

When I felt like I'd finally finished pouring myself into her, I collapsed next to her. We both lay there for a few minutes, attempting to catch our breaths.

"That…was…amazing. Let's…do that…again," Courtney said in between breaths of air.

I let out a laugh and rolled over to her. "As much as I'd love to do that again, I don't think it's humanly possible for me to go again so soon. At least give me an hour."

She turned her head and looked at me as she laughed. "I've never felt so amazing. Thank you." She rolled over to face me, and then she ran her hand through my hair.

"So, not too bad for a tree-loving, cultivating-plant pussy, huh?" I said with a wink.

She busted out laughing and pushed me away from her as she said, "No, not too bad at all."

She placed her hand on the side of my face, and I leaned my head into her hand.

"Thank you, Reed. Thank you for just being you. Thank you for loving me, and thank you for not giving up on me."

I pulled her hand away and gently kissed her. "You want to ride Tink?"

Her eyes lit up, and she began nodding her head quickly. She jumped up from the bed and headed toward the door. She turned around and put her finger in her mouth as she smiled. "I know something else I want to do."

I sat up and smiled as I looked her naked body up and down. "Oh yeah? What is it?"

She shook her head and said, "Just bring a blanket with us on the ride. I'll meet you in the kitchen in ten minutes. I need to go get dressed." She slowly backed out of the room and made her way downstairs.

I fell back on the bed and pulled a pillow over my head as I kicked my feet around in excitement. I was acting like a high school girl with how happy I was, but I didn't care. I hopped out of bed and began getting dressed for our late-night ride.

I took one look at my dick before I slid my jeans up. "Don't fail me now. I need you to function at your best performance. We haven't had sex in so long, buddy. You've got some making up to do."

I shook my head, surprised I'd lasted as long as I had in the shower. Just the idea alone of making love to Courtney should have made me come in a minute or less. There was also the fact that I hadn't slept with Anna for months before we broke up. Ever since I'd gotten the tattoo on my chest, I just couldn't bring myself to have sex with her while I was so in love with Courtney.

I thought back to when Courtney and I had figured out that Layton and Whitley had set us both up to stay at the house at the same time. I was going to give Layton a big ole kiss when I saw him tomorrow—or later today actually. I looked at the clock and quickly put on my boots before heading downstairs.

The moment I walked into the kitchen, I saw Courtney leaning over while looking in the refrigerator, and I stopped dead in my tracks.

Damn, that girl has a nice ass.

She started moving it back and forth as she began humming some song. My dick jumped, making it clear he was definitely down for a marathon tonight. I leaned back against the doorjamb and watched as she wiggled around while Lulu and Midnight just sat there, waiting. Then, she started singing "Oops! I Did It Again," and I noticed she was listening to her iPod.

I stepped around the corner and stood in the living room as I listened to her. My cheeks were beginning to hurt from smiling so big. I peeked around the corner and saw she had a pickle in her hand while she was now dancing with the dogs running around her. I let out a laugh, and Midnight came running over.

Courtney spun around and saw me. She kept singing as she began moving toward me. When she walked up to me, she started grinding her hips against me as she continued singing.

Good God. It would have helped if she had a terrible voice, but she actually had a beautiful voice.

I grabbed her hips and pulled her closer to me. She raised her eyebrows when she felt my erection, and she let out a giggle.

"Ready so soon, huh?" she said as she pulled out her earbuds.

"You sure you want to go for a ride? I could easily take you right here on this kitchen island."

She looked over her shoulder and then back up into my eyes. She bit down on her lower lip. "I'd rather make love on your kitchen island at the cabin."

I sucked in a breath of air and smiled. "I love you, Court. I hope you know that I will do everything in my power to never hurt you—ever."

Her smile faded for a quick second before she flashed it back at me. "Let's go riding."

I grabbed her hand. "Come on, mutts. Y'all want to go?"

"Oh, Reed, they won't run away, will they?" Courtney asked.

I grinned. "No, baby. I always take them when I ride. They love it."

She let out a sigh and started skipping out of the house with both dogs and me in tow.

I watched as she and the dogs made their way over to the ranch truck. She pulled the tailgate down, and the dogs jumped into the bed of the truck. She shut it and turned back as she smiled.

I walked up to her and held up the blanket. "Will this work?" I leaned down and gently kissed her.

"Oh, yes, that will be perfect," she whispered against my lips.

As we rode along, the light of the moon lit our pathway. I glanced over, and my breath caught as I saw Courtney with her head thrown back and a smile on her face.

"Damn…it's so cool out, and that breeze feels amazing. I've always wanted to ride at night!" Courtney said with a giggle. She snapped her head forward and then looked at me. "What?" she asked.

I slowly shook my head and smiled. "I just don't want this to be a dream. If it is, I don't ever want to wake up."

She started laughing. "I feel the same way." Her smile faded, and she brought Tink to a stop. "Do you think we could stop here and…talk for a bit?"

The seriousness in her voice scared the shit out of me. "Sure." I jumped off my horse and grabbed the blanket as I looked around for somewhere to sit.

"Just let Tink roam?" Courtney asked.

"Yeah, Tink and Rascal are good horses. They won't wander far, and the dogs will end up just lying near us."

I looked over her shoulder and saw a giant elm tree. I walked over and laid out the blanket. My heart was racing. I could hear it in Courtney's voice that she was nervous about something.

Please don't let this just be a fling for her. Please, God, don't let her say this all ends tonight.

We both sat down on the blanket, and Courtney pulled her knees up to her chest as she finally looked at me.

She took a deep breath and slowly let it out. "Reed, I need to tell you about Noah."

Noah…the guy she was dreaming about. I took a deep breath in and said, "Okay. Who's Noah?"

The moment I saw the moonlight hit the tear rolling down her face, I died inside.

Whoever he is, I plan on hurting him.

NINE

Hearing Noah's name coming from Reed's lips killed me. I'd never told anyone—*no one*—about what happened with Noah. Reed was different though. I knew I wanted to spend the rest of my life with Reed. I knew I loved him more than life itself, and I didn't want to keep anything from him.

I quickly wiped the tears away and took in a deep breath. "Noah is my brother's best friend. He's two years older than me, and he was my high school crush."

I stopped and looked at Reed. His eyes were fixed on mine, and I'd never had anyone give me such devoted attention before in my life.

"When I was sixteen, he asked me to go to his senior prom. Needless to say, I was overjoyed, and I said yes. I was just happy that he'd finally noticed me," I said with a weak smile.

I swallowed hard as my mind went back to that night. I closed my eyes, and when I felt Reed take my hand, I jumped.

I shook my head and opened my eyes. "Noah always stayed at our house when his parents would go out of town, which was often. His dad worked for the government, doing something. I never did understand what he did. Anyway, Noah was staying with us for the weekend, and I was so excited because that meant I got to see him all weekend. I was still jazzed from him asking me to the prom. That same night, he came into my bedroom in the middle of the night."

Reed's grasp on my hand tightened.

I closed my eyes and prayed that I could get through this without crying. Opening my eyes, I took in another deep breath and slowly let it out. "I asked him why he was in my room, and he said he was there to…to…make me his," I barely said.

"No," Reed whispered.

"I told him to leave, and if my father or brother caught him in my room, they would be mad. Noah put his hand over my mouth and pushed me onto my back. He…he, um…" I stopped for a second to regain my composure.

"He told me if I said anything, he would hurt my brother, and Tyler would lose his football scholarship. So, I promised to be quiet. Then, he started touching me. He slid my panties down, and I grabbed his hands as I asked him to stop. I told him that I didn't want this, and he just kept telling me that I did, that he saw the way I looked at him, so he knew I wanted him." I began shaking my head. "I didn't, Reed. I didn't want my first time to be like that, so I begged him to stop. I said that I didn't care what he did to my brother, but then Noah…he…"

Reed started to move closer toward me. I knew he just wanted to take me into his arms, but I needed to do this.

I put my hand up to stop him. "No, wait. I have to get this all out, Reed. Please," I said as I looked into his tear-filled eyes.

Taking in a shaky breath, I closed my eyes and slowly opened them again. I needed to think about my future with Reed. I wanted a future with him. I wanted kids. I wanted to finally let go of this darkness that was buried so deep inside of me. I had to get this all out.

"He told me he would hurt my parents, and then he would go after my younger sister, who was only fourteen at the time."

Reed sucked in a breath of air and whispered, "Fucking bastard."

"So, I promised him I wouldn't make any noise, and I wouldn't tell anyone our secret. The moment I felt him down there, I just kind of got lost in my own world. I started repeating my favorite book quotes over and over in my head."

"My God, Courtney," Reed whispered as he reached up and wiped away my tears.

I squeezed his hand, my knuckles turning white. "He started staying at our house more and more. Each time he came into my room, I would just try to disappear into another world. I tried to pretend I was with the love of my life, but it never worked. He just destroyed me more and more after each time."

I took a deep breath in and then let it out. "It went on for three months until I couldn't take it anymore. One night, I was watching my father clean his guns. I told him I wanted to learn more about how to clean them. I had gone hunting with my father a lot, so it made sense to him that I was interested in knowing more about guns. After that, I only needed the combo to his gun safe."

Reed began shaking his head.

"I got the combo, and the next night Noah stayed with us, I snuck into my father's office and took a handgun. I checked to make sure it was loaded, and it was. I brought it up to my room and put it under my pillow. I had the safety on the whole time. I was ready to put a stop to all of it. When Noah came into my room that night, I didn't care what I had to do."

I took a second to look at Reed. His eyes were filled with such sadness, but there was also something else there—anger.

"He told me to get undressed and said that we were going to try something new."

Reed pulled his hand from mine and ran it down his face. I could see his anger growing more and more.

He began shaking his head. "I want to kill him, Courtney," he said as he looked me in the eyes.

My heart started beating faster, and I wanted nothing more than to be in his arms. "Reed," I barely whispered, "I just need to get this all out…please."

He slowly nodded his head and took my hand in his again.

Praying to get through this, I began again. "So, anyway, I stood up with the gun, faced him, and pointed it at him. I told him it all stopped right then and there. I was willing to spend the rest of my life in jail if it meant he would leave me alone."

"Your sister?" Reed asked in a whispered voice.

"I told him I would sit outside her door with the gun every night if I had to. He never stayed with us again. He somehow talked his parents into letting my brother come to his house when they went out of town. After Noah and my brother left for college, they hardly ever came home. When they did, they stayed at their girlfriends' places, so I didn't have to worry about my sister."

Reed cleared his throat and looked away before glancing back at me. "Did he ever…your sister?"

I shook my head. "I don't think so. I asked her once if Noah had ever approached her in a way that made her uncomfortable, and she said no before asking me why I would ask her that. I'm almost a hundred percent sure he never touched her."

"Wait…Court, you never told her about what happened?"

I slowly shook my head and whispered, "I've never told anyone."

Something I'd never seen before moved across Reed's face. He pulled back and looked down a little to the side, like he was thinking about something.

"What Whitley said to me that night…" His face snapped up, and he looked me in the eyes.

I looked at him, confused. "What are you talking about?"

"Baby, you never even told Whitley?" he asked.

The concern in his voice and the knowledge that I'd actually told someone hit me like a brick wall, and I began crying hysterically.

"No. You're the…first person…I've told," I said in between sobs.

He grabbed me and pulled me onto his lap. He held me as he gently ran his hand up and down my back. He didn't say a word. He didn't have to. I just needed him to hold me right now. I felt so incredibly safe in his arms.

I wasn't sure how long Reed held me while I cried. Something happened though, and the more I cried and the tighter he held me, the more free I felt. That dark, dirty secret I had held on to for so long was finally lifting away.

"Courtney, I'm so sorry that happened to you, baby. It kills me to know that you've been hurting for so long. I…"

I heard him hold in a sob, and my heart started pounding. I couldn't look at him, or I would start crying again.

"I want to love you forever, Courtney. I want to give you what you deserve and do nothing but make you feel my love for you every single day."

I slowly pulled away and looked at him. I just stared at him as I took in everything he'd said. *This is what I've always dreamed of.* Reed, my Prince Charming, was going to rescue me and love me for the rest of my life.

He pushed a piece of hair behind my ear and gave me the sweetest smile. "I love you, Courtney. I'll always love you…forever," he whispered.

"I love you, too, Reed. Forever."

He started to move me off his lap, and I instantly missed his warmth. He stood up and reached down for my hand. As he helped me up, he whistled, and both horses began walking over to us.

I looked at the horses and then back at Reed. "Holy shit, that was awesome. Will that work for you, too?" I said with a wink.

He smiled bigger as he placed both hands on my face, and he brought me in for the most amazing kiss of my life. It was so gentle and filled with so much love. I'd never in my life experienced anything like it.

"I want to give you what you deserve, Courtney," he said as he moved his thumbs gently across my cheeks.

All I could get out was, "Okay."

The ride back went by quickly once Reed had picked up the pace, and we let the horses trot back the whole way. By the time we got back to the stables, I was exhausted from the whole evening. I leaned against Tink as Reed took care of the saddles and the horses. The dancing, the laughing, the lovemaking, the crying while telling Reed about Noah—all of it just hit me at once. I moved to a hay bale and drifted off to sleep.

When I felt Reed's arms around me, I couldn't help but smile.

"Shh, go back to sleep, angel," Reed whispered into my ear.

I wrapped my arms around his neck and nodded off to sleep again. My dreams were filled with nothing but my Prince Charming.

TEN

REED

My cell phone vibrated, and I looked down at it sitting on the counter.

Layton: Hey, dude! Did you survive three weeks with Court? We landed a little bit ago and will be there in a couple of hours.

Reed: Welcome home! All I can say about the last three weeks is that I've never been this happy in my entire life.

Layton: No shit! Y'all together?

Reed: Dude…I don't kiss and tell.

Layton: About damn time. Whit is screaming next to me right now. I have a feeling they will want some girlie time when we get home.

Reed: Probably. What about you? You enjoy your three weeks?

Layton: One word—heaven. Getting in my truck now. See ya soon.

Reed: Awesome. Drive safe.

I smiled as I thought about Layton and Whitley spending three weeks alone together. I only hoped I could give Courtney that kind of an amazing honeymoon. Shaking my head to clear my thoughts, I let out a laugh. Just imagining marrying Courtney was causing my dick to jump again.

I poured two glasses of orange juice and set them on the tray next to the plates covered in scrambled eggs, toast, and fruit. Making my way upstairs, I heard Courtney on the phone. I slowed down and stopped at the door. I wasn't sure who she was talking to until I heard her let out a little scream.

"Oh, Whitley, I have so much to tell you. I mean, at first, I hated you like there was no tomorrow because y'all set us up like that, but"—she let out a sigh—"Reed is so amazing, so…*so* amazing. Oh yeah…that kind of amazing, too."

I smiled, and if I weren't holding a tray loaded down with food, I would have done a fist pump.

"Well, I don't really want to kiss and tell," Courtney purred into the phone.

I let out a small chuckle because that was exactly what I'd said to Layton. I started to make my way into the bedroom, and her eyes caught mine. I was pretty sure I let out a moan when she smiled at me.

"Okay, well, be careful driving and see you soon. Oh, trust me…I will. Later, girl."

She ended the call and tilted her head as she looked me up and down. I had on nothing but a pair of boxers.

She closed her eyes and said, "Please tell me I'm not dreaming…because I'm pretty sure I just had the most amazing night of my life last night."

I set the tray down on the side table and made my way over to her on the bed. With her eyes still closed, I gently kissed her on the lips and then sucked her bottom lip into my mouth. I pulled back slightly as she opened her eyes and looked into mine.

"If you're dreaming, then so am I, and this is one dream I don't ever want to wake up from."

Her eyes filled with tears as she gave me the sweetest smile. "Reed…" she whispered.

"I think we have time before they get here," I said as I looked down at her lips.

She pulled her lower lip in between her teeth and nodded her head. As she lay back on the bed, I stripped off my boxer shorts and then slowly began kissing her body everywhere.

"Courtney, you're so beautiful in every way."

She let out a small moan that traveled straight through my body and to my dick. I slowly began teasing her with my tip as we found each other's lips and began a sweet dance with our tongues.

I just wanted to freeze this moment in time. I needed to go slow and enjoy every second with the woman I loved. I needed her to feel special, wanted, and adored.

As I began making love to Courtney, that familiar fear of me hurting her crept back into my mind. I pushed it aside and focused on doing nothing but making her feel good. I covered her body in kisses and then focused on each of her nipples, sucking and then pulling each one with my teeth, and she let out moan after moan.

"Reed…oh God, that feels so good."

When she fell apart in my arms, I rolled her over until she was on top of me. The feel of her on me, moving in such a way that was practically driving me mad, caused me to have one of the most intense orgasms of my life. It felt like it went on forever.

Courtney leaned down and kissed me before she whispered, "Thank you for swooning me."

I smiled bigger, and inside, I was like a little boy jumping up and down for joy.

"Nick swoon-worthy?" I asked.

She made a funny expression and then looked up, like she was thinking hard. "Not quite but oh-so very close. I think you'll need more practice…lots and lots of practice."

She began grinding on me, and I swore I felt my dick growing harder.

I let out a laugh as I pulled her to me and rolled over. Pinning her to the bed, I began tickling her. It wasn't long before Lulu came running in and jumped on the bed. I immediately stopped and looked at her, and then I looked down at Courtney.

"Holy shit, we didn't crate them last night." I jumped up and started getting dressed.

"Wait, you didn't let them out when you were making breakfast?"

"No! I forgot about them, but I was sure we—"

"Courtney? Courtney, honey, are you upstairs? The front door was unlocked, so I just came in."

Courtney's eyes got so wide, and the face she was making caused me to start laughing. She hit me in the stomach and quickly started looking for clothes to put on.

"Oh. My. God! It's Mimi," Courtney said in the midst of running around.

"Mimi? What is she doing here? Why was the front door unlocked? Did she let out the dogs?" I asked, standing there like an idiot.

Courtney stopped and looked at me. She shook her head. "Um…she wanted to bring Layton and Whit their wedding gift before they got home. I think I forgot to lock the front door yesterday morning after I checked the mail."

"Man, we suck at this house-sitting thing," I said.

I slowly smiled as I pulled her to me and kissed the shit out of her. She let out a small moan and ran her hands through my hair. When I pulled away quickly, she was trying to catch her breath.

"Wow. What was that for?" she whispered.

"No reason. I just love you so damn much. How we didn't see this long ago is beyond me," I said in a low voice.

She wrinkled up her nose and asked, "See what?"

"How we are made for each other. We fit together so perfectly, Courtney. I love you so much."

She let out a sigh and lifted the left corner of her mouth. She quickly gave me a kiss and said against my lips, "That was Nick swoon-worthy."

She turned and began putting on a pair of my sweatpants and one of my T-shirts. She grabbed her hair, twisted it somehow, and piled it on top of her head. "Come, Lulu, let's go say good morning to Mimi."

"Wait…*that* was *Nick* swoon-worthy?" I called after her, confused.

She stopped right outside the door and smiled. "Oh yeah, Mr. Moore." She winked and bolted down the stairs.

I stood there, more confused than ever.

I sat down on the bed and said, "So, the horseback riding in the moonlight was not swoon-worthy, but telling her we fit together was Nick swoon-worthy?" I rubbed the back of my neck and shook my head. "Fuck, I need to read more. Clearly, I'm missing something."

I sat at the kitchen island, smiling, as Mimi told me all about this book she'd discovered and how she hadn't been able to put it down all night.

"I'm telling you, it was amazing, Courtney. You should really read it."

I nodded my head and took a sip of tea. All I could really think about was how Reed had just made the most amazing love to me. It had been so slow and romantic. It was like he hadn't wanted it to end any more than I had.

"What's the name of the book?" I asked.

"Oh, darn…I can't remember. What is the name of that book? Oh, it was so funny. Crap."

I started thinking about last night and this morning—Reed falling in the field, Reed naked, Reed and me in the pool, Reed and me in the shower, Reed and me horseback riding, Reed telling me we were made for each other. I touched my lips gently and felt the ache growing between my legs.

"Courtney? Courtney, are you even listening to me?" Mimi asked.

I snapped my head up and looked at her. "What? Of course I'm listening to you."

She leaned back in her chair and folded her arms. "Really? What did I just say then?"

"Um…you were trying to remember the name of this really good book you read," I said with a small smile.

"Wrong answer. I was telling you that you looked lost in thought, and then I asked what in the world you were thinking about because the blush on your cheeks was a beautiful red."

I instantly put my hands on my face. "What?"

Just then, Reed walked in, and the room felt like it was filled with electricity. I even found myself catching my breath.

He sauntered up, leaned down, and kissed Mimi on the cheek. "Good morning, Miss Mimi. You look as beautiful as ever."

Mimi let out a little giggle. "Oh, Reed, you always were such a sweetheart."

Reed gave her that smile of his that had been driving me insane for months. He turned and looked at me. He placed his finger on my chin, leaned down, and gently kissed me. "I missed you," he said on my lips.

"I've only been gone for a few minutes," I barely got out, totally forgetting that Mimi was sitting right there.

"Doesn't matter. I still missed you."

The moment he moved away, I felt the longing for his touch grow ten times worse.

"There goes that beautiful red blush again," Mimi said.

I couldn't pull my eyes away from Reed. *Has Reed always been such a gentleman like this?* I tried desperately to remember him with Mimi in the past, and then it hit me. *He has always been this way. I just chose not to see it.*

When Reed laughed, I was pulled out of my trance. I looked between him and Mimi. *Is this really happening? Are we finally together?*

I felt a hundred times better after telling Reed about Noah. And how Reed had made me feel last night after I told him was amazing. He was amazing. *He's better than any book boyfriend could ever be.* I decided to keep that little bit of information to myself.

"Court, I'm going to go make sure Ryan and Johnny have everything ready for the feeding. I won't be gone too long," Reed said.

I chewed on my lower lip and nodded my head. We were in public now, and I had a feeling as soon as Reed stepped out the back door, I was shark food for Mimi.

As he began walking away, I called out, "Be careful. I love…um…" I turned to Mimi and then back to Reed, who was standing there with his cowboy hat in his hand, smiling. I couldn't help but smile back. "I love you, Reed. Be careful."

His smile grew about ten times bigger. "I love you, too, Courtney, and I will."

After he left, I waited a good five to ten seconds before I turned and looked at Mimi.

She was grinning from ear to ear. "Well, land sakes alive, it's about damn time."

"What's about time?" I asked, knowing she was talking about the exchange I just had with Reed.

"Oh, don't play coy with me, young lady. You and Reed, huh?" She wiggled her eyebrows up and down.

My mouth dropped open. "Mimi! You didn't just—"

Right then, we heard a gunshot.

"What in the hell? Was that a gunshot?" I jumped up and looked out the window. I let out a small scream when I saw Reed lying down on the ground with Ryan standing next to him, holding a shotgun. "Oh my God! Reed!" I yelled as I ran out the back door.

I started calling out Reed's name, and it should have registered in my head that he was okay when he jumped up and turned around, but my heart was beating so fast.

I skidded to a stop and looked him up and down. "Are you…have you been shot? Are you hurt? Oh my God." I didn't see any blood anywhere on his body. I quickly looked back and forth between Reed and Ryan.

Ryan looked confused as hell.

"Who did you shoot? Why did you shoot?" I asked Ryan. I looked all over Reed's body again. *Nope. Still no blood.*

Reed grabbed on to my shoulders. "Court, baby, look in my eyes. I'm not hurt. Ryan was trying to shoot a rattlesnake, and I was looking to see if it had gone under the car."

I shook my head and tried to calm my beating heart. "What? A snake?" I asked.

Mimi was laughing behind me.

I took a deep breath in and let it out. "Wait, what if it had struck you?" Tears were burning my eyes, and I wasn't sure where this pussy-ass girl had come from. The thought of losing the man I'd waited so long for overtook my body, and I lost it. "Reed, I don't ever want to lose you—*ever*. God, I was so scared when I saw you on the ground, and I thought…I thought…"

I choked back the tears as Reed grabbed me and pulled me into his arms.

"Oh, baby, I'm so sorry you got scared. It was stupid of me to look under the car, and I promise not to do stupid shit like that. I don't want you to be scared. I'm so sorry."

Then, he started laughing.

I pulled back and looked at him. "Why are you laughing?"

"Uh…I'm not really sure."

I put my hands on my hips and looked at Ryan, who was now in a full-out laugh.

"Miss Will, you should have seen your face. You were freaking out!" Ryan said before laughing harder.

My mouth dropped open, and I glanced back to see Mimi's shoulders bouncing up and down. When I turned back to Reed, he was at least attempting not to laugh anymore.

I pointed to him and said, "I take back that you were Nick swoon-worthy."

Reed's face dropped, and I was so pleased that I wanted to hug myself.

I'd absolutely fallen more in love with Reed when I saw him reading my favorite book. I'd known why he was reading it, and nothing had touched me more, so I knew taking back his swoon moment would gut him.

"*What?* You can't take that back."

Smiling bigger, I said, "Oh, I do believe I can, and…I just did."

"Um…" Reed said as he looked around.

I let out a small scream when Layton honked his horn as he was driving up before he parked.

"I'll help Mr. Morris with his luggage, Mr. Moore," Ryan said as he carefully engaged the safety before setting the gun down.

"Oh, look at her face. She's glowing," Mimi said as she took off toward Whitley and Layton.

When I turned back to look at Reed, I slowly smiled and walked closer to him.

"Did I really get it revoked?" he asked as he pulled me to him.

When he pressed himself against me, I felt how hard and ready he was for me.

I let out a giggle. "No, you didn't, but don't ever scare me like that again. Reed…I just can't even begin to tell you what these last few weeks have meant for me. Thank you."

He leaned down and kissed me oh-so gently and then barely pulled back from my lips. "I feel the same way, Courtney. I can never lose you now—*ever*. You're mine for always."

I swallowed hard and looked into his eyes. He had my stomach doing all kinds of crazy shit. All I wanted to do was jump into his arms and beg him to make love to me.

"You've been reading more, haven't you?" I asked as I winked at him.

The crooked smile that spread across his face said it all.

"Um…excuse me, but we're home!" Whitley said.

I spun around and faced my beautiful best friend. I let out a gasp when I saw her. She looked stunning. We both screamed as we ran into each other's arms and hugged. I couldn't wait to tell her everything that had happened with Reed and me.

She moved her mouth toward my ear and whispered, "I take it, you and Reed made it public? Glad to see y'all made nice with each other."

I pulled back and smiled. "Oh hell, we made more than nice! I had fucking shower sex."

Whitley's hands sprang up to her mouth as she let out a small scream. Her eyes quickly looked over at Reed, who was now helping Ryan and Layton with the luggage. He had a huge smile on his face, and the next thing I knew, Layton dropped a suitcase and slapped him on the back. He brought Reed in for one of those bro hugs and then said something in his ear.

"Well, I'm going to let everyone get settled, and then I plan on throwing a big barbeque in a few weeks to celebrate your marriage," Mimi said. Before heading to her car, she stopped and kissed each boy on the cheek, and then she turned back to look at Whit. "I'll call you, Whitley, with the details."

"Yes, ma'am. Talk to you soon!" Whit called back to Mimi.

Whit turned back around and hooked her arm with mine, and then we made our way toward the main barn.

She called back over her shoulder, "If you'll excuse us, gentlemen, we need some girl time."

I turned around, and my eyes caught Reed's. We smiled at each other, and the way he smiled back told me he would miss me as much as I would miss him. When he winked, my heart melted, and my stomach took a nosedive.

After walking into the barn, out of earshot from everyone, Whitley pushed me onto a wooden bench. "Oh. My. God! Finally! Tell me everything," she said as she jumped up and down and clapped her hands.

Two of the horses nickered, excited at the chance to go for a ride.

I rolled my eyes at her and tried to play it off. "Nothing really to tell. I mean, we fought some, hung out together, fought some more, went horseback riding a few times, Reed ran around some cows while he was naked, made mad, passionate love—"

Whitley held up her hands in a motion for me to stop talking. The smile on her face was making it hard for me not to smile from ear to ear.

"Okay…I'm pretty sure I don't want to know why Reed was naked while running around cows. Although my curiosity is getting the better of me on that one, I want to hear about the mad, passionate love!" She dropped to her knees, put her elbows on my legs, and propped up her chin, ready to hear a story.

"There really isn't much to tell," I said with a shrug of my shoulders. Just thinking of being with Reed was causing the want between my legs to return.

"Bitch, don't even try it. I've been waiting for months for this shit to happen. I want details, Lollipop—*now*."

I threw my hand up to my chest and said, "You want me to kiss and tell?"

"Uh…hell yeah, I do, and the sooner, the better before my hornier-than-hell husband comes looking for me! He actually wanted to pull over and have sex in the truck on the way home."

I covered my mouth and let out a laugh before I said, "My God, you just spent three weeks together on your honeymoon. Did y'all not have sex? Speaking of honeymoon, how was it?"

The way the blush moved across her cheeks made me so happy. I knew they both wanted a baby, so I had no doubt in my mind that a lot of babymaking had happened during those three weeks.

She put her head in my lap and let out a long sigh before looking back up at me. "Oh, Court, it was amazing. He made it so incredibly romantic the whole time. Gah! The places he made love to me were unreal. I don't know how many times, but the things he whispered in my ear melted me on the spot." She shook her head and smiled bigger as if she was remembering something.

"Whitley, I'm so happy for you. You deserve your happily ever after more than anyone I know."

She looked up at me, and tears filled her eyes. "So do you, Courtney."

I let a small smile play across my mouth as I nodded in agreement. I ignored the familiar sick feeling in my stomach that I'd been feeling for the last couple of days. I'd been waiting to wake up to find this all had been a dream.

"We can talk about the honeymoon later. Court…you and Reed?"

I shook my head and then dropped it back as I let out a long sigh. I pulled my head forward and looked into her eyes. "I love him so much, Whitley, and that scares the shit out of me, but when we're together…" I slowly smiled bigger. "My God, when we're together, I feel so…so…"

"Safe? Loved? Peaceful and content?" Whitley asked with a smile.

"Yes! He makes me feel all those things. I never felt that with Mitch or any other guy I dated. Reed's touch…it does things to me and makes me feel like a horny teenager."

Whitley giggled and sat back as she nodded her head for me to keep going.

"I feel this connection with him, and a part of me is so scared by it, but the other part of me wants to just take off running with it and never look back."

Whitley raised her eyebrow and whispered, "Tell me about the first time."

I smiled and wiggled my eyebrows up and down. "Well, two words—wall sex!" I said as I began bouncing up and down on the bench.

"Oh my God! You finally got your wall sex!" Whitley screamed.

I slapped her across the head. "Jesus, tell the whole damn countryside, why don't you?"

She gave me a look and asked, "Was it good?"

I closed my eyes and pictured the moment when Reed had called out my name as he came. Opening my eyes, I slowly nodded. "It was beyond good. It was amazing…wonderful…magical."

I felt myself beginning to choke up as I remembered Reed whispering in my ear how much he loved me and how I felt like heaven. I looked down at my best friend, and her smile made my stomach take a small dip as I thought about Reed's love for me. I began chewing on my lower lip.

Whitley got up and sat down next to me. She grabbed my hands and turned me, so we were facing each other. "Why do you look worried?"

"I, um…I just don't want it to end, and I'm scared he will leave me, or something will happen, and I'll mess this up. Whitley…Reed is the second guy I've ever been with, and well—"

She let out a gasp and pulled back. "What? You mean, Mitch was your first?" She shook her head and looked confused. "But…you've dated, and…you were a virgin when you began dating Mitch? Courtney…I thought…"

My heart started pounding. *Shit! Shit! Shit! How did I let that slip? Son of a bitch.*

Just then, I heard Layton and Reed talking and laughing as they rounded the corner. I instantly felt better when Reed looked at me and smiled. I went to stand up, but Whitley pulled me back down.

"Courtney, what's going on? The look on your face just then scared me."

I tried to smile. "Maybe we can talk later, okay?"

I quickly stood up and walked toward Layton. He smiled bigger, so I was pretty sure Reed had already filled him in on what happened between us. I walked into Layton's arms and welcomed him home.

He whispered in my ear, "It's about damn time. I've never seen him this happy before, Court."

I pulled back and grinned. I stepped back and looked at Reed, who was smiling from ear to ear. I walked up to him, and he pulled me into his arms.

He quickly kissed me before pulling back and saying, "I had to tell him."

I chortled and said, "I had to tell Whit, too!"

Layton slapped his hands and made his way over to Whitley, who was still looking at me with a puzzled expression. I knew she was confused because I had always talked about having sex with guys I dated. I tried to give her a reassuring smile, but it didn't work.

"I picked up a bunch of steaks for grilling, if y'all are hungry," Reed said as he pulled me closer to him.

Being in his arms made every fear and doubt just melt away. I looked at Whitley. She was trying to smile but doing a shitty job of it.

"Oh, hell yeah, I'm starved," Layton said.

Reed kissed me on top of the head before he began walking out of the barn with Layton.

"You must be starving and tired from the long trip. You want me to make a salad, too?" I said to Whitley as I began to follow Reed and Layton.

"Courtney?"

I stopped and closed my eyes. *I can't do this right now.* I slowly turned around and gave her a weak smile. "Whit, give me a couple of days, and we'll talk, okay?"

The concern flooding her eyes made me feel terrible. I knew she was wondering why I'd never told her about my sex life, or lack thereof, but right now, I just couldn't tell her, not when I was so happy.

She slowly nodded her head. "Okay." She smiled and walked up to me. "So, tell me about this whole Reed-running-around-the-cows-naked thing."

We both began laughing as we walked out of the barn. Reed turned around and looked at me with so much love that it caused my heart to skip a beat. He winked before turning back around, and then he slapped Layton on the back.

I put my arm around Whitley and began telling her about last night with Reed and how he had done all the things I liked.

"I knew it! I knew he would be romantic like Layton!" Whitley said with a giggle.

We made our way into the kitchen where all of us talked about the honeymoon, Reed's new job with Layton, and how happy we all were.

When I glanced over at Reed, he mouthed, *I love you.*

There goes my stomach again…and my heart…and the blush on my cheeks. I got up and walked over to him. I leaned against him, and I could feel his hard-on as he pulled me closer to him. I instantly smiled.

"I love you, Courtney," he whispered.

I reached up on my tippy-toes and kissed him on the lips. "I love you, too, Reed."

I just wanted to stay in this bubble forever.

But something was telling me that my bubble was going to be popped…and sooner than I wanted.

TWELVE

REED

A couple of months had passed since Layton and Whitley came back from their honeymoon, and tonight, Mimi and Frank were finally throwing them a barbeque. I decided to get a cup of Court's favorite coffee for her before heading over to her house to pick her up.

I pulled up to the coffee shop, jumped out of my truck, and made my way in. I couldn't help the smile on my face. I was thinking about last night and how we had finally made love on the kitchen island in the cabin. It couldn't have been more perfect. As I stood in line, the memory flooded my thoughts.

"Courtney, I can't take it any longer. I want to make love to you, baby," I whispered as I pulled her body closer to mine.

We were painting the kitchen a different color than the one my sister had picked out. The moment Court had mentioned the color she wanted in her kitchen at home, I'd decided it was going to be the color in the kitchen at the cabin.

I looked down at her face and let out a chuckle. She had paint everywhere—in her hair, on her nose, and even on the tip of her ear. I brought my lips down and crushed them against hers, and she let out a small moan. I pulled back and picked her up, and then I set her down on the kitchen island.

"Oh God, Reed, I can't seem to get enough of you," she whispered.

I saw the look of lust fill her eyes at the idea of me making love to her on the island. The first time I'd shown her the house and she'd run her hand along the granite, I'd pictured me inside her, making love to her on top of the island. With the way her cheeks had flushed, I had been pretty sure that she was thinking the same thing.

As I began taking off her sneakers, the smile spread across her face. I started to unbutton her shorts, and when she lifted up her ass, I took both her shorts and panties off in one fast movement.

"Shit! The granite is cold," she said with a giggle.

"I'll heat you up, baby." I licked my lips as I began taking off her T-shirt.

She was wearing a white lace bra, and her nipples were hard and so ready for me to suck on them.

"Courtney, I want you so much," I whispered.

"Yes. Please, Reed. I need you," she said as she took off her bra.

She began moving back on the island as I quickly stripped out of my clothes. This was not the time for sweet lovemaking. I wanted to fuck her hard and fast, and I couldn't get in her quickly enough.

"Courtney, I want to fuck you hard and fast," I said before I even thought about how she would react to me talking to her like that.

Her eyes lit up, and she arched her body as she pulled me to her. "Yes. Shit, that turns me on even more when you say it like that," she panted.

Okay…she liked it. Now, my dick was even harder and beginning to hurt because I wanted her so badly.

I leaned down, took her nipple into my mouth, and began sucking on it. She whispered my name as I gave each nipple equal attention.

"Damn it, Reed…touch me now."

I reached my hand down, and when I touched the inside of her thigh, she jumped with anticipation.

"I'm not going to last two minutes, Court."

"You better. I want it hard, Reed."

I let out a moan as I slipped two fingers into her wet, warm body. "Jesus, Courtney…you're always so ready."

She pushed her hands through my hair. "Yes, I'm always ready for you." She pushed her hips up and let out a whimper. "Reed. *Please.* Fuck me now."

I swallowed hard and pulled my fingers out of her. I grabbed her hips and slammed my dick inside her in one quick move. She let out a cry, and I stopped in fear of hurting her.

"No! Don't stop. Faster, Reed. Oh God, go faster and harder."

I did just that. I moved so fast and hard, and I fought like hell not to come before she did.

She began moving her hips right along with me as she called out, "Harder!

So, I gave her just what she'd asked for.

"Oh God, Reed! Feels…so…damn…good."

"Court…come for me, baby. Please…I can't hold off much longer," I said between pants.

"I don't want it to end. Oh God…oh my God. Yes! Right there. I'm going to come, Reed!"

I pulled almost all the way out, and then I slammed my dick back into her as she began screaming out my name over and over. When she looked into my eyes and said my name, I lost it. I exploded in her, and I couldn't believe how it felt. I'd never in my life experienced such an orgasm as I did just then. It felt like I was never going to stop pouring myself into her body. As I lay there, holding my body weight off of her, I could feel my dick still twitching inside her. I didn't want to pull out. I wanted to stay buried inside her forever.

"Don't move yet," she whispered as she held on to me tightly.

"I never want to move, Court. I want to stay this way forever." I moved my lips along her neck and up to her lips where I began kissing her.

We were both so lost in the kiss.

When I pulled away and looked down at her, I whispered, "I want to marry you, Courtney."

I watched as she swallowed, and her eyes filled with tears. For a few seconds, I regretted saying it out loud while she just kept staring into my eyes, not saying anything, but then I could see the love in her eyes.

"Will you promise to fuck me like this at least once a week? And teach me about plants?" she asked as she raised her eyebrows.

I smiled and let out a laugh, feeling my dick growing inside her. "I promise." I began moving in and out of her again, each movement causing my dick to get harder and harder.

She let out a soft moan before she wrapped her legs around me, pulling me closer to her. "Then, it's a done deal. With a promise like that, I'd be a fool not to want to marry you."

I shook my head and gave her my crooked smile that I knew she loved. "I'm going to make love to you now, angel. I love you, Courtney."

"I love you, too, Reed, so very much."

"Are you not even going to say hello to your old man?" a voice said, snapping me out of my daydream.

I looked to my right and saw my father standing there. A girl, probably around my age, was standing next to him, eye-fucking the shit out of me.

"Oh my, your son is just as handsome as you are, honey," she said.

She bit down on her lip, and my stomach turned.

"Reed, it's been a while," my father said as he put his hand out for me to shake.

I looked down at his hand and then up into his eyes. "What are you doing here?" I asked, panic filling my whole body. *If he's even thinking about going to see my mother, I will kick his ass.*

"I came to see Paul, Wesley, and you, of course. Maybe your mother, too, if I have time."

I grabbed his shirt and pushed him. "You stay the fuck away from her and Paul and Wesley. No one wants you here. You made your choice years ago when you left us all for some slut." I looked at the girl and smirked. "I see you found a new one."

She gave me a dirty look.

My father grabbed me and got right in my face. "Don't you talk to her like that. You think you're better than me, Reed?"

I pushed his hand away. "Yes, sir, I do. I'd never leave my wife and kids—*ever*."

He threw his head back and laughed as Jim, the owner of the coffee shop, came walking up.

"Reed, Mr. Moore, is everything okay here?"

My father looked at Jim and smiled. "Jim, good to see you after all these years. Yeah, all is well. I was just letting my son here know that the apple doesn't fall far from the tree."

With that, he grabbed the slut by the hand, and they started to make their way out of the coffee shop. My heart was pounding, and that familiar fear that I'd thought I had pushed away came creeping back.

Jim put his hand on my shoulder. "Don't listen to him, Reed. You are nothing like him. Nothing."

I glanced over at Jim and tried to smile as I nodded my head. "Thanks, Jim. I think I'll skip the coffee."

I turned and headed to my truck. The moment I got in, I felt like I couldn't breathe. I never wanted to hurt Courtney—*ever*.

I grabbed the steering wheel hard and yelled out, "Fuck! Why the fuck did you come back?"

I reached for my cell phone, and with shaking hands, I hit my sister's number.

"Hey, big bro. I'm just about to pull up to Mom's to pick her and Paul up, and then we will be heading out to Mimi and Frank's place."

"Wesley," was all I could get out.

"Reed, what's wrong? Are you okay? Is Courtney okay?"

I tried to talk, but I couldn't.

"Reed! You're scaring me!" she yelled over the phone.

"He's back. Dad is back," I whispered.

"What?"

"I just ran into him at the coffee shop. He was with some bitch our age. Wesley, he told me that I was like him. I can't be like him. I promised Courtney that I'd never hurt her." I barely got the last few words out while I fought to hold back a sob.

"You listen to me right now, Reed. You are *nothing* like that man. Our mother raised you to be a gentleman and to treat women with respect, and I've never in my life seen you not do just that."

I let out the breath I'd been holding and put my head down on the steering wheel. "Wesley, I've done things, things I'm not proud of. If Courtney ever found out—"

"Stop this, Reed. Stop this right now. I know Courtney, and I know how much she loves you. What you did in the past has nothing to do with how you feel about her. We all make mistakes, Reed. Please…please don't let him do this to you. Promise me."

I sat there and thought about what I'd done in my past. I needed to tell Courtney, or I'd never be able to shake this fear of losing her if she ever found out.

"Reed? Please talk to me," Wesley whispered.

I cleared my throat. "I'm here. I promise, Wesley."

"Don't let him ruin your happiness. He doesn't deserve it. I'll let Paul know that Dad is back in town. Are you still going with us to take Paul back to school?"

I nodded my head even though I knew she couldn't see me. "Yeah, I'm still going. I think Court wants to come along as well."

"Perfect! I know Mom really loves Courtney, so it will be nice for her to spend time with the whole family. I gotta run, honey. Please don't worry about Dad. Reed, you are nothing like him. Just always remember that," Wesley said as I heard her punching in the gate code to our mom's place.

"Yep. Talk to you later, sis." I hit End and sat there for a few minutes.

Then, I started driving toward Courtney's house as I thought about how what I was about to tell her could possibly end my whole future.

THIRTEEN

I sat on Mimi and Frank's porch swing, looking out over the pasture, lost in thought.

Whitley walked up and hit me on the shoulder before sitting down. "Hey, what's wrong?" she asked as she pushed the swing.

We began swinging back and forth, and I shook my head as I kept staring straight out.

"Courtney, did something happen with you and Reed?"

I turned and looked at her, giving her a weak smile. "I don't think so. I mean, after we made love last night, he told me he wanted to marry me."

Whitley gasped and threw her hand up to her mouth. "What? Did he ask you?"

I smiled and shook my head. "No, he just said he wanted to marry me, that's all."

Whitley let out a gruff laugh. "That's all? Um…that's pretty big. So, if he's saying he wants to marry you, why are you sitting out here, looking like someone just killed your dog? Or worse yet, like someone took your Kindle."

I laughed. "I think something has changed. When he picked me up earlier, he was very distant—I mean, scary distant. He's hardly talked to me at all, and I keep wondering if maybe he has changed his mind. Maybe he just blurted it out, and he didn't really mean it," I said as I shrugged my shoulders.

Whitley put her arm around me and let out a sigh. "No, Reed doesn't act on impulse. I know that for a fact. Besides, I heard him talking to Layton earlier. I wasn't going to say anything to you, but with how you're filling your mind with doubt, I have to."

I turned and looked at her. The smile on her face made me giggle. "What do you know?"

"Promise that you'll never, ever repeat what I'm about to tell you. Ever!"

I nodded my head quickly, and hope began flooding back into my heart.

Whitley clapped her hands and leaned closer to me while looking all around. "Mimi asked me to grab more sausage for the grill. I went to the kitchen, and the back door was cracked open. Layton and Reed were in there, and…well, they didn't hear me coming in. I overheard Layton ask Reed…" She threw her hand up to her mouth and smiled even bigger.

"Oh my God. He asked Reed what?" I grabbed her hands.

"I feel like I'm going to ruin your surprise if I tell you."

I pulled back and shot Whitley the dirtiest look I could. "Really, Whit? You're going to go that far and then say you shouldn't tell me? Spill the beans, bitch, or no new book recommendations from me for three months."

Whitley let out a gasp and then quickly spilled the beans. "Layton asked Reed if he had picked up your ring yet from the jeweler in Austin. Layton said something about it being sized and cleaned."

Whitley had spit it out so fast that I had to sit for a few seconds to process it.

"Wait, what?"

Whitley quickly shook her head and looked at me like I was crazy. "What do you mean, *what*? He picked up a ring. He told you he wanted to marry you. He's going to ask you to marry him, you idiot! I don't think he's changed his mind."

My heart started racing, and my stomach took a dive straight down to the ground. "Do you think?"

Whitley rolled her eyes and giggled. "Yes! Courtney, stop letting fear creep into your mind. Reed loves you, sweetheart. Everyone who looks at the two of you knows how much you love each other."

I smiled and looked at her as I tilted my head. "Just like when they look at you and Layton. The love pours off of y'all. Speaking of, you two have been awfully giddy today. I mean, the way Layton keeps looking at you and smiling is turning *me* on. What's going on?" I gave her my best mom look.

A beautiful blush instantly covered her face, and her eyes lit up.

"Oh. My. God. You're pregnant," I said as I jumped up and stared at her.

"What? How in the world did you know?" Whitley asked with a startled look on her face.

I let out a small scream as I grabbed her hands and pulled her up into a hug. "I don't know. I just saw the look on your face, and you just seemed…different!"

We kept hugging each other.

She pulled back and gave me the biggest grin I'd ever seen. "Yes, I'm pregnant! I went to the doctor yesterday, and they confirmed it. It looks like I'm about eleven weeks along."

I put my hand up to my mouth and let out another scream before I got myself under control. I took a deep breath and asked, "Your honeymoon night maybe? Oh my God, how romantic, Whitley!" I pulled her into another hug and whispered to her, "I'm so incredibly happy for you both."

She was laughing when we finally sat back down on the swing. "I didn't think it would happen so fast, especially with me stopping the pill just the day before the wedding."

"Well, ya know what they say—it only takes one time," I said with a wink. "How is Layton taking it?"

Whitley's head dropped back, and she let out a sigh as she looked at the clear blue sky. "He is so happy, Court." She looked back at me and shook her head. "I mean, I don't think I've ever seen a man so happy in my life as when the doctor came in and said the test was positive. Then, we did an ultrasound, and you could see the little angel on the screen. It was the most amazing moment of my life."

I grabbed her hand and squeezed it as I used my other hand and wiped away the tear rolling down my cheek. "I bet it was. I'm so happy for both of you."

Her smile faded for just a second before she said, "You can't tell anyone though, okay? Layton and I agreed we wouldn't tell anyone for at least another week or so. You can't even tell Reed."

"What? I can't keep that from Reed," I said.

"Oh, yes, you can. I promised Layton. *Please.* For me?" she begged in her famous whiny voice.

I crossed my heart with my index finger and stuck my pinkie out. "Fine, I promise, but don't make me wait too long. I'm dying to start buying her clothes!"

We both started laughing when Reed and Layton walked up. I glanced over and caught Reed's eyes. He was smiling, but his eyes were filled with so much sadness. I tried not to worry, but a part of me had a very bad feeling that something was about to happen, and Reed might very well break his promise to me about never hurting me. I took a deep breath as I stood up.

Whitley grabbed my arm and pulled me back to her. "Courtney?" she asked with concern.

"Yeah?" I said without pulling my eyes away from Reed.

"When do you think we can talk, Court? You keep delaying what we started to talk about that day when I came back from my honeymoon."

I quickly turned and looked at Whitley. From the shocked look on her face, I was pretty sure all the blood from my face had drained away.

"Um..."

"Hey, angel. Do you want to take a walk with me?" Reed asked as he walked up and took me into his arms.

Oh God. My heart started pounding.

I looked back at Whitley and tried to smile. "Tomorrow?"

She slowly nodded her head. "Promise me?"

I grabbed on to Reed and barely said, "Yes."

I wasn't sure how long Reed and I had been walking in silence before he finally stopped and turned me to him. He looked over my shoulder, and when I turned to see what he was looking at, I noticed an old bench sitting under an oak tree.

I turned back and smiled. "Want to sit down?" I asked.

He nodded, and we made our way over to the old bench. We sat down, and Reed took in a deep breath.

"I ran into my father right before I picked you up."

Shit. I closed my eyes and let out the breath I had been holding. *That explains why he has been so distant. He's upset.*

Wesley had told me one night about how their dad had left them and how heartbroken their mother had been. I knew Reed had a fear of hurting me. He'd told me time and time again how he needed me to believe he would never hurt me in any way.

"Where? Did you talk to him?" I asked as I reached for his hand.

"At the coffee shop. I stopped to get you a cup of coffee, and there he was with some twenty-five-year-old slut hanging on to him while eye-fucking the shit out of me."

I instantly got jealous, but I pushed the feeling aside.

"We talked for a couple of minutes, and that was it." He turned and looked at me, and then he grabbed my face with his hands and brushed his thumb across my lips. "You have to believe me when I say I'm not like him. I'd never leave you. I'd never, ever leave you or hurt you. I saw what he did to my mother, and I promise you, I'll love you until the day I die."

When I saw a tear slide down his face, my whole world stopped spinning. I reached up and put my hands on top of his.

"Reed, I know you would never hurt me or leave me. I believe that with my whole heart. I love you so much, and I would never doubt your love for me—ever."

He closed his eyes, and my heart was just breaking for him.

"Reed, I know your heart. I know how kind, gentle, and wonderful you are. I don't think you would ever do anything wrong, or—"

"Stop. Please don't say anything else."

His eyes snapped open, and I instantly became nervous. There was something in his eyes, and I didn't know what it was, but it scared me.

"Please don't say what a wonderful person I am. You don't know the terrible things I've done."

I shook my head, confused. "What do you mean? What terrible things?"

He dropped his hands, and I instantly missed his touch. He stood up, jammed his hands through his hair, and then slid them down his face. I wasn't sure why, but I loved whenever he did that. When he looked back at me, he was crying as he shook his head, and I sucked in a breath of air.

"I'm so afraid that I'm about to lose the one thing I've waited for my entire life. You're the only person I've ever loved, and if I lost you..." His voice cracked, and he turned away.

Holy shit. What in the hell is going on? "Reed, you're really scaring me. Please talk to me."

He looked back at me, and the hurt in his eyes killed me.

"I can't lose you. You're my entire life."

I stood up and grabbed his hands. "You're not going to lose me. I promise you. Nothing you say is going to make me stop loving you—ever."

"I did things...things I'm not proud of." A sob escaped from his lips.

"Reed, what you did in the past is in the past. You don't have to tell me anything. I love you for the person you are right now, today, not the you before me."

He ran his hand through his hair again and then leaned over as he dropped his hands to his knees. "I have to tell you. I have to tell someone because I can't take the guilt any longer."

My heart was pounding. I had no idea what he was about to say to me, but I knew it had to be big if he was worried it would push me away from him. I slowly sat down and looked up at him. "Reed, just tell me, and please know that I love you and will always love you."

He gave me a weak smile and sat down next to me. He must have sat there for a good five minutes before he took a deep breath and slowly let it out.

"There was this girl...Kelsey. I met her in college, and we went out a few times. It was nothing serious, but one night at a frat party, we both had too much to drink, and one thing led to another."

A one-night stand? He's worried about a one-night stand? "Okay, so y'all slept together. Reed, you're not the first person to have a one-night stand." I placed my hand on his knee.

He closed his eyes and whispered, "She got pregnant. I'm not even sure how because I wore a condom, but..."

It felt like someone had pushed a knife into my stomach. *Reed has a child?* I couldn't say a word. I just sat there and waited for him to keep talking.

"When Kelsey told me she was pregnant, I didn't hesitate to tell her that I would help with the baby. I had no intentions of marrying her because I didn't love her, but I knew I would help out with the baby the best I could. She told me she didn't need my help because she had decided to...to..."

Oh. God. Oh God…please don't say what I think he is going to say. "Reed…" I whispered.

"She told me if her parents found out, they would disown her and stop paying for college. She came from a very strict Catholic family. She didn't want to disappoint them, and she didn't want this to ruin her life. I tried to talk her out of it. I told her we could put the baby up for adoption, or I'd take the baby…but she wouldn't listen to me."

He put his head in his hands and began sobbing. "I just let her do it. I didn't try hard enough to talk her out of it. She told me it was her body and her decision, and when I tried to say I had a part in the decision as well, she said I didn't, and she had already made up her mind. She asked me to take her…and…*oh God*."

I felt the tears running down my face as I grabbed on to Reed and held him as he cried. I'd never in my life felt such heartache as I did at this very moment.

Reed was now sobbing while trying to talk. "I took her to the appointment, Court. I waited there and did nothing while they did it. I took her home, and her roommate just smiled at me and told me she would take care of Kelsey. I turned and walked away, and I never saw Kelsey again."

"Reed, you don't have to say any more."

He began shaking his head as he looked up at me. "I do. I need you to know everything because I never want there to be anything between us—ever."

I took a deep breath and nodded my head.

"I kind of just lost it after that. I began drinking and partying more, and I hooked up with a bunch of girls those first few months after."

My stomach felt sick at the idea of Reed sleeping around with a lot of women, but at the same time, I understood.

"I woke up one morning with a girl in my bed, and I decided right then and there that I needed to stop. The last thing I wanted to do was end up getting another girl pregnant. I stopped with the partying and concentrated only on college." He turned and looked at me, sadness filling his eyes. "I'm so sorry. None of them meant anything to me, and I felt so guilty for using them all for sex. I never promised them anything, and they were all one-night stands. They meant nothing."

"Reed, it was in the past. It was long before me, and it means nothing to me now. I love you."

I placed my hand on his chest, and he closed his eyes as he sucked in a breath of air.

"I love you for the man you are today, not who you were in college. I'm so sorry for what you went through. I can't even imagine." I shook my head. My heart broke for Kelsey as well.

The next thing I knew, Reed was on his knees in front of me. "I'm so sorry. I'm sorry that another girl, who I didn't even love, was the first to carry my child. That should have been you. I want the mother of my children to be you, Courtney. My only dream was to find you, the love of my life, the one girl I'd lay my life down for and do anything to make her happy. I don't want my dream to be broken because of something I did in my past or for the stupid way I behaved."

He began crying harder, and I dropped to my knees next to him.

I placed my hands on his face and made him look at me. "That will be me. That *is* me. Reed, I'm not going to take away the fact that a precious little angel in heaven would have been your first child, but we will have all our dreams come true, you and me together. I want nothing more than to give you your first child. I can't wait to give you that gift. Reed, our dreams are no longer broken, not when we have this kind of love together. I love you so much."

I began kissing him, and at first, he wasn't responding. I moved my tongue along his lips, and he finally opened them up to me. Our kiss quickly turned passionate, and then it became something even more. I needed him to be inside me. I needed him to know how much I loved him and how I would always love him. Nothing would ever change that. I unbuttoned his pants and then pulled off his T-shirt.

"Courtney..." he whispered as he looked at me and pushed down his pants.

I smiled as I pulled my shirt up and over my head, and then I slipped my panties off from under my skirt. "I love you, Reed. I need to feel you inside me."

He pressed his lips against mine and frantically began kissing me. He pulled away once and looked into my eyes. "I don't deserve you."

I reached down and began stroking his dick as I gave him the sexiest smile I could. "Oh, Mr. Moore, how wrong you are...how very wrong you are."

He gently laid me back and pushed himself into me. He moved in and out slowly, and I was completely lost in his lovemaking. He kept repeating how much he loved me, and my heart broke at the idea of him being so scared of hurting me. I was so touched that he'd shared what happened with Kelsey, but at the same time, I was devastated for him, for all those years he'd carried around that guilt.

I wasn't sure how long we lay there on the ground, wrapped up in each other. We talked for a bit more about what we both wanted.

"Maybe I should bring some items over to the cabin?"

He smiled so big and nodded his head like a child. "Why don't you just move in?" he asked with a boyish grin on his face.

"We've only been officially going out for a few months. You don't think it's too soon to move in together?"

He smiled and said, "Nope."

When he pulled away from me and began getting dressed, I sat up and just stared at him. *Damn, how did I get so lucky with him?* I reached for my clothes and started dressing. I was pretty sure that I was going to end up with grass burns from our little lovemaking session, but I didn't care. It had been beyond perfect, and somehow, I thought it had helped Reed even more that we'd made love after all that he told me.

I stood up and looked around for the hair band that I'd had. I thought I'd wrapped it around my wrist. I turned around, about to ask Reed if he'd seen it, when I saw him down on one knee, holding a ring box.

Oh. My. God. Oh, holy hell. I placed one hand on my stomach as the other one came up to my mouth.

"Courtney, I had this all planned out, and I wanted to make it so special for you, but something just came over me, and I…well, shit…I couldn't wait another minute. I love you, Courtney. I want to love you for the rest of my life. I want to wake up to you every morning and lie down next to you every night. I want to make love to you on our kitchen island as much as we want to. I want to sit with you on the back porch and watch you while you're lost in one of your books. I want to see your stomach getting bigger with our kids, and hell, I even want to fight with you and then have make-up sex. I want the world for both of us, and more than anything, I want to make all your dreams come true. I want to be your Prince Charming, Courtney. I want to be your everything. Will you marry me?"

I stood there, stunned. I slowly dropped to my knees and looked into his eyes. *He is dead serious. He is really asking me to marry him.* My head started spinning. The logical side of my brain was telling me this was way too fast, and we needed to slow down. The romantic, crazy fool side of my brain was screaming for me to say yes. *Yes! Yes! Yes!*

"Um…Court…with you not really responding and all, I'm kind of getting really nervous that my unplanned, spur-of-the-moment proposal was a bad idea."

I closed my eyes, and I did the one thing I'd never done before. I listened to my heart instead of my head. When I opened my eyes again, I smiled, causing Reed to flash me that drop-dead gorgeous smile of his. Even though we'd just made love, I wanted him again, more than ever.

"Reed, the first time I ever looked into your eyes, I felt something I'd never felt before. I knew I wanted to be a part of all your dreams. I think I've always known you are my Prince Charming. Nothing would make me happier than to be your wife."

His smile grew bigger. "Really?"

I nodded my head and said with a smile, "Really."

He looked down and opened the box. My eyes followed his, and I let out a gasp when I saw the ring. The pale pink oval diamond was breathtaking. It was surrounded by a row of smaller diamonds that continued down both sides of the platinum ring.

I quickly looked back up into Reed's eyes. "I've…I've never seen anything so beautiful in my life. The diamond is pink! It's breathtakingly beautiful."

Reed's smile just about knocked me over. "It was my grandmother's ring. After I graduated from college, my mother gave it to me in hopes that I would someday find a love like my grandparents shared."

After he pulled the ring out of the box, he gently took my hand in his. I quickly wiped away my tears and looked into his piercing blue eyes. They sparkled like diamonds, and I didn't think I'd ever seen such happiness in them before. The moment he put the ring on my finger, he gently placed his hand on my face, bringing my lips to his, and he began to kiss me.

"I found that love with you. You've made me the happiest man on earth, Courtney. I love you so very much."

I launched myself into his arms and started kissing him like a crazed fool. *I'm engaged! I'm engaged to the man of my dreams! And it's a pink diamond. Holy shit. Best. Day. Ever.*

Reed started laughing as he pulled back and looked into my eyes. "Are you happy, angel?"

My heart was pounding so loud that I was sure Reed could hear it. "I've never been so happy in my life. I just…I just don't even know what to say, Reed. I want to spend the rest of my life with you and…" I looked down at the beautiful ring on my finger. "And it's a pink diamond!"

Reed started laughing. "Wesley told me you would freak when you saw it. I just hope I didn't move too fast, and I'm sorry I didn't make it more special. The moment just seemed so right."

I moved to where I was sitting on him, straddling him. I felt his erection, and I was pretty sure my panties were soaking wet at this point. "You could have asked me anywhere, and it would have been perfect because it would be you asking."

Reed kissed me on the tip of my nose and whispered, "Do we go back and tell everyone?"

Without even thinking, I blurted out, "Yes! With this news and Whitley being pregnant, I think we need to—" I slammed my hands up to my mouth. *Oh shit.*

Reed's eyes grew bigger. "Whitley told you? Oh…Layton is gonna be pissed. She wasn't supposed to tell anyone."

I dropped my hands and tilted my head. "Wait, you know? Layton told you?"

Reed's expression dropped. "Um…"

I pushed him back until he was lying down. "What do you mean, Layton is gonna be pissed? He told you? Neither one of them was supposed to tell anyone."

Reed started laughing and pushed his hips into me. The friction his hard-on was causing instantly had me needing more. I began grinding my hips into him, and he let out a long, soft moan.

"Fuck," Reed hissed.

I threw my head back and whispered, "Yes, please."

Before I even knew what was happening, Reed was standing us up, pulling my panties down, and then unzipping his pants. He picked me up, and I wrapped my legs around him as he backed me up against the giant elm. The moment he brought me down onto him, filling my body, I felt instant relief.

"Reed, you feel so good."

"What do you want me to do, Court?" he whispered in my ear.

"Please…move, Reed…God, please move," I begged.

Reed pulled out some and then slammed back in, causing me to let out a moan so loud that I was sure everyone within a mile could hear it.

"I'd do anything for you," Reed said as he fucked me hard and fast against the tree.

I never wanted this moment to end. Being with Reed was like nothing I'd ever experienced before. I loved it more than anything when he made sweet, passionate love to me, but when he made love to me like this—fast and hard, like he just couldn't get deep enough inside me—it drove me insane with desire.

I began to feel my orgasm building, and I couldn't hold back when it hit.

"Reed…I'm coming." I could hardly breathe. Every inch of my body felt like it was pulsing. "Holy shit! I can't…oh God…oh God!" This had to be the longest orgasm in the history of orgasms.

I could feel myself squeezing Reed, and the way he was saying my name over and over was more than I could take. Right as I started coming down, I felt him getting bigger.

He pulled out and slammed into me again as he cried out with his release. "Courtney…oh God, baby, I'm coming. Feels…so…fucking…good."

"Yes," was all I could manage to get out.

I wasn't sure how long we stood up against that tree. I could feel him twitching inside me as I held him closer to me. Nothing felt as amazing as having Reed inside me. Each time after we'd made love and he had pulled out, I would feel like I was missing a part of me.

"Don't move. Please…I just want to stay like this forever," I whispered.

"I love you so damn much, Courtney. That felt…"

We both said at the same time, "Amazing."

I giggled and pulled back to look at him. "Will it always be like this? This incredible, this hot?"

He smiled as he nodded. "I'll do everything in my power to always make it this way. Being with you, Courtney…" He shook his head and grinned bigger. "I just don't even know the words to say how it feels when I'm making love to you."

I closed my eyes to keep the tears back. I opened them and looked into his eyes. "I feel the same way, Reed. I hate that we wasted so much time by being so stubborn and fighting our feelings for each other. If we had only known how we would lead each other out of the dark…"

Reed pushed a piece of hair behind my ear and whispered, "And into the brightest light ever where there is nothing but love and hope for the rest of lives."

I choked back my sob and said, "I've never felt so whole in my life."

"Marry me, Courtney."

I chortled and said, "Nothing would make me happier than to be your wife, and I'm pretty sure I already said yes."

Reed leaned his forehead against mine, and I could almost feel all of the guilt, anger, hurt, and fear leaving his body.

He slowly pulled out of me, leaving me with that familiar empty feeling. "We better head back."

As we started to make our way back, I had the most remarkable feeling wash over my whole body.

For the first time since I was sixteen years old, I was finally walking toward the light.

FOURTEEN

REED

I pulled my truck up and parked behind Layton's. He had called me this morning, asking me to meet him, because he had something he had to do and didn't want to be alone for it.

As I walked into the barn, I saw Layton in Blazin' Dreams's stall. "Hey, dude. How's he doing?"

Layton turned and looked at me with the biggest shit-eating grin ever. "I think this big guy is going to make some serious money. Lucky just brought him back this morning. His first race is in a month."

I walked up to the horse and smiled. "He sure is one beautiful boy, isn't he?"

Layton nodded his head as he gave the horse a few pats on the side, and then he began walking out of the stall. He ran his hand through his hair and reached down into a cooler to grab a beer. "Want one?"

"Sure, I'll take one."

Layton tossed me one and sat down on a bench.

I opened up the beer and took a quick drink before sitting down next to him. We sat there for a good two minutes in silence.

"Talk to me, Layton."

He reached into his back pocket, pulled out a piece of paper, and handed it to me. I took one look at it and knew what it was.

"The letter?" I asked as I looked over at him.

"Yep. He asked that I not read it until I found out I was going to be a father. I guess that means I have to read it now."

"You haven't read it yet?" I asked as I watched the pain fill his eyes. I hadn't seen that in his eyes for some time now, and it gutted me to see it there again. I glanced down at the letter in my hands. *Shit. What in the world did his father write to him?*

"Nope, I can't bring myself to read it, Reed. I can't. I need you to read it to me."

I snapped my head over at him and dropped my mouth open. "Huh? You want me to read it to you? Layton…I'm not sure…"

Layton stood up and downed his beer. "I'm well on my way to getting drunk, Reed. I was short with Whitley this morning, and I ended up walking out after a fight. I have been in this damn barn ever since. I had Lucky bring me a couple of twelve packs of beer. I can't do this alone. I can't read it."

When I saw the tears filling his eyes, I jumped up and walked over to him. "Layton, you're married to the woman you're going to spend the rest of your life with. You're going to be a father, and you and I both know that you will be a damn good dad. *Nothing* in this letter will change any of that. Do you understand that?"

He slowly nodded his head and gave me a weak smile. "This is why you're my best friend. I need you to do it though. I need to know what he wanted to say to me and why he felt like he had to wait until I was going to be a father."

I turned and sat back down on the bench as I began to open the letter. I took a deep breath and looked up at Layton. "You ready?"

He nodded. "Yeah."

I cleared my throat and began to read the words Layton's father had written down on paper.

Dear Layton,

I want to first say congratulations, son. There is nothing more amazing than becoming a parent. The first moment you hold your child in your arms is one of the most wonderful experiences you will ever have.

If you are reading this letter, then I have moved on to be with your mother. I want you to know, Layton, I loved you and your brother more than anything. I know it doesn't seem like it, and if I could go back and do it all over again, I would change so many things. But I can't, so I won't dwell on my mistakes.

I've seen you with Whitley, and it warms my heart. The love I see in your eyes is like looking into a mirror. It is the same love I had for your mother. She was my entire world, Layton. When she left us...I couldn't breathe. I didn't want to exist without her, and I did the only thing I knew how to do. I ran away. I ran from the memory of her. I ran from my two beautiful sons because in their eyes, I saw her eyes, and it gutted me. Was it the right thing to do? No. I'd give anything now to go back and fix the biggest mistake of my life.

When I found out that Mike had died, I wanted to reach out to you so badly, but I had been gone for so long that I didn't know how or even if I should. A part of me thought you were better off without me in your life. Then, I found out Whitley had moved to Llano, and I knew it was your mother who had brought her to you. She'd somehow brought me to Whitley all those years ago, and then she brought Whitley to you. I just had a small part in that plan.

As reality set in that my days were numbered, I knew what I had to do.

I've sat down many times, trying to begin this letter, only to just get up and walk away. Now, I know what I need to say.

I'm sorry. I'm so sorry I walked away from you and your brother. I'm sorry I wasn't there to help the two of you with the things that you needed most in this life. I'm sorry I missed the birth of my first grandchild. I'm sorry I wasn't sitting right next to you during Mike's funeral. You don't know how many times I had to keep myself back, hiding behind everyone, while I watched my son suffer...again. I'm sorry I missed your wedding. And I'm so sorry I won't be there when you welcome your first child into this world.

I need you to know something, and I need you to believe it with all your heart. You and your brother were so loved, so very loved by your mother and me. Remember all the times the four of us spent together, Layton. Remember the picnics. Remember the trips to the coast with you and your brother fighting and your mother offering bribes to both of you for some peace and quiet. Remember every birthday when we would come into your room with your birthday cake and sing "Happy Birthday" to you. Remember every soccer game and football game and how we cheered you on from the sidelines. Remember every Christmas morning and how your mother would be up before anyone, making blueberry muffins.

Please don't remember one foolish, stupid mistake I made. I have no doubt in my mind that you will be an amazing father. I saw Mike with Kate on more than one occasion. I saw the love he had for his daughter, and I know you will be the same. I might have messed things up, but you had an amazing mother, and I know that her love spilled over into your blood, Layton. You will be an amazing father. Learn from my mistakes and from your mother's unconditional love.

I don't deserve to be called your father, but please know this—I love you, Layton. You have made me one very proud father with everything that you have done. You made that ranch into more than anything I could have ever dreamed of. I'm so very proud of you, son.

Congratulations again, Layton. Enjoy every second of this journey. Don't ever take a single day for granted, and make sure Whitley knows how much you love her every second of every day.

Love, Dad

I looked up at Layton and had to catch my breath. He was leaning against a stall…crying. I quickly wiped away the tear slowly making its way down my face. I waited a few minutes before I said anything.

"Layton? You okay?" I asked as I stood up.

He looked at me and slowly smiled as he nodded his head. "Yeah, I'm more than okay. That's all I ever wanted, Reed. I only wanted him to say he was sorry and that he loved us." He looked down and kicked the dirt. "That's all I ever wanted," he whispered again.

I walked up to him, grabbed him, and pulled him in for a hug. "I love you like a brother, Layton. I'm always here for you."

"I know, Reed. Thank you for always being there for me. It means more to me than you know. You know I love you like a brother, too."

"Am I interrupting some bonding time here with you two pussies?" Kevin said from behind us.

After slapping each other's backs harder than we needed to, Layton and I stepped back and shook hands as we smiled at each other.

"Fuck off, Kevin," I said as I handed Layton the letter.

He pushed it into his back pocket and started laughing. "You want a beer, Kevin?" Layton asked as he reached into the cooler and pulled one out.

"Hell yeah, I do. So, what's going on? I got your text, Layton, saying you had something to tell me. I rushed over, but I'm not so sure I want to know what it is after walking in on the two of you…sharing a *moment*." He rolled his eyes and then let out a chuckle.

I laughed as I sat down on the bench and downed my beer. I glanced up, and the smile on Layton's face had me smiling. I knew exactly what he was going to tell Kevin—Whitley was pregnant.

"I've got some good news, dude, but you can't tell Whit that I told you," Layton said.

I started laughing. *He's worse than a girl.*

"Oh, hell no. I don't want that girl getting mad at me. You just keep your secret to yourself until the girl says you can spill the beans on whatever it is."

Layton shrugged his shoulders and sat down next to me. "Okay, but Reed knows."

Kevin was about to take a drink of his beer but stopped right at his lips. "Reed knows the secret you're not supposed to be telling?"

I nodded my head and laughed. "Yep, I sure do. It's a good one, too."

Kevin dropped his head back and let out a sigh before looking back at Layton. "Shit. I promise not to tell Whitley you told me. What's the damn secret?"

Layton smiled bigger, if that were even possible, and said, "Whit is pregnant."

Kevin slapped his leg, jumped, and yelled out, "Damn, I knew it! When I just saw her, she looked different! She looked so happy. Ah hell, Layton."

He walked over toward Layton as he stood up. They shook hands and then hugged quickly before Kevin pushed Layton back. Layton threw his head back and laughed.

"Congratulations, dude. You must be over the moon," Kevin said.

"Oh, man, you have no idea. I've never been this happy before in my life. I honestly don't think I could be any happier," Layton said with a goofy-ass grin on his face.

"This is the best news. Y'all, we need to celebrate this shit!" Kevin said.

"Celebrate what?"

All three of us turned to see Whitley and Courtney standing there. The moment I saw Courtney, my stomach did that same damn funny thing it had been doing for the last year.

This girl drives me crazy.

"Uh…" Layton said as he looked at me and then at Kevin, willing one of us to help him out.

I glanced over toward Whitley, who now had her hands on her hips with her head tilted, giving Layton a look. Courtney was trying to hold in her laughter as she looked everywhere but at us.

"Layton, did you tell them? You promised," Whitley said with a little bit of a whiny voice.

"You told Courtney," Layton said.

I closed my eyes and waited.

"Reed Nickolas Moore, you weren't supposed to say anything!" Courtney said.

I peeked over at Courtney, only to see Whitley staring at her now.

"You told Reed?" Whitley asked Courtney.

"Um…wait, this is not about me. This is about Layton telling all of his friends and planning a party to celebrate," Court said as she pointed to Layton.

"Hey!" Layton said as he pointed to Kevin. "The party was his idea."

Kevin began laughing as he walked over to Whitley. He grabbed her and spun her around. "Girl, congratulations. Now, let's get down to business. We have a damn party to plan."

Whitley smiled and then looked at me and winked. "We have more than one reason to celebrate."

Kevin stepped back and looked around at everyone, stopping at Courtney. "Is someone else pregs?"

Courtney and I both said, "No!"

Whitley grabbed Courtney's hand and held it up, showing the engagement ring. Court and I had decided not to tell anyone at the barbeque yesterday.

"Holy shit." Kevin turned and looked at me with a stunned expression on his face. His mouth dropped open. "Reed, you're getting married to my girl?"

Courtney started laughing as she made her way over to me.

I grabbed her and pulled her next to me. "I'm afraid I am, dude. You moved too slow."

Kevin looked down at Courtney and then back at me. He shook his head and stuck out his hand. "Damn, y'all. It's about fucking time."

I reached for his hand, and he pulled me in for a hug.

He leaned in toward my ear and whispered, "I'm so happy for you, Reed." He slapped me on the back and stepped back, and then he looked down at Courtney. Kevin pulled her into a hug and said, "Damn, girl, I thought we had something. I guess I'll let you go, but only because I love this guy like a brother. I'm happy the two of you finally got your shit together."

Laughing, Courtney punched him in the stomach.

"So," Kevin said, looking around at everyone, "pontoon party?"

Layton started laughing. "Babe, you feel up to it?"

Whitley smiled and nodded her head. "Why not? We have a lot to celebrate."

Courtney jumped up and down, kissed me quickly on the cheek, and headed back to the house with Whitley.

Kevin slapped me on the back again, and then he reached for Layton and pulled him over to us. "All right, my brothers, let's make this the best damn pontoon party ever."

I smiled as I looked at Layton. He seemed happy, really happy, and I was glad that his father had given him what he finally needed to completely move on.

As we were about to make our way out of the barn, Layton pulled me back. "Hey, Kev, I'm gonna talk to Reed for just a couple of minutes. We'll meet you back up at the house."

"Sure thing. I'll start making some calls," Kevin said as he turned and walked out of the barn.

I peered over at Layton, who now had a serious look on his face.

"Is everything okay?" he asked.

I smiled and nodded my head. "Yeah. Why wouldn't it be?"

"You and Courtney just started dating, Reed. You don't think y'all are moving too fast with the engagement?"

For some reason, Layton asking me that instantly pissed me off. "I've been in love with her for much longer than a few months, Layton. No, I don't think we are moving too fast. I'd marry her tomorrow if I thought she would."

The smile that spread across his face caused me to smile.

"That's all I needed to hear. You know I love you like a brother, and I love Court like a sister. I just want y'all both to be happy." He looked down and then back up at me as he kicked the ground. "You doing okay after running into your dad? Wesley told me that it kind of threw you for a loop."

I rolled my eyes and silently cursed my sister. She always ran to Layton anytime she thought I was having a rough go of things. I knew she'd had a thing for Layton years ago, and she had used it as an excuse to talk to him more than anything, but now, this running-to-him shit was getting old.

I shrugged my shoulders and quickly looked away. I thought back to what Courtney had said to me, and I grinned slightly. I looked back up at Layton. "I'm good. I'll admit that some things from my past crept up on me, but I talked to Courtney, and"—I let out a small chuckle—"we worked everything out. It just hit me, Layton. It was the right time to ask her."

Layton nodded his head. "It's just that you talked about asking her at Christmas, so this sudden engagement came as a surprise. I'm happy for you though, Reed. You know I am."

I nodded and slapped him on the back. "Layton, I've never been so sure of something in my entire life. Courtney is my entire world. I don't even want to imagine my life without her in it."

The smile that spread across Layton's face told me he knew exactly how I felt.

"Let's go throw the best damn pontoon party ever. I'm going to be a father. Holy shit," Layton said as he shook his head and laughed.

"God help the future generation of girls if you have a boy."

As we walked toward the house, a strange feeling hit me. It was almost a panicked feeling that something bad was going to happen.

Courtney walked up to me with that beautiful smile of hers. "Are you all right?" she asked as she tilted her head and looked at me.

"Yeah, I've never been better. Ready to tell everyone that you're mine and officially off the market?"

She jumped up and down and let out a little squeal. "Hell yeah, I am!"

I picked her up and swung her around in a circle before setting her down. I kissed the tip of her nose and then said, "Let's go make it official."

FIFTEEN

I looked around and let out a sigh. I could not believe how many people were at this party.

"Gesh, when these boys throw a party, I think the whole damn countryside shows up," I said as I glanced over at Whitley, who was looking out at the makeshift dance floor.

I turned, and the first thing I saw was Kevin holding Kate while he was dancing with Jen. "You know what I think? I think Kevin and Jen would make a cute couple. What do you think?" I asked Whitley.

I looked back at Whitley. She was still peering out at the dance floor, but this time, she had a very pissed-off look on her face. My heart started pounding, and I was wondering who she was looking at.

Olivia? Maybe even Anna?

I didn't want to look, but I followed Whit's eyes, only to find Layton dancing with Wesley, Reed's sister. They were both laughing about something, but the way Wesley was looking at Layton seemed a little off to me. It was almost like she—*oh shit.*

I walked and stood in front of Whitley, breaking her eye contact with them. "Earth to Whitley. Did you hear what I said about Kevin and Jen? Don't you think they would make a cute couple?"

Whitley peeked around my shoulder and whispered, "That bitch."

I quickly turned to see Wesley embracing Layton a little too close. Layton quickly moved back, creating more distance between the two of them.

"Whitley…" I said with that motherly tone my mother would use on me right before I was ready to lose my shit on someone.

Whitley quickly looked into my eyes. "Spill it," she said.

I gave her a confused look. "Spill what?"

Placing her hands on her hips, she tilted her head and gave me that you-know-what-I-mean look. "Wesley and Layton—did anything ever happen between the two of them?"

My mouth dropped open, and I just stood there for a second. "Well, how in the hell would I know that?"

"You're engaged to her brother," Whitley said, like that meant I should know everything about Wesley's sex life, present and past.

"So? I've hardly talked to her. I mean, we've gotten a bit closer these last few weeks, but before that, I barely said two words to her, except for *hello* and *see ya around*."

Whitley looked back out on the dance floor. I looked over my shoulder, praying to God they had stopped dancing. The music had changed to a slower song, and Layton was still dancing with Wesley.

Stupid ass. What in the hell is wrong with him?

"What in the hell does he think he's doing? He's danced with her for three songs now," Whitley said.

"Three?" I said with almost a gasp.

Whitley looked pissed and started to make her way out to the dance floor.

I grabbed her arm and said, "Whitley, calm the hell down and just think about this, okay? You're married to him and about to have his baby. He's known Wesley for…how long? She is his best friend's sister. I'm sure it is all innocent."

"Oh, hell no! What is *she* doing here?"

Shit! Shit! Shit! I was hoping we could have one event where Olivia wouldn't try to come between Layton and Whitley. I let out a breath as I turned around, and immediately, I saw her…talking to Reed.

"Anna," I whispered. The panicked feeling hit me so hard that I had to hold on to Whitley to keep my balance. "What's she doing here?"

"That's what I just asked. I'm going to have to talk with Kevin about who he invites to these things. Everyone in the damn county is here!" Whitley shook her head and turned toward the truck.

"Wait, where in the hell do you think you're going?" I asked.

She stopped and turned around with a smile. "I'm going to put on my bikini. I might be pregnant, but my ass still looks good in a two-piece."

I let out a giggle and directed her to Reed's truck. "Please. Bitch, have you already forgotten? When I pack, I come prepared. I have two itty-bitty bikinis in Reed's truck."

Whitley gave me that evil, crooked little smile of hers as we made our way over to Reed's truck.

Fifteen minutes later, we were walking out from behind a group of trees where we had changed, and we were strutting our New York City–girl asses, dressed in bikini tops, short-ass shorts, and our cowboy boots.

As we walked up, Layton was leaning against a table, talking to Wesley.

"Houston, we may have us a serious problem," I said.

"And Houston knows just how to fix it," Whitley said as she walked toward Layton.

The moment he laid his eyes on her, anyone could see how in love with her he was. Whitley walked right up to him and pushed her body into his, and then she kissed the living shit out of him.

Oh yeah, I taught her that shit. I let out a giggle as I watched Layton practically melt in Whitley's arms.

One quick look at Wesley, and my suspicions were confirmed. She was glaring at Whitley.

Time to have some fun.

I walked toward Wesley and bumped her on the arm. "Hey, future sister-in-law."

She quickly looked at me and plastered on a fake-ass smile. "Hey, Courtney. Congratulations again. Anyone can see how much you and Reed love each other."

I smiled and said, "Thank you, Wesley." I peeked over at Layton and Whitley, who were still pawing each other all up. "I've never before seen a couple so madly in love like Layton and Whit. They light up a room with their love."

I slowly looked back at Wesley. I was pretty sure she had steam coming from her ears.

"To be honest, I never really thought Layton was the settling-down-and-marrying kind with his player ways," she said.

Interest piqued. "Player ways?" I asked.

She started to make her way over to where everyone was playing horseshoes. "Between you and me, of course, Layton was always a bit of a player. I mean, he never cheated on Olivia, but after they broke up, he must have hooked up with a dozen girls, each one hoping to capture his heart."

"Really? Were you one of them?" I asked.

"Excuse me?" she asked, trying to seem offended.

"Were you one of those hookups?"

"God, no! I mean, I've always liked Layton, but no, we've never been anything more than friends."

I glanced up and saw Anna walking toward Reed. I'd totally forgotten about Anna talking to Reed earlier.

"I just wish Layton would have seen me as more than just his best friend's sister."

I snapped my head back at Wesley. *What in the hell is she talking about?*

She was staring at Layton again. I needed to be sure to share this with Whit. Wesley clearly had a thing for Layton, and the fact that he was married and getting ready to have a baby didn't seem to matter to her.

"Wesley, you do realize that he is married to the love of his life. He's about to be a father. My advice to you is to move on. Layton doesn't want anyone but Whitley."

She looked at me and gave me a weak smile. "Of course I know that." She looked around and waved to someone. "Excuse me, Courtney. I see someone I haven't seen in a while. We really need to go out to lunch and get to know each other more."

I nodded and smiled as I watched her turn and walk up to some built guy who picked her up and spun her around. I shook my head and looked back at Reed. Anna was still standing there, talking to him. He glanced over and smiled at me. The look in his eyes caused me to suck in a breath of air.

I can't believe he is finally mine. I slowly smiled and started to make my way over to him.

I walked up, and Anna finally looked to see who Reed was staring at. Her smile instantly fell.

She looked me up and down and smirked. "Courtney, don't you look…like you're ready to go for a swim?"

I smiled and looked up at Reed. "Oh, I'm ready for something, but I don't think it's swimming."

Reed laughed as he pulled me closer to him.

Anna cleared her throat and said, "Well, I see now is not a good time to talk, Reed. Maybe later. Lunch or something?"

Oh. No. She. Didn't.

Reed pulled me tighter against him, and I instantly felt calmer.

"I think now is as good of a time as any, Anna. I don't keep secrets from Courtney, so what you have to say, you can say in front of her."

Anna shot me a dirty look and stood up straighter. "Fine. I just didn't like the way we ended things. I mean, I think we both overreacted. I thought maybe this *thing* you have going on with Courtney would have played out by now, but I see it hasn't."

"You bitch," I blurted out. I tried to make my way over to her, but Reed was holding me back.

She rolled her eyes at me and let out a small laugh. "Nice, Courtney. Really classy. Are we in high school?"

I balled up my fists. I was ready to knock the shit out of her. "What? You just—"

Reed pulled me back and stepped in front of me. "Anna, I broke up with you because I love Courtney. I've loved her from the moment I first saw her, and I'll love her until I take my last breath. I don't appreciate you talking to my fiancée like that, so please, I think it would be best if you just left."

My stomach did a little dip when Reed said his reason for breaking up with her had been because he loved me. Then, I took great pleasure in watching Anna's jaw drop to the ground when she found out we were engaged.

"Wait, you're engaged? When?" Anna asked as she stumbled on her words.

"That's what this party is for, Anna—to celebrate Court and me getting engaged and Layton and Whitley expecting their first child."

Anna shook her head and looked around. She looked back at me and then at Reed. She finally came to her senses and gave him a smirk. "You just made the biggest mistake of your life."

Reed let out a small chuckle. "No. The biggest mistake of my life was not admitting my feelings for Courtney from the very beginning."

Anna let out a huff as she turned and stomped away toward all the cars and trucks. I watched as she stormed off, and I prayed that would be the last time she would try to cause problems.

Brett Eldredge's "Mean to Me" began playing, and Reed grabbed my hand and brought me out to the dance floor.

As we began dancing, he leaned down and brushed his lips against my neck before whispering in my ear, "I love this song. I think of you every time I hear it."

I was silently cursing that I couldn't remember how the song had started, but as we were dancing, I listened to the words. I buried my head into his chest and just took it all in. I'd never felt so loved in my entire life.

I'm engaged to my Prince Charming.

"You're so beautiful, Courtney. I have to control my temper right now, and let me tell you, I'm being tested big time."

I pulled back and looked up at him. "What do you mean, you're being tested? Why do you have to control your temper?"

Reed looked around and then back down at me. "All these cowboys are drooling over you. The moment I saw you walking up, dressed like that, I wanted nothing more than to leave and have my wicked way with you."

My heart started to pound in my chest, echoing in my ears, and I was pretty sure Reed could hear it. He ran his knuckles down my face, and I wanted him to take me right there, to hell with all the people.

"I love you," I whispered.

He reached down and brushed his lips against mine, causing me to let out a soft, low moan. I pushed my hand through his hair and grabbed a handful, and he let out a moan of his own. It moved over my body like a warm blanket, and I needed him more than ever before.

"Courtney…" he whispered in such a seductive voice that I trembled. "I need to make love to you…right now."

I pulled on his hair more, and before I knew what was happening, he picked me up and started walking toward his truck. It took a few seconds for it to sink in that everyone was whooping and hollering. I buried my face into Reed's shoulders and started giggling.

"Reed, everyone knows why we are leaving." I peeked over his shoulder and saw Layton and Whitley watching us with the goofiest smiles ever on their faces.

I waved good-bye to Whit, and she threw her head back and started laughing. Layton pulled her to him and whispered something into her ear. If I knew those two, it wouldn't be long before they left as well.

By the time we got to Reed's truck, I almost wanted to put my hand down into my panties and ease the intense pressure between my legs. He set me down, grabbed the seat belt, and buckled me in.

I laughed and pushed him away. "I can buckle my own seat belt, cowboy."

He smiled, and when I felt his hand touch the inside of my thigh, I jumped.

Jesus, the way he makes me feel is unreal.

I looked him up and down. He was dressed in jeans that fit his ass so damn good. The light blue T-shirt he had on made his eyes look stunningly blue.

I could totally lose myself in this man's eyes.

"Tell me what you want, baby." He moved his fingertips up and down my thigh oh-so lightly.

I closed my eyes and pushed his hand up to ease my need. "I want you to make love to me—*now*."

When I opened my eyes, I looked into his, and they were on fire.

"I can get us to my place in ten minutes," he whispered as he looked down at my lips.

I purposely licked them and sucked my bottom lip in between my teeth. He let out a moan before he quickly shut my door and ran around the front of his truck.

As he jumped in, I glanced back at the party. "Reed, what about all these people? Y'all invited them, and now, we're leaving."

Out of the corner of my eye, I saw Layton and Whitley walking. When I looked at them, they were heading to Layton's truck, and Whitley was smiling from ear to ear.

"Oh. My. God. They're leaving their own party!" I said as I shook my head.

He started laughing as he put his truck in drive and hit the gas pedal. "So are we, baby, and I'm pretty sure all these people couldn't care less. Besides, Kevin is here. He loves this shit more than Layton and I do. He can handle it."

I looked over at Reed and chuckled. "I guess that's true. I feel bad for leaving though."

He shook his head and said, "I don't. I want to be inside you much more than I want to stand around, drinking beer and talking to everyone."

I squeezed my legs together and dropped my head to the back of the seat. *Oh God.* Nothing was more like heaven than having Reed buried deep inside me. I closed my eyes and started to daydream about Reed making love to me. The things that began running through my mind were driving me insane.

"Courtney, if you keep making noises like that, I'm not going to be able to make it home without pulling over and fucking you on the side of the road."

Oh my. The idea of getting Reed so worked up turned me on even more. *I wonder how far I can push him.*

We were about five minutes from his house when I decided to kick it up a notch.

I reached up and began playing with my nipple through the light fabric of my bikini top. "Oh…oh God…I'm so horny," I whispered.

I tried not to smile when I heard Reed's sharp intake of air. *A little more, Courtney, and you've got him.* I was hugging myself internally. I slowly moved my hand down and unbuttoned my shorts before sliding my hand inside. The moment I touched my overly sensitive clit, I let out a gasp. *Oh God…I just need to come. It feels so good.*

I closed my eyes and let out a moan as Reed made a sharp turn and slammed on the brakes. I opened my eyes, and we were pulled off to the side of his driveway. I quickly looked to see how close we were to the road, but I couldn't even see the road from where we were parked.

Reed threw open my door and unbuckled my seat belt. He reached in and took me out of the truck. I was still reeling from touching myself and being so close to coming that everything was happening so fast. He set me down against his truck and pulled my shorts and bikini bottoms off in one quick movement. How in the hell he'd gotten them both over my boots, I had no idea. I was standing there in nothing but my bikini top and cowboy boots. Reed's eyes moved up and down my body as he licked his lips hungrily.

"You drive me so insane, Courtney, so fucking insane." He reached down and pushed two fingers inside me as he closed his eyes and whispered, "Court, you're so wet."

"Ah…Reed…please. I need to feel you inside me right now."

Before I could even wrap my legs around him, he was picking me up and pushing into me.

"Motherfucker," he said, moving in slowly and pulling out just as slowly.

"Reed…I need more," I said.

He pulled out and then slammed into me before he began moving harder and faster. I placed my hands on his shoulders as I tried to contain the moans of pleasure he was bringing out of me. The feeling of Reed moving in and out of my body in such a frantic way was beyond amazing. It was so intense that I could barely breathe. I never wanted it to stop.

Then, I felt it starting. "Reed…oh God…I'm about to come."

He dug his fingers into my hips as he pulled almost all the way out and then drove back into me.

I let out a scream and dropped my head back. "Yes! Reed…harder…"

He gave me just what I'd asked for, and I began calling out his name. The idea of being outside, knowing someone could come up on us as Reed was fucking me against his truck, caused my orgasm to hit me faster and stronger. I'd never in my life had such a powerful orgasm.

I couldn't help but scream out, "Oh God…Reed, I'm coming. Oh God! Feels. Amazing. Yes…oh God, yes!" I wasn't even sure what I was hollering out at this point. All I knew was that I was having the most intense orgasm of my life, and I couldn't believe how long it was lasting. It was taking my breath away as my body trembled from head to toe.

Reed held on to me even tighter as he called out, "Courtney, I'm comin', baby. Ah…*fuck*…it feels so good."

I swore I could feel every single ounce of him as he poured his hot come into my body. I held on to him as he slowly stopped moving his body. I wrapped my legs around him tighter as he put one hand against his truck and attempted to catch his breath. I'd read about hot sex like this in all those damn books, but never had I ever dreamed that I would be fucked outside against my fiancé's truck. Just the idea of it made me start grinding against Reed.

He pulled his head back and looked at me with a smile. "Not satisfied, baby?"

I smiled and said, "Oh, believe me, I'm very satisfied. That was the most incredible orgasm I've ever had. You just make me want you every damn second of the day. I feel you moving inside me, and just the thought of what we just did…well, it turned me on again."

He gave me that panty-melting smile of his. "Let me take care of that for you then."

I let out a whimper at what he could possibly have in mind. "What are you thinking of?" I asked with an innocent smile.

He laughed. "I know my girl, and I know how well she packs. I bet there is something other than your Kindle in that bag of yours. Perhaps a toy?"

My heart dropped to my stomach. *Oh Lord…does he want to play with me and a…vibrator?*

The thought had me pushing him out of me, and he put me down.

I'd never moved so fast in my life. I opened the back door, and then I reached for my bag and stuck my hand inside, looking for the vibrator. The moment I felt the rubber, I smiled. "Yes!" I instantly felt the heat move into my cheeks as I realized that I'd said that out loud.

I looked down at the vibrator in my hand and smiled. Whitley had told me how turned-on Layton had gotten when he watched Whitley use the vibrator on herself, and I was betting Reed would be the same way. I turned around and held it up. When I looked down and saw Reed's dick getting harder, I let out a giggle.

"Why, Mr. Moore, look at you…my very own ready-on-command. Do you get this excited when you play with your plants or feed the cows?" I used my hand holding the vibrator to exaggerate my words.

Reed's eyes were glued to it as he shook his head. "Baby, no plant could ever have my dick coming up this soon after having sex with your—"

"Choose your words wisely," I said as I gave him a look.

I quickly looked around. We were just down from the house, but I knew there was no way in hell I could make it even just for two minutes. I turned back around and pushed my bag onto the floor of the backseat. Thank God Reed's backseat was roomy. I climbed in and slowly lay back. Reed's eyes grew bigger as he jumped up and climbed into the truck with me.

"Court…what are you doing?" he asked, his voice cracking.

I bit down on my lip and then smiled. "I'm going to use this vibrator and play with myself as you watch."

He swallowed hard, and I wanted to hug myself—one, because I knew this was turning him on big time, and two, for being so brave. I'd never before used a vibrator in front of a guy, let alone allowed a guy to play with me with a vibrator. BOB was my toy and only for me to enjoy. No man had ever been worthy enough to share me with BOB. But Reed was not an ordinary guy. He was my everything.

I reached down and stuck two of my fingers inside me quickly. I smiled at how wet I was, and then I smiled bigger when I saw Reed's eyes about to pop out of his head. I moved the vibrator slowly down my chest, making sure I rubbed it on one of my nipples. Reed let out a moan, and then I slid it down my stomach and finally between my legs. I slowly began working it in and out of my body.

"I think I've died and gone to heaven." Reed quickly looked up at me and licked his lips as he pulled his shirt off.

"Not yet," I said as I turned it on and arched my back. *Oh shit, I'm going to come fast.* The damn thing had fresh batteries in it, and I was so worked up that a stick would probably make me come fast.

"Jesus Christ, Courtney…" Reed whispered as I was moving the vibrator in and out.

I had my eyes closed, and when I felt Reed sucking on one of my nipples, that was my undoing.

"Oh, Reed…I'm going to come," I called out.

Reed pulled back, and I opened my eyes. Our eyes caught, and as I called out in pleasure, he smiled so big that I couldn't help but smile back. He reached his hand down to mine and pulled out the vibrator. He moved my body farther into the truck and slowly began rubbing on my clit with his hard dick.

"I can't…not again…Reed, I can't," I said between gasps of air.

When I felt him slowly slide in, I wanted to cry. Something about this whole thing felt so…magical. As he moved in and out of me, he kissed me across my chest, up my neck, and along my jawline.

When he reached my right ear, he whispered, "I love you, Courtney. I can't wait to spend the rest of my life with you. I can't wait to see your stomach growing bigger with my child."

I began crying hard as I wrapped my arms around him. "I love you, Reed. God, I love you so much."

Then, Reed pushed into me so deep that I sucked in a breath of air. The moan that he let out told me he was coming, and I felt him pulsing inside me, giving me everything he had. I took all of it as I squeezed around him. He stopped moving and held himself above me for a few minutes before I moved over and turned on my side. He lay behind me and pulled me against him, and he held me as we lay there in silence. Something wonderful had just happened between us, and I wasn't really sure what it was. Once Reed's breathing became normal again, I turned around on the small seat and faced him.

"How fast can we get married?" I asked.

I'd never seen Reed smile so big in my life. It was like I'd just told him he won a million dollars.

"I'll marry you right now if you want."

I looked down at his tattoo on his chest—*my heart*—and then back into his eyes. I gave him a wink and said, "I've always wanted to go to Lake Tahoe."

SIXTEEN

REED

I watched as Courtney ran up the stairs in her house to pack a suitcase.

She stopped at the top of the steps and looked down at me. "Do you want to call Layton? Or should I call Whit?"

I smiled and said, "I'll call Layton. You just pack, angel."

The smile she flashed caused me to take in a sharp breath of air.

"Oh. My. God. We're really going to do this, aren't we?"

"I'll do whatever you want, Court. We can do this, or we can invite five hundred people to a church. As long as I can marry you, I don't care how we do it."

She gave me a wink and made her way into her room. I pulled out my cell phone and hit Layton's number. I walked into the living room and sat down on the sofa. I took a deep breath and got ready to do the one thing I'd been so terrified to do since my father walked out on my mother.

"Hey, dude. You and Court ever make it back to the party?" Layton asked with a chuckle.

I smiled and asked, "Did you and Whitley?"

"Fuck no. Did you see how my hot pregnant wife was dressed? I took her home and performed my husbandly duties."

I made a face and tried to shake the image out of my head. "Jesus, too much information, you ass."

"I don't even think anyone noticed when we left, to be honest. I'm pretty sure everyone is gone now," Layton said.

I heard Whitley talking to someone in the background.

"Who is Whit talking to?" I asked as I pushed my hand through my hair. I was nervous as hell to tell Layton that Courtney and I were on our way to Austin to catch a plane to Reno.

"Jen. She stopped by to say good-bye before she left with Kate."

"Oh."

"Spill it, Reed," Layton said as I heard Jen's and Whitley's voices fading.

He must be walking away from them. "Um…"

"Reed, is everyone okay? Did something happen between you and Courtney?"

I smiled as I looked out in the hallway. "Oh yeah, something pretty damn big happened."

Layton let out a small chuckle. "Well, are you going to fill me in or make me stand here and guess?"

I slowly took in a deep breath and let it out. "Court and I wanted to know if you and Whitley…if y'all wanted to…" *Fuck, I can't breathe.*

"If Whitley and I want to what? Reed, what in the hell is going on?"

Shit. What if I hurt her? What if I can't make her as happy as she makes me? I closed my eyes and thought back to just a little bit ago and how amazing making love to her had been. I would do everything in my power to never hurt her—ever. From this point on, my goal was to make Courtney happy and keep her safe.

"Reed? Are you still there?" Layton asked.

"Yeah, um…Court and I want you and Whitley to go with us to Lake Tahoe," I blurted out so fast that I was sure he would need me to repeat it.

"Oh, hell yeah! I'd love to take Whitley to Lake Tahoe. When are y'all thinking of going?"

I looked down at my watch and said, "In about five hours."

Silence.

"Layton?" I practically whispered.

"Five hours? Holy shit…is this what I think it is?"

I nodded my head and slowly said, "Yeah…and I'd like nothing more than for you to be there when I marry the love of my life."

"Son of a bitch. Reed, what in the hell? Y'all are eloping?"

I heard Whitley let out a small scream.

"What? Oh my God. I want to talk to Courtney! When? Where?" Whitley was yelling out.

I couldn't help but laugh as I imagined Whitley running for her phone to call Courtney.

"Uh…Whitley is calling Courtney right now," Layton said.

Not even thirty seconds later, I heard Courtney scream from upstairs.

"I think Court is talking to Whit now," I said with a chuckle.

"Reed, are y'all sure? You don't think you're moving too fast? Courtney doesn't want a wedding?"

"Layton, I know I want to spend the rest of my life with Court. It was her idea to get married as soon as possible. I want to spend the rest of my life with her, and this feels so completely right. I mean, I'm scared as hell, but at the same time, nothing has ever felt so right in my life."

I wished I could see Layton's face right now.

He let out a small breath. "What airline? And what time does the flight leave?"

I jumped up and did a fist pump. "Thank you, Layton. Shit, you don't know what this means to me to have you there."

He let out a laugh as I heard Whitley yelling something about packing a bag.

I gave Layton the flight information and told him that we would meet them at the Austin-Bergstrom airport. By the time we were done talking, I turned around to see Courtney standing there. She was dressed in a pair of jeans and a white T-shirt that had a green alien holding a gun in one hand and a book in the other with the words *Take Me to Your Reader* written in black under the alien.

I let out a laugh and shook my head. *Damn, I love this girl.*

She tilted her head and gave me that smile of hers that had my stomach doing that damn flipping thing.

"I like your T-shirt, baby," I said as I walked up to her and pulled her to me.

She stood on her toes and put her hand behind my neck. She pulled my lips to hers and gently kissed me. "Reed, are you sure?" she whispered as she barely pulled back from my lips.

I smiled and brushed my lips back and forth across hers. "I've never been so sure of anything in my life. Are you sure, baby?"

"Oh yeah. I really can't wait to let my mother know that we're eloping."

I pulled back and gave her a questioning look. "Why?"

She let out a giggle. "My mother has been planning my wedding since I was, like, five years old. Every year on my parents' wedding anniversary, she would pull out her wedding dress and show it to my sister and me. She would tell us that whoever got married first was going to get to wear the dress and have the biggest wedding ever."

My smile faded. "Courtney, we can plan a wedding. I don't mind—"

She put her finger up to my lips to stop me from talking. "The only thing I want is for someone to say that I am Mrs. Reed Nickolas Moore. It doesn't matter to me how or where that happens. I just want to marry my Prince Charming."

I smiled as I brushed the back of my hand down the side of her face. She pulled back and turned to grab her suitcase.

She looked over her shoulder and said, "Besides, my mother's wedding dress is the most hideous dress I've ever seen. With me eloping, it falls to my sister to wear it in her wedding." She spun around and started to make her way out the front door.

I stood there for a second, trying to decide if she really wanted to get married right away or if she was trying to get out of wearing her mother's wedding dress. I quickly decided that it didn't matter. Soon, I would be making love to my wife, and that was all that mattered.

I set the house alarm and shut the door. I ran up and took the suitcase from Courtney. I put it in the backseat before shutting her door and running around to the driver's side of my truck. When I jumped in my truck, panic took over, and my stomach dropped.

I looked over at her and said, "I don't have the wedding bands."

She winked and said, "We'll figure it out, baby. Let's go get married."

I watched as Whitley and Courtney walked ahead of Layton and me in the Reno airport. They had not stopped talking since we met them at the airport in Austin.

"What in the hell are they going on and on about?" I asked as I looked over at Layton.

He started laughing. "My guess would be the wedding."

I got that feeling in my stomach again. *What in the hell are we doing? No plans, no dress, no tux, and no wedding bands.* I stopped walking and just stood there, frozen.

Layton stopped and turned to look at me. "What's wrong?"

"What in the hell are we doing, Layton? I don't even have a wedding band to give to her. She has no dress. What kind of a wedding could I possibly give her? We're flying by the seat of our pants." I felt sick and wished I could sit down.

Layton walked up to me and smiled as he put his hand on my shoulder. "Reed, do you want to marry Courtney?"

I looked at him like he had grown two heads. "Of course I do. I want nothing more than to marry her."

He slapped me on the back and let out a laugh. "Then, don't sweat the small shit. Courtney seems to be flying high, dude. I don't think she's too worried about it all." He glanced back at Courtney and Whitley as they stood there, waiting for the luggage.

Courtney was on her cell phone, and her hand was waving all over the place. I had no idea who she was talking to, but as soon as the plane had landed, she was on her phone.

I took a deep breath as Layton and I began walking over to where the girls were standing.

Whitley came running up and jumped into Layton's arms. "Oh my God! My best friend is getting married."

Layton started laughing and gave her a quick peck on the lips. "I think my boy here is feeling a little nervous," he said as he gestured toward me.

"I'm not nervous. It's just that we don't have anything planned, and maybe we should have thought this through, and—"

Layton had set Whitley down, and she quickly walked up to me and put her hand over my mouth.

"Stop right there. Are you having doubts?" she whispered.

What is with everyone asking me if I have doubts? "No. It's just that I want this to be perfect for Court."

I looked over at her on the phone. The smile on her face instantly had me relaxing.

I glanced back down at Whitley and smiled. "You know what? As long as Courtney is happy, that is all that matters to me. It will be perfect. I'll make sure it's perfect."

Whitley smiled and gave me a wink. "That is so the right answer." She quickly looked back at Courtney before turning back to me. "If there is one thing you need to know about Courtney, the girl can plan shit. Just relax, Reed. I promise you, she is so happy right now."

I smiled and nodded my head, knowing Whit was right. I'd seen Courtney work under pressure, and she was always on top of everything.

Layton and I walked up to the baggage carousel and looked for all the suitcases as we talked about the ranch. Once we had them all, we started heading toward the car rental. Courtney was still on the phone as she stood off to the side. This time, she didn't look so happy. She looked over at me as I was making my way to the rental counter. The smile she gave me caused my stomach to drop, and my pants felt a size or two smaller.

Damn…the hold this girl has over me.

Whitley put her hand on my arm. "Don't worry. She's talking to her mother, who happens to be slightly upset that Court decided to elope."

Layton and I both said at the same time, "Oh shit."

Layton slapped me on the back and chuckled. "Way to welcome yourself into the family, dude."

I snapped my head and gave him a go-to-hell look. "Fuck off, asswipe."

Whit and Layton both started laughing as I began talking to the rental car agent.

All it took was one flash of my smile and a little bit of innocent flirting, and I had upgraded our car rental at no extra charge.

As the agent handed me the keys to our BMW X5, she asked, "What brings you to Reno? Maybe we could meet for a drink later, and I can…show you around."

I smiled. "I'm sorry, but can't. I'm actually here with my fiancée. We're getting married."

It wasn't lost on me how her smile faded, and she looked like she was about to take back the car keys.

I quickly flashed her a smile and said, "Thank you so much for the warm welcome. Have a wonderful day."

I turned to see Layton shaking his head with a smile on his face before he looked away.

As I walked by him, he said in a low voice, "At least you know you still have a way with the girls."

I quickly looked at him and winked before I walked up to Courtney. She was finally off the phone and talking to Whitley. Courtney smiled at me as I made my way to her. The look on her face caused me to smile. She looked so happy and beautiful.

When she began walking up to me, I mouthed, *I love you.*

She picked up the pace and slammed into my body. I dropped our suitcases and held her as she began crying.

"What? What's wrong, baby?" I pulled back and saw her smiling as tears were streaming down her face. "Court? Baby, talk to me. I'm slightly confused by the tears and the smile."

She wiped away her tears and shook her head. "Everything is perfect. Well, besides the fact that my mother is pretty pissed off at me right now, but she'll get over it. My father's best friend is someone big at The Ritz-Carlton hotel, and he owed my dad a favor, so my dad called him on it. We are all set for a sunset wedding on the beach tomorrow. I called a local bridal shop, and they have the dress I want. Whit can pick out a bridesmaid dress when we get there. The florist at the hotel is taking care of the flowers, and I told her to keep them simple. The only thing left to do is get our wedding bands."

I was pretty sure my jaw was on the floor. She scrunched up her nose in that cute way she does, and my dick instantly jumped.

"You did all that…since we got off the plane?"

She threw her head back and laughed. "No. I called my father before we left, and I asked him to find out about The Ritz-Carlton to see if they could make it work. After we landed, I was on the phone with the bridal store, the florist…and my mother." Her smile faded.

"So, should I be afraid when you bring me home to meet the parents?" I said with a chuckle.

She took a deep breath. "Probably. My parents both think I'm pregnant, and that's why we're rushing the wedding. I told them I wasn't, but my mother is being crazy. She demanded I take a pregnancy test and show her the results."

"What?" I said.

Courtney shrugged her shoulders and smirked. "I almost want Whit to take one, so I can freak my mom the hell out."

"Wait, is your mom serious? She wants you to send her a picture of a pregnancy test?" I asked.

Courtney nodded her head and simply said, "Yep."

I didn't know whether I should be really worried or really scared for my life. "What about your dad? How does he feel about this?" I asked, silently saying a prayer that her dad had been cool with it. Then, I thought about how I hadn't even told my own mother yet.

"Let's get to the car, so we can check in at the hotel and then go to the bridal store. I'll fill you in on what my parents said, I promise."

By the time we got all the luggage into the car and entered the hotel address into the GPS, I was sweating bullets. Whisking Court off to Lake Tahoe and marrying her was not a good way to make an impression on her parents.

Driving to the hotel, I was the only one not talking. All I kept thinking of was how we had disappointed her parents. *What is my own mother going to think? Shit! I need to call her.*

When Courtney placed her hand on my leg, I instantly felt a warmth there before it spread throughout my whole body. I looked over into her sparkling eyes, and I immediately felt better. I didn't care what her parents thought. I wanted to marry her, and she wanted to marry me, and this was how we were going to do it.

I'll deal with the parents later. Right now, it is all about my beautiful bride-to-be and our wedding.

She moved her hand up to the side of my face and began brushing the back of her hand on my cheek. "So, what do you want to hear first—my father's threat to you or my mother's?"

SEVENTEEN

I tried so desperately to hold in my laughter when Reed's head snapped over and looked at me. His mouth had dropped open, and he couldn't even talk. Layton and Whitley were laughing in the backseat, and I wanted to just hug myself for freaking Reed out.

I might love him more than life itself…but I love fucking with him, too!

"I think I should go with my mother's first," I said in a nonchalant manner.

Reed slowly looked back to the road, and the light turned green. We were not very far from the hotel, and my nerves had been getting the better of me.

I can't believe I'm getting married tomorrow.

To calm myself down, I'd thought I would jack around with Reed's nerves.

Reed cleared his throat and said, "Wait, your parents threatened me? How? Why?"

I took in a deep breath and quickly let it out. "It's pretty simple. They feel like you're depriving them of seeing their daughter get married. So, they're flying out tonight, and they will be here for the wedding tomorrow."

Reed pulled into a parking lot and slammed on the brakes. "What?" he yelled out as he looked at me with nothing but panic in his eyes. "Your parents are coming here? For the wedding?"

I slowly nodded, and the next thing I knew, Reed sprang out of the car and began pacing. Layton jumped out, and Whitley hit me on the back of the head.

"Stop it, Courtney. He is a bundle of nerves as it is. Why are you doing this to him?"

I let out a laugh. "'Cause it calms my nerves!" I looked out the car window and saw Reed leaning over with his hands on his knees.

"Is he…" I started to ask as Whitley said, "Oh my God, you made him sick."

Oh shit. I got out of the car and ran over to Reed. "Are you okay?"

He looked up at me. "No. I'm not okay. Maybe we shouldn't be doing this."

I took a step back, and now, I was the one feeling sick. "What?" I barely got out as I took another step away from him.

"Reed…" Layton said in a warning tone.

Oh my God. What if he's changed his mind? What if he isn't sure he wants to marry me? I looked around and saw The Ritz-Carlton across the street.

"Reed, just take a few deep breaths. Everything is going to be okay," Whitley said as she walked over to Reed.

I turned and walked to the car. I grabbed my purse and made my way across the street to the hotel.

"Courtney!" Whitley called after me.

I turned and gave her a weak smile. "I'll meet y'all at the hotel."

I picked up my pace as I heard Reed call out after me. There was no way I could talk to him right now. By the time I got halfway across the street, I began running toward the hotel until I came to a stop in the massive lobby. All I could hear was Noah's voice in my head, saying over and over that no one would ever want me like he wanted me.

One quick look around, and I found the ladies' restroom. I barely made it in time before I began throwing up. When I finally couldn't throw up anymore, I stood up and leaned against the stall. When I closed my eyes, I saw Reed, and I bent over and panicked.

No. I'm not okay. Maybe we shouldn't be doing this.

Then, I saw Noah again. This time, he was on top of me, saying how much he wanted to be inside me, how only he belonged there, and how no man would ever want me.

My eyes snapped open, and I began crying as I placed my hands over my ears. I whispered, "Please go away. Please just go away."

I began reciting my favorite quotes from *The Marriage Bargain* over and over until all thoughts of Noah were gone.

I banged my head against the stall and whispered, "I'm so stupid. I rushed Reed. He said he would marry me tomorrow, but maybe he didn't really mean *tomorrow.*"

I wasn't sure how long I had been in the stall before I walked out. I rinsed out my mouth and washed my hands. One quick look in the mirror revealed a mess staring back at me. My eyes were red and swollen, my face was flushed, and my hair was a mess. I reached into my purse, pulled out a hair band, and threw my hair up into a ponytail.

I swallowed and took in a deep breath. *How stupid of me to think how romantic it was for Reed to just whisk me away and marry me on a moment's notice.*

I looked at myself in the mirror again and whispered, "Life is not like the books you read, Courtney."

I closed my eyes, and Noah's face appeared.

He smiled and said, *No one will ever want you like I want you.*

I snapped my eyes open and quickly wiped away my tears. I pulled out my phone and saw I had six missed calls from Reed and three from Whitley. I also had one text message from Reed.

Reed: Courtney…baby, please call me. I'm really worried about you. I didn't mean that the way you thought. It's just that you freaked me out by telling me your parents are coming and that they are really pissed. I just want to make you happy. Please call me. I love you so much, Court.

I looked at the time on my phone. "Oh shit!" I'd been in the restroom for almost an hour.

I splashed some cold water on my face before I walked out of the restroom and to the lobby. I walked up to the counter, gave the woman standing behind the front desk my name, and asked for my room. I smiled when she told me I was in one of the presidential suites, and then she gave me a key.

Oh, Daddy, I'm going to owe you a big kiss and hug.

I sent Whit a text message, saying that I was on my way to the elevator.

Courtney: Hey, I'm heading up to our room. I'm so sorry. I didn't know how much time had passed.

Whitley: Oh my God, Courtney. Reed is a complete mess. We are in the room with him. I let him know that you're on your way up. What in the hell happened? Why did you run away? We have an appointment in an hour for your dress. I'm so pissed at you right now.

Courtney: Duly noted. I'm sorry. I didn't mean to worry you guys. I'm almost there.

When the elevator opened, I turned to the right and started making my way to our suite. My heart was pounding, and I wasn't sure how Reed would take it that I had only been kidding with him about my parents. I hadn't realized how nervous he was.

I stopped outside our door and sucked in a breath of air, preparing myself to hear Reed say that we were no longer getting married. I slid the key in and opened the door. When I saw Reed sitting there, looking completely destroyed, my heart dropped to my stomach, and I dropped my purse.

He jumped up and made his way over to me so fast that I didn't even have time to say anything before he pulled me into his arms.

"Please don't ever leave me like that again. *Please.* I'm so sorry, Courtney. I didn't mean for you to think that I don't want to get married. I just want everything to be perfect for you, and if you'd rather have your parents here…"

I pulled back some and looked into his eyes. *Has he been…crying?*

I quickly looked behind Reed and saw Layton and Whitley. Whitley was standing there with her hands on her hips, looking ready to rip me a new one. I looked back into Reed's eyes, and my heart actually began hurting, knowing that I had hurt him so much by foolishly running away like that.

"I, um…I felt sick, so I went to the restroom. I felt so guilty for making you feel that way, and then, um…" I looked away and whispered, "*Old memories* came back, and I just…lost track of time."

Reed placed his finger on my chin and turned my face up to his. The love in his eyes warmed my heart and filled my soul with peace.

"I just freaked, angel, that's all. I was worried that I was rushing you, and then you said your parents were upset and all. I'm so sorry I said anything to hurt you."

My breathing picked up, and I couldn't believe what he was saying. I had been a bitch and purposely made him worry, and here he was, saying such wonderful things to me.

"You lost track of time?" Whitley said from behind Reed. "Really? That's the best you can come up with, Court? You deliberately said that bullshit to Reed to make him upset, and then you take off when he freaks out. I just—"

Reed turned and held up his hand. "Whitley, it's okay."

Whitley started shaking her head as she walked over toward Reed and me. "No, it's not okay, Reed. So, because you had some stupid old memories come up, you caused all of us to worry?"

I sucked in a breath of air, and Reed grabbed on to me tighter.

He turned and gave me a questioning look. "You haven't told her yet?"

I felt the tears burning my eyes. The last thing I wanted was for Noah to invade my world, especially these next few days when I should be the happiest I'd ever been. The moment I felt a tear roll down my cheek, I quickly wiped it away.

I looked down and whispered, "Not yet."

"Courtney…" Reed said as he pulled me closer to him. "Baby, I love you so much."

I pulled back and looked at Whitley. Her anger had turned to concern.

"Told me what? Is this what you were supposed to tell me but kept putting off?" Whitley asked.

Layton came walking over. "I hate to be the one to say this, but if we want a wedding dress and tuxes, we need to get going."

I tried to give Layton a smile, but I was afraid it came off fake as all get-out. I should have been excited to get my wedding dress. Instead, I was filled with panic, guilt, anger, and love. All the emotions were beginning to build up, and I was afraid they would break the dam at any moment.

"Whitley, Layton, can y'all give us just a few minutes? Then, we will head out to the bridal store," I said.

They both nodded their heads.

Whitley walked up to me and brought me in for a hug. She whispered in my ear, "I'm so sorry. I was angry, and these pregnancy hormones make me crazy with my emotions. Please, Court, please talk to me, okay?"

When she stepped back, I cleared my throat and said, "I will. After we get our dresses, okay?"

She nodded, and then she turned and followed Layton out of the room.

Before Layton shut the door, he said, "We'll meet y'all down in the lobby in ten minutes."

Once the door shut, I lost it and fell into Reed's arms, crying hysterically. I started to just spit everything out, like I only had moments to say it all. "Why? *Why* is he invading my thoughts now, Reed? I want him gone. I *need* him gone. I'm so sorry. I was kidding. My parents never threatened you. Okay, that's a lie. My father did threaten to hurt you if you hurt me, but they're not coming here. They were never coming here. I'm so sorry. I never meant to make you so upset. I'm so, so very sorry."

He pulled me in tighter and began moving his hand up and down my back. "Shh…angel, please don't cry. It's okay. I promise, it's all going to be okay. I'm here for you, Courtney, and I will never leave you. I'll never let him hurt you. I swear to God…I'll never let him hurt you again, Courtney."

I looked into his eyes that were filled with so much love, and I instantly felt a warm sensation run through my whole body. I wanted him inside me so badly. I needed to feel him close to me. I needed him to love me.

"Make love to me," I whispered.

He smiled and kissed the tip of my nose. "We don't have time, Court."

I pushed myself into him and felt his growing erection. "We can be fast…please." I batted my eyelashes at him.

He stepped back and held up his hands. "As much as I want to bury myself inside you and make you feel nothing but love, we can't."

I attempted to give him my best pouty face, but it didn't work.

I reached down and grabbed my purse. "Fine, but if you think I'm putting out for you the night before our wedding, you're crazy."

I turned and started for the door. Reed walked up and spun me around, and then he slammed me against the door. Before I could even register what was happening, he had my pants down, and he was finger-fucking the hell out of me. I couldn't believe how fast my orgasm was building. I was beginning to think that all this man had to do was touch me, and I'd have an orgasm.

"Oh God, Reed…"

"Does that feel good, baby?" he asked as he pulled my leg up and pinned it against him.

I dropped my head back and began thrusting into his hand. "Yes! Oh…faster, Reed…please go faster."

Then, it hit me. The feeling washed over my body so fast and so hard that it took everything out of me not to start screaming out. I bit down on my lower lip and let out whimper after whimper while his fingers moved in and out of me, bringing me to such an incredible high. Then, he slowly brought me down as he whispered how much he loved me.

Once I was able to start breathing normally again, he looked into my eyes as he pushed a stray piece of hair behind my ear. "I love when you call out my name when you're coming."

I smiled as I brought my arms up, and I wrapped them around his neck, pulling him closer to me. He brushed his lips back and forth against mine before sucking in my bottom lip and biting down on it gently.

"I guess since you're being old-fashioned and not putting out later, I'll just have to wait until tomorrow night to feel how warm and wet you are for me."

I let out a chuckle. "Being old-fashioned is overrated."

He threw his head back and laughed, and then he reached down and helped me put my pants back on. "You ready, Miss Will?"

I nodded my head. "Yes, I am, Mr. Moore. Yes, I am."

EIGHTEEN

REED

Layton and I were about to try on tuxes when Courtney decided we should just wear jeans and white shirts with a charcoal tie. Whitley's dress was charcoal, and I had to admit that she looked beautiful in it. I was amazed that they would only have to make one minor adjustment to her dress. Courtney wouldn't let me watch as she tried on her dress, but Layton and I both heard the girls let out a gasp as Courtney tried it on.

Then, I heard Court yell out, "Motherfucker, it's the perfect dress!"

I glanced around the store and just shrugged my shoulders. "That's my future wife. She's a little excited."

I got one smile and three dirty looks.

Fifteen minutes later, Courtney and Whitley came walking out, holding dress bags and smiling from ear to ear.

Courtney came walking up to me, and she kissed me so hard and fast on the lips that I let out a laugh afterward.

"Are you sure you're happy with this, Court?"

She smiled that adorable crooked smile of hers as she placed her hand on my chest. "I've never been so happy in my entire life. I cannot wait to be Mrs. Reed Nickolas Moore."

My heart almost burst with love when I heard her say *Mrs. Reed Nickolas Moore.*

"Say that again," I whispered.

She tilted her head. "Which part?"

"Your name."

She let out a giggle. "Mrs. Reed Nickolas Moore."

I smiled bigger and placed my hands on the sides of her face. I brought her lips up to mine, and I kissed her. I wanted to pour as much love into this kiss as I possibly could.

When I pulled back, she whispered, "Wow."

I took a step back to put space between us. The heat coming from both our bodies was driving me insane, and I was pretty sure she felt the same way.

"Layton and I are going to go watch some football for a bit while y'all take the dresses back to the rooms. I made y'all appointments at the spa and then dinner reservations at Manzanita. I figured you needed some girl time," I said.

The look in her eyes caused my stomach to do a few flips and flops and one big dive.

"Reed, you're making all my dreams come true."

"I hope so, angel. I really hope so."

After we got back to the hotel, Layton and I made our way to the hotel bar to give the girls some time to talk. Courtney had promised me that she would tell Whitley everything about Noah, and I knew she would this time. She needed to in order to help her move on.

"You're lost in thought, dude," Layton said as he set a beer down in front of me.

I tried to smile. I swore nothing ever got past Layton.

"Talk to me, Reed. What happened to Court today? Since I've known her, I've never seen her so upset and lost."

I took a deep breath and let it out as I looked around. "When y'all were on your honeymoon and Courtney and I…well, when we finally got together, she told me something that night, something she had been carrying around with her since she was sixteen years old. She'd never told anyone, not even Whit."

Layton sat up and appeared to be holding his breath. "Okay, so it's something serious. You know you can trust me to keep it between us, but if it is something really big, I won't hide it from Whitley."

I gave him a smile. "I wouldn't ask you to, and that's why I haven't said anything. I wasn't even sure that Court had told Whitley yet. I figured she hadn't since you never said anything to me about it. Courtney is telling Whit tonight."

Layton nodded his head and waited for me to continue.

"Fuck, I don't even know how to say it." I shook my head, and when I closed my eyes, I was brought back to the night when Courtney had told me about Noah. "His name is Noah, and he's Courtney's brother's best friend."

I opened my eyes and fought like hell to keep the tears at bay. Just knowing what that fucker had done to Court made me want to hunt his ass down and kill him.

"He came into her room one night and threatened her whole family if she didn't do what he wanted her to do."

"No," Layton whispered.

I looked down at Layton's hands balling into fists. He thought of Courtney as a sister, and I knew after telling him, he was going to feel the same way I felt, and I felt nothing but pure hate and anger.

"How long did it go on?" he asked, his voice cracking.

"A few months. One night, he came in, and she pointed one of her father's guns at him. She told him she'd rather go to jail than be put through what he was doing to her." I looked away and then back at Layton. "I want to hurt him so bad, Layton. You have no idea how hard it's been for me not to call her brother and tell him. He still hangs around the fucker. They're best friends. I want him to know what his so-called friend did to his sister."

I saw the look of horror move across Layton's face.

"Courtney's younger sister…" he whispered.

"Courtney said she's almost positive he never touched her sister. He seemed to wait until Court was older. Once she turned sixteen, he started."

Layton looked down at his beer. "Motherfucker. What kind of a monster does that to another person?"

I let out a long, drawn-out sigh. "I don't know, but if I ever lay eyes on him, he better run in the opposite direction."

Layton snapped his head over. "Isn't her brother getting married in a few months? Is she going back for the wedding? If this Noah guy is her brother's best friend, won't he be at the wedding?"

"That was the first thing she asked her brother—if Noah was going to be in the wedding or at the wedding. Her brother told her no. He said that Noah had to go out of the country on a business trip that week, and he couldn't change the dates. I guess her brother and his fiancée couldn't change the date of the wedding because this place has a really long waiting list. That's the only reason Court is going back home for the wedding."

Layton ran his hand through his hair. "Damn. Poor Courtney. She's never talked to anyone about this?"

I shook my head. "Nope. I'm the only person she's ever told. She's only been with this guy, Mitch, and me."

"Shit," Layton said as he dropped his head back. He looked back at me, and his eyes were filled with sadness. "Reed, she really needs to talk to someone about it."

I looked down at my beer as I ran my finger along the glass. "I know. I asked her if she wants to. I even told her I would go with her, but she insists that she doesn't need to. I'm hoping that maybe when she talks to Whitley about it, it will help Court move on even more. I think the secret has been slowly sucking the life out of her more and more. I could almost feel the release when she told me. It was like a huge weight had been lifted off her shoulders."

My cell phone started ringing, and I pulled it out of my pocket to see it was Courtney calling.

"Hey," I said with a smile.

"Hey back, handsome. What are you boys up to?" Courtney asked.

"Sitting at the bar, drinking a few beers, shooting the shit, and watching football. You know, typical guy stuff."

Courtney let out a giggle. "We just left the spa. I feel amazing. I'm so very relaxed. Thank you for that," she said in a seductive voice.

"You're very welcome. Dinner now?" I asked as I looked down at my watch. "Your reservation isn't for another forty-five minutes. The spa didn't take as long as I thought it would."

"No, it's good. We're actually going to take a walk around the property and…talk…"

When her voice trailed off, I knew she was scared.

"Court?"

"Yeah?"

"I love you. I love you more than anything. You're the strongest person I know, and every day, you amaze me. Thank you for loving me."

She choked back a sob. "Jesus, what is with me and the crying?"

I smiled, picturing her trying to wipe away her tears before anyone saw her crying.

"I love you, too, Reed. Thank you for loving me. I've got to run. Whitley is out of the restroom now."

"All right. Y'all be careful, and don't wander off the paths, okay?"

She let out a laugh. "Okay, Dad."

"Give me a call when you get to the restaurant, okay?"

"Okay. Hey, Reed?" she said in a hushed voice.

"Yeah?"

"Thank you for showing me that I have the courage to do this."

I tried to swallow the lump in my throat. "Courtney," was all I managed to get out.

"Talk to you soon. I love you. Bye."

I had to look away and stare out the window. I saw her walking out with Whitley, but she didn't see me.

"I love you, too, Courtney. Bye, baby." When I hit End, I wanted to just throw my phone and scream. There wasn't anything I wouldn't do to take away what had happened to her.

When I felt Layton put his hand on my shoulder, I remembered where I was. I took a deep breath, turned back around, and tried to give him a smile.

"Reed, you can't take away the pain and hurt, no matter how hard you wish you could. Just be there for her. Listen to her when she needs to talk.

Love her when she needs to be loved, and make her happiness your number-one goal in this life."

I nodded my head and grabbed my empty beer, holding it up, so the bartender could see it. I held up my fingers, indicating we wanted two more.

"Shit, let's change this mood around. I'm getting married tomorrow." I punched Layton on the side of the arm.

Oh shit, I'm getting married tomorrow. "Oh, dear God, what if she wants us to say our own vows?" I asked as I reached for the full bottle of beer that was just placed in front of me.

Layton let out a laugh. "I wouldn't be surprised at all if Court decided for y'all to say your own vows."

I just stared at Layton.

"What in the hell am I going to say?" I brought the beer up to my lips and practically drank it all in one drink.

Layton threw his head back and laughed. "You say what is in your heart. Don't worry though…I already asked Court if y'all were saying your own vows, and her exact words were, 'Oh, hell no.'"

My mouth dropped to the ground as I glared at my best friend. "What is with y'all today? Are you trying to cause me to have a heart attack?"

Layton shrugged his shoulders and took a sip of his beer. "You're just so much fun to fuck with when you're a basket case."

"Thanks. I'll remember that when you're pacing back and forth, waiting for the birth of your child."

Layton's head snapped over to me, and he was just about to say something when two girls walked up to us. I looked them both up and down. They barely had on any clothes. They couldn't have been more than twenty-two years old.

The blonde, who was wearing a short-ass skirt with a practically see-through white tank top, smiled. "Do I detect a Southern accent there, boys?"

Layton rolled his eyes. "Yes, ma'am, you do. We're from Texas to be exact."

The redhead leaned in closer to me and brushed her tits up against my arm. "I've always wondered what a Texas cowboy would feel like inside me. I do love a good ride," she said, trying to sound seductive.

Holy shit, talk about blunt. A year and a half ago, I would have been all over this girl, but now, all I wanted her to do was get the fuck away from me.

"I'm getting married tomorrow, so it looks like this is one cowboy you won't be riding," I said with a wink.

Her smile faded, but then she looked at Layton. "What about you, cowboy? You look like you could be pretty fast and hard." She stuck her finger in her mouth and began sucking on it.

Layton let out a laugh. "No, thanks. I'm happily married to a beautiful woman who is carrying my child. If y'all don't mind, do you think you could move on, please?"

"Your loss, assholes," the blonde said.

Then, they both turned around and walked away.

I looked at Layton and began laughing. "Damn. I don't think I've ever had a girl come on to me that blatantly."

Layton chuckled. "She's just lucky that Courtney didn't see her rubbing her tits all over you. Poor girl would have had to crawl out of this bar."

I let out a laugh and raised my beer up to Layton. "To being off the market."

Layton held his beer bottle to mine and said, "A-fucking-men."

NINETEEN

I sat there, holding Whitley's hand, waiting for her to say something. She had started crying about two minutes into me telling her about Noah.

"I'm…oh God, Courtney." She pulled me to her and hugged me. "I'm so sorry I wasn't there for you. I'm so sorry I didn't know the nightmare you were going through. I knew something was wrong. I *knew* it!"

She began crying harder, and I pushed her away and looked into her eyes.

"I should have kept asking you. I should have been a better friend. I should have known something was going on. I'm so sorry you went through all that alone…that you've been dealing with this for so long all alone."

I smiled as I wiped away her tears, and she wiped away mine.

"I'm no longer alone though. Telling Reed helped me to move on and let go of the pain and guilt. Telling you has also helped me in more ways than you will ever know."

Whitley took a deep breath and blew her nose in one of the tissues I'd grabbed on the way out to the courtyard. I'd figured we would both break down crying and need them.

"If I ever see him…oh my God, I swear, I'll kill him, Court."

I let out a giggle. "I think Reed will beat you to it, and I'm pretty sure Reed is telling Layton about it tonight, so you might have to wait in line."

She gave me a weak smile. "I'd be willing to let Reed and Layton deal with Noah first, but I'm finishing his ass off if I ever see him again." Then, she threw her hands up to her mouth and said, "Your brother's wedding! Reed will kill him!"

I shook my head. "Noah won't be there. I already asked my brother, and he said Noah had a business trip he couldn't change, so he has to miss it. My brother is pretty upset about it, but it would have been either me or Noah missing the wedding. There is a still a chance he could end up going though if his trip is canceled so there is always the chance I might not go."

"Oh, thank God. Court, you never told your parents? Why?"

"I don't know. Guilt…or mostly embarrassment because I let someone do that to me. If I had known then what I know now, I would have screamed for my father that night, but I didn't know any better, and I can't turn back time. I think I'm slowly starting to realize that it wasn't my fault and that I didn't do anything wrong."

Whitley let out a gasp. "No, you didn't! It was all him, Court. He took advantage of you. I wish you had shot his ass. I never did like that prick."

We both started laughing, and I needed to move us on to another subject.

"I'm getting married tomorrow. I want to focus on the future and not the past." I reached into my purse and pulled out two pregnancy tests.

Whitley's eyes grew bigger.

I laughed. "Don't even go there. My silly mother wants me to take a pregnancy test to prove that I'm not pregnant, but…" I wiggled my eyebrows up and down.

Whitley let out a giggle. "You are so mean. You want me to pee on one, don't you?" she asked as she stood up.

I laughed my evil laugh as I stood, and we hooked arms on the way to the restroom.

I set the tests down on the counter and opened one. I took a picture of it and sent it to my mother.

Courtney: Taking the test, Mother. I hope this proves to you that I'm NOT pregnant!

Mom: How do I know it's you peeing on the test?

Courtney: Do you really want to go there, Mom? I'll film myself pissing on a stick if you really want me to.

Mom: No. I raised you right. I trust you.

I rolled my eyes and made my way into the stall. "You go on the other test," I said as I shut the door.

"But I don't have to pee. I just went," Whitley said.

"Seriously, Whit? You've had to pee all night! And the one time I need you to pee, you can't?"

She let out a giggle. "Sorry. Maybe if I run the water."

She turned on the water, and I began peeing on the stick. I couldn't believe my mother thought I was rushing to get married because I was pregnant. I pulled out some toilet paper and set the test down, and then I began pulling up my pants.

"I think the water is making me want to go," Whitley said.

I smiled as I went to reach for the test. My hand stopped just short of it. *Why are there two lines?* My heart began pounding so loud that it was hurting my ears.

"Okay, I've got to go now," Whitley said.

I grabbed the test and threw open the stall door. "Stop! Don't use that test!" I screamed.

Whitley froze in place as I walked up to her, and I grabbed it out of her hand before going back into the stall.

Fuck! Fuck! Fuck! I don't have to pee anymore.

"Turn on the water! Make it warm!" I yelled out.

"Um…okay. But why warm?" Whitley asked.

I let out a sigh and said, "Gesh, Whitley, everyone knows warm water makes you want to pee." My hand was shaking so bad that I could hardly hold the test. I looked at the other test. *Yep, still two lines.*

"Uh…I hate to be the one to break it to you, Court, but that only works if you actually stick your hand in the warm water."

I looked around and made a face. "Shit, that's right."

Once Whitley turned on the water, I willed myself to pee.

"Oh! Yes! Oh, yes, yes, yes!" I screamed out.

Then, someone other than Whitley said, "Well, I never."

"Oh no. Oh no, ma'am, she's alone. Wait! I mean, it's not what you think!" Whitley said as she called out to the lady.

I heard Whitley's footsteps moving closer to the door.

"Whitley! Don't leave."

I opened the stall door, and Whitley was laughing so hard that she could hardly breathe.

"Oh. My. God. She thought…she thought…"

I gave her a fake smile. "She thought I was masturbating. Ha-ha."

Whitley finally got herself under control and looked at me. Her smile faded. "What? What's wrong, Court?"

I swallowed hard. "Nothing will be wrong if you tell me two lines means not pregnant."

Whitley grabbed the box. "Um…nope. Sorry, I'm pretty sure that two lines means preg—" Her head snapped up, and she looked at me.

I held up both tests for her to see. Her mouth dropped open, and we both just stood there, staring at each other.

When someone walked in, Whitley yelled, "Out! You can't be in here!"

The poor lady quickly turned and walked out.

"Whitley! Why did you tell her to leave?" I asked.

Whit shook her head as if she was trying to clear her thoughts. "Where did you buy the tests?"

Why does she want to know that? Oh…

"The lobby store," I barely whispered.

Whitley turned and walked out of the restroom. I paced back and forth until she finally came back, carrying two bags. She dumped the contents of one bag out into one of the sinks.

I looked into the sink and then back at Whitley. "Six? You bought *six* pregnancy tests?"

She shrugged her shoulders, handed me a bottle of water, and began to open one of the tests. I downed the water and then began drinking another bottle.

"I have an idea. Open a few. That way, if I start peeing, I can try to stick as many as possible under the stream." I drank half of another bottle of water.

We placed a bunch of paper towels on the floor of one of the stalls and lined up all six tests. Every time someone came in, we blocked that stall.

Then, it hit me. "Shit! I have to go."

Whitley pushed me into the stall, and I jumped over the tests.

I pulled my pants and panties down and went to town. "Ah shit, I pissed on my hand! Ew…gross!" I yelled out.

Whitley started laughing. "Just go fast. Get them all under the stream. You can wash your hands when you're done."

After I placed the last test down on the paper towel, I sat there and watched as each test came up with the same result. All six of them had double lines.

Whitley knocked on the stall door. "Court?"

I stood up, slowly pulled up my panties and pants, flushed the toilet, and gathered up my collection of pregnancy tests.

When I opened the door, Whitley was smiling from ear to ear. "Welcome to the club."

"Court, you really need to eat, honey," Whitley said.

I looked up at her and tried to smile.

"I mean, you're eating for two now."

I shot Whitley a dirty look. "Funny. What in the hell, Whitley? I'm on the pill. I can't be pregnant."

Whitley took a bite of her food and rolled her eyes. "Please. Courtney, you know that isn't one hundred percent. Did you maybe forget to take a pill?"

I shook my head. "No." I thought about it a little harder.

I was terrible with my pills. I never took them at the same time of day like I was supposed to do, and I'd missed pills before. *Did I miss a pill and just not think about it? Shit!*

"At least, I don't think I have. Fuck, I don't know. I've missed them before, and I just don't think about it." I looked down at the plate of food in front of me. I couldn't even think about putting a thing into my stomach.

Whitley touched my hand, causing me to jump. "Have you missed your period, Court?"

My heart started pounding when I realized I hadn't started yet, and when I looked up at Whitley, she smiled that big, stupid smile again.

"I was, um…I should have…last week. I should have started last week. I guess I wasn't paying attention. It's all been such a crazy ride, and I wasn't even…" Then, I thought about Reed again. *Oh. My. God. Reed. What's Reed going to think about this?* I felt the tears building in my eyes. "Well, hell, I guess this explains why I keep getting all emotional," I said as I wiped away a tear.

"Are you not happy about this, Court?"

I shrugged my shoulders. "I think I am. I mean, I guess I'm just in shock, ya know? Reed and I haven't even talked about kids. What if he…what if he gets upset? We haven't even gotten to spend time together, and now…" I brought my hands up to my face and attempted to stop myself from crying. Then, another thought hit me. I dropped my hands and started laughing.

Whitley looked at me like I was crazy. "Oh shit, you're going to be fun through this pregnancy. You're laughing and crying at the same time, Courtney."

"My mother, Whitley! I told my mother I wasn't pregnant, and here I am…" I started laughing harder. "It's like karma. I was going to tease her with your pregnancy test, and here I am, pregnant after all!" I started laughing so hard that I couldn't breathe.

That got Whitley laughing, and before I knew it, we both had tears streaming down our faces.

I glanced up and saw Reed. I instantly stopped laughing and wiped away my tears. I jumped up, almost causing my chair to fall backward.

"What are you doing here?" I asked in a panicked voice.

Whitley cleared her throat. "Court, settle down, honey."

Reed brought me into his arms and whispered in my ear, "I missed your warmth."

I instantly felt my need for him and let out a low moan. "Oh God, Reed," I whispered.

He pulled back and smiled before looking down at my plate. "What's wrong with the food?" He looked at Whitley's almost cleared plate and then back at my full plate.

"I, um…I wasn't really hungry. I couldn't eat."

I looked at Whitley as she grinned in the most obvious way.

Reed winked at me and asked, "Are y'all about finished?"

"Yes!" Whit yelled as I screamed, "No!"

Layton and Reed both started laughing.

"Whit says yes, and Courtney says no. This should be fun," Layton said.

Whitley stood up and put her hands on her stomach. "Whew, I just all of a sudden got so tired. We have such a big day tomorrow. I should head up to the room and take it easy for the rest of the night."

I gave her the dirtiest look I could muster up. *Traitor.*

Layton pulled Whitley closer to him. "That sounds like a wonderful plan. What are y'all going to do?"

Reed looked into my eyes. "Probably head up to the room. I need to make sure my princess gets her beauty sleep."

Whitley let out a gruff laugh. "Yeah, right. I highly doubt either of you will sleep tonight."

I snapped my head over and glared at her.

"Sex, Court. I'm talking about pre-wedding sex." She wiggled her eyebrows up and down as she started making her way over to me. She pulled me into her arms and said in my ear, just low enough for only me to hear, "Tell him tonight. He's going to be over the moon, I promise you."

When she stepped back, I instantly missed her calming touch. I nodded my head and said, "I promise, I will."

Layton walked up, leaned down, and kissed me on the cheek. "You're going to be beautiful tomorrow, Courtney. Get some sleep, sweetheart."

I smiled a weak smile. "Thanks, Layton. I will. Take care of my girl, or I'll bust you in the nuts."

Layton's smile faded for a second, and then he started laughing. "God, I love you, Courtney. You always catch me off guard."

Reed laughed as he pulled out some money, set it down on the table, and then grabbed my hand.

I quickly turned to get my purse and felt dizzy. *Shit.* The room began spinning. I had to hold on to the chair until everything stopped moving.

"Court? Are you okay?" Whitley asked.

Reed held on to me to steady my swaying body.

I nodded my head. "Yeah, I'm fine. I just spun around too fast and got dizzy, that's all."

As we walked to the elevators, Layton and Reed were planning something for after the wedding tomorrow.

I had a million things running through my head. *How in the hell do I tell Reed? When do I tell Reed? Do I tell him before or after the wedding? If I tell him after the wedding and he is upset with the idea, he might think I trapped him. Shit! Shit! Shit!*

My cell phone went off with a text message notification. I pulled it out and sucked in a breath of air.

Mom: Well, how long does a pregnancy test take?

I peeked up at Whitley and mouthed, *My mom.*

She smiled and winked at me.

Nice. Some friend she is.

She thought the whole thing was romantic and sweet—not to mention, funnier than shit.

I mouthed back, *I hate you.*

She made a heart with her hands and giggled.

"Who's the text from, baby?" Reed asked.

I panicked. *He was with me when I bought the tests. He's going to ask if I sent my mom a pic of the test.*

"My mom," I barely said.

"Oh yeah? Did y'all ever trick her by sending her a pic of Whit's positive pregnancy test?" Reed asked as he let out a small chuckle.

"So mean, Courtney, but so you," Layton said as we stepped into the elevator and headed up to our suites.

Whitley finally snapped out of her happy fairy-wonderland state. "What did y'all do this evening while we pampered ourselves?"

Layton grabbed on to Whitley as he said, "Suffered without our women, fought off girls left and right, drank a few beers, and watched football."

"Wow, sounds like a busy evening," Whitley said as she pushed Layton away and punched him in the stomach.

"Man, it was rough." Layton pulled Whit in and kissed her.

They soon got lost in their kiss, and I had to look away. I glanced up at Reed, and the passion in his eyes caused that familiar buildup deep in the pit of my stomach. I wanted to feel him inside me so badly. I *needed* to feel him inside me. It was the only time I ever felt completely whole.

When the elevator doors opened, Reed grabbed my hands, pulled me out of the elevator, and practically dragged me down the hallway to our suite. "Night, y'all," he called out.

Layton and Whitley both laughed.

I turned and gave them a small wave, and Whitley gave me a thumbs-up before the bitch started giggling. I knew she was going to tell Layton, so I had to tell Reed tonight before he saw Layton tomorrow.

When Reed opened the door, I let out a gasp.

"Oh my." I looked around the room in awe. I hadn't really paid attention to the room the first time I was in it. Now, I was taking it all in.

It was beautiful, and every available countertop was covered in vases filled with white and red roses. The smell in the room was heavenly. The massive fireplace had a fire going in it. I put my hand up to my mouth and looked at the rose petals arranged into two paths on the floor.

"Oh, Reed, this is so…it's so…"

Reed walked up behind me and pulled me to him. "Nick swoon-worthy?"

I let out a laugh as I felt a tear slowly slide down my cheek. "No, this is better."

Reed rested his chin on top of my head. "There's something better than Nick swoon-worthy?"

I turned around and pulled his lips to mine. Before we kissed, I whispered against his lips, "Yes. This is Reed swoon-worthy. Nothing is better than that."

Reed's eyes lit up with passion, and he captured my lips with his. The kiss started off slow and sweet, and then it quickly turned more heated. He walked me backward until my legs bumped into the sofa, and he slowly began pushing me down.

I tried to push everything out of my mind, but I couldn't do it. *I can't do this. I can't pretend and go on like everything is okay.* I pulled back from Reed's lips, placed my hands on his chest, and then barely pushed him away.

He looked confused. "What's wrong, baby?"

I took in a shaky breath and slowly let it out. "Reed, I, um…I need to talk to you before we do anything else."

He pulled back and sat up. I sat up and pulled my legs into my body as I looked into his eyes. Just a few seconds ago, they had been filled with so much love, and now, they were filled with…concern.

"Please tell me you haven't changed your mind about getting married," he whispered.

What? "No! Absolutely not. I want nothing more than to marry you, Reed."

His body instantly relaxed.

"I'm sorry. I didn't mean to make you think I was having doubts. I've never wanted something so much in my life," I said as I smiled at him.

I wanted nothing more than to crawl into the safety of his lap and just tell him everything, but I knew if I touched him, I'd let him make love to me, and I really needed to tell him about the baby.

"I feel the same way, Courtney. I have to admit that you're kind of still making me worry here. Angel, please talk to me."

I closed my eyes, said a silent prayer, and just went for it. "Okay, so you know how I was going to have Whitley pee on one of the tests to play a joke on my mom?"

He nodded his head. "Yeah."

"Well, I didn't need Whit after all," I said with a weak smile, waiting for it to click in Reed's head.

Nothing.

He just stared at me, like he was expecting me to keep going on with the story.

"Is there more to the story?" he asked as he scrunched up his nose.

He is so damn sexy. I wanted to jump him just for scrunching up his damn nose.

I let out a giggle and shook my head. "Not really."

"Why didn't you need her? Did your mom tell you not to do it?"

I tilted my head. "No. She's still waiting for me to send her a picture of a negative test."

He looked so confused, and it was so damn cute.

"Why haven't you sent it yet?"

I smiled bigger. "Because all the tests were positive."

"All the tests were…"

Then, it clicked. *Bingo! He's finally got it. God, please don't let him be angry.*

He stared at me for a few seconds before his smile matched mine. "Court…are you saying what I think you're saying?"

I stood up and walked over to my purse. I grabbed all eight tests and placed them on the coffee table. "I hope you're not mad. I was just as surprised as you are. I didn't believe it. Oh God, I'm so sorry, but I might have missed a pill…or two. I'm so bad about taking them, and…well, I had no idea, and I'm not that late, so…"

Reed got up, never taking his eyes off the tests. He just stood there, staring down at the table. The longer he stayed silent, the more scared I got. He finally looked at me, and I gave him a smile.

He smiled back and asked, "We're having a baby?"

I nodded my head and pointed to the tests. "Unless they're all wrong. Are you upset?"

The next thing I knew, Reed was pulling me to him and picking me up. He started walking us toward the bedroom.

"What are you doing?" I asked.

He looked at me and let out a laugh. "I'm going to make love to you, Courtney. I didn't think you could ever make me as happy as I have been, but you just made me the happiest man in the world."

He walked up to the side of the bed and slowly let me slide down his body. I could feel how much he wanted me. My heart was beating so fast, and I had the strangest feeling in my stomach.

He's happy?

He's happy.

I bit down on my lower lip. "You're not upset? I was so afraid you'd be upset with me."

He placed his hands on the sides of my face, and I watched as his eyes moved all over my face until his eyes locked with mine.

"I could never be upset about something like this. Do you know how many times I've dreamed of you having my child? How many times I've thought about how wonderful it would be to make love to you when your stomach is full and round with our baby? You're my whole world. You're my dreams come true." He took his thumbs and gently wiped away my tears. Then, he leaned down and kissed me on the forehead. "I pray to God every night that this isn't a dream and that I don't fuck this up in some way and make you leave me."

I shook my head and tried to talk, but I was so choked up that I couldn't get anything out. Reed gave me that crooked smile of his as he took a few steps back. He reached down and picked something up. I didn't want to pull my eyes from his, so I didn't know what he was doing until I heard Norah Jones singing "Come Away with Me."

He walked back over and began undressing me. "Do you know what my goals are for us, Court?"

I whispered, "No."

After removing my shirt, he reached behind me and unclasped my bra. He slowly pushed the straps off my shoulders, and every inch of my skin he touched was on fire.

Please don't let me be dreaming.

He took one nipple into his mouth as his hand played with the other one.

I dropped my head back and moaned, "Oh God."

He moved his lips up and began brushing them along my jawline. I was completely on fire at this point and ready to combust.

"My goals for us are as follows…"

He dropped down to his knees and began taking off my pants. My legs felt like lead while I lifted each one up as he slipped off my pants and panties. He sat back on his heels and looked my body up and down as he licked his lips.

Jesus…

I could almost feel my orgasm building just from him idolizing my body the way he was.

"You're so beautiful," he whispered as he reached out for me and pulled me closer to him.

He leaned up and began kissing my stomach. I let out a gasp and ran my hands through his hair.

He kissed all over my stomach and then said, "I'm going to make you the happiest woman on earth."

"I'm so happy, Reed. You have no idea how happy I am right now," I said as my breathing became needy.

"My first goal is to love you completely." He lifted my leg and put it over his shoulder.

My whole body began trembling as I anticipated what he was going to do next. "Yes…" I whispered.

He began kissing the inside of my thigh. "My second goal is to make every single one of your dreams come true," he whispered.

I grabbed a handful of his hair and pulled on it as I begged, "Please, Reed. Please touch me."

He took his tongue and teased my clit with one fast movement. I jerked my hips and let out a moan.

"My third goal is to make you scream out my name in passion…often."

"Like now! Now would be a good time to do that," I said as I tried to push his face into me.

He licked my clit again and slid two fingers inside me. He slowly moved them in and out, and I felt my world beginning to unravel.

"My fourth goal is to wake up every morning to the sound of your heartbeat, and I will always tell you how beautiful you are and how happy you make me."

My breathing was getting so ragged with the way he was teasing me with his fingers.

"Okay…Reed…please…I can't…I need you…"

He started kissing my clit, and my hips began thrusting harder against him.

Oh God, yes. I need this so badly.

He pulled back, and I let out a whimper.

"No…no, no, no…please don't stop."

"I'm not done with my goals, baby," he whispered as he began fucking me harder with this fingers.

"Yes…Reed, faster."

He slowed down and pulled his fingers out, and then he began to tease my clit with them. "My last goal is to make love to you all the time, Court, but I'm also going to give you a good fuck when you need it, too."

My eyes widened as I said, "Now, Reed. I need it now!"

He stood up quickly and spun me around. He bent me over and leaned into me as he whispered, "I'm going to fuck you from behind, Courtney. Don't come."

What?

He slammed into me, and I almost came on the spot. He dug his fingertips into my hips as he began thrusting so hard and fast. I felt that familiar feeling beginning to build.

"Don't. Come. Courtney," Reed said in between thrusts.

"I can't stop myself from coming! Oh God, Reed…please…"

I started to move my hand down to touch myself, but Reed pulled out some and stopped.

"No! Why are you doing this?" I yelled out.

He slowly began moving in and out of me, and I'd never felt such pleasure. There was no way I could stop myself from coming. When he reached around and pinched my nipple, I let out a gasp.

"Reed! I need to come."

He began kissing my back as his fingers dug into my hips again, and then he started slamming in and out of my body. I felt it start in my toes. I was so close.

Fuck!

"Courtney, you feel so good," Reed said as he picked up his pace. "Come now, baby…I'm so close."

Yes! Finally!

I pushed myself against him every time he slammed into me. I could feel the buildup as I prepared for an intense orgasm.

"Court…I'm close, baby."

"Deeper, Reed. Harder!"

Somehow, Reed pushed my one leg out more, causing him to go deeper into me.

Heaven. Pure heaven.

Then, he moved his right hand and brushed the cheek of my ass before he grazed down the middle of my ass. As he pushed harder, he said, "Someday, I want this, too, baby."

The moment he pushed on my ass, it was my undoing, and the orgasm hit me so hard that I let out a scream and began calling out his name.

"Reed! Oh God, Reed! Yes! I'm coming. Oh God…ah…oh God, oh God, oh God." I could hardly even form any words. I just cried out the same thing over and over.

Then, I felt Reed getting bigger inside me as he began to come.

"Ah…shit…Courtney, it feels so good." He kept thrusting as he reached around and began playing with my clit.

I instantly had another orgasm as his fingers assaulted my clit over and over again. Reed pulled out of me, and we both collapsed onto the bed. I was still trying to catch my breath as I came down from my second orgasm. Reed was lying next to me, attempting to catch his breath as well.

I rolled over and looked at the ceiling. "That was so fucking hot."

He laughed. "It sure as hell was." He turned and looked at me. "That was fun," he said with a wink.

I let out a giggle, rolled over, and snuggled up into his side. I began moving my fingertips lightly across his chest. "Wow, that was amazing. I really like your goals, especially that last one."

He pulled me closer with his arm and kissed my forehead. "I love you, Courtney. I can't believe we're having a baby."

I smiled, and my stomach did that funny little dip, like the one from a first kiss. *I'm having Reed's baby. I'm marrying Reed tomorrow and having his baby.* My insides were jumping for joy as I thought about tomorrow and the baby.

Resting against his chest, I placed my chin on the back of my hand and looked into his eyes.

He smiled and asked, "What are you thinking about?"

"This."

He let out a chuckle. "This?"

I smiled. "Us. Sometimes, I think I'm dreaming, but then you touch me. I feel the fire from your touch, and I know nothing in this world could feel that amazing and be wasted in a dream."

"I'm sorry," Reed said as his smile faded briefly.

I moved to sit up, and I wrapped the cover around me. "What are you sorry for? I loved what we just did. It was amazing and sexy and…amazing!"

Reed let out a laugh. "You already said amazing."

"That's because it was so amazing that I had to say it twice."

He looked away as he took a deep breath. "I'm sorry for hurting you that day in the old cabin. And I'm sorry for sleeping with Anna when I was trying to forget about you. I'm sorry for fighting my feelings for you for so long and for pushing you into the arms of Mitch." He began shaking his head as he turned back to me and closed his eyes. "I've hurt you so much. I don't deserve your love."

My heart literally hurt from hearing the pain in his voice. I let go of the cover and moved on top of him. He snapped his eyes open, and we held each other's gaze for a few minutes. As I felt him growing bigger and harder underneath me, neither one of us moved or said a word. I slowly began grinding myself against him, as I felt the heat building between us again.

"I'm just as guilty for hurting you and for fighting my love for you. But that's all in the past now, Reed. I've never in my life felt so complete in every possible way. You're my own personal drug for so many different things."

I got up on my knees a bit and moved until I felt his tip seeking entry into my body. I slowly sank down onto him, and we both let out a moan.

"Nothing feels as amazing as having you inside me, as you loving me," I said as I began moving up and down slowly.

Reed touched my stomach, and I jumped. Goose bumps covered my whole body, and he smiled.

"I love what my touch does to you," he whispered.

He moved his hand down and began playing with my clit as I brought my hands up and started playing with my nipples. I knew it drove Reed mad to watch me touch myself, so I slid my right hand down and pushed his hand away as I began playing with my clit while I so slowly moved him in and out of my body.

"Fuck me, Courtney."

I smiled as I looked down at him. "Mr. Moore…right now, it's time for slow and steady lovemaking. The fucking will come later."

He sucked in a breath of air and flipped me over onto my back. He began moving in and out of me even slower.

"Ah…it feels so good." I wrapped my legs around him and lost myself in his lovemaking.

Nothing in this world could ever top this night.

TWENTY

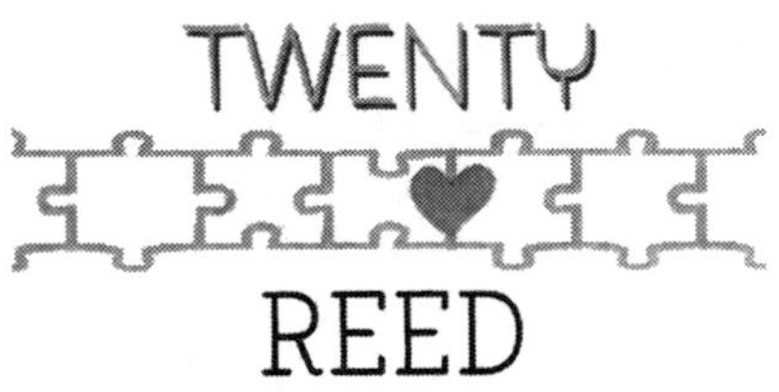

REED

I stood in the small building just outside the hotel where the sweet and bossy Kendra had told Layton and me to wait. I walked back and forth, wringing my hands together. Layton was kicked back in a chair, humming some stupid tune. I tried blocking him out of my head, but he was beginning to drive me crazy.

"Stop. With. The. Humming," I said between gritted teeth.

Layton stopped and looked up at me. "You don't like that song?"

I shook my head. "I don't even know what song you're humming. Just stop!"

Layton whistled and leaned back his chair. He drew in a deep breath and said, "Dayum, you a little on edge, Reed, my boy?"

I stopped and glared at him. If he wasn't my best friend, I'd punch the shit out of him right now. Layton stopped smiling and dropped the front legs of the chair back down to the floor.

"Reed, what in the hell are you so nervous for? You're marrying the love of your life in one of the most beautiful places on earth. You're going to be a father, and a damn good one at that, I might add." Layton stood up and walked over to me. He grabbed me by both shoulders and gave me a little shake. "Just relax, and take a deep breath."

I instantly felt better…until Kendra banged on the door.

"Mr. Moore? Mr. Moore, are you still in there?" she screamed from the other side of the door.

I rolled my eyes as Layton laughed.

I pulled open the door and stared down at her. "Yes, Kendra?" I flashed her my signature smile.

My patience was running out with this girl, and I thought she was starting to see that.

Her face immediately flushed. "Oh, um…we're ready for y'all to take your places on the beach now. Miss Will is about ready."

I let out a sigh of relief. "Thank you, God. I was going crazy in this small room."

Layton slapped me on the back. "Let's do this thing!"

We headed down to the beach, and I smiled at the white arbor covered in red and white roses. I had made a call to the florist at the hotel as soon as I could after we arrived to change up the flowers Court had arranged. I'd also had them bring the flowers up to our suite last night. When Courtney had asked me why I wanted white and red, I'd told her that the two colors done together signified unity. I smiled, thinking back to her saying that I had scored another swoon-worthy moment.

"What in the hell are you thinking about? Wait, never mind. I don't want to know." Layton walked up to the preacher and began talking to him.

I turned and looked out over the beautiful blue waters of Lake Tahoe. I couldn't wait to see Courtney's eyes with this blue all around us.

Layton walked up behind me. "Reed, it's time, dude."

I turned to see my best friend smiling like a little kid in a candy store. I couldn't believe we had both gotten what the girls called our happily ever afters. Layton deserved to be happy, but I still wasn't a hundred percent convinced that I deserved Courtney's love.

I looked down and kicked the sand as I let out a laugh. "Holy shit, I'm about to get married."

Layton grabbed me and pulled me in for a quick hug before he pushed me away and walked over to his place. I followed him and said a quick prayer that I didn't mess this up for Courtney. I wanted to make this day special for her, and I was pretty sure what I had planned would be a swoon-worthy moment for sure.

I moved up next to Layton and smiled at the preacher.

"Are you ready, son?" he asked in a fatherly tone.

I nodded and said, "Yes, sir. I've never been more ready for anything in my life."

When the music began playing, I glanced up and saw Whitley walking down the aisle. She looked breathtaking, and I heard Layton suck in a breath of air.

He whispered, "My girl."

She was dressed in a charcoal-colored dress that Courtney had said was a perfect fit. She had also said something about it being perfect for a beach wedding with its cocktail length and satin sheath. Whit made her way up to us on her bare feet. She smiled and gave me a wink as I smiled back at her.

Then, something in the air changed, and I looked back down the aisle of red and white rose petals. My heart stopped beating. Courtney was standing there, wearing a beautiful strapless white dress that hugged her body perfectly. My eyes moved up and down her body as she began walking toward us. The bottom of the dress was lower in the back and higher in the front, so she had no problem walking through the sand in her bare feet. She was carrying a huge bouquet of white and red roses. Her hair was pulled up with a few strands hanging down, blowing gently in the wind. She looked so beautiful.

When she walked up to me, I had to remind myself to breathe before I passed out. She held out her hand, and I took it and kissed the back.

"You take my breath away, Courtney. You look so beautiful."

Her blue eyes sparkled, catching every single bounce of light coming off the crystal-blue water. She bit down on her lower lip and then whispered, "I feel like a princess."

I placed my hand on the side of her face. "You're my princess."

The preacher cleared his throat and began with the ceremony.

I wasn't even sure that I knew half of what he was saying because I was so lost in those beautiful blue eyes. They were filled with so much love. The fact that I was marrying Courtney while she was pregnant with our baby was doing all kinds of weird shit to my stomach. I knew I was nervous, but at the same time, I'd never in my life felt so…complete.

We exchanged vows, and right before the preacher was about to officially announce us as man and wife, he did what I had asked him to do.

"Courtney, Reed would like to say a few words to you."

Her face lit up, and the tears she'd been able to hold back finally broke free.

I held on to her hands tighter and took a deep breath. Then, I began speaking from my heart, "Courtney, you've made me the happiest man on earth by becoming my wife, and you're also giving me the greatest gift I could think of." I looked down at her stomach and then back into her tear-filled baby blues. "I've been wandering around lost and broken for so long, thinking that none of my dreams would ever come true…but then you walked into my life and made it a living hell for so many months."

Court, Layton, and Whitley all let out a laugh.

"There was something about you though, and I knew it the moment I first saw you. I felt it in my heart and soul, but I fought it for so long until I finally figured out that nothing could keep love from happening. It always finds a way." When my voice started cracking, I had to stop talking, so I could get my emotions under control.

Courtney's thumbs were rubbing back and forth so fast on the backs of my hands that it was causing a sensation to run up my arm.

"I'm not perfect, and I've done things in my past that have haunted me for years, but when I'm with you…" I smiled as I reached up and wiped away her tears. "When I'm with you, Courtney, I'm a better man. You've filled my heart with so much happiness and love, and I'll never be able to thank you enough for that. I absolutely cannot wait to see what our lives together bring. I love you. I love you so very much."

Courtney began crying harder, and I was pretty sure I heard Layton sniffling behind me. I turned around to see him wiping away a tear, and I just looked at him.

"What? Dude, that got me…that got me good," Layton said.

Whitley, Courtney, and the preacher all let out a chuckle. When I looked back at Courtney, she had the most amazing smile on her face. I couldn't help but smile back at her.

"Courtney, Reed, I now pronounce you man and wife. Reed, you may kiss your bride."

I placed my hands on the sides of her face, and I brought her lips up to mine. I kissed her softly and tenderly. I wanted to turn the kiss into something more, but I needed to keep this gentle and loving. When her hands moved up and around my neck, she pulled me in to deepen the kiss, and I did just that.

I wasn't sure how long we were lost in our kiss.

Layton tapped me on the shoulder and said, "Uh…I think the good preacher needs to get to another wedding, y'all."

I pulled back just a little bit and whispered against Courtney's soft lips, "I love you, Mrs. Moore."

She smiled and said, "I love you, Mr. Moore. Thank you for making all my dreams come true."

I winked at her. "I've only just begun."

TWENTY-ONE

I sat at the bar, drinking water and staring down at my wedding ring. Reed had picked out a beautiful platinum wedding band with diamonds surrounding it. It was beautiful and looked breathtaking against the pink diamond on my engagement ring. My whole body came to attention when I felt Reed's hot breath on my neck.

"Are you happy?" he whispered against my skin.

"Yes," I barely whispered as my stomach dipped.

He turned me around, and when I looked up into his eyes, my body reacted immediately.

How long is this incredible need to have him buried inside me and make me his going to last?

"What's the plan now, y'all?" Whitley asked as she leaned back onto Layton's chest.

Layton had not stopped yawning since we sat down.

"Are you tired, cowboy?" I asked with a wink.

Whitley's face turned ten shades of red.

"Your best friend here had me up almost all night," Layton said as he wiggled his eyebrows up and down.

"Court, do you realize we are going to have our babies so close together?" Whitley said with a huge grin on her face.

I smiled, but then panic set in, and my smile faded. Reed and I hadn't told our parents yet that we were pregnant. My mother had been texting me all night and this morning.

What if Reed's mom thinks I trapped him with this? What if she doesn't believe that we just found out?

I peeked up at Reed, and the happiness on his face told me all I needed to know. He was over the moon about me being pregnant. I knew how much this meant to him, and honestly, I didn't give a shit about what my parents or his mother would think.

All that mattered was us—Reed and me.

I closed my eyes and thought back to what he'd said during the ceremony. I wanted so badly to tell him that he had swooned the hell out of me, but I could barely talk.

"What are you thinking about, angel? Your face is flushed," Reed whispered before kissing me softly on the cheek.

I opened my eyes and stared into his. "What you said to me during the wedding. It was amazing."

When his eyes lit up and that crooked smile played across his face, I knew what was coming next.

"Swoon-worthy?"

I slowly nodded my head. "Oh, yes, very much so."

I laughed when he did a fist pump, and then he pulled me off the stool and took me into his arms.

"I want to go dancing." He looked over at Layton and Whit. "Y'all want to hit the club? Have a little fun before we head back to Texas tomorrow?"

"Yes! Dancing sounds amazing!" Whitley said.

Layton nodded. "Sounds good to me, but I need a nap."

Whitley turned around and hit Layton in the stomach. "Come on, let's head back to the room, so you can call Kate and see how her horseback riding competition went."

"That's right! I forgot Katie Mac was in a show this weekend. Shit! I can't believe I forgot, and we missed it," I said as I pulled out my phone. I sent Jen a quick text message, saying I was sorry for missing Kate's show.

Layton grinned and pulled me in for a hug. "Don't worry. I told Jen about you and Reed, and she was so happy for y'all. She said that Kate will have plenty of shows. Now, you and the old man go have a bit of fun before we all meet up again later. Our flight is early tomorrow, so we can't stay out too late."

I giggled. "Okay, Dad."

While Reed and Layton talked about something to do with the ranch, I hooked my arm with Whit's, and we made our way to the elevator. Every now and then, someone would stop Reed and me and congratulate us on our wedding. I was honestly getting tired of smiling.

Gesh. What would I have done if we'd had a big wedding with guests, like my mother wanted? I would have died.

"Have you told your mom yet?" Whitley asked with a smirk.

"Ugh, no. Honestly, I'm scared to tell her. She was pretty upset that we'd decided to elope and that we were getting married so soon."

Whitley shrugged her shoulders. "She'll get over it soon enough. I bet they are going to want to throw a big reception though."

I let out a sigh as we walked into the elevator. "Yep. She wants to have a dinner or something for us when we come up for Tyler's wedding. I just hope we'll be making it to the wedding…ya know?"

Whitley knew why and didn't even have to ask. It was kind of nice that she knew about Noah now. If I hadn't told her, she would be asking me fifty million questions about me not going to my own brother's wedding.

I'd already been going over excuses for why I wouldn't be able to make it if Noah's business trip got canceled.

Whitley and I rode up to the top floor in silence as we listened to Layton talking about a racehorse he needed Lucky to work on. Then, he went on about something to do with the cows and calves and fences that needed mending. Reed worked more now than he ever had with his job at the Texas Parks and Wildlife Department, but he loved every minute of being partners with Layton. They worked so well together. Layton had hired Frank and Mimi's former ranch hand to take Mitch's place, and from what Reed had said, this guy was ten times better than Mitch.

Reed glanced my way, and when our eyes met, he licked his lips, and I let out a soft moan, regretting it the moment it escaped my lips. Layton was too busy talking, and Whitley was staring up at Layton. She was so lost in his words that she hadn't noticed my slip.

Gah, I just want to feel Reed's lips on my body…everywhere.

By the time the damn elevator doors opened, I was on fire and needing Reed more than ever, but Layton was still going on and on.

I grabbed Reed's hand and pulled him away. "Sorry, Layton. If you'll excuse us, Reed has his husbandly duties to fulfill."

"Really, Court? I didn't need that visual," Whitley said.

I turned around and walked backward as I smiled at Layton and Whitley.

"Go take care of your wife, Layton," I said.

A smile spread across Layton's face. "With pleasure, Mrs. Moore," he said as he reached down and swept Whitley off her feet. He began carrying her back to their room as she laughed and kept telling him to put her down.

When I turned around, I was pretty sure I had a goofy-ass grin on my face.

Reed was just about to put the key into the slot when he lifted my chin. "What's with the big smile?"

"Layton called me Mrs. Moore, and it sounded so wonderful," I said as I felt the stupid tears building in my eyes again.

"Well, I'm glad to hear you love it so much since I intend on you keeping that name for the rest of your life. Now, let's get on with these husbandly duties I have to fulfill."

Reed reached down and picked me up, and I let out a small scream. He opened the door and carried me in while giving me a sweet, soft kiss. The smell of all the roses in the room was intoxicating. He brought me into the bedroom and set me down on the edge of the bed.

"I really love that wedding dress, but it has to come off now."

The flood of wetness between my legs caused me to let out a whimper. I couldn't wait to feel him moving in and out of me, and I was more than ready for it. He got down and took off one of my shoes. He brought my foot up to him and began rubbing it before making his way up my leg. I instinctively spread my legs wider for him, and he let out a moan when his fingers made their way into my panties.

Reed closed his eyes and said, "Damn…you're always so wet and ready, Court."

I dropped my head back. "Only for you."

He pulled his fingers away too soon, and I let out a huff.

He slowly moved his hands down my other leg and removed my other shoe. "I want to taste you on my lips."

I could hardly stand it. I wanted to reach down and touch myself, but then he reached for my hands and pulled me into a standing position.

"Turn around, angel."

I slowly turned around, but I kept looking at him over my shoulder.

He reached up and placed his hands on my shoulders as he whispered, "So beautiful."

I looked straight ahead and tried to keep my thoughts from going crazy. Something about Reed talking like that turned me on even more. He began unzipping my dress, and I felt the goose bumps all over my body.

"This dress looked so amazing on you, Courtney…so incredibly amazing."

I closed my eyes and smiled. The moment I had seen the dress, I'd known I wanted it. I'd been lucky enough that a bridal store in Tahoe had the damn thing, and I'd gotten even luckier that they had it in my size. I'd only needed a few simple alterations on it. The dress was an Alfred Angelo embroidered lace princess-line dress. The dropped waist and high-low hemline hugged my curves in all the right places. I paired the dress with a pair of Louboutins that I'd worn after the ceremony. I'd accessorized the dress with white pearl drop earrings that Whitley had bought for me and a pearl necklace that was my grandmother's.

Reed let the dress drop, and when he let out a gasp, I wanted to hug myself. I was wearing a light baby-blue corset with matching baby-blue thongs. I slowly turned around, and the hungry look in Reed's eyes had me wanting to do a fist pump.

"I, um…I take it this is your something blue?" Reed said as his eyes moved up and down my body before locking on to my eyes.

I knew the light blue in the corset would make my blue eyes pop even more, and when Reed sucked in a breath of air, I knew I was well on my way to driving him crazy.

"Your something new?" He took his index finger and traced along the top edge of the corset, barely touching my breasts in the process.

My breathing became slightly unsteady as I said, "The earrings."

He leaned down and kissed along the exposed part of my breasts, which Whitley had said were practically pushed up to my chin.

"Something old?" he whispered against my skin.

I sucked in a breath of air and replied, "The, um…the necklace. It was my grandmother's."

He slowly began unclasping each hook on the corset, and I had to admit defeat. Here I was, wanting to drive him insanely crazy, and he was turning the tables on me.

"Something borrowed?" He pulled my corset down, cupped one of my breasts, and brought my nipple into his mouth.

He sucked on it so hard that I let out a whimper.

Shit on a brick. My breast is so tender.

I let out a long, soft moan as I ran my hands through his hair, pushing his head down. I needed his lips to ease the throbbing between my legs.

He stopped and looked up at me. "Courtney…"

I was so lost in the passion that I could hardly think. "Yes?"

"Your something borrowed, baby?" he said in the most seductive voice.

"Oh God…Reed…please. Please touch me."

He continued to unclasp the last few hooks, and once the corset fell open and dropped to the floor, I let out a sigh of relief.

"Thank God. That bitch was so fucking tight."

Reed laughed against my sensitive skin, causing a chill to run across my whole body. He dropped to his knees and buried his face in my panties as he blew hot air against them.

"*Please,*" I begged.

He placed his hands on my stomach, and I snapped my eyes open and looked down at him.

"You haven't told me your something borrowed yet, Court."

"Um…my, um…it's…"

The way he was rubbing his hand on my stomach was causing my mind to race in a million different directions. I was so turned-on, but just this sweet, small gesture had me almost dropping to my knees to tell him how much I loved him.

"Wait, what was the question?" I asked as I looked into his beautiful blue eyes.

They were almost the same color as my corset right now.

Reed smiled and kissed my stomach, never taking his eyes from mine. "Something borrowed?"

"Right. The hair comb in my hair. Whitley wore it in her hair when she got married."

As soon as I finished talking, he ripped my lace thongs off and pushed me back onto the bed. I didn't even have time to recover from how fucking hot it was seeing him rip off my panties before his face was buried between my legs, and his tongue was moving in and out of my body.

Holy fucking shit.

Reed was the only man who had given me oral sex, and right now, I was so damn happy about that. To know this was one thing only he would ever give me filled my body with such passion. I grabbed on to his hair and held him as I began thrusting my hips against his face.

"Yes! Oh God, yes!" I screamed out as my orgasm hit me.

I wasn't sure what Reed was doing differently, but he did something that made it feel like an orgasm hit on top of my current orgasm.

"Oh my God!" I yelled out as I almost came off the bed. "What? What…are you…doing? Don't stop! Reed…oh God."

My head was thrashing back and forth, and I was experiencing the longest, most intense orgasm of my life. Everything was clenching down, and my legs even felt like they were tingling. I never wanted it to stop, but at the same time, I almost needed it to stop because it was so intense.

It took a few moments or so to even realize that Reed had moved me up the bed, and he was now making love to me. He was moving so slow and gentle when I finally came back to my senses. I wrapped my legs around him and lost myself again in his sweet passion. He covered my face in kiss after kiss as he whispered how much he loved me. The slower he moved in and out, the more love I felt between us. I'd never imagined it would be this wonderful, this amazing, and this breathtaking.

"Reed…" I whispered.

He quietly said my name as he poured himself into my body.

When I opened my eyes, the room was completely dark. Reed and I were wrapped all around each other, and the sound of him breathing made me smile. Then, I thought about my orgasm and Reed making love to me. I tried to work myself out of the tangled mess of arms and legs without waking Reed up. Somehow, I managed, and I tiptoed into the bathroom. I took one look at the bathtub and let out a low moan.

"Oh God, to soak in that would be heaven," I whispered.

"Do you want me to start it for you?" Reed wrapped his arms around me.

I smiled and shook my head. "What time is it? We should check to see if Layton and Whitley have called." I turned and wrapped my arms around his neck. I just wanted to pinch myself to make sure I wasn't dreaming.

Reed's eyes locked with mine, and we both smiled at the same time.

My smile faded some as I thought about the question I'd wanted to ask Reed since I told him last night I was pregnant. "I know we've moved fast, and now, we're married and going to have a baby and all. Are you upset that we didn't get more time to be together, just you and me?" I asked.

His smile faded for one brief second before it reappeared, and this time, it was bigger. He slowly shook his head. "I'm not going to lie. I would have loved being just a couple for a little bit longer. There were so many places I wanted to take you and things I wanted to do with you. I think the key will be making sure we spend time alone together after the baby is born. I don't mean like taking off for weeks at a time, but we just need to make sure we get in some…alone time." He raised his eyebrows.

I let out a giggle. "Well, ya know…it takes nine months, and I'm not that far along, so I bet we have a good eight months to enjoy each other."

Reed threw his head back and laughed. "Damn, I have a hell of a lot to show you and do with you in the next eight months." He tapped the tip of my nose with his index finger.

He was just about to lean down to kiss me when the phone in the room rang.

"Shit!" Reed turned and made his way to the phone.

After I used the bathroom, I headed out into the living room area where Reed was still on the phone.

He looked up at me and asked, "Are you hungry, baby? Do you want to get dinner first?"

I nodded my head like a crazed person. I was starving.

Reed hung up the phone, stood up, and made his way over to me. "Apparently, Whitley is hungry enough to eat Tink, so she needs food immediately."

I let out a laugh. "It's all that sex they're having. Jesus, I've never heard of two people who have sex as much as they do." I spun around and headed into the bedroom to get dressed.

"Gross, I didn't need that image in my head. I'm still trying to get the image of them in the truck out of my head."

I stopped and turned toward my husband. "In the truck? Having sex? When?"

Reed slipped on a pair of jeans as he tilted his head as if he was thinking hard. He shrugged. "I don't know. Maybe right after they got together. Oh yeah, it was the day Layton gave Tink to Whitley."

I let out a gasp and put my hands on my hips. "What? She had truck sex with Layton, and that bitch didn't tell me about it?"

Reed looked at me like I was crazy. "Um…I guess so? Does it matter?"

I walked my naked ass over to my suitcase, flung it open, and looked for the perfect dress to wear. *There it is—my favorite strapless blue dress, the one that fits me like a glove. Oh…I think I'll go sans panties as well.* I hugged myself and smiled as I thought about how Reed was going to flip when he saw me in this dress and my cowboy boots.

Now, back to the matter at hand. "Yes, it matters. She's my best friend. She should have told me she had sex in the truck and that you caught them. You know what this means, don't you?"

Reed pulled a green T-shirt over his head and looked at me.

Holy shit.

It was tight on him and showed every inch of his muscles. I moved my eyes up and down his body, and when they landed on his messy dark brown hair, I sucked in a breath. I loved when he had that just-fucked look to his hair. I licked my lips as I looked back at his chest. He had the perfect muscular body.

Oh Lord, and his tattoos drive me crazy. On more than one occasion, I'd traced them with my fingers and my tongue.

"Court? Hello? Earth to Courtney? Where are you?"

I let out a sigh and said, "Lost in your hotness."

He laughed as he slipped on his cowboy boots, stood up straight, and winked at me.

Bam, just like that, and he was ready to go, looking all hot and shit.

Damn him.

He walked up to me and cupped each of my breasts, and I let out a gasp.

"Oh my gosh, they're so sore."

As he began sucking on one of my nipples, I totally lost my train of thought. He sucked one hard and pulled back until he made a popping sound with his mouth. He peeked up at me as he was about to move to the other nipple.

I quickly shook my head and pushed him away. "Okay, stop. I need to think, and I can't think with you being all sexy and everything."

He held up his hands as he stood up straight and then moved to sit down on the bed. I pulled the dress over my head and went to say something, but Reed cut me off.

"Whoa. Hold up for a second. You don't have a bra on."

Confused, I looked down at the dress and then back up at him. "So? I never wear a bra with this dress."

Reed stood up and started going through my suitcase.

"What are you doing?" I asked as I tried to push him away.

"I'm looking for a goddamn bra. Your nipples are showing through that thing."

I looked down and smiled. "That's because you just turned me on by sucking on them, you dipshit."

His mouth dropped open. "Well, I plan on turning you on a lot tonight, so no, I don't want other men seeing my wife's nipples."

Oh, wow. Oh my. Hearing him call me his wife did things to me.

I slowly smiled as I began playing with my nipples through the fabric of the dress. "So, you wouldn't want me to do this while we are at the club?"

His eyes widened, and he licked his lips. "Court, you better stop, or I'm going to take you right here."

The rush of wetness I felt between my legs caused me to moan. "God, I'm so horny all of a sudden," I purred as Reed took a step closer to me. Then, I remembered what I was going to say.

I held up my hands and yelled, "Stop!"

He immediately stopped and said, "What?"

"I remembered what I was going to say. You know what this means—Whitley having public sex in Layton's truck and not telling me? I need to one-up her."

Reed looked at me, confused. "Huh? What do you mean, one-up her?"

I looked at him with a serious face. "We have to have public sex…in a better place than she did."

"What?"

I nodded and quickly took off the dress. I reached into my suitcase, pulled out a strapless bra, and put it on. When I glanced over at Reed, he was standing there with his mouth hanging open. I slipped the dress back on, hoping he wouldn't notice that I hadn't put on panties.

"So, be on the lookout tonight for a good place." I made my way into the bathroom where I sprayed on some perfume.

When I walked back into the bedroom, Reed still had his mouth hanging open. He closed his eyes and shook his head.

"No. Absolutely not. No way." He ran his hand through his beautifully messy hair.

"What do you mean, no way? Yeah, we are. We are having public sex tonight, and you will enjoy it, damn it!" I said as I slipped on a pair of high heels, deciding I needed to sex it up for him if I was going to make this work. I quickly swept up my hair and pulled down a few strands, so it looked almost the same as it had during the ceremony.

Reed walked over to me, grabbed my arm, and spun me around. His beautiful blue eyes were searching my face for any signs that I was kidding. When he didn't find any, he let out a sigh. "Courtney, I'm not fucking my pregnant wife in public. No way in hell is that going to happen."

Aww…he looks so cute when he's frustrated…if only he knew how wrong he is. Play it cool, Court. You got this.

I slowly put my finger in my mouth and bit down on it as I looked at him with sad puppy eyes. "Reed, come on. You don't think it would be sexy as hell to have sex in public? We don't know any of these people."

For one brief second, I thought I had him convinced when his eyes filled with lust, and he looked my body up and down. Then, he closed his eyes and shook his head quickly as if he was trying to clear an image from his brain.

"No! No, Court, I don't think that would be sexy as hell." He turned, grabbed his watch, and put it on as he mumbled something about me being crazy, and it was a good thing he loved me so much.

I smiled and gave myself a quick hug, thinking about how I was going to get him so hot and bothered tonight he would be begging for me. He turned around and looked at me, waiting for me to agree.

I shrugged my shoulders. "Fine, if that's the way you want to be." I reached for my clutch and innocently smiled at him.

"Thank God. Jesus, Court, you freaked me out there for a few seconds. I'm glad you came to your senses."

He placed his hand on the small of my back, causing goose bumps to invade my skin. I smiled as we made our way out the door.

Oh, Mr. Moore…clearly, you don't know your wife very well.

TWENTY-TWO

REED

The club in the hotel was unbelievably packed with people. Layton was guarding Whitley like a hawk, and it didn't help that Whitley was in a dancing mood.

I glanced over at Whitley and Courtney talking. I couldn't help but smile when I thought back to dinner when Courtney had tried like hell to play with me under the table. She looked at me and smiled as I smiled back at her. I knew what she was up to.

Layton walked up, handed me a beer, and slapped me on the back. "Holy shit, man. This place is packed. I'm just glad Whit is taking a breather from dancing."

I smiled as I nodded my head and looked around the club. "Shit."

I saw the two girls who had approached Layton and me at the bar the other day. They were out dancing on the dance floor.

Great. Hopefully, they see us with the girls and stay away from us.

Layton got closer to me and started yelling, "What is Courtney up to? She has that look in her eye, and trust me, dude, when she gets that look, you better watch out."

I let out a laugh as I shook my head. Courtney thought I hadn't noticed her not putting on panties as she got dressed, but I'd noticed…and I'd been fighting my hard-on all night while just thinking of her with no panties on.

I shouted at Layton, "Oh, believe me, I know she's up to something. I've got my guard up to Defcon level one."

Layton chuckled and took a drink of his beer.

The song changed, and Selena Gomez's "Slow Down" started.

Layton and I both said, "Shit."

Both girls loved that damn song and would play it all the time.

Layton downed his beer and set it down. Then, he looked at me and shrugged his shoulders. "Let's do this!"

He slapped his hands together and grabbed Whitley when she walked up to him. They made their way to the middle of the dance floor, and Court and I were right behind them. I tried like hell to keep my laughter in as Courtney's dancing got more and more provocative. She was trying like hell to get me turned-on.

As long as I don't touch her too much, I'll be okay.

I glanced over at Layton and Whitley, and they were all over each other. I rolled my eyes and noticed one of the girls from the other night walking toward me. I grabbed Courtney and pulled her up against me. The girl stopped in her tracks, made a face, and turned to walk away.

I let out the breath I'd been holding and looked down at Court. She had the biggest grin on her face. The song ended, and I was again breathing a sigh of relief until "Cyclone" by Baby Bash started playing.

Fuck me. It's the song from our first night together.

The look in Courtney's eyes changed. She turned around and backed her ass right up next to my poor hard dick that I'd been trying to keep under control all night. She began grinding and rubbing her hands all over her body.

Come on, Reed. You've got this. This is the same girl who called you a tree-loving, cultivating-plant pussy. Stay strong. Don't touch her.

Courtney turned around and was sucking on her damn index finger. I looked away and caught a glimpse of Layton and Whitley.

Holy shit.

Those two were practically having sex on the dance floor. I quickly looked away and tried to look everywhere but at Courtney. Then, she reached down and grabbed me. I jerked my head and looked at her as she started moving her hands all over me while she danced like I'd never seen her dance before. I'd never seen anyone so fucking sexy in my entire life. She moved her whole body up and down my body, and then she turned around and started with the whole ass-grinding again. My dick was so hard that it was beginning to hurt. She placed her head back against my chest.

I leaned down and said, "You're driving me crazy, Courtney."

The dance floor was packed, and the damn place seemed to be getting darker. Before I knew what she was doing, she grabbed my hand and pushed it under her dress. I sucked in a breath of air and closed my eyes as I brushed my fingers across her lips. I quickly slipped one finger in, and she was soaking wet. I pulled my hand out, and she turned around and looked at me.

"I want you, Reed."

Oh, motherfucker, she's good. Stay. Strong.

She pulled me down and put her lips up to my ear. "Now is one of the times I just need to be fucked…by my husband."

I'd underestimated my wife.

Janet Jackson's "If" started playing, and I knew I was toast. Courtney smiled as she grabbed me by the shirt and began walking off the dance floor.

Just stop your feet from moving, Reed.

She turned and looked over her shoulder, and the smile she gave me was my undoing. I looked up to see where she was going. I smiled when I saw she was leading us to a dark little nook by the restrooms at the back corner of the club. She turned and backed herself into the corner. She began moving her hands up and down her body while the beat of the song was pounding in my head.

She pulled me to her and yelled, "Now, Reed!"

I looked her up and down and decided right then and there that this girl had a power over me. I put my hand on the wall next to her head and placed my other hand on her thigh. She bit down on her lip and dropped her head back against the wall. I lightly brushed my fingertips up and down her thigh, slowly making my way up to the treasure that was waiting for me. She grabbed my hand and pushed it up. I slipped two fingers inside her and started working her.

Shit…she's dripping wet.

I used my thumb and began my assault on her clit. She began thrashing her head back and forth, and I knew the moment she was coming when she clenched down on my fingers. I moved my fingers in and out faster as she brought her hands up and cupped her breasts.

Fuck it.

I pushed her around the corner of the nook and quickly unbuttoned my pants. I was thanking God that I had gone commando tonight. I lifted up her dress and pulled up her leg. She gave me a shocked look.

"Remember my goals, baby. I intend on making you happy, and if having sex in public will make you happy, then that's what I'll do."

The beat of the song changed, and I slammed my dick into her, causing her to let out a scream. The music was so loud that there was no way anyone would hear her. She grabbed on to my arms and matched me thrust for thrust. It didn't take me long at all before I felt the buildup.

I leaned down and said, "I'm gonna come, Courtney."

We both began calling out each other's name. She began squeezing my dick and taking every drop I was giving her. I pulled out quickly and dropped her leg as I pulled her dress down. She had her head leaning against my chest as she attempted to catch her breath. She leaned back against the wall, and I began buttoning up my pants as I looked around. I let out a laugh because not a single person was paying attention to us. I glanced back at Courtney. Her face was flushed, and she had the most beautiful smile on her face. The song stopped, and another immediately began playing.

She quickly said, "Oh. My. God. That was the hottest thing *ever*! That shit needs to go in a book!"

I laughed as the next song pounded its bass in my head. I grabbed her hand and walked down the hallway to the restrooms. I stopped at the ladies' room and grinned at her as she pushed open the door and headed in. I fell back against the wall and ran both my hands through my hair.

Holy shit. I just had sex with my pregnant wife…in a club…in front of hundreds of people.

I looked down the hallway at everyone lost in their own little worlds, and I wondered if anyone had caught a glimpse of what Courtney and I had just done. The restroom door opened, and before I knew what was happening, some girl was pushing herself into me.

I quickly grabbed her and said, "What the fuck?" as I gave her a good push back.

"Oh, baby, come on. I saw the way you were looking at me. Ditch the blonde, and let's go find somewhere to…play."

The next thing I knew, she dropped out of my sight, and I saw Courtney standing there. She was looking down, so I followed her gaze. The girl was down on the ground, bitching about Courtney pushing her. I snapped my head back up and looked at Courtney, who used her index finger to motion for me to follow her. As we walked back out into the club, I took her hand in mine, and we made our way back to the bar. Layton and Whitley were standing there, attempting to talk to each other.

I leaned over and said in Layton's ear, "I've got to get out of here, dude."

He nodded and motioned to Whitley that we were leaving. As we left the club, both girls decided they needed food, so we headed out to find them something to eat. When we got outside, I took a deep, cleansing breath of mountain air.

Layton slapped me on the back and then grabbed me around my neck before pulling me off. "Where in the hell did you two go? We were looking everywhere for you. One minute, you were dancing, and the next minute, you were gone."

I peeked over at Court. She was laughing at something Whitley was saying.

I never took my eyes off of her as I said, "I'll fill you in later. I'm still trying to let it soak in."

I looked at Layton, and he gave me a questioning look.

"Trust me, you don't really want to know." I made my way over to the rental car.

"Well, hell, now you've piqued my curiosity, dude!" Layton called out to me.

I sat there in the restaurant and watched Whitley and Courtney eat like they were starved. I just shook my head and smiled. The moment Whitley and Courtney got up to use the restroom, Layton went on the hunt for information.

"Spill it," he said with a wink.

I rolled my eyes. "Trust me, dude. I don't think you really want to know."

He let out a laugh. "I'm pretty sure I want to know. Whitley was in an uproar when you two disappeared."

I let out a sigh and said, "Will you drop it if I tell you? And you have to promise never to bring it up again—ever."

He gave me his crooked smile. "You know me better than that. Spill it."

"Fine. I said something to Court about driving up on you and Whit that day when you were getting it on in the truck. Court freaked that Whitley had never told her about it, and Court said she had to pay Whit back by having sex in a public place…a better public place."

Layton's smile quickly vanished, and it was replaced by a look of…terror.

I slammed my hands on my face and dragged them down. "Oh God…what did I do?"

"Holy motherfucking shit. You didn't?" Layton whispered as he looked all around.

I looked around. "What are you looking at? It's not like I had sex with her in here!"

Layton sat back and stared at me. "You're right. I didn't want to know."

I gave him a look and said, "I told you. And you can't tell Whitley."

Then, the bastard started laughing. "Dude, she has you wrapped around her finger."

Wait, what? "What? No, she doesn't," I said.

He tilted his head and lifted his eyebrows. "Hmm…yeah, she does. She talked you into having sex in a club."

I sat back and took it all in. Then, I smiled at Layton. "It was hot as fuck though, I'll tell ya that."

Layton snarled his lip and grabbed his water. "Don't need the visual, thank you very much." He took a drink and looked around. "I bet it was though. Whitley was driving me fucking crazy with the way she was dancing."

I let out a chuckle. "Just don't tell Whitley."

Layton nodded his head as Whitley said, "Don't tell Whitley what?"

Both Layton and I snapped our heads up. One look at Courtney's face, and I knew I was in trouble.

I think I see our first fight as a married couple coming on.

"Reed! You didn't tell him, did you?" Courtney gasped.

"Um…" I looked at Layton for a little bit of help.

He just sat there, smiling.

Oh, you bastard. You wait.

Whitley sat down next to Layton and looked around. "What's going on?"

Courtney sat down, and she glared at me and then Layton. For a second there, I was pretty sure I saw fear in Layton's eyes.

"Hello? Will someone tell me what in the hell is going on that I don't know about?"

"Reed and Court here…"

I pointed at Layton. "Don't do it, Layton. We're best friends. We share a common bond. Dude, really?"

Layton looked at Whitley, who shot him an innocent, sweet smile.

"Don't look at her smile! Don't look into her eyes!" I shouted.

Courtney hit me on the shoulder and whispered, "I can't believe you told him! He's going to tell her first before I get the chance to rub it in!"

Rub it in? My mouth dropped open. "You used me? You used me to get back at Whitley. I feel so…so dirty now." I stared at her in shock.

She looked at me and smiled. "No, I didn't use you, not really. I mean…pesh…please. You enjoyed it."

"Someone tell me what in the hell we are talking about," Whitley said as she slammed her hand down on the table.

Layton was just about to tell Whitley when he yelled out, "Ouch! What the fuck? You kicked me, Courtney?"

She put both hands on the table and looked at Layton. "Listen here, cowboy. I warned you…don't mess with me. You will not take this away from me. You got that?"

Layton shut his mouth and held up both hands.

Courtney turned and looked at Whitley. "So, missy, sex in Layton's truck, huh?"

Whitley's eyes widened. "Did you see us?"

Courtney was stunned for a second as was I.

Then, Court tilted her head and asked, "How many times have y'all had sex in Layton's truck?"

Whitley's face turned red. "Um…" She shrugged her shoulders and said, "I don't know. Four maybe?"

"Four? Where? Besides the first time when Reed caught y'all in the dirty little act, and you never told me about it."

I placed my head in my hands and mumbled, "Oh, this is not going to turn out well for me. I just know it."

"I'm waiting, Mrs. Morris," Court said as she sat back and folded her arms across her chest.

"I never told you about that? Are you sure? I'm positive I did," Whitley said.

"The other three, please," Courtney said as she snapped her head over at Layton, who quickly looked away.

Whitley leaned over the table and said, "Court. Really? Can we talk about this maybe another time?" She jerked her head over toward me and made a face.

Courtney shook her head as she continued to stare at Whitley.

"Fine. The second time was in the parking lot of a movie theater, the third was on the side of the highway after I picked Layton up at the airport, and the fourth time was in the ranch truck as we were making rounds around the ranch."

I shot my head up and looked at Layton. "Really? In the ranch truck, Layton? I'm never gonna be able to drive or sit in that truck again."

Layton started laughing as I sat there, shaking my head.

Courtney leaned forward. "You *never* told me about all those times. How could you? I'm your best friend! I told you about me and Reed having sex in Layton's pool while y'all were getting the food ready for the cookout two weeks ago."

Shit.

"*What in the fuck?* You had sex in my pool, dude? While I was home? That is so beyond messed-up," Layton said as he pointed at me.

At this point, I chose to stay silent. I had a feeling this train was about to wreck at any moment.

"Courtney, does it really matter? And can you keep your voice down, please?" Whitley said as she looked around.

"Well, Reed and I had sex in the dance club tonight," Courtney spit out.

Yep, train derailing now. I slid farther down in my seat as I looked around.

"What? How? My God! Where in the club?" Whitley's hands went up to her mouth as she let out a gasp. "Is that where y'all disappeared to? You were having sex?"

Courtney leaned back and smiled as she nodded her head. "Yep," she said as she popped her P.

Whitley's eyes got big as she moved in closer and whispered, "Oh my God…was it hot? Oh, I bet it was hot as hell."

"What?" Layton and I both said at once.

Courtney giggled. "Oh, you have no idea how hot it was."

I looked back and forth between each of them.

"Did anyone see?" Whitley asked with a giggle.

"Wait, what?" Layton said as he looked at me.

I shrugged.

"I don't know, and I don't care. I screamed like all get-out, too!" Court said.

Layton slammed his hands over his ears. "Stop! Oh, for the love of all things. Stop!"

Whitley looked at Layton and pulled his hands down. "Oh, stop it."

Layton pointed at me while I was still sitting there in a state of shock from Court screaming out that we'd just had sex…in the club. Then, he pointed at Courtney.

"I don't want to picture them doing it against the wall in the dance club tonight. Change of conversation," he said.

Whitley smiled. "Come on, Layton, let's be crazy and have—"

"No!" Courtney yelled out.

Two tables full of people turned and looked at her.

"Oh no. No more public sex until Reed and I catch up."

I choked on my own spit. "What?" I yelled out.

Courtney stood up, reached for my hand, and began pulling for me to stand up.

I started panicking. "Where…where are we going?" I asked her as I saw nothing but determination in her eyes.

"We're going to have sex in the rental car in the parking lot." She turned and started walking toward the door.

My mouth dropped open, and I looked at Layton and then Whitley, who was trying to hide the fact that she was giggling.

"Oh my God. What happened to the girl I married?"

Layton shrugged his shoulders and lost it, laughing. Whitley followed his lead and laughed her ass off.

"Reed! Come on!" Courtney called out before walking out the door.

"What's…what's happening?" I said as I slowly followed Courtney outside.

I stood next to the rental car and waited for Reed to make his way over to unlock it.

Ugh. I can't believe Whitley. Some best friend she is.

Reed walked up to me and gave me a weak smile. "Um…Courtney, you're kind of freaking me out here."

I placed my hand on my hip and looked at him. "Why?"

He put his hand behind his neck and began rubbing it while twisting his head like crazy. "Courtney, what happened in the club was hot—*very, very hot.* But something like that will never happen again. Baby, what's gotten into you? Please tell me this is just some crazy thing because you're pregnant, and you're not thinking straight."

I dropped my hand and leaned against the car. I stood there for a few moments before looking at Reed, horror filling my eyes. I slowly put my hand up to my mouth and said, "Oh my God. What were we thinking? We're gonna be parents!"

Reed closed his eyes and whispered, "Thank you, God. She's coming back to me."

I tried not to giggle. "We should have at least gone into the restroom and done it in a stall."

Reed snapped his eyes open and gave me a shocked look. "What?"

I started laughing uncontrollably.

"What is so damn funny?" he asked.

"You! I wish you could have seen your face just now." I pushed off the car, walked up to him, and placed my hand on his chest. "Okay, I'll admit that I got a little crazy with the whole thing. I'm a bit…competitive."

Reed smiled and pushed a piece of my hair behind my ear. "A bit?"

I let out a giggle. "Okay…a lot. I had no intentions of having sex in the rental car. I just wanted to see your face…and Whitley's."

Slowly shaking his head, Reed pulled me closer to him and placed his finger under my chin, slowly pulling it up until our eyes locked with each other. "I love you so much. Do you know that?"

"I think you should show me."

He leaned down and took my lower lip in between his teeth, and then he sucked on it as I let out a moan. He let it go and began kissing me so sweetly. When his hand moved around my back and pulled me in closer, I wanted to fall apart in his arms. Being in Reed's embrace, feeling his love pour into my body, was the most wonderful place in the world.

He pulled back and whispered, "I'm ready to take you home to Texas. I have a wedding gift for you."

I wiggled my eyebrows up and down, and then I made a sad face. "I didn't get you anything."

He threw his head back and laughed. "I think we can find something I'd like for a present."

Layton and Whitley came walking out of the restaurant, laughing.

"I knew you were totally bluffing, bitch!" Whitley said as she walked up and pushed me gently. "I'm exhausted and still need to pack for the flight home."

After we packed up our suitcases and got everything ready for the flight home tomorrow, I was exhausted.

"We still need to let your parents and my mom know we are expecting," Reed whispered in my ear as we lay in bed.

We were both too exhausted to even think of having sex.

I pulled the pillow over my head and let out a cry. "No! I don't want to. Can I just text her?"

Reed snorted and said, "No. If we have to tell my mom in person, you have to tell your mom over the phone at least."

I pushed the pillow off and grabbed my cell phone from the side table. "Fine, but when the shit hits the fan, you're going down with me."

He shook his head and let out a small laugh. I hit my mother's number and held my breath.

"Well, it's about time. I never did get that pregnancy test picture, my dear. What about pictures? Do we at least get to see what you were dressed in?"

I rolled my eyes and let out the breath I had been holding. "Yes, Mom. I'll send pictures when I get back. The ceremony was beautiful. Daddy's friends did an amazing job."

"Oh, I'm so happy to hear that, honey."

I could almost hear the smile in her voice.

"Courtney, you know your father and I are so very happy for you. If this is truly how you wanted to get married, then you know we stand behind you one hundred percent."

I smiled as I looked at Reed. He must have heard her because he smiled and winked at me.

"Thank you, Mom. It really is. I know this seems fast and all, but I've been in love with Reed for so long, and we both fought our feelings, and…well…you know how you've always told me when you know something is right to follow your heart. I just followed your advice, Mom."

I heard her sniffling, and that caused me to choke back a sob. I placed my hand on my stomach and got ready to drop the bomb.

"About those pictures…"

She let out a giggle. "Oh, Courtney. I wasn't being serious, sweetheart. Okay, well, a part of me was, but I believe you when you say you're not pregnant."

I let out a fake laugh. "Well, about that. You see, when I took the test, I was planning on having Whitley take one also. I was going to mess around with you and all."

My mother let out a gasp. "Courtney Marie…that is not funny."

I nodded my head even though I knew she couldn't see me. "Yeah, I know, but the joke was on me, Mom. When I took the test, I had to take seven more."

"What?" my mother asked, confused.

"Yep. The first test showed two lines, and—"

My mother screamed loudly. "Steve! Oh my God, Steve! Get down here!"

All right then…clearly, my mother knows that two lines mean pregnant.

I pulled the phone away from my ear and hit Speaker. "Mom, please stop screaming in my ear."

"Hush now, Courtney! Steeeve!"

I rolled my eyes as Reed began laughing.

"Is that Reed I hear?" my mother asked.

"Yes. I had to put your ass on speakerphone, so you don't break my eardrum."

"What in the hell, woman? Why are you screaming about Marie?" my father said.

I looked at Reed and whispered, "She put me on speakerphone!"

"Steve, it's Courtney," my mother said in an excited voice.

"How was the wedding, princess? Did that little fucker do you right?" my father said. My mother must have hit him. "What? He stole my baby girl, my second-born. He is a little fucker."

"Dad, I have it on speakerphone, and the little fucker is sitting right here."

Reed sat up and said, "Hello, Mr. Will, sir."

My father cleared his voice and said, "You'll know how I feel some day, son, when some little fucker—oh, I mean, when another man takes your daughter's heart."

I laughed as Reed's expression turned to one of horror.

"Um…yes, sir, I'm sure I will."

"He's a polite boy. Keeps calling me sir. I like that."

I shook my head and said, "Daddy, please."

"Steve! Oh my God, Steve!" my mother started again with the yelling.

"Ten Hail Marys and twelve Our Fathers, woman. Settle the hell down."

I covered the phone. "Catholic, remember?" I whispered as Reed's look of terror turned to one of pure confusion. "My father has always said that. No one really knows why, but just go with it."

"She's pregnant!" my mom finally spit out.

Then, came the silence. Reed began sliding back down in the bed, and I started to join him. We pulled the covers over us, thinking it would protect us in some way.

Then, I heard my father choke back a sob. "Court? Baby girl…you're…you're…"

I instantly felt the tears building. "Daddy…I'm gonna have a baby."

The sound of my father crying over the phone instantly made me cry. Reed immediately pulled me into his arms and began running his fingers through my hair.

"I found out yesterday when I was going to send Mom a picture of the test, and…" I couldn't talk. I buried my face into Reed and cried.

Reed whispered, "Please tell me those are happy tears."

I shot my head up and looked into his tear-filled eyes. "Yes," I whispered back.

"Um…please remember your mother and father are listening to everything right now. I really don't want to hate this boy before I even meet him," my father said as he cleared his throat a few times.

Reed and I both laughed. I took the phone off speaker and talked to my father and then my mother for a few minutes. By the time I got off the phone, I was emotionally exhausted. I snuggled into Reed's side as he lightly brushed his fingers up and down my side.

As I began to drift off into sleep, I kept seeing a figure standing in a corner, but it was dark, and I couldn't make it out. I strained to see who it was, but finally, exhaustion took over.

I sat at Whitley's kitchen table, sipping a cup of tea, as I listened to Mimi go on and on about the latest book she'd read that I had suggested.

"How could you, Courtney? I've never cried so hard in my life."

I smiled and shrugged my shoulders. "It was a good book."

Mimi turned and looked at Whit. "What did you call it, Whitley? What kind of crying did you do when you read it?"

Whitley let out a giggle. "I ugly cried."

"Yes! I ugly cried," Mimi said as she pointed at me and shook her finger around like she was drawing a circle in the air.

I laughed and sat back. "Did you read the other book, *From Ashes*? I promise you won't ugly cry with her second book."

Mimi took a deep breath and looked away. I sat up and smiled.

"You did read it, didn't you? So, tell me, Mimi, did Gage get you hot and bothered? I know how you love those Texas boys."

Whitley started laughing as Mimi jumped up, walked over, and poured herself another cup of coffee.

"I have no comment for you, missy. Besides, I don't kiss and tell. Never have, never will."

I took a sip of my tea. "Mimi, have I ever showed you the website for Lelo?"

Whitley dropped a plate, causing it to break, sending broken pieces of glass everywhere. She looked at me with a shocked expression on her face.

"Oh, dear! Whitley, darling, are you okay?" Mimi said as she quickly bent down and began picking up pieces of the plate.

I stood up, and Whit mouthed, *No,* to me.

I smiled and winked at her as I bent down and helped Mimi. As we picked up the broken pieces of the plate, Reed and Layton came walking in. I glanced over at them and about fell over.

Oh damn.

They were both covered in sweat with their T-shirts stuck to their bodies while they were both laughing. Reed's laughter moved through my whole body and caused me to shudder as I attempted to tame the clenching feeling between my legs. I couldn't pull my eyes away from him.

The next thing I felt was Mimi placing her finger on my chin and saying, "Let me shut your mouth for you, dear."

Reed looked down and jerked his head back. "Why are y'all on the floor?"

Mimi laughed and said, "Whitley here dropped a plate. Now, Courtney, what is this Lelo website you were talking about?"

Reed and Layton both stopped and looked at me. Layton grabbed on to the counter to steady himself as he gave me a serious what-the-hell look. I slowly moved my eyes back over to Reed and took in every square inch of him.

"Um…Mimi, now might not be such a good time to discuss that."

Whitley pushed me, causing me to lose my balance, and I landed on my ass.

Reed bent down and tugged on my ponytail. "Talking book boyfriends again, are we, angel?"

"I, um…I was just…"

We'd been back for two weeks now, and every time he looked at me like that, I thought I would come on the spot. I had asked Whitley if she found herself hornier while being pregnant.

She'd shrugged her shoulders and said, *I don't think so.*

Bitch. She was just horny, no matter what.

Me, on the other hand—I couldn't keep my hands off my husband.

"I…we were talking about—"

"Books," Mimi said as she got up and began making sweet tea for both Layton and Reed.

I nodded my head and smiled. "Yep, books."

Reed reached for my hand and helped me up. "I'd give you a hug, babe, but I'm all sweaty."

I bit down on my lip and peered up at him through my lashes. Reed's mouth opened just a little, and I knew he was having the same thoughts I was having.

"I have something to show you at our house," he whispered before he leaned down and kissed me.

I moved my arms around his neck and deepened the kiss. I was completely and utterly lost in his love until Layton cleared his throat. We pulled back a bit and smiled at each other.

"We can finally go home?" I asked.

Since we had been back home, Reed would not let me come back to the log cabin. We'd either stayed at my house, or we'd stayed with Layton and Whit.

He tapped the tip of my nose and laughed. "Yep. I can finally carry you over the threshold."

I did a little jump and started to run out of the kitchen.

"Court? Where in the hell are you going?" Reed asked.

I stopped, turned around, and looked at him like he was crazy. He'd just told me we were heading home, so I was going to pack up to leave.

"I'm packing up my stuff!"

Reed laughed and shook his head. "Okay, we'll have to hurry up. I don't want it to get dark."

I glanced at the clock. It was five in the afternoon. "I'm pretty sure the sun doesn't go down at six, babe." I spun around and rushed upstairs. I was so ready to finally get settled and work on the room for the baby.

I grabbed Reed's duffel bag and began shoving his clothes in it. He wouldn't mind. I still didn't see how he could put his clothes in that thing. I was about to call for him to help me when he appeared in the doorway.

"You in a hurry?"

I nodded my head and walked up to him. If I could crawl into his body, I would. The only time I ever really felt completely safe and happy was when we were making love.

"I just want to make love in our house…as a married couple…on every single surface," I said as I raised my eyebrows up and down.

"Every surface?" he asked in almost a whisper.

"*Every*. Surface."

He grabbed both bags and started heading downstairs. I did a little hop and hugged myself. I loved when I was able to turn him on like that. As I followed him downstairs, he walked through the kitchen and right out the back door without so much as a good-bye. I stopped and looked around at everyone.

"Okay…I guess we're leaving," I said with a giggle.

I hugged Mimi and Whitley good-bye.

"Call me later if you're not too…busy," Whitley whispered in my ear. "I remember when Layton and I came home from our honeymoon, and let me tell you, there are a lot of rooms in this house!"

I pulled back and let out a chuckle. As I started to walk outside, Layton joined me. We walked out onto the back porch, and I glanced over and saw Reed putting the bags in his truck.

"Hey, Court?"

I spun around and looked at Layton. "Yeah?"

"Thank you," he said with a smile.

I smiled back and asked, "For what?"

"For making my best friend the happiest I've ever seen him in my life."

I felt the tears building in my eyes. "I should say the same thing to you."

He let out a small laugh. "You have—after you threatened to cut off my balls if I ever hurt her in any way."

I winked at Layton and said, "That still holds true." I blew him a kiss good-bye and made my way over to the truck. I had never been so excited in my life.

Okay, that's a lie.

I had felt more excited when Reed and I went to the doctor the other day. We'd had our first sonogram, and we'd seen our little peanut on the screen. I would never forget Reed's reaction for as long as I live. The moment I'd seen the tear slide down his cheek, I'd fallen even more in love with him.

I hopped in the truck, and Reed gave me that panty-melting crooked smile of his.

"Ready, Mrs. Moore?"

I nodded. "Ready, Mr. Moore!"

TWENTY-FOUR

REED

"Reed? What are you so nervous about?" Courtney asked as she reached over and touched my knee.

Instantly, the electricity shot through my body. I was tempted to ask Layton if he still felt like that with Whitley, but I wasn't in the mood to have him call me a pussy.

"I'm not nervous," I said as I attempted to clear the frog in my throat.

What if she doesn't like it? What if she didn't really mean it when she mentioned it that day? Shit! I should have asked her about this.

I pulled over about two miles from the house.

"What's wrong? Why are you pulling over?" Court asked.

I looked at her and smiled. I pointed to the glove box and said, "Baby, will you open that up?"

She looked at me and smiled as she turned and opened the glove box.

There was a silk scarf in there that I had bought in one of the boutiques in Tahoe.

"Will you take out that scarf?"

She pulled it out and looked at me. "Whose is this?"

I could see the hurt in her eyes. *Shit. She thinks it belongs to another girl. Thank God I kept the tag with the boutique's name on it.* "I bought it for you in Tahoe. I was going to wait to give it to you at Christmas, but…"

She gave me that smile of hers that just melted my heart.

There isn't a damn thing I wouldn't do for her.

"May I see it?" I asked as I smiled at her.

She slowly handed it to me as I unbuckled my seat belt and winked at her. "I need you to turn around, angel."

"Um…why?" she asked.

"I need to blindfold you. There is something I want to surprise you with, and I don't want you to see it."

She bit down on her lower lip and let out a giggle. I chuckled at how easy it was to make this girl giddy. She turned around, and I wrapped the scarf around her eyes, snugly tying it.

"Can you see?"

She shook her head. "Nope."

"Are you sure?" I asked as I ran my finger down the back of her exposed neck.

She shuddered, and I couldn't help but smile.

I leaned over and put my lips up to her ear. "I'm thinking this might be something fun to try for later," I whispered before pulling her earlobe with my teeth.

"Mmm…that sounds like a good idea," she whispered.

I sat back and pulled my seat belt back on, and then I drove the longest two miles of my life. I parked the truck and said, "Hold on, baby. Let me get the door and help you out."

I ran around the front of the truck and opened her door as she held her hand out for me to help her down. I guided her to the side of the house over toward the giant oak. I stopped her back far enough to where she would be able to see it as soon as I took off the blindfold.

"Are you ready?" I whispered in ear.

She nodded her head and clapped her hands. "The surprise is outside?"

"Yep." I started to untie it and said, "Don't open your eyes until I say so." I let the scarf drop from her eyes as I watched her face. "Open your eyes, Court."

She took a deep breath and opened her eyes. Her mouth dropped open, and she brought her hands up to her mouth. When I saw the tears building in her eyes, I knew I had done the right thing by surprising her. I knew how much she loved surprises.

She just stood there and stared up at it. She dropped her hands and turned to look at me. The tears were streaming down her face as she said, "You remembered what I said about the tree house. When? I mean…how? I mean, did you build this, Reed? It's amazing. It's the most breathtaking tree house I've ever seen," she said between sobs.

I nodded my head. I was afraid if I tried to talk, I'd start crying like a pansy-ass. She threw herself into my body and held on to me as tight as she could. I must have held her for a good five minutes while she cried and kept saying thank you over and over. She pulled back, and I used my thumbs to wipe away her tears, and then I gently kissed her on the lips.

"That day I brought you out here to show you around, I knew I would be building this for you. When we got back to Layton's, I began drawing out the design. Then, when you told me you were pregnant, I knew I would be building it as soon as we got back home."

She sucked in a breath of air and said, "This is what you've been doing?"

I smiled and nodded my head. "Layton and I have been taking care of the ranch in the mornings and then meeting Kevin and Richard over here in the afternoons to build it. I've been nervous as hell to show it to you."

She pulled back and gave me a shocked look. "Why in the world would you ever be nervous to show it to me?"

I shrugged my shoulders and said, "I was worried you weren't serious or that maybe you would want to be a part of the design. I just always want to make you happy. There is nothing in this world that I love more than making you smile."

When the corner of her mouth lifted and she peeked up, I knew what she was thinking.

"I know the first surface that needs to be broken in," she said.

I let out an exaggerated gasp. "Our future kids' tree house? You want to have sex in our future children's tree house?"

She slowly nodded her head and said, "It's ours for a little while."

I glanced up at the tree house and then back down at Court. My dick jumped at the idea of making love to her up there. I grabbed her hand and pulled her over to the staircase that snaked around the tree and led us up to the deck of the tree house. Courtney let out a giggle and mumbled something about not being able to wait to tell Whitley.

As I pushed open the door, I looked back to see her face.

"Oh, Reed," she said in a hushed tone as she looked in every direction.

We had built the tree house all around the tree. The main room contained a few beanbag chairs. There was a flat screen TV on the wall, and under that was a wall that contained built-in cabinets.

"Oh my God. There is a TV in here?" Courtney said.

I laughed and said, "Layton and Kevin insisted. They said the kids wouldn't be able to use it for a few years, so we might as well make it fun for us. We just put these chairs in here until you pick out some other stuff."

She looked at me, stunned. I took her hand and led her into the other room that had two sets of bunk beds that Kevin had made out of cedar. All the wood was cedar, and it smelled so damn good. Courtney put her hand up to her mouth and shook her head.

"I didn't have a chance to buy any mattresses or anything like that."

"Reed, what about the weather? Won't the heat and cold ruin this stuff?" she asked as she looked around the room.

"No, baby. The whole thing is insulated, and we have it ready to add air and heat."

She spun around and stared at me with her mouth dropped open. "What the hell? Our kids' tree house is going to have air and heat? They're not even born yet, and you're spoiling the hell out of them already!"

I threw my head back and laughed. I didn't want to say anything, but I loved how she also kept referring to multiple kids. "Well, I figured we can enjoy it until they get older."

Courtney walked up to the ladder and asked, "Where does this go? To a bathroom?" she said with a giggle.

I walked up and whispered in her ear, "This leads to my favorite part of the whole tree house, the crow's nest. Here, you go first. I don't want you slipping and getting hurt. There is a small landing at the door. Just open the door and step on out."

As she climbed up, my heart started pounding.

"Why does it have a lock on it?" Courtney asked as she looked down at me.

"Well, I figured when the kids are little, we will want to keep it locked, so they don't go up here without us. I've built up the walls pretty high to keep them from falling over. This is the only area that does not have windows."

I made my way up to the landing and stood there while she smiled at me.

"Reed, you're going to make an amazing father."

I gave her a weak smile and said, "I hope so."

I reached around her and pushed open the door. She turned around and let out another gasp.

Rose petals covered the floor, and white lights were draped across the walls. The sun was beginning to sink into the western sky, and the colors of the sky were amazing. The view would only get better the closer we got to sunset. In the corner was a blanket, a bottle of grape juice, two wine glasses, and Courtney's favorite thing right now, chocolate-covered grapes. I gagged every time I saw her eat them, but she loved them.

She spun around and looked at me with the most adorable smile on her face. She scrunched up her nose and said, "You planned this. How did you know I'd want to make love in the tree house?"

I made my way over to her and took her in my arms. I placed my finger on her chin and brought her soft lips to mine. I kissed her slowly and gently before pulling back some. "I figured you for sure would want to look at it. I was hoping I could have my way with you, and you would go along with it."

She pushed her fingers through my hair and looked into my eyes. "I love you so very much. I don't even have words to tell you what this means to me that you built this. My heart is aching because it's filled with so much love for you."

I took her lips in mine and began kissing her like I couldn't get enough of her. Our hands were all over each other's bodies. Before I knew it, we were spreading the blanket on top of the rose petals, and I was burying myself into my wife's body. I slowly began letting go, losing myself in her love. I felt whole when I was making love to Courtney, and I knew she felt the same way. The way we stayed together for so long after we made love, almost like we were afraid to break the connection, was one of my favorite things. Nothing would ever come between us. I would never hurt her, and I'd kill anyone who tried to hurt her.

"Reed?"

I was lying on my side with Courtney pulled up next to me, her soft skin feeling like heaven to me. "Yeah, angel?"

"I think I'm ready to go break in our shower."

I smiled as I kissed her on the head. "Oh yeah?"

She turned around and made a funny face. "Yeah. You really stink from all that sweaty work you did today."

My mouth dropped open before I started laughing. I looked down at my body, picked up my arm, and gave myself a good smell. *Holy shit, I really do stink.*

I stood up and quickly began getting dressed as I watched my beautiful wife get dressed. We grabbed the blanket, grape juice and grapes, and headed back down the tree house. I took her hand in mine as we made our way to the front door. I unlocked the door, opened it, and then bent down and picked up Courtney. I carried her into the house and kicked the front door closed before I walked straight back to our master bathroom.

It didn't take long before I had her up against the wall in our shower.

"Heaven…you are pure heaven," I said as I came inside her while listening to her say my name as she came at the same time.

After sex in the kitchen, sex in the living room, sex up against the hallway wall, and then sex in our bedroom again, we were exhausted. We both lay on the bed, panting.

"I don't think my dick is going to work for a week," I said, trying to catch my breath.

Courtney laughed and rolled over as she began running her fingertips up and down my chest. "I hope not. We have a couple of more bedrooms, the dining room area, the laundry room—"

"Stop! Stop the madness. Holy fuck. I'm getting tired from just thinking about it."

Courtney dropped onto her back and said, "I think I'm going to sleep for at least twelve hours."

"Agreed," I said as I pulled her body next to mine.

The last thing I remembered was Courtney saying, "We can't forget about the other bathroom and the half bath, too. Next week, we can tackle those."

I woke up to Courtney's phone ringing. She had thrown her purse on the window seat of our bedroom, and it had gone off three other times. I knew she was tired from the rough night she'd had. She must have thrown up five times. I slowly got up and rubbed my hands down my face.

"Make it stop, Reed. Please make it stop."

I smiled as I stood up and looked down at my beautiful angel. Even when not feeling good, she was breathtaking. It had been a month since we got married, and it still felt like yesterday.

Standing up, I made my way into the bathroom, only to stop when Court's phone started ringing again. I headed over toward her purse and reached in to grab her phone. One quick look revealed it was her brother, Tyler, calling.

"Court, it's Tyler," I said with a yawn.

"Fuck him! It's Saturday morning, and I don't feel good," Courtney said in a whiny voice.

I laughed as I answered it. "Hello, Tyler. It's Reed. Yep, but she is still half-asleep. If you really want me to wake up the sleeping beast…she, um…had a tough night last night. Okay…here she is."

I tapped Courtney on the shoulder, and she flopped over and glared at me. She slowly sat up and gave herself a few seconds to see if she was going to get sick again.

She must have been feeling better since she reached for the phone and said to me, "Traitor. No sex for you today."

"Uh-huh. You already told me at three this morning that you were never having sex with me again because I made you sick."

She gave me a slight smile and put the phone up to her ear. "This better be good, you dickhead, for waking me up so early on a Saturday."

I started to make my way into the bathroom.

"Reed…"

I stopped and waited, just incase Tyler was going to tell Court that Noah was coming to the wedding after all. I made my way back over to her and sat down.

"I'm so sorry we didn't RSVP, Tyler, but I didn't really think I had to since I'm your sister and in the wedding. No…I haven't talked to Mom, and no, I haven't bought my tickets yet. Um…who all is in the wedding party?" She closed her eyes for a few seconds and then snapped them open. "Yeah, that's a real shame about Noah still not being able to make it." She nodded her head and reached for my hand. "Oh, that's a shame. I'm sorry to hear that."

She rolled her eyes and shook her head. The slight smile on her face told me that Noah was still not attending the wedding.

"Okay. Reed and I will book the flights today, I promise. I'll be there, I promise. I know I told Mom we might not be able to make it, but we will. Yes. I can't wait to see y'all, too. I love you, too, Ty. Later."

She hit End and let out a breath. "He's not going to be there."

Her chest was heaving up and down, and I pulled her to me.

"Oh, thank God. He's not going to be there, Reed."

"Good, because I would have killed him. I hope you know that," I said as I gently moved my hand up and down her bare back.

She pulled back and looked at me. "I just figured he'd somehow try to be there. I already had my excuse ready for why we couldn't attend, but now..." She smiled bigger. "Now, you can finally meet my family, and I can see my brother get married."

Something doesn't feel right about this whole thing. "He's still on that business trip he couldn't get out of?"

Courtney took in a deep breath and slowly let it out. I knew just talking about him upset her.

"Yep. When Tyler suggested changing the wedding date, Meg freaked. The place they are getting married at has a year-long waiting list." She let out a giggle and said, "I never thought I would love Meg as much as I do right now!"

"So, I guess we're heading to New York in two weeks."

She smiled and said, "I can't wait for you to meet my family." Her smile faded, and she looked away.

"Hey, what's wrong?" I asked as I turned her face back toward me. I hated seeing her upset or frightened.

"Shit. I just realized something. This whole time I was preparing not to go to the wedding, and now that we are, I only have two weeks to prepare you for my dad."

My heart dropped in my stomach as I watched Courtney get up and head toward the shower. She was mumbling something about her dad, his guns, and his baby girl.

Oh yeah. That sick feeling just got about ten times worse.

The moment we stepped foot into my parents' house, Reed had my mother, my sister Sissy, and Meg all wrapped around his finger. My father, on the other hand, kept calling Reed the *little motherfucker*, even when I begged him to stop. I knew, deep down inside, he loved Reed. My dad could see how happy Reed made me, and that was all my father cared about—my happiness.

I was sitting in a chair next to my grandmother as she showed me how to crochet. I was attempting to make a baby blanket. I would do about ten rows, and then Grams would check it and rip out at least three rows, saying I was doing it too loose or too tight. I was beginning to get pissed-off.

Tyler came and sat down next to me as I worked on my pale yellow blanket.

"Hey," he said as he hit my knee.

I smiled up at him and replied, "Hey yourself. Are you getting nervous? Tomorrow is the big day."

His eyes lit up, and I knew that look. I'd seen it almost two months ago in my own eyes.

He shook his head and said, "Nah. I'm just ready to make Meg happy until the day I die."

I smiled and nodded my head as I looked out into the kitchen. Reed was laughing at something my father was saying, and when he looked at me and winked, I had to catch my breath.

"He makes you happy," Tyler said.

I snapped my head back and looked at him as I smiled probably the goofiest smile ever.

"He makes me so happy. I'm the happiest I've ever been in my life," I said as I peeked back at Reed.

Tyler took in a deep breath and ran his hand through his hair. "Courtney, can I ask you something?"

"Sure. You can ask me anything."

"What happened between you and Noah? I mean, I really thought you liked him, and I know he liked you. I know something happened because Noah told me he was in love with you, and you destroyed him."

My breathing picked up, and my hands started to shake. I quickly looked at Reed, but he'd moved, and now, his back was facing me. *I need him. Reed, please turn around.*

"Court? Are you okay?" Tyler asked as he touched my hand.

I jumped and pulled my hands back.

"Jesus Christ, Court. What in the heck is wrong? You look like you saw a ghost."

I swallowed hard and somehow built up the courage to talk. The whole time, I kept my eyes on Reed. "Tyler, I don't want to talk about Noah—*ever*. Please just let it go. It was in the past, and I'd like to keep it there."

"He was right."

I snapped my head and glared at Tyler. "Excuse me?"

"Noah—he told me if I tried to talk to you about him, you would get mad and say you didn't want to talk about it. Court, I have to ask. Did you cheat on him or something? He's still hung up on you after all these years. I mean, he's moved on finally, and he is engaged now…"

That poor girl. If she only knew what type of a man she was marrying…

"And he seems happy now, but when he asked me not to—"

I was pulled out of my moment of daydreaming, and I stared at Tyler. "When he asked you not to what?"

Tyler stood up and gave me a weak smile as he slowly shook his head. "Nothing. Never mind. I'm just really glad you're here, Court. I love you and Sissy more than anything."

I smiled as I stood up and set my piece of work to the side. "I love you, too."

"Congratulations on the baby again. I'm really glad you found Reed and that he makes you happy."

I gave him a kiss on the cheek and grinned. "Thank you, Tyler, and yes, Reed makes me beyond happy."

As I watched him walk away, I had the strangest feeling come over me. I felt like that sixteen-year-old girl again, deathly afraid to be alone because *he* might be here. I found myself looking around.

Tyler was saying good-bye to everyone. He was heading to his bachelor party. He had asked Reed to go, but then he'd made the comment that Reed would most likely feel out of place. Tyler had almost seemed like it bothered him to say that, but he'd said it. Reed had no desire to go, but it still pissed me off, and I had every intention of talking to Tyler about it after the wedding. My parents had made me promise to wait. They had also been upset by how rude Tyler had acted, and it took everything out of me not to junk-punch him.

I watched as Tyler walked out the door. I turned and looked out the window as I watched him walk down the sidewalk and up a little ways. He jumped into a Toyota 4Runner that took off down the road. I glanced over to my right, only to see Reed staring at the retreating 4Runner also. I put my hand on my stomach and tried to push down that awful feeling I hadn't had in so many years.

He's out of the country, Courtney. He can't hurt you any longer.

When I looked back at Reed, he was staring at me. He smiled that smile of his and made his way over to me.

When he pulled me into his arms, he whispered in my ear, "Let's stay at a hotel tonight."

I closed my eyes and held on to him harder. I had told my mother that I didn't want to stay at the house. I couldn't bear the thought of Reed being in the same bed where Noah had done those things to me.

I hadn't even had to tell Reed my anxiety over it. The first night we had gotten here, he had gone up to my room ahead of me. When I'd walked into my room, I'd seen he had built a little tent on the floor. When I'd crawled into it, blankets and pillows had been on the floor. I'd looked at him, and he'd told me we would be camping for the next few nights. I had thrown my body into his as I'd cried and told him how much I loved him.

When I stepped back, I opened my eyes and nodded my head.

"I'll let your mother know our plans."

I couldn't talk. I just stood there and watched him as he walked into the kitchen and said something that made my mother laugh. Then, her smile faded, and she looked at me. I was scared shitless she would start screaming about us wanting to leave and go to a hotel. She turned back and smiled at Reed as I watched my father shake Reed's hand.

Wait, what's happening? What did he tell them?

Reed walked up and took my hand as he said, "Let's go pack up. I'll call and make reservations at a hotel."

I followed him up the stairs in silence. When we got in my room and Reed shut the door, I finally found my voice. "What did you tell them? Are they mad we're leaving?"

He laughed as he put both suitcases on the bed and shook his head. "I simply told them that I was uncomfortable being under their roof, and that due to my respect for you and them, I just simply couldn't make love to you while being here. And that since we are newlyweds still, I was going to have to take you to a hotel."

My mouth dropped open. "You didn't," I whispered.

He looked at me and said, "Oh, yes, I did."

"And my father didn't kill you?"

Reed shrugged his shoulders. "Nope. He said he respected me for being honest and for thinking about their feelings on the matter. Married or not, he said you are still his little girl."

I sat down on the bed and tried to let it all sink in.

That's it. Reed Nickolas Moore has powers, very strong powers, that not only control my heart, soul, and libido, but apparently, he has the power to make my family fall so in love with him that he can do no wrong.

This is bad, very bad.

After we checked into the hotel and made our way to our room, I was exhausted. My cell phone began ringing, and Reed and I both moaned, "Not again."

"She's already called you three times since we left…an hour ago," Reed said.

I collapsed onto the king-sized bed. I rolled my eyes as I hit Answer. "What is it now?"

"Excuse me, young lady, but that is no way to talk to your mother. I just want to make sure you asked the hotel to give you a wake-up call."

I let out a long, drawn-out sigh. "Yes, Mother, I did. I have my alarm set, Reed has his set, I set the alarm in the hotel room, *and* the hotel is calling with a wake-up call. I will be there at six."

"Did you leave your dress here? Oh, I hope you did, so it won't get wrinkled. Meg, did she leave her dress?"

I heard Meg start laughing in the background.

"Mom, will you just chill the hell out? You're going to drive Meg insane before she is even an official member of the family."

Reed began rubbing my feet, and I let out a soft moan.

"Mom, I have to go. I'm exhausted. Do you want me to have bags under my eyes tomorrow?"

"Oh no, Court! You should call down and get some tea bags right now. Be sure to get a good night's sleep. Take a hot bath, sweetheart, and make sure you are here by five forty-five."

Reed was slowly moving his hand up before he began drawing circles on my inner thigh. I closed my eyes and willed him to put his lips on me.

I popped my eyes open and said, "Wait, now, it's five forty-five, Mom? Are you crazy?"

She let out a laugh and said, "We have a lot to do to set up and get ready. Tyler is not coming back until right before the ceremony tomorrow, so we all need to pitch in and get things ready."

I sat up. "What? Why does he get out of work? It's his fucking wedding."

"Language, please."

"I'm pregnant! I deserve special treatment, too."

Reed let out a giggle as I continued to argue with my mother.

"Where is the baby staying tonight anyway?" I asked as I flopped back down and pouted. Even though she couldn't see me, I wanted her to feel my dissatisfaction.

"I'm not sure. He just said he was staying with a friend. Courtney, I need to ask you something," my mother whispered.

I could tell she was walking outside when I heard the screen door opening.

"Sure."

"Your brother was acting weird. Even Meg noticed it. Do you think he is having second thoughts?"

I smiled and shook my head. "No, Mom. He's just nervous. He acted weird to me, too, before he left. I think he will be fine after the ceremony, and I'll be able to kick his ass for being rude to Reed."

My mother let out a sigh. "Yes. I'm still upset that he did that to Reed. It's just not like your brother. It's almost like he was…hiding something."

My stomach dropped, and I had the same feeling sweep over my body as I had earlier. "Yeah. I thought the same thing, but…everything will be okay, Mom."

"Courtney, he wouldn't tell Meg who he is staying with. She's beginning to have things run through her mind, and I don't know what to tell her."

"Why didn't he tell her?" I asked as I looked at Reed nodding off to sleep. *Great. There goes any hope of sex for me tonight.*

"I'm not sure why he wouldn't tell her. She is trying to act like it doesn't bother her, but I know it does. She almost seems—"

"What? She almost seems what?"

My mother let out a sigh and said, "Never mind. I think I'm just a nervous wreck. Is it wrong I'm secretly hoping Sissy elopes like you did?"

I let out a gentle laugh, so I wouldn't wake up Reed. "Nope, not at all. I'm heading to bed, Mom. I love you. Night."

"Night, sweetie. Sleep good," she said with an evil little laugh.

I could almost picture her wiggling her eyebrows up and down.

"Night, Mom."

I hit End and set my phone on the side table. I turned to look at my passed-out husband. I watched his chest moving up and down. Each breath caused me to relax more and more until I could no longer keep my eyes open. As sleep took over, the pit in my stomach slowly started to go away.

He's not here, Courtney. He can't hurt you anymore.

The wedding was starting in two hours, and I was pretty sure my mother was going to have a breakdown. Meg had been too quiet all day, so I made my way up to my parents' room where she was getting her hair done.

I knocked on the door and barely heard her say, "Come in."

I opened the door to see her sitting there, alone, staring out the window. When she looked at me, she gave me a weak smile.

"Hey, you. Is everything okay?"

She patted lightly on the seat next to her. As I walked over toward her, I couldn't help but notice how sad she looked.

I'd known Meg since high school. She was a year older than me and a year younger than my brother. They had been dating since Tyler's senior year and her junior year of high school.

I sat down and followed her gaze. I wasn't sure how long we sat there before she began talking.

"Have you ever carried a secret so dark that you felt like you were drowning in it?"

I snapped my head over at her. *Does she know?* I quickly looked away and nodded my head as I said, "Yes."

Now, it was her turn to look at me. "Sometimes, I just want to run away."

I looked at her and gave her a weak smile. "Are you having second thoughts?"

She looked down and said, "I don't deserve your brother."

"What? Meg, of course you do. He's damn lucky to have you. How you put up with his ass, I'll never know."

She laughed slightly and said, "I've tried talking him into moving to Texas. I just want to leave New York. I hate it here." She looked back out the window. "The memories here are too…painful."

I grabbed her hand and held on to it as I took a deep breath. "Meg, is there something you want to talk about?"

She turned, and when I saw the tears in her eyes, I caught my breath.

"Something happened. It was a few years back, but I never told Tyler, and the guilt is killing me."

My heart started pounding. "Did you cheat on him?"

Her eyes widened, and she shook her head. "No! God, I would never do that to Tyler." She quickly wiped the tears away. "I've never told anyone, and I just can't do this anymore. I'm so scared, Courtney."

"You can trust me, Meg. I promise you."

She was just about to start talking when the door opened, and my mother, Sissy, and Meg's mom all walked in.

"Oh hell, Megan, your eyes are going to be all puffy now." Meg's mother stood there with her hands on her hips, looking at her daughter, clearly not caring that her daughter was upset.

Meg pulled her hand from mine and stood up. She wiped away any evidence of sadness and replaced it with a smile. I recognized that smile. I'd seen it a million times on my own face.

"Sorry, Mama."

She started to walk away, but I grabbed her hand. She gave me a look, and I dropped her hand.

Sissy walked up to me and whispered, "Those did not look like happy tears. Is everything okay, Court?"

I gave her a reassuring smile and said, "Nerves, that's all."

I had tried to talk to Meg again, but we were never alone. Now, it was nothing but running back and forth between rooms, getting hair and makeup done. Sissy was zipping up my dress when little Lizzie Sue, the flower girl, walked up to me.

I bent down, and she said, "Um…Weed is waiting for you in the libwary."

I smiled and said, "Thank you for letting me know, angel."

I stood up, and Sissy turned her back to me, so I could get her zipper.

"Lucky bitch. I wish I had weed waiting for me. I don't smoke the shit, but if Mom doesn't cut out the crazy-ass behavior, I'm going to be picking it up."

I hit her shoulder and laughed. "Reed is waiting, Sis, not weed."

She turned and winked at me. "I knew what she meant. You better hurry if you want to sneak in a quick fuck."

My mouth dropped open as I stared at her. "Oh. My. God. Really?"

She shrugged her shoulders and said, "Listen, I'm just saying if my hotter-than-hell husband was waiting for me downstairs, you better believe I'd be ditching my panties on the way down." She turned and walked over to our mother but not before turning and winking at me. She held up her hand and mouthed, *Five minutes.*

I hugged myself as I headed to the hall bathroom and followed my little sister's advice. I walked into the library, closed the door behind me, and locked it. It was dark in there since my father had the curtains drawn.

"Reed? Baby, I got your message, and I have a little surprise for you."

I saw someone move in the corner. I smiled as I made my way over. I stopped when I saw Noah step out into the small amount of light coming in through the curtains.

No.

"It's been a long time, Courtney. I've missed you."

I just stood there, frozen. I willed my feet to move, but I couldn't. "Wha-what are you doing here?"

"Funny how I had a change of plans right at the last minute, isn't it?"

I shook my head as I took a step back.

"You see, I knew you wouldn't come to the wedding if you knew I was going to be here, so I hatched up the whole being-out-of-town-for-the-wedding excuse. I knew Meg would never change the date even though Tyler had asked her to so that his very best friend wouldn't have to miss the wedding. That fucking bitch hates me. She tries everything she can to keep Tyler and me apart."

My head began spinning. "Does Tyler know you're here?" I whispered.

He threw his head back and laughed as he took another step toward me. "Of course he does. Who do you think threw his party last night? He stayed at my house last night, too. Naturally, I asked him not to tell you about me being here. With our history and all, I told him you would be upset, and I just wanted to get through this as easily as possible. You know…with how you devastated me and all by breaking up with me."

I went to turn and walk away, but he grabbed me and spun me around. He held on to my shoulders and began backing me up until I hit the wall.

"You're crazy. We were *never* together! Let me go, or I'll scream."

"Now, Court, if you scream, you'll regret it. Did Tyler happen to mention that I've taken Sissy out? We went out twice, and she sure is a sweet little thing even though she's a few years younger than me. I'm now engaged though. Sweet girl, Lilly is, but she sure isn't you."

I looked at him, confused. "Stay away from my sister."

Noah laughed. "Please. Your sister is a bitch. I have no interest in her at all."

I let out a sob and placed my hand on my stomach.

He looked down, and when he looked back into my eyes, his eyes were filled with anger. "You let him get you pregnant, you bitch. You. Are. Mine. You've always been mine, Courtney. I was your first."

I closed my eyes and prayed Reed would come find me. "Please…please just let me go."

He grabbed my face and got so close to me that I could feel his hot breath and smell the alcohol. "Did you tell that fucker about us?"

I closed my eyes as he squeezed harder, and I let out a small whimper.

"Look at me."

I opened my eyes and tried to smile. "Yes."

He laughed and whispered, "Liar. Don't fucking lie to me, you bitch!"

He placed his hand on my stomach, and I pushed it away.

"Don't touch me."

He grabbed my hands and put them over my head as he held on to them with one hand.

Fuck. He is so strong.

He used his finger and began moving it along my cleavage.

"Please stop," I whispered.

He moved his hand down my body, and my eyes snapped shut. I forgot that I had taken my panties off. He reached his hand up under my dress and slowly started to touch my inner thigh.

"Reed, please…I need you," I whispered.

Noah instantly stopped moving his hand. "What in the fuck did you just say?" He pulled his hand out and grabbed my face again before he began trying to kiss me.

I tried turning my head. The moment his lips touched mine, I wanted to throw up.

Reed! Please, Reed, help me! I need you!

In that one second, I knew what I had to do. I needed to show Noah that he could no longer control me.

Reed…I need you…please hurry.

TWENTY-SIX

REED

I walked down the hallway, heading back to Court's bedroom. I had left my Kindle in her room, and I wanted to make sure I got it before we left to head back to Texas. A bedroom door opened, and Sissy ran right into me.

"Shit," we both said as we hit each other hard.

"Damn it, Reed! What in the hell?"

I laughed and said, "Sorry, Sissy. I was heading to Courtney's room to get my Kindle that I'd left here. I don't want to forget it."

She smiled and said, "Wow, are you two done already? That was fast."

My smile faded as I looked at her, confused. "What do you mean?"

"You and Court…you know…getting it on in the library. She got your message to meet her in there."

My heart dropped to my stomach. "I never sent her a message to meet me in the…" I turned and started running down the stairs.

"Reed? If it wasn't you, who was it?"

I called back, "Oh God…Noah's here. I have to get to Courtney."

Sissy started running after me. "Why?"

I ran down the stairs as fast as I could. I stopped and looked at Sissy. "Shit! Where is the library?"

She just stood there, looking at me, confused.

I grabbed her shoulders. "Sissy. *Please.* Your sister is in danger. Please tell me where it is."

Her face dropped, and she took off running down a hall as I followed her. We ran right by Tyler, and I almost knocked him over.

"What the fuck? What's going on?"

Sissy said as she pointed, "Last door on the left, but, Reed…"

I ran past her and tried the door. It was locked. I stepped back and kicked it open. As soon as I walked in, I looked to my left, and a guy was doubled over, holding himself.

"You fucking bitch!" he yelled out.

"Courtney!" I yelled.

She let out a scream and ran to me. "I knew you would come for me! I knew you would come!"

She slammed into my body, and I held her. I looked at the fucker as he stood up. He gave me a smile as he ran his hand through his hair. I pushed Courtney back and looked her up and down.

"What in the fuck is going on here? Someone please tell me!" Sissy said.

"Baby, are you hurt? Did he touch you anywhere?"

Courtney began shaking her head quickly. "No, but he almost…he almost…oh God, Reed, thank God you showed up when you did. I didn't know what else to do, so I kicked him. He almost…he had his hand up my dress with my hands pinned above…above…" She began crying again.

I turned around and motioned for Sissy. "Take care of her for me, please."

Sissy grabbed Courtney, who was crying hysterically.

Court reached for me and yelled out, "Reed, no! He's not worth it."

I turned back to see that Noah was beginning to walk toward the door.

Tyler walked into the library, took one look around, and asked, "What in the hell is going on?"

Noah laughed. "Nothing. Your sister wanted to talk to me, and—"

I lost it. "You lying piece of fucking shit." I launched myself at him and grabbed him before he could move. I pulled my fist back and hit as hard as I could.

He stumbled back and fell but quickly jumped up.

From the corner of my eye, I saw Meg come in.

"We heard someone scream, and—oh my God. What are you doing here, Noah?"

Noah turned, looked at her, and winked. When I looked at the expression on Meg's face, it felt like I was looking at Courtney all over again. She had the same look of fear on her face.

I turned back and looked at Noah. "You son of a bitch."

I jumped on him, knocking him to the ground. I just began hitting him over and over again as I heard Courtney, Meg, Tyler, and Marie yelling for me to stop. Tyler tried to pull me off Noah, but there was no way I was letting this asshole get away with what he had done to Courtney.

"Courtney, stop your husband, for God's sake!" Tyler yelled.

I kept hitting the son of a bitch over and over again. Each hit was for Courtney and the pain he'd caused her. Before I knew it, four guys, including Tyler and Steve, were holding me back as Marie was helping Noah up.

Marie turned, looked at me, and asked, "Why? Why would you do this, Reed?"

I looked at Courtney, who was just standing there, stunned. I faced Meg, who was now crying. She looked at Courtney and put her hand up to her mouth.

She walked over to Courtney and placed her hand on Courtney's shoulder. "Oh my God, Courtney. Did Noah do it to you, too?"

My knees felt weak, and the guys holding me back were now actually holding me up.

Courtney snapped her head and looked at Meg. "Is that what you were talking about earlier?" she barely said.

Meg slowly nodded her head.

Tyler said, "What in the hell are you two talking about?"

"How old were you, Courtney?" Meg asked.

Courtney looked at me before looking back at Meg. "Sixteen."

Meg sucked in a breath of air and began saying, "Oh God, no." She turned toward Noah and walked up to him. She began hitting him on the chest as she screamed over and over, "How could you, you dirty rotten bastard? She was a baby!"

Marie stood there, stunned. Tyler let go of me and grabbed Meg, who was still screaming at Noah.

"Meg! Meg, what are you talking about?" Tyler held on to Meg as she dropped to the floor, crying.

I just noticed that she was wearing her wedding dress. She had been minutes away from getting married.

"Reed, if we let you go, will you please stay calm until we figure out what is going on?" Steve said.

I nodded my head and stared at Noah, who looked scared shitless.

Tyler was pushing pieces of hair out of Meg's face as she cried. I looked at Courtney. Sissy was still holding her, and I thought Sissy was the only one who had put two and two together because she was now crying.

"He's a monster. I've tried telling you so many times, but he kept threatening me," Meg said in between sobs.

"Who, baby? Noah?" Tyler looked up at Noah.

Tyler looked back at Meg when she said, "Yes. He said you'd hate me if you found out."

Tyler's head snapped back to Noah. "What did you do?" Tyler hissed through his teeth.

Noah stood there in silence.

Tyler pulled Meg's chin up and whispered, "Baby, please tell me what is going on."

Meg looked at Courtney, who seemed to be in shock.

Shit. Her whole family is about to find out what happened to her.

"Noah…he…he forced me…and Courtney…to have sex with him. Oh God, Tyler…Courtney was only sixteen! I was at least older. He threatened…he said…he would hurt you if I said anything."

Courtney let out a loud cry and began falling to the floor. I quickly ran to her and grabbed her as Courtney began crying hysterically.

"Baby, I'm here. I promise you, he will never touch you again. I promise you," I said as I held her to me.

Tyler tried to stand up but stumbled backward. "Noah, is it true?"

Noah wiped the blood from his mouth and said, "Courtney wanted me. I saw it in her eyes."

I was about to go after him again, but Courtney grabbed me tighter, and before I knew it, Tyler was on top of Noah, beating the hell out of him.

Steve pulled Tyler off of Noah while Tyler screamed, "That's my baby sister! You motherfucker! What did you do to my sister and Meg? I'll kill you!"

"Get Tyler out of here now!" Steve yelled at the other guys standing there in shock. "Marie, get Meg and Courtney out of here."

Marie had tears running down her face as she and Sissy helped Meg up. I slowly picked up Courtney and carried her out of the room. She was crying so hard that she seemed to be having a hard time breathing. I followed Sissy into the living room and set Courtney down on the sofa.

I placed my hands on her face and made her look into my eyes. "Angel, I need to go back into the library, okay?"

She grabbed my hands and shook her head.

I wiped her tears away with my thumbs and brought her forehead down to my lips. "I promise you, I will be right back, but your father cannot be alone with Noah, okay?"

She just continued to cry as she looked into my eyes.

"I promise you." I looked up at Sissy and said, "Will you stay with her?"

She quickly wiped away her tears and sat down next to Courtney.

I turned to head back to the library when Sissy called after me. "Reed?"

I turned around and looked at her.

"Please don't let my father do something stupid."

I nodded my head as I gave her a weak smile. I spun around and headed back toward the man I wanted to kill more than anything.

As I walked by the kitchen, Tyler was arguing with a few of his friends. "Just let me go. I just want to go see Meg and my sister. Please just let me go."

My heart broke for him. His fiancée and his sister were both victims of this fucker.

The library door was open, and when I walked in, I saw Noah sitting in a chair as Steve was talking to some guy I'd never seen before. The guy looked up at me and then nodded before he started walking out. Steve turned and saw me. As the guy passed by me, he placed his hand on my shoulder and gave me a caring look. I smiled back and gave a quick nod in return.

"Reed, shut and lock the door, please," Steve said.

I glanced over at Noah. He had a terrified look on his face, and I almost wanted to smile. I did as Steve had asked. I stood back away from both of them. If I got too close to the asshole, I'd just want to beat the shit out of him again.

Noah looked at me and smiled. I balled my fists together and looked at Steve before glaring back at Noah.

"What in the fuck are you smiling at?" I asked Noah.

Noah's smile faded as he looked everywhere but at Steve.

"I want to know what you did to my daughter," Steve said through gritted teeth as he sat down in front of Noah.

"Nothing she didn't want," Noah bit back.

I started making my way over to him. "You motherfucker! She was sixteen, for fuck's sake!"

Steve held up his hand to stop me. "Don't worry, Reed. I'm going to make sure you have some alone time with this lowlife. Just give me my time."

I stopped and barely said, "Yes, sir."

"I'm going to ask you again. What did you do to my daughter?"

Nothing.

Noah wasn't saying a word.

I cleared my throat and said, "I know what he did to her, Steve."

Without ever taking his eyes off of Noah, he said, "Tell me."

I swallowed hard and took a deep breath. "Court just turned sixteen, and Noah had asked her to the prom. He snuck into her room and told her he was going to have sex with her because he saw the way she would look at him, and he had waited until she got older. He threatened her by saying he would hurt Tyler, you, Marie, and worse yet…he would go after Sissy." I stopped talking when I saw Steve making fists.

"How long did it go on for?"

"Three months."

Steve's head dropped, and his shoulders began shaking. I fought like hell to hold back my tears. I tried to place myself in his shoes, but I couldn't. As much as I wanted to kill this fucker, I couldn't imagine how Steve felt.

I sucked in another breath and continued, "One night, Courtney went down to your gun safe. She got out a pistol and waited for him. When he came into her room, she told him she would kill him, and if she had to sit outside Sissy's door every night, she would. She told me Noah stopped staying over, and Tyler would instead stay at Noah's house when his parents were out of town."

Steve sucked in a shaky breath. "Did you ever touch Sissy?"

Noah looked up at me. "She told you everything?"

I nodded my head, and he looked away.

Steve yelled, "Did. You. Touch. Sissy?"

"No. Never."

I was pretty sure Steve and I both let out the breath we had been holding, but I didn't trust this bastard.

"The only reason I'm not walking over to my gun safe right now is because I love my family, and they need me. Otherwise, you'd be dead right now."

Noah's face dropped, and I could see the sweat running down his forehead.

"If I so much as ever see your face or find out you are attempting to talk to anyone in my family, I'll find some way to make it happen. Do you understand me?"

Noah nodded his head and whispered, "I understand you. What are you going to do?"

Steve stood up and turned to look at me. "I'm going to leave you alone with the man who loves my daughter, and you better pray the police get here fast."

"Think about Courtney," Steve said to me as he made his way past me and to the door.

As the door shut, I turned and looked at Noah. He just stared at me as I made my way over to the same chair Steve had been sitting in.

"Why don't you just get it over with?" he said as he looked away.

I sat down in the chair and let out a gruff laugh. "Believe me, asshole, I'd like to beat you until you're barely breathing."

He gave me a cocky smile and said, "Then, why don't you?"

"Because I love Courtney, and I won't do anything to harm our future. Besides, I'm the winner in this."

"You're the winner? How do you figure?" Noah said as he touched the side of his eye that I had split open when I hit him over and over.

"I'm married to the most amazing woman, and we're going to have a baby in April. I'm going to give her everything she has ever dreamed of. I'm going to make love to her every single chance I get. Each morning and each night, I'm going to cover her in kisses while I tell her how much I love her. I'm never going to take her love for granted, and I will adore her always."

He smirked and said, "I'll always be her first."

I jumped up and grabbed him by the shirt as I got in his face. "You were never her first. You were nothing but a nightmare that I intend on making sure she never has to worry about again. I swear to God, if you ever attempt to contact her, you will regret it. I would go to jail for the rest of my life to protect her and my child."

Noah quickly looked away.

"Do you understand how lucky you are? There are three men here right now who would love to kill you. I suggest you leave and never look back."

The door opened, and Noah's head snapped up. He closed his eyes as he dropped his head.

"Reed?"

I took a few steps back and turned around to leave. There was another man standing next to Steve. He looked like an older version of Noah.

"Noah's father is here. Courtney is asking for you."

I nodded my head and walked past the two men. As I made my way out, I turned in the opposite direction of where Courtney was and made my way to the guest bathroom. I shut the door and turned on the cold water. I splashed water on my face over and over again as I lost it and began crying.

After a few minutes of trying to get my breathing under control, I heard a knock on the door. I cleared my throat and held out my hands. They were barely shaking now, so I opened the door. Marie and Steve were standing there.

"Courtney is asking to leave, Reed," Marie said as she wiped a tear away. "Oh God. I only wish we had known."

Marie broke down crying as she fell into Steve's arms. He looked at me, and I gave him a knowing nod. I knew exactly how he felt. He just wanted to take all their pain away.

"I'm going to get Court and take her back to the hotel."

Steve nodded and began walking with Marie.

As I headed to the living room, I heard Tyler and Meg talking. My heart ached for them. It was supposed to be one of the happiest days of their lives, and it had turned out to be nothing but a nightmare.

I walked past the kitchen, and Tyler called out for me, "Reed! Please…wait."

I stopped and took a deep breath.

"I just wanted to say I'm sorry. If I had just known what Noah had done, and…I mean…" He began choking back a sob. "He asked me not to tell Meg, but that didn't surprise me because Meg had made it known that she didn't like Noah, but I…I didn't…fuck. He didn't want me to let Court know he was here either, and now, looking back, I fucked up so bad. I don't know why I didn't see the signs." He fell back against the wall and said, "My own sister and girlfriend. Oh God…"

I placed my hand on his shoulder and said, "I think you and Meg should spend some time alone together. If she hasn't talked to anyone about this, she is really going to need you now more than ever."

He nodded his head. "Court won't talk to me. She wouldn't talk to anyone but Mom, Dad, and Sissy. Do you think she hates me, Reed?"

I shook my head and gave him a weak smile. "No, Tyler. She just needs some time. Just give her some time."

He slowly nodded his head and attempted to give me a smile.

"Listen, I need to get Court out of here. Is Meg okay?" I asked as I looked around him and into the kitchen. I was guessing it was her mother and father who were in there with her.

Tyler looked back at Meg and said, "Yes and no. But we're gonna be okay. I'll do everything in my power to help her in whatever way she needs."

"I know you will." I reached out my hand and shook his before I headed to my girl.

She was curled up on the sofa, and Sissy was sitting on the floor. Courtney was running her fingers through Sissy's hair. When Sissy saw me, she turned, gave Courtney a kiss on the cheek, and whispered something to her.

Sissy walked up to me and gave me a hug. "Please take care of her."

I brushed away the single tear from her cheek and smiled. "Forever and always."

I gave her a kiss on the cheek and then made my way over to my angel. I bent down and ran the back of my hand down the side of her face. When she smiled, my heart began pounding harder.

She sat up and said, "I need to get out of the house."

I reached for her hand and helped her up. I reached down and swooped her up into my arms.

She let out a little giggle. "I can walk, you know."

I winked at her and said, "Any reason to have you in my arms, and I'm taking it."

We walked through the house and out to the rental car. I placed her into the passenger seat and walked around the front of the car. I knew exactly what I was going to do next.

TWENTY-SEVEN

Reed and I drove back to the hotel in silence. Every time he came to a stoplight, he picked up his phone and texted someone. I didn't want to close my eyes because every time I did, I saw Noah. I wanted to ask him what he'd said to Noah when they were alone, but the faster I forgot about what had happened, the better.

Reed reached for my hand, and I felt those familiar goose bumps cover my body. He rubbed his thumb back and forth on the back of my hand, and with every motion, I began to relax.

Reed pulled up to the valet and said, "We'll be right back down. We're just changing."

I looked at him, confused. All I wanted to do was crawl into bed and go to sleep. Reed smiled at me as we walked into the hotel. Making our way over to the elevator, I looked up at him. He was smiling from ear to ear.

"Reed, I'm so tired. Where are we going?" I said with a whine.

He squeezed my hand and motioned for me to get in the elevator. "Somewhere fun," he said as he pushed the button for our floor.

"I don't want to do something fun. I just want to crawl into bed and sleep."

He looked down at me. "I know you do, babe. I know. Will you please just trust me on this?"

I wanted to argue with him, but I just didn't have it in me. I was emotionally exhausted and honestly too tired to care. We walked into the hotel room, and I made my way over to the bed and collapsed. I watched as Reed got undressed and quickly slipped on a pair of jeans. He slipped on a T-shirt and then put on his sneakers.

He looked at me and said, "Come on. Change out of that dress and put on something comfortable."

I stood up and stomped my foot before I began taking my dress off. It wasn't lost on me that Reed was staying across the room.

He always at least touches me when I get undressed.

What if he is appalled at the idea of Noah touching me? What if Reed thinks I let Noah touch me?

I slowly turned and walked over to my suitcase. I pulled out a pair of Victoria's Secret sweatpants and a long-sleeved T-shirt. I slipped them both on and fought like hell to keep the tears at bay. I instantly felt calmer when Reed wrapped his arms around me.

"I know what you're thinking, and please stop. The only reason I stood on the other side of the room is because I knew if I was close to you when you undressed, I'd want to make love to you."

I dropped my head back onto his chest. "Please, Reed. I need you, and nothing makes me feel better than being with you."

He leaned down and kissed my cheek as he slipped his hand down my pants. "Put your leg on the bed, Courtney," he whispered in my ear.

I did what he'd said, and the moment his fingers swept across my lips, I let out a moan.

"I'm going to make you come, Courtney, and then we're leaving, okay?"

I nodded my head as I bit down on my lower lip. Reed slipped his fingers inside me and began moving in and out slowly.

"Faster," I said as I pushed my hips into his hand.

He brushed his thumb against my clit, and I let out a long moan.

"Yes. Oh God, that feels so good."

When he began moving faster and his thumb pressed just a little harder, I came hard and fast. I felt my leg wobble, but Reed grabbed on to me and held me while I fell apart with my orgasm.

He kissed along my neck and then nibbled on my earlobe. "Did that help?"

"A little," I said as I turned and wrapped my arms around his neck.

He leaned down and began kissing me so sweetly. I wanted it to be more passionate, but he pulled away, reaching up and removing my arms from his neck.

"Come on, we're late."

I looked at him, confused. "For what? We should be at a wedding, so I know damn well you didn't make plans for tonight."

He let out a laugh as he opened the door to our room. He waited for me to walk out.

As we rode the elevator down, I noticed he was texting someone. I wanted to ask, but a part of me was worried he had been talking to Layton. I hadn't grabbed my purse, so I didn't have my phone. I knew if Whit had found out what had happened, she would be calling, and I really didn't feel like talking. After telling my parents everything and seeing them both cry and blame themselves, I knew I couldn't take any more tonight. As I sat down in the car I put my head back and closed my eyes as I thought back to Reed making love to me for the first time.

I felt Reed put his hand on my leg, and I slowly opened my eyes and looked around. "Shit. I fell asleep."

Reed let out a chuckle and got out of the car. He walked around to my side and opened the door. When I got out, I noticed where we were.

I gave him a confused look. "Laser tag?"

He smiled and nodded his head. "You said one of your favorite things to do was play laser tag against your brother. So, we're about to go kick some serious ass. It's couple against couple."

I looked back toward the laser tag entrance and let out a gasp. My parents, Tyler, Meg, Sissy, some guy I didn't know, and one of Tyler's friends with his wife were all standing there, talking.

I put my hand up to my mouth and turned to look at Reed. "You planned this? When?"

He smiled and let out a small laugh. "On the way to the hotel, I sent a text to Tyler and asked if he felt like having a little bit of fun."

I threw myself into his body and held my tears back. "I love you, Reed Moore. I love you so damn much!"

"I love you, too, angel."

I pulled back, and Reed lifted my chin up and looked into my eyes. "Swoon-worthy?"

I let out a giggle and said, "Very swoon-worthy."

We walked up to the entrance, and Tyler walked up to me and took me into his arms. We didn't say anything to each other, and no one else said a word.

When I finally pulled back, I smiled and kissed Tyler on the cheek. "Reed and I are going to kick your *ass*."

Tyler threw his head back and laughed and then looked at Meg. "Oh, I beg to differ, but bring it on, baby sister…bring it on."

My father let out a gruff laugh. "Please, your mother and I might not seem like we can keep up with you guys, but trust me, you're all going to be eating our dust."

My mother did a weird little fist pump and yelled, "Yeah! Eat our dust!"

Everyone laughed as we made our way into the building. I glanced over at Reed, who winked at me and gave me a thumbs-up.

How did I get so lucky with him?

I wanted to ask him what he'd said to Noah when they were alone, but the faster I forgot about what had happened, the better.

I wasn't the least bit shocked when we got in there, and Reed pulled me off to the side to give me the strategy on how we were going to take everyone down.

"If you have to, use the I'm-pregnant card on your mother, father, and your brother only. Anyone else is not going to care."

I nodded and said, "Got it."

Reed went over the hand signals, and we even made up our own little handshake.

"What? Do you have a damn team cheer also?" Tyler said as he walked by.

Meg was smiling from ear to ear, and my heart just broke for her. She should be dancing at her wedding right now. I hit Tyler on the shoulder, and Reed and I took off in different directions.

I wasn't sure how long we had played, but Reed and I made one hell of a good team. When we won four games in a row, Sissy declared that she and her friend Ryan were officially quitting. My parents had given up after two games. Now, it was down to Reed and me, Tyler and Meg, and Tyler's friend and his wife.

I ran around a corner, and Tyler was standing there.

I almost panicked but played it cool. "Oh my God! I just felt the baby move!" I yelled out.

Tyler dropped his gun down to his side and said, "What? I want to feel."

As soon as he took a step closer, I started shooting the shit out of him. I let out an evil laugh and took off running.

Reed and I met up in our meeting place, both of us fighting to catch our breath.

"They're dropping like flies," Reed said between pants.

Reed and Tyler were really getting into this. I smiled, just thinking of how Reed was kicking Ty's ass.

Oh, how I love my husband.

"Ty's friend's wife said she was bored, so they stopped playing, and now, the only other couple is Tyler and Meg," I said.

Reed gave me a quick peck on the lips and said, "Let's get these bastards!"

I gave him a funny look, shrugged, and said, "Okay! Let's do this! Brother or not, he's got to go down."

And down he went. With my little stunt I'd pulled about feeling the baby move, it pretty much sealed the deal for us. When we won the last game, Reed and I might have celebrated a little too much.

As we walked out of laser tag, my parents were making arrangements for everyone to go to dinner.

"Mr. and Mrs. Will, I've already made dinner arrangements for all of us," Reed said.

I smiled at him. I wanted to attack him and cover him in kisses. Reed looked at me and smiled as my heart thumped in my chest.

Meg walked up to me and hooked her arm through mine as we walked toward the rental car.

"I'm so sorry, Meg. Maybe if I had said something, he wouldn't have touched you."

She gave me a weak smile and said, "No, Courtney. Don't say that. None of this is your fault or my fault. Please don't ever think that, okay? I'm just ready to move on, and knowing he will be forever out of my life is amazing. He's finally going to get what he deserves."

I couldn't even begin to understand how it had been for Meg to see Noah day in and day out, having him over for dinners, parties, vacations. *Yuck.*

By the time we got back to the hotel, I was spent. I looked into the mirror and frowned. *I look like shit.* My hair was pulled up in a sloppy ponytail, and I was dressed like I'd just rolled out of bed. I could see the pain buried in my eyes, and I closed them in hopes that when I opened them, everything with Noah would just be a dream.

The moment I felt Reed's arms wrap around me, the love just flowed from his body into mine.

"You're so beautiful," he whispered against my neck.

I let out a giggle and opened my eyes to see him staring at me in the mirror. "You must be looking at a different reflection than me," I said with a weak smile.

He pulled his head back while he looked my body up and down in the mirror and slowly shook his head. "The reflection I see is the most amazing woman I've ever met, one who has such an incredible passion for life and love. I see the most beautiful woman I've ever laid my eyes on. I see the mother of my children, the woman I'm going to spend the rest of my life with, and the woman who—for some crazy reason—took a chance on love with me. I also see the luckiest man on earth standing next to her."

I bit down on my lower lip and closed my eyes as I sank back into his body. "I love you, Reed. I knew you would come for me. I knew you wouldn't let him hurt me again."

He turned me around and held on to me while I cried. I wanted to forget everything that had happened, but I couldn't until I talked to him about it.

"He was going to touch me, and there was no way I could let him. I was pleading with him to stop while I was praying for you to find me and make him stop."

Reed sucked in a breath of air. "I'm sorry it happened in the first place, baby. I'm so sorry."

I placed my hands on the sides of his face. "Don't say you're sorry. Just tell me he is forever gone from my life."

He placed his hands on mine and smiled. "I promise you, he will never bother you ever again. I promise you, baby."

When I saw the tear roll down his cheek, my heart exploded. I'd never loved anyone like I loved Reed, and I knew I never would.

As I showered and got dressed for dinner, I was beginning to long for Texas. New York no longer felt like home. Texas was home now, and all I wanted to do was sit on my front porch, crochet my blanket, and drink some tea as I watched my sexier-than-hell cowboy work on a fence or do some cowboy shit like that.

"What are you thinking about?" Reed asked as he pulled the rental car up to the valet parking at the restaurant.

I shrugged my shoulders. "I'm just sad that Tyler's wedding was ruined."

Reed gave me a smile that caused my breath to stop. He quickly placed his hand behind my neck and pulled me in for a kiss. "Ya never know…this might just turn out to be one of the best days of Tyler's and Meg's lives."

"Yeah. Maybe."

We got out of the car and made our way into the restaurant.

Reed walked up to the hostess and said, "Hi. Reed Moore. I called earlier."

The young lady smiled bigger and looked at me. I smiled and wondered what in the hell Reed was up to.

"Mr. Moore, yes. It was tough, but we managed to get it all down." She turned to another girl and said, "Please show Mr. and Mrs. Moore upstairs to the private dining room."

Private dining room?

"Reed, what is going on?" I asked as I began looking around for my parents, Tyler, or Sissy.

Reed grabbed my hand and practically pulled me up the stairs. When we walked into the large banquet room, I let out a gasp. One side of the room looked out to the mountains. It was breathtaking. I quickly looked around and saw the whole room was filled with white lights and all the flowers from my parents' house. My mouth dropped open when I saw all the tables had been set up, and on the far side of the room was the arbor that had also been at my parents' house. And Father Mike was standing there, talking to Tyler's friend, Bob.

Bob saw Reed and started walking up to him. "Man, it's a good thing you had everyone at laser tag, so we could get everything out of the house and here. We just told Tyler that we took it all out. We didn't tell him why or where we were taking it."

Reed nodded his head and looked around. "Thanks for picking such an amazing place," he said.

I stood there in shock.

"Ty asked Meg to marry him here, so Kat and I thought it would be the perfect place."

I shook my head to clear my thoughts. "Wait. Just wait one second. Reed, what in the world is going on here?"

Reed looked down at me and said, "My heart broke for Meg and Tyler. I got Bob's cell phone number earlier this morning, and after everything went down, I asked him if he wanted to help me pull this off."

I bit down on my lower lip, fighting to keep back the tears that were forming. "You did all this? You planned everything? Why? Reed, why would you do all of this?"

Reed shook his head as he reached down and gave me a kiss. His lips were still against mine when he whispered, "Because I love you. I did this for you and your family because I love you, Courtney."

I choked back a sob and pulled away. I looked around and asked a waitress where the restrooms were.

She pointed to the other side of the room and said, "Back right corner."

I grabbed Reed's hand and pulled him in that direction. I walked up and scanned each door. *Perfect.* I walked into the family restroom, pulling Reed in with me. I shut the door and locked it. I quickly spun around and found myself looking into Reed's very confused eyes.

"Please tell me you aren't mad, Court. I thought I was—"

I held up my hand for him to stop talking. "I'm so happy I decided to wear a dress this evening."

Reed tilted his head, looking more confused than ever. "What? Court, are you angry with me?"

I shook my head as I reached up under my dress and slowly pulled my white lace panties off. I never took my eyes off of Reed.

He licked his lips and said, "Wha-what are you doing, Court?"

I bit down on my lip and whispered, "I need my husband—now."

Before I knew what was happening, Reed was all over me. His hands were on every inch of my body, moving frantically, like he couldn't get enough of me. He pushed the dress all the way up and over my head while he used his other hand to push my bra up, releasing my breasts in one movement, causing me to let out a moan. He quickly put one nipple in his mouth and began sucking and gently biting on it as I unbuttoned his pants and exposed him to me. I grabbed on to his length and felt it throbbing in my hand. He let go of my nipple and picked me up as he pushed me against the wall. I wrapped my legs around him and moaned when I pushed myself against him. I needed relief, and only Reed could provide it.

He placed his tip just at my entrance while he held me up. "Court? Are you sure you want to do this? I mean, here?"

I looked into his eyes and said, "I need you so much, Reed. *Please*."

I bucked my hips into him, and the look in his eyes changed to nothing but pure lust. Seeing it turned me on even more, and when he pushed himself inside me, I had to attempt to hold back the scream I wanted to let out.

"This is gonna be fast," Reed said as he began moving in and out of me, hard and fast.

"Yes! Oh God, yes, Reed," I whispered as I dropped my head back against the wall. I bit down hard on my lip. I could feel the buildup, and all it was going to take was one more—

Reed pushed into me hard and deep, and I lost it. I grabbed on to him and began moving my hips along with him. My orgasm hit me so hard and so fast that I let out a whimper as Reed hissed through his teeth and came with me.

He stood there for a minute, not moving, while he caught his breath. He gently put me down and zipped up his pants, never once looking anywhere but in my eyes. My chest was heaving up and down, and I was desperately trying to catch my breath. Reed turned and grabbed a handful of toilet paper. He bent down and lifted my leg as he began cleaning me.

"It feels so good when you touch me," I whispered.

Reed stood up and turned to throw the paper out. He walked up to me and placed his hands on either side of my head as he leaned closer.

"This makes two wedding days when we've had sex in a public place."

He held my panties out in front of me while I chuckled and hugged myself inside.

"We totally have Layton and Whitley beat!" I said as I raised my eyebrows.

Reed laughed.

I walked up and looked in the mirror as I fixed my hair. Spinning around, I took my panties and shoved them into his pocket. "Better keep it easy access…just in case."

Reed let out a small whimper as I reached for the door and opened it quickly. I glanced back at Reed as I made my way out of the restroom and into the hallway. I ran into someone and turned to see my sister, Sissy, standing there with her mouth hanging open.

"Dear God Almighty. Did you…did you guys just…in the restroom?" She kept looking back and forth between Reed and me. She put her hands on her hips and said, "Here you ask me for help, and I bust my ass to get here and make sure all is ready, and you're making fun with my sister…in a public restroom?"

I smirked at my sister as I grabbed Reed's hand and started to move us past her. "Wasn't nearly as hot as having sex in a nightclub in a dark corner," I said.

Sissy let out a gasp as we kept walking. I did a little inner jump and fist pump.

"What? Seventy-five Hail Marys and a gazillion Our Fathers! You can't say that and walk away from me! Court? Courtney!"

Reed dropped my hand and placed his arm around my waist and said, "Why do I get the feeling that being married to you is going to be nothing but an adventure?"

I peeked up at him with a coy smile and said, "Hold on, baby. It's going to be one hell of an adventure."

TWENTY-EIGHT

REED

I rolled my eyes as Courtney let out another curse word. As if the noise from the plane wasn't bad enough as I tried to read, Courtney kept sighing every five minutes. I glanced over at her, and she was pulling out yet another row she had just crocheted.

"What am I doing wrong? *Shit.* I don't remember how to do a double crochet." She pulled out the pattern again and whispered, "What in the hell does back loop only mean?"

I looked back down at my Kindle and tried to tune out Court as I got back into my story.

"Wait, I think I remember how to do the double crochet. I take the hook and—oh wait, do I? Or was that knitting? Shit on a brick, why did she show me both?"

I let out a sigh and turned off my Kindle. "Can I see it?" I asked as I held out my hand.

Courtney just looked at me and let out a small laugh. "You want to try crocheting? Please, Reed. I don't even know what I'm doing, let alone know how to show you how to do it."

I closed my eyes and took a deep breath. I knew what I was about to do could end up causing me grief in the future, and Courtney would have a lot of fun with it, but I had to. She was driving me crazy. I opened my eyes to find her holding up the blanket.

"Why are there holes in it?"

I reached for it and took the hook from her. "Because you're not keeping the same tension throughout. If it is too loose, you'll get the holes, and if it is too tight, you'll have a hard time attaching the next row. Here, look…this is how you do the double crochet." And I began crocheting.

I looked over at Courtney, and she was sitting there with her mouth hanging open, staring down at what I was doing.

Her eyes moved up and looked into mine. "How…wait. Wait just a damn second here. You know how to crochet?"

I nodded my head and said, "Are you watching?"

She let out a laugh and quickly covered her mouth. "You know, if I had known this a year ago, I would have totally called you a tree-loving, cultivating-plant pussy, crocheting cocksucker!"

I dropped my hands and looked at her. "What?"

She shrugged her shoulders and said, "Cocksucker was the only thing I could quickly think of that started with a C."

If I didn't love her so much, I would be so pissed at her. "Here, if you don't want my help…"

I handed everything back to her, and her smile dropped.

"Wait! Show me again."

I rolled my eyes, took everything back, and showed her again.

"May I ask you something?" she said.

"Not if you are going to make jokes about it."

"I promise, I won't," she said as she attempted to hold back a giggle. "Um…where did you learn to crochet?"

"And knit. I know how to knit, too," I said as I whipped out two rows on the blanket.

Courtney busted out laughing, and I turned and glared at her.

She used both hands to cover her mouth. "Sorry! Okay, I'm sorry. I won't laugh."

"My grandmother taught me, Paul, and Wesley all how to crochet, knit, and…" I lowered my voice and said, "Darn."

Courtney leaned in closer to me and said, "I'm sorry. What did you say? I couldn't hear you."

I looked away and then back at her quickly. "Darning."

"What in the hell is darning?" Courtney asked.

I let out a long sigh and said, "It's a sewing technique for, um…well, for repairing holes and worn-out areas on fabric and stuff." I shrugged and returned the crochet hook and yarn to her.

She began chewing on her lower lip, and I was regretting even telling her.

She held up her hands and said, "I'm trying. Really, I am, but…Oh. My. God. That is too funny!"

I picked my Kindle back up and turned it on while Courtney sat next to me, having a laughing fit. When she finally settled down and tried to start crocheting again, she busted out into another laughing fit. I ended up turning off the Kindle again and closing my eyes. It didn't take long before I ended up falling asleep to the sounds of my wife giggling next to me.

I jerked my eyes open when I felt something moving on my leg. I lifted my head and looked around. Courtney was looking out the window, and her nails were now digging into my leg.

Ouch! Son of a bitch. We must be landing. "Court, angel, you're going to put holes in my leg."

She snapped her head around and looked at me with a scared expression on her face. "We're landing."

Courtney loved flying, but she hated the takeoff and landing parts of it. I grabbed her hand and began kissing it, and then I ran my fingers up and down her arm.

Once we were on the ground and getting off the plane, Courtney took my hand and said, "I have to tell you, I'm super turned-on right now."

I looked at her, surprised. "How come?"

She scrunched up her nose and said, "For some reason, knowing my big ole cowboy knows how to crochet, knit, and darn…well, it just turns a girl on."

I let out a laugh and said, "Oh yeah? Maybe I should crochet, knit, and darn in the nude for you."

Courtney let out a laugh. "That might be fun!"

When we pulled up to the house, I wasn't surprised to see Layton and Whitley sitting on our porch swing. Courtney had called Whitley before we left New York and filled her in on everything that had happened. Courtney jumped out of the truck and ran up to Whitley. The next thing I knew, they were making their way over to the tree house and climbing the steps. I glanced over toward Layton, and he gave me a weak smile.

I walked up to him and stuck out my hand.

"Welcome home, dude."

I shook my head and let out a sigh as I ran my hand through my hair. "Thanks. Nothing like being on Texas soil."

Layton grabbed two suitcases, and I took the other two, and then we made our way into the house.

"Just set them in the living room. I'll grab us some beers, and let's head out back."

Layton and I sat down on the rockers and looked out over the garden Courtney and I had been working on.

He let out a small chuckle and nodded in the direction of the garden. "It amazes me how these two have just melted right into country life."

I smiled and nodded my head. "Shit, Courtney's parents' house, I swear, is bigger than yours, dude. I got fucking lost in it twice."

Layton threw his head back and laughed. "Did you like New York?"

I tipped my beer back and got a long drink. "Nope. Hated it. I mean, it was pretty and all, and it had its moments, but…"

Neither one of us said anything for a few moments before Layton cleared his throat and said, "Are y'all okay, Reed? I mean, I know you are okay as a couple, but…are you okay?"

I looked down at the ground and then back out over the countryside. "I had this one moment when I wanted to kill him. I mean, I really wanted to kill him, Layton. I know you know what I mean with what you and Whit went through with Roger." I shook my head as I thought back to seeing Layton shot and how scared Whitley was.

"What made you stop?" Layton asked.

"Courtney, the baby, and the future I promised her. I felt so much anger—not only at him, but at myself for not protecting her from him in the first place. I promised her I would never let him hurt her, and I failed her. I knew something felt wrong in my gut, but I didn't listen to it. I let him get close to her, and I feel like I let her down. I can't shake that guilt." I peered over at the tree house and then looked at Layton. "I can't ever hurt her, Layton. I'd rather die than hurt her."

He nodded his head and looked back over at the tree house before turning back and looking at me. "Reed, you're not your father."

I nodded my head and said, "I know I'm not."

Layton leaned forward and grabbed my shoulder. "I see how much you love Courtney. I've seen a change in you these last few months. You're happy and content, and hell, dude, you even seem peaceful, if that makes sense. As much as we want to protect both those girls, we need to understand that we just can't protect them from everything. We can try like hell, and I know you do as much as I do. You're a good guy, Reed. You're a good husband, and I know you'll make one hell of a good father."

I cracked a smile and said, "Thanks, Layton. You know I've always looked up to you, and that means a lot to me for you to say that." I glanced up when I heard the girls laughing as they were coming down from the tree house. "Layton, I'm really happy for you, too. I'm really glad Whit's car broke down that day."

Layton let out a chuckle and looked over at Whitley and Courtney as they headed our way. "So am I, dude. So. Am. I."

Courtney smiled at me, and I couldn't help but smile at the stupid, crazy feeling that happened in my stomach every time she looked at me.

She walked up, sat down on my lap, and gave me a quick kiss. "I missed you," she whispered.

I let out a small laugh and said, "You were only up there a few minutes."

She shrugged her shoulders and said, "I missed your touch."

Whitley walked up and gave Layton a quick kiss. "I have to go potty."

Layton let out a loud laugh. "Are you practicing baby talk, Whit?"

Whitley crinkled up her nose in a cute way and nodded her head. "Think about dinner. You have two pregnant women who want to eat," she called over her shoulder as she walked into the house.

We had decided on barbeque, so we headed into town. Layton and I talked about the ranch as Whit and Court talked about some baby store in Austin they wanted to go to. We were walking into Cooper's Old Time Pit Bar-B-Que when I heard a familiar voice calling my name from behind us. My heart started pounding as I turned around to see my father standing there.

"Well, if it isn't my oldest son, Reed. Reed, this is Candace. Candace, this is my oldest son, Reed."

Is he really introducing me to his girlfriend? I haven't seen him in months.

"Reed, aren't you going to introduce me to your girlfriend?"

I just stood there, frozen. I would never understand how he could make me feel like a ten-year-old in trouble.

Courtney walked up to him and said, "I'm Courtney Moore, Reed's wife."

"Blake Moore. It's a pleasure, Courtney." He smiled at Courtney and then looked back at me. "Married, huh?" He glanced back at Courtney and laughed. "My son treating you good?"

Courtney hooked her arm through mine and gave my arm a squeeze. "Like a princess, but then again, he is my Prince Charming."

When she smiled at me, I instantly felt better.

Layton's voice filled my head. *You're not like your father, Reed.*

I glanced at the girl on his arm. She was a different girl than the last one I'd seen him with a few months ago.

"If you'll excuse us, we were just about to order."

"How's your mother?" he asked as I went to turn around.

I glared back at him and said, "Why would you care? You walked out on her and your three kids years ago. You left us with nothing, and Mom struggled for years to turn things around while you were out having yourself a good time. You didn't seem to care how she was back then, so why care now?"

His face dropped, and he pulled his head back, like he was surprised I had talked to him that way.

"You know, it's probably a good thing you left us," I said.

He didn't say anything for a few seconds as he just stared at me. "Why's that?" he asked.

"Because you showed me the type of man I never want to be. That's about the only good thing that came from you." I grabbed Courtney's hand as I turned and walked away.

The farther I walked away, the better I felt. Something had happened just then, and I wasn't really sure what it was, but it felt like a weight had been lifted off my shoulders.

Layton slapped me on the back and said, "Fucking awesome. About time." He turned and wrapped his arms around Whitley as we waited in line.

I peeked down at Courtney. She was looking up at me, smiling.

"What?" I asked as I pulled her closer to me.

She snuggled her head into my body and said, "It looks like we both buried the ghosts that haunted our dreams."

I nodded my head and placed my hand on her stomach. "Nothing but happy memories from here on out, angel." I reached down and gently kissed her on the lips.

She let out a sigh and said, "Total swoon-worthy moment with the whole hand on the pregnant stomach and all."

I threw my head back and laughed. "Damn, I'm getting good at this."

"Mmhmm. I wouldn't say good…better maybe," she said with a wink and a crooked smile.

I leaned down, put my lips up to her ear, and let out a hot breath. I saw her whole body shudder, and I instantly felt my dick jump. "Wait until I get you home later. I'm going to swoon the hell out of you in bed."

She bit down on her lip and placed her hand on her stomach. "I don't think I'm hungry anymore," Courtney said as she went to try to get out of line.

I grabbed her arm and pulled her back. "Oh no, Mrs. Moore. My son wants some brisket, and brisket he will get."

Courtney smiled the biggest smile I'd ever seen on her face. "Son? What makes you think it's a son?"

"Pesh, it's my sperm. It'll be a boy for sure," I said as I looked at her like she had grown two heads.

Courtney placed her hands on her hips and swung her right hip out. "Well, it's my egg. Maybe my egg only wanted to fornicate with female sperm."

I shook my head. "No. The sperm decides the sex, and my sperm is dominated by sexy male cowboy genes."

Layton and Whitley both turned and looked at us.

"Really? This is the conversation y'all are going to have in the line at Cooper's?" Whitley said as she used her hand and gestured toward the people standing in line behind us.

I didn't even bother to look to see how many people were behind us. I shrugged my shoulders and looked at Layton. "Dude, don't you think you're having a boy?"

Layton smiled. "Hell yeah, I'm having a boy. My sperm—" He looked at Whitley and quickly said, "I mean, I don't care. As long as the baby is healthy, I'm happy."

I just looked at him and shook my head. "Pussy," I said.

Layton shot me the finger. Whitley hit Layton on the shoulder, and Courtney started laughing.

We sat down to eat, and I'd never seen two women eat so fast and so much in my life.

"Where did the sausage go?" Layton asked.

I pointed to Courtney. "Miss I Am Woman, Hear My Eggs Roar over here ate it all."

Courtney gave me a look and said, "Ha-ha, Mr. My Sperm Is All Manly-and-Sexy Cowboy Sperm. Keep it up, and your cowboy sperm isn't going to be having any fun tonight. Oh my God…I can't *believe* I forgot to tell you, Whitley! Reed and I had sex in the family restroom at the restaurant where my brother got married. We did it right before the wedding." Court jumped in her seat and pointed at Whitley. "Ha! We totally have y'all beat for public sex, and let me tell you it was—"

I saw a middle-aged woman stand up and walk over to our table.

She leaned over our table and said, "Excuse me?"

We all looked at her as Courtney smiled and said, "Yes?"

The lady pointed to Whitley and then Courtney. "Are you girls both pregnant?"

They both smiled and said, "Yes," at the same time.

The lady nodded her head and said, "I see. Well, may God help your children." She turned, walked back to her table, and sat down.

I glanced between Courtney and Whitley, and both had their mouths hanging open. I peeked over at Layton, and he was laughing uncontrollably.

Courtney turned and looked at me as she whispered, "What in the fuck did she mean by that?"

I started laughing as I shrugged my shoulders. I looked over at the lady as she and her family stood up to leave. She looked back at Courtney and shook her head.

Courtney snapped her head back and looked at Whitley. "Did she just insinuate that we are going to be bad mothers?"

Whitley slowly nodded her head. "I think so, but then again, you and Reed were talking about your eggs and his sperm and fornicating and how you had sex in a *family* restroom before your brother's wedding. I'm gonna guess that one pushed her over the edge. No wonder she said something to you."

"To me? Oh no, no, no! She pointed to both of us, sweetheart. She said you were going to be a bad mother, too. It was not just me."

"No, I'm pretty sure she was directing it to you, Court," Whitley said as she sat back and put her hands on her stomach. "I am full."

Layton was still laughing as Courtney turned and watched the lady walk out of Cooper's.

Courtney let out a huff and crossed her arms over her chest. "Bitch. I'll show her. I'm going to be the best mother ever."

Lying in bed, I felt Reed wrap his arms around me as he began running his hand over my stomach. I was now almost twenty weeks pregnant and had what Reed called *the cutest baby bump in the whole world.* I smiled as I felt my skin tingle everywhere he touched.

"What time is it?" I asked in a sleepy voice.

Reed covered my back with kisses as he mumbled, "Six."

I let out a moan and rolled over, looking at my handsome husband, who had the biggest smile on his face. "Reed! Why? You said you were going to sleep in, baby."

"I did sleep in. Six is sleeping in on Christmas, Court."

I rolled my eyes and looked up. "Lord, please let our children take after me and sleep in on Christmas morning and not wake me up at four, and then five, and now six."

He laughed and placed his hand on my stomach again.

"What did you just do?" I asked.

He looked at me and said, "What do you mean?"

I made a funny face and shook my head. "Never mind. I thought I felt something, but it must be gas or something moving through my stomach."

Reed leaned over and took one of my nipples in his mouth. He sucked on it as he moved his hand down between my legs.

Oh, yes. This is how I wish to be woken up every Christmas morning.

Reed slipped his fingers inside me, and I bucked my hips frantically into him. I needed more. He slowly sucked on my nipple as he moved his fingers in and out.

Nothing. Ugh.

I thrashed my head back and forth and said, "Wait! Stop."

Reed stopped and pulled his fingers out as he looked at me, confused.

"Cleopatra?" I said with a shy smile.

Reed's face lit up, and I'd never seen him move so fast in my life. He ran into our bathroom, opened up the cabinet, and then came running back with one of my vibrators.

He held it up and wiggled his eyebrows. "Is this what my angel wants for her first Christmas present?"

I nodded my head and put my finger in my mouth. Reed spread my legs open wider and began inserting the vibrator, slowly at first, and then he began working it in and out faster. I let out a moan as he reached up with his other hand and pinched my nipple while he turned the vibrator on.

"Oh God!" I was shocked at how fast my orgasm hit me. "Reed…oh…feels…oh God!"

Right as I was coming down from my orgasm, Reed quickly pulled the vibrator out and buried his face in between my legs. The moment his tongue flicked my clit, I lost it again. This time, it was more intense and lasted longer. By the time I came down again, I realized I was turned over, and he was taking me from behind. Feeling him move in and out of me was nothing short of heaven.

I started to feel the buildup again, and I moaned. "Can't. Take. Another. One," I whimpered.

He pulled back and pushed in farther, hitting right where I needed it. I called out his name as he called out mine, and we came together. He slowly pulled out of me and kissed my back. Then, I rolled over and lay down on the bed.

"Oh. Wow." I was panting for air now, and my body still felt like it was quivering from my multiple orgasms. I turned and looked at Reed, who was now lying next to me. "It keeps…getting better."

He let out a chuckle and nodded his head. "Yeah, it does." He quickly turned and tapped my nose with his finger. "Can we please get up, get dressed, and open presents now?"

I let out a gasp and said, "Did you just butter me up with…sex?"

Reed smirked and said, "Maybe?"

I was just about to say something when my cell phone rang.

"Who in the hell is calling you this early?" Reed asked.

I rolled my eyes as I rolled over and grabbed my phone. *Yep. It's exactly who I thought it was—Whitley.* I cleared my throat and said, "What?"

"Merry Christmas! Have y'all opened presents yet?" Whitley said in an all-too-chipper voice.

"No. It's not even six thirty in the morning. I want to go back to sleep."

"Oh my gosh…you sound like Layton! Come on. I want to know what you got. Layton is in the kitchen, bitching, while making us some tea and blueberry muffins."

"Huh…sounds like I got the better end of the deal this morning. At least Reed tried to bribe me with sex."

Whitley let out a sigh and said, "Damn. I'll have to remember that next year. Maybe add a little bit of extra fun for him, like a blow job to get him up earlier."

"Gross. I don't need to hear your detailed plan. I think I just threw up in my mouth a little bit when that image popped in my head."

Whitley giggled and said, "Come on, Court. You better get used to getting up early once the baby gets old enough to come wake you up."

I let out a sigh and then stretched. I sat up, and Reed jumped up and started getting dressed.

"I'll go make some coffee." He practically skipped out of the room.

I smiled at how excited Christmas got him. I was excited, too, but I didn't want to come off like I was.

I went to say something to Whitley when I felt the flutter in my stomach again. *Oh. My. God. Is it…the baby?*

"Court? Did you hear me?"

I quickly put my hand on my stomach. "Whitley, be quiet."

"Um…okay."

I sat there for a few seconds.

Nothing.

I went to say something, but then I felt the flutter again, and I let out a scream.

"Holy shit! Why did you scream in my ear?" Whitley said.

I jumped up from the bed and began jumping up and down. "I think I just felt the baby moving! What does it feel like?"

Whitley started laughing. "Okay, you know when Reed touches you, and you don't expect it? That funny feeling you get in your tummy, like a flutter? It kind of feels like that…or gas, but I like the sweet flutter-feeling description better."

Reed came running into the room and then skidded to a stop. I was standing before him, butt-ass naked.

"Yep, that was it!"

Whitley let out a scream of her own. I was sure she was paying me back for my earlier scream.

Payback is a bitch.

"Okay, Whit, I'm gonna have to let you go, so I can celebrate with my husband."

Whitley giggled and said, "Okay. Call me later! I want to know what you got."

"I will. Promise." I hit End and smiled at Reed.

"Why…why did you scream, but when I came in, you were smiling? I'm confused."

I bit down on my lower lip and said, "I felt the baby move."

His mouth dropped open, and then that panty-melting, drop-dead gorgeous smile of his spread across his face.

Damn. That smile was the first thing I'd noticed about him, and every time I saw it, all I wanted to do was jump on him. *Gah! He drives my body insane with want. I just had three amazing orgasms, and here I am, wanting him again.*

"You felt the baby?" he asked as he placed his hand on my stomach.

I nodded and instantly felt sad that Reed couldn't feel what I was feeling. I wasn't sure how long it would be before he could feel the baby.

"I should be able to feel him around twenty-two weeks or so," he said.

My heart dropped, and I fell even more in love with my husband.

"What?" I whispered.

Reed was still looking down at my stomach as he talked, "At twenty-two weeks or so, I should be able to feel him."

He looked into my eyes, and I had to suck in a breath of air.

He's really mine. I'm married to this man and going to have his baby.

I launched myself at him and began kissing him frantically.

He pulled back, laughing, and said, "Damn. What did I do to deserve that?"

"Pinch me."

Reed raised his eyebrows and smirked. "You want to play rough, huh?"

I slapped him on the chest and said, "No! I mean, pinch me, so I can make sure I'm not dreaming."

When Reed pinched me, I yelled out, "Ouch! Why did you pinch me?"

"What the hell, Court? You just told me to pinch you."

I rubbed my arm where he'd pinched me and gave him a dirty look. "I wasn't being serious, you ass."

He pulled me into his arms, and I could feel his dick getting harder.

"I'm sorry, angel. I didn't mean to pinch you that hard, but you did ask for it."

I dropped my head to the side, exposing my neck, so he could kiss it. I did this often, and Reed knew how much I loved for him to kiss my neck.

"Reed?" I whispered as he moved his lips up and down my neck.

"Mmm?"

"Do you ever ask yourself if this is all real?"

He pulled back and looked at me as he slowly smiled. "Every day when I wake up and see you next to me."

"Will you make love to me?" I asked.

Reed tilted my chin up and looked into my eyes. "Yes…but only after we open presents."

He quickly kissed my lips, and then he reached around and slapped my ass, causing me to let out a scream and jump.

"Now, get your beautiful pregnant ass dressed and in front of the Christmas tree in five minutes, woman, or no sex for you."

I let out a laugh as I watched my husband retreat from the bedroom to go back to the kitchen. I headed into the bathroom, brushed my teeth, and got dressed in my comfy sweatpants from Victoria's Secret and one of Reed's T-shirts. As I started to walk out of the bedroom and toward the kitchen, I was stopped in my tracks.

Is that Christmas music? I walked closer to the kitchen and stopped again as I placed my hand over my mouth.

Reed was in the kitchen…singing.

I leaned up against the wall and tried to settle my beating heart. His voice was amazing.

How did I not know my own husband has such an amazing voice?

When he walked out of the kitchen, he stopped and looked at me. "What's wrong? Are you okay, Court?"

I nodded my head and wiped away my tears. "I'm more than okay. I'm so more than okay."

Reed smiled as he held out his hand, and I placed mine in his. We walked out into the living room, and I let out a gasp. I looked around at all the gifts and started to cry again.

"Where? When? How did you get all this here?" I looked around and saw a swing, a bassinet, a crib, a changing table, and an endless amount of presents under the tree.

My eye was drawn back over to the crib. I walked up to it and ran my hand along it. It was the most beautiful crib I'd ever seen. "Reed, is this handmade?"

He nodded his head and said, "Yep, by a guy in Fredericksburg. His name is Josh. Super nice guy, and he does amazing work. He made all the furniture in both Layton's office and mine."

"It's so beautiful. I just don't even have words for it. What type of wood is it?"

Reed smiled as he walked up to the wood crib. "It's hickory, and you can use it in three stages as they grow."

The crib had a paneled backboard with the most amazing details carved on it. The base and feet had curved embellishments that were elegant but still simple.

"Do you like it? The changing table is the same wood and design."

I felt the tears building, and I fought like hell to control them. I nodded my head and whispered, "I love it. I love all of it."

I turned and looked into his eyes. They were filled with tears as he smiled that beautiful smile of his. Right in that moment, I felt the flutter in my stomach again, and I lost it and began crying. Reed's smile disappeared as he reached for me and pulled me over to him. He sat down on the sofa, and I sat on his lap.

"Baby, are those happy tears?" He pushed a strand of hair behind my ear and then ran his hand down the side of my face.

I quickly nodded my head and wiped away my tears. "I felt the baby again, and seeing you smiling at me and…" I pointed to all the gifts. "Well…I just love you so much. Reed, I really hope you know how much I love you."

He smiled as he pulled me down to kiss him. The kiss was slow and passionate and filled with nothing but love flowing from each of our bodies.

He pulled back and said, "I just have to know something."

"Anything," I said.

"Are you as happy as Alexa?"

"Alexa?" *Why is he asking about a fictional character in a book?*

"Yeah, from *The Marriage Bargain.*"

"Oh, Reed…" I quickly moved and straddled him. "You do know that I would never, ever compare you to a fictional character, right? I love you for who you are"—I placed both my hands on his chest—"in here. I love you for how incredibly sweet, caring, stubborn, hardheaded, oh-so romantic, and hardheaded you are."

"You already said hardheaded," he said with a smile.

"Don't interrupt me when I'm on a roll," I said with a wink.

Reed looked down and then looked back up into my eyes. His blue-green eyes were sparkling, and I found myself getting lost in them.

"Do you remember all those things I promised you? My goals for us?" he asked.

I smiled and nodded my head. "Yes."

He took a deep breath and said, "The most important one for me is making you feel safe and happy. I want to give you your happily ever after, Court. I just want to love you with everything I have."

I swallowed hard and slowly took in a deep breath. I leaned into his body, and I pulled his lower lip with my teeth. He let out a soft moan that moved through my body, like silk sliding against bare skin.

I let go and whispered against his lips, "I never dreamed I would be this happy, Reed. You've already made so many of my dreams come true." I placed his hand on my stomach. "This one has to be at the very top though," I said with a giggle. "Don't you see, Reed? The first time you held me in your arms and told me you loved me was the beginning of my happily ever after. Your love is my happily ever after."

His eyes were dancing in the sunlight as he smiled and said, "And my swooning?"

I giggled as I shook my head. "Nick who?"

"That's right, baby," Reed said as he moved me to a lying position on the sofa.

He began kissing me everywhere as his hands moved all along my body, and then he slowly undressed both of us. When I finally felt him enter my body, I let out a moan.

I'd never felt so free in my life. Every fear, hurt, and confused memory vanished from my mind. Reed making love to me was almost like a healing process. Each time, I felt more and more whole, and now, I felt complete.

"Reed…" I whispered as he moved in and out of my body slowly. "I'm yours—completely."

He looked at me as he came to a stop. Feeling him twitch inside my body was like a drug to me. I needed to feel him every single day.

He placed his hands on the sides of my head and said, "I'm completely yours." He captured my lips, and we slowly made love. When he moved his lips to my ear, he whispered, "I'm about to come, angel."

I lost it. I softly called out his name as we lost ourselves in each other…completely.

THIRTY

REED

When I heard my truck driving down the road, I looked and then glanced over toward Layton. He jumped up and pulled out his cell phone. Courtney put the truck in park and got out of it. She waved to us as she made her way over. She looked so damn cute in her overalls and pregnant belly. She smiled at me, and my stomach dropped a little, doing that little flutter. I loved how she could still make me feel this way, even when I'd just seen her a few hours ago.

"Is Whit okay?" Layton called out.

Courtney rolled her eyes and made her way over toward us. "Yes. The little moody bitch is just fine. She was driving me insane, and I had to get away from her. How in the hell do you live with that?"

Layton smiled and said, "True love."

"Or great sex," Courtney said as she attempted to sit on the tailgate.

I walked up to her, lifted her up, and then set her down onto the truck tailgate as she grabbed my cell phone to keep from sitting on it.

"My oh-so strong hubby," she said as she smiled at me and then looked back at Layton. "So, I'm going with great sex since you decided to remain silent on that one."

Layton shook his head and grabbed the fence pullers as I let out a laugh.

"So, what did my beautiful bride do to make you so pissed at her?"

Courtney dropped her head back and closed her eyes. "God, the sun feels so good." She let out a sigh and said, "She wants me to run into town and buy her crunchy peanut butter."

Layton stopped and looked at Courtney funny. "I just bought some, like three days ago."

"Wait, I bought her some last week," Courtney said as she looked at me.

I held up my hands and said, "Don't look at me. I haven't bought her anything but the mint chocolate ice cream last night."

Courtney's mouth dropped open. "You bastard."

Oh shit.

"You bought that bitch ice cream and didn't buy any for me?" She looked down at her stomach and pointed. "Um…hello, Daddy? Mommy is pregnant, too, and likes chocolate and ice cream and is sick of flowers!"

Layton let out a giggle, and I turned and glared at him.

I looked back at my beautiful wife, who was due in a little over a month. Her skin was glowing, and since she became pregnant, her eyes were the most beautiful blue I'd ever seen. My mother had sworn to me that Court's eyes had not changed colors, but I swore the blue in her eyes was brighter.

"You don't like my flowers?" I said, trying to sound hurt.

Courtney snapped her eyes up to mine, and I tried like hell to make my eyes water. She dropped her mouth open a little.

I turned and walked away. "I'll be right back."

"No! Reed, wait. Shit! Reed…I was just…damn it. Layton, get your ass over here and get me off this tailgate."

I kept walking as the smile spread wider on my face. I walked around my truck and leaned against it as I put my hands on my knees and dropped my head.

"Reed, you know I was just kidding. Oh my God, I love my flowers more than anything. Please. I'm so sorry I said that. I really didn't mean it."

I looked away and held my hand up, like I couldn't talk.

I'd planted a garden behind our house, and every morning, I would go out and pick a small bouquet of flowers. Then, I'd put them next to Courtney's side of the bed, so she would see them as soon as she woke up. I knew Courtney understood my passion for plants, and she loved helping me in the garden, so I knew this would get her good.

"Oh God, Reed. I…I…I didn't mean it."

I was just about to let her know I was kidding when Layton yelled, "Reed!"

I jumped up and ran over toward him. "What? What's wrong?" I said as I skidded to a stop.

Layton held his phone out for me, and all it said was, *My water just broke.*

I smiled as I looked at Layton. He was standing there, frozen stiff.

I snapped my fingers in front of his eyes and said, "Dude, snap out of it."

Nothing.

"What's wrong?" Courtney said.

"Whit's water broke, and Layton here is frozen, like a stone."

Courtney slapped the side of Layton's face to snap him out of it.

Still nothing.

"Hey, that was kind of fun," she said with a snicker.

I grabbed him by the shirt and pulled him over to the passenger side of his truck. I shut the door and looked at Court, who was looking at my cell phone. She glanced up at me, and her eyes were filled with hurt, but I didn't have time to tell her that I had only been kidding about the flowers.

"Babe, can you follow us back in my truck?"

The moment I saw the tears build, I knew she thought I was upset with her. *Shit. Shit. Shit.* "I just don't want to leave it out here for a few days until I can get it."

I jumped into the truck and started it up. I pulled up next to my truck. Courtney was pulling herself up and into my truck. I tried to quickly tell her that I was not upset, but she shut the door. I honked the horn, but she wouldn't look at me.

Ah hell, I know better than to kid around with a pregnant woman. "Shit," I whispered as I took off toward the house.

The whole way there, I tried to get Layton to talk to me, but he was in a comatose state.

"Jesus, dude, you better snap the hell out of it before we get to the house. You're gonna freak Whitley out."

Layton turned and looked at me. "Her water broke. Do you know what that means?"

I tried hard not to laugh as I said, "Um…she's fixin' to have a baby?"

I came around the corner and pulled up, and Layton jumped out of the truck before I even stopped. Mimi came out with a huge smile on her face. I let out a laugh and shook my head. I knew Courtney would never leave Whitley alone being so close to the due date, but she was going to be pissed this had happened right when she left.

Speaking of, Courtney came barreling up in my truck and skidded to a stop before she got out of the truck. As she walked by, she shot me the finger.

"What the fuck?" I whispered as she walked by.

I jumped out of the truck, ran up to her, and grabbed her by the arm. "Courtney, why did you just do that?"

She looked away from me, but I turned her body around, so she was facing me.

"Fuck you, Reed. I hate you." She had tears streaming down her cheeks.

My heart dropped to my stomach. "What?" I whispered. I dropped my arms and took a few steps back.

She looked so angry.

"Courtney, I was kidding, baby. I swear to you, I wasn't upset about what you said about the flowers. Why are you acting this way?"

The next thing I knew, she threw my cell phone at me. "Just don't talk to me until we get Whitley to the hospital. Until then, I don't want to look at you. Prick."

She turned and walked away. I picked up my cell phone and saw she had opened my text messages.

Reese: Hey. Do you want to meet sometime this week? I know we've been keeping this a secret from the wife, but I'm really excited to see you. This is going to be amazing.

I looked up at Courtney as she was walking toward the porch.

Fuck me. She thinks I'm cheating on her.

I ran up to her, but Layton came out, helping Whitley. Court walked up to her and took her other arm as she helped her.

"Court, I have to talk to you—now."

She shot me a dirty look and turned back to Whitley. "Remember to breathe, baby girl. That's it. You got this."

"Courtney?" I said.

She let go of Whitley and turned to look at me. "What you have to say is not nearly as important as Whitley having a baby with her husband—her husband who is loving and caring and *faithful* to her."

Layton and Whitley both stopped, and Layton turned and looked at me.

"What's going on?" Whitley asked as she held her stomach.

Courtney glared at me. "Nothing important."

As she turned to walk away, I yelled out, "I didn't cheat on you, Courtney. Reese is not a girl, for fuck's sake. It's a guy."

Layton really looked confused now. "Are you talking about Reese Michaels? The guy I got Lulu from?"

I let out a sigh and dropped my head. *There goes my surprise.*

I looked up, and Courtney had stopped walking.

She slowly turned around and looked at me. "Reese is a dog breeder?"

Layton said, "Yeah. I was wondering why you'd asked me who I got Lulu from. Y'all are getting a dog?"

"Oh, yay!" Whitley said before she bent over and let out a little yell.

Everyone ran up to her and helped her into Layton's truck. Whitley sat in the backseat with Courtney, and I jumped up front with Layton.

"Wait!" I yelled. "I better bring my truck just in case. I don't want to be stuck at the hospital or leave you stuck there."

Almost forty minutes later, we were at the hospital in Fredericksburg. Things were so crazy, and I was waiting for Layton to pass out any minute.

When the nurse asked Whitley if she wanted anyone in the room, she said, "Just Layton."

I looked around for Courtney but couldn't find her.

Layton started to follow the nurse, but I grabbed his arm and said, "Layton?"

He turned and looked at me. "Yeah?"

"Take in every moment."

He smiled and nodded his head before heading to where they had taken Whitley. I pushed my hands through my hair as I pulled out my phone. I sent Reese a quick message back about meeting him this week, but the cat was out of the bag. Right when I shoved my phone into my pocket, it began ringing. I pulled it out and saw it was—

Courtney?

"Court? Where in the hell are you?" I heard her sniffle. "Angel, are you okay? Please tell me where you are."

"I'm in the courtyard. I needed fresh air."

I looked all around and saw a sign that said, *Outdoor Courtyard.* "Baby, I'm on my way."

I practically ran through the hospital and out the doors. She was sitting on the grass next to a tree. I walked up to her and sat down. When she looked in my eyes, I was gutted.

I always end up hurting her somehow. "I'm so sorry I always hurt you," I said as I reached out to touch the side of her face.

"What?"

I shook my head. "I'm always hurting you, and I don't know why."

She grabbed my hands and said, "Why in the world would you say that? You don't ever hurt me—*ever.*"

"Courtney, I swear to you, I was just playing around with you. I didn't mean for you to think I was upset, and then you read that text, and for you to think that I would ever cheat on you…I guess I just thought maybe I'm not loving you enough and—"

"Stop." She choked back a sob. "Please stop. Reed…I'm so sorry I even thought that. I was just already upset, thinking I made you upset, and when I saw that text, I just…" She looked down and then back up at me. "Those old memories came flooding back, and I'm so sorry I just assumed, and it kills me that I did. You have no idea how upset I am with myself that I jumped to conclusions too soon, and I just didn't ask you. It's all these hormones, and we haven't had sex in so long."

I let out a chuckle. "Baby, it's only been four days."

When her eyes captured mine, I sucked in a breath of air.

"You don't understand. I need you, Reed. I need to feel you close to me. Sometimes, it scares me so much that I need you like I do. Nothing makes me feel better than you making love to me. You're like my drug."

I smiled as I gently ran my hand down the side of her face. "Come on, let's go wait in the waiting room. The nurse made it sound like it wouldn't be too long."

I stood up and reached down to help her up. As she stood up, she gave me that look.

I tilted my head and looked at her. "Court?"

She bit down on her lower lip and said, "We can really win it."

I rolled my eyes because I instantly knew what she was talking about. She and Whitley were bound and determined to be the winner in this whole public-sex thing.

"Reed, come on. Public sex…while pregnant. We've got this!"

My mouth dropped open. "We already did that. In the nightclub, remember?"

"Not while I was this pregnant. This pushes that one out the door."

I started to walk off. "No, Courtney. I'm not fucking you while you are eight months pregnant in the hospital where our best friends are having their first baby."

She started following me and said, "Well, when you put it like that…"

I smiled as we headed back to the waiting room. All I could think about was how I wanted nothing more than to find an empty room and give her exactly what she needed.

THIRTY-ONE

Reed had his hand on my stomach as we both watched in amazement while an elbow moved across one side to the other side of my stomach. We both looked at each other and started giggling.

"Oh God, I can't wait to see her."

"Or him," Reed said with a smirk.

I let out another chuckle and said, "Or him."

Reed kissed me on the cheek as he picked my legs up and scooted out from under them. "Want something to drink?" he asked as Gracie jumped up with excitement.

Reed about busted his ass as he tried to maneuver around the twelve-week-old black lab he'd bought me the weekend Taylor was born. I smiled when I thought about Whit holding her daughter and how happy she was. I swore that Layton and Whitley had hardly left the house ever since they brought Taylor home.

"Damn it, Gracie. We are not playing again," Reed said as he jumped over her.

I smiled and watched them walk into the kitchen. "What's it going to be like when we have two babies in the house?" I called out.

Reed let out a moan. "Oh, I totally forgot. My mom told me to tell you that she has that baby blanket she ordered you."

I would have jumped up and screamed if I wasn't so pregnant. I hugged myself and let out an inner scream.

"Why did you have her order it?"

Oh shit. Shit, shit, shit! "Um…I don't remember why I had her order it. I think I had left my purse in the car or something, and she just took care of it. I already paid her back for it though."

I attempted to get up off the sofa, so I could grab my cell phone. "Reed? Will you cut me up an apple, please?"

I heard a loud crash, and Reed yelled out Gracie's name.

"Sure, babe!"

I waddled my way over to my cell phone and quickly sent Reed's mom, Melanie, a text message.

Courtney: Melanie, OMG! Did you get it?

I wasn't surprised when she texted me back almost immediately.

Melanie: Yes. What does OMG mean? Anyway, I have it, and it looks amazing. The colors are beautiful, Courtney. Reed is going to love it. Should I have Paul bring it over?

Courtney: Yes! If he doesn't mind. I'd love to hang it in the baby's room and see how long it takes Reed to notice it. Oh…OMG means, oh my God or oh my gosh…however you want to say it.

Melanie: Why not just say, oh my God?

Courtney: OMG is faster!

Melanie: Dear Lord.

I laughed and put my cell phone down. I turned around to see one very excited puppy looking up at me. "Gracie! Do you want to play, baby girl? Will Daddy not play with you?" I said as I raised my voice higher than normal.

She began barking, and I started laughing when she ran to the front door.

"I'm telling you, this dog is brilliant. She learns so fast. I think we picked the best one from the litter," I said. I made my way to the front door, opened it, and watched Gracie take off running.

Reed walked up and handed me a glass of sweet tea. I practically downed the whole glass as Reed watched me and smiled.

I pulled the glass away, took a breath, and said, "What?"

He chuckled and shook his head as he handed me my apple. "Nothing. I just love you more than life itself, that's all."

As he stepped off the porch, I tilted my head and smiled. The butterflies that went off in my stomach still amazed me. I was just about to tell him to make love to me when I felt a sharp pain in my stomach again. I placed my hand on my stomach, and it was rock hard the whole time the pain lasted. Once it let up, I let out a breath. This had been going on almost all morning.

Motherfucker. That was not comfortable.

I sat down on the rocking chair and watched Reed wear out poor little Gracie. She was so tired that she ended up just flopping down on the ground. Reed walked up to her and picked her up. He flipped her over and held her like a baby.

"What are you going to be, baby? A boy or a girl?" I whispered as the cool April breeze relaxed every inch of my body while I rubbed my hand on my stomach.

When another contraction hit, I grabbed the sides of the rocking chair and tried to breathe it out. Reed was now running around with Gracie, who had quickly gotten her second wind. I heard a car driving down the driveway and looked up. I didn't think it could be Paul already. When I saw Layton's truck, I tried to smile.

Reed grabbed Gracie and waved as he walked back over toward the porch. Layton parked and jumped out of the truck. Reed set Gracie down and walked over.

He shook Layton's hand and slapped him on the back. "Where is my goddaughter?"

Layton let out a laugh. "Home. Napping with her mama. Whit asked me to bring some lasagna over to y'all." When Layton turned and looked at me, he tilted his head a bit and gave me a funny look. "You okay, Court?"

I smiled and stood up. "Yep! Just tired. Haven't been sleeping much. Want some tea?"

Layton nodded and said, "Yes, ma'am, that would be awesome."

I turned and made my way into the house and to the kitchen. I grabbed the home phone and quickly dialed Melanie's number.

"Hello, darling," Melanie said.

"Melanie, it's me, Courtney."

She must have heard it in my voice because she instantly knew without me even telling her. "Okay, sweetheart. Have you told Reed you've started having contractions?"

I felt the tears building in my eyes. "No," I whispered.

I wanted my mother here. She was supposed to fly down two days ago, but she had gotten held up with some stupid benefit dinner for Daddy's office.

"Melanie, I'm so scared," I barely said.

I wasn't sure what in the hell was wrong with me, but for the last two weeks, I'd been scared to death about giving birth to the baby. I had talked to both my mother and Melanie about it. I needed to stay strong for Reed, but I couldn't when I was so terrified.

"How far apart are they?"

"Um…maybe twenty minutes or so…give or take. I've been having small contractions all day, but I thought they were just the Braxton Hicks ones. They're getting stronger and coming quicker."

I heard her cover the phone and yell something to someone. "Court? Baby girl, I want you to hang up the phone and call your doctor. Then, you need to let Reed know, okay?"

I nodded my head even though she couldn't see me.

"Then, I want you to have Reed call me when y'all are leaving for the hospital. Courtney?"

I sucked in a breath of air as I attempted not to get upset. "Yeah?"

"You are one of the bravest women I know. You've got this, okay? I promise you."

"What if I do something wrong?" I said as I wiped a tear away.

"Oh, baby girl, you won't. God knew what he was doing, and just like that, you will automatically know how to take care of that baby. You will know what to do to bring her into this world."

I smiled. "Or him," I whispered, thinking of Reed.

Melanie let out a laugh. "Yes, or him. Hang up and call the doctor, sweetheart."

"Okay. But you'll be at the hospital, right?"

"Yes, I'm going to leave now. Paul already left, so I will text him and tell him to hang up the frame in the baby's room and then meet us there."

"Okay. I'm gonna call Dr. Miller now."

I hung up with Melanie, called Dr. Miller's office, and told the nurse everything. She told me to head into the hospital. After I hung up with her, I quickly went to my cell phone and texted my mother. If I talked to her, I would break down crying.

Courtney: Mom, I'm in labor. Heading to the hospital.

I took a deep breath and headed outside. When I walked out, I caught a glimpse of Reed. Sometimes, I would just watch him without him knowing, and I would become so overwhelmed with the feelings I had for him that I would just cry. There was nothing stronger in this world than our love. With Reed by my side, there wasn't anything I couldn't do.

Another contraction hit, and I held on to the post and tried to breathe. Reed must have sensed I was there because he turned and looked at me. I tried to smile, but his face turned white, and he immediately ran over to me.

"What's wrong?" he said as he grabbed my face with both hands.

"Um…contractions. We…we…need…to…leave now."

His eyes moved all over my face before they landed on my lips and then slowly looked up to my eyes. "What?" he said.

I saw something change in his eyes. I nodded my head and smiled.

"Court? When did they start?" Reed asked.

Layton came walking up and smiled. "Courtney, where is your suitcase?" he asked.

I couldn't even talk. The look in Reed's eyes took my breath away. He looked so happy, the happiest I'd ever seen, and I knew it was because our baby was about to be born.

"It's in the truck already," Reed said.

He leaned down and kissed me. I'd never experienced such an amazing kiss. Something was so different about it. It felt like every fear I had been feeling for the last few months just disappeared. He gently pulled back just enough to where his lips were barely touching mine.

"I love you so much, and I'm so honored to be your husband and the father of this baby. Thank you, Courtney."

I sucked in a breath of air and felt a tear slide down my cheek. Reed used his thumb to brush it away, and the next thing I knew, he was picking me up and carrying me to the truck. I buried my face into him and took a deep breath. I loved Reed's smell. I often found myself going to his dresser and pulling out a shirt to smell it on the days when he would work long hours at the ranch. Something about his scent calmed me, just like it did right now.

When he set me down in the truck, he pushed my hair back away from my face and whispered, "Don't be scared, baby. I'm going to be by your side every single second."

I smiled and let out a small sob. I covered my mouth and tried to regain my composure. I slowly placed my hand on his face and said, "I love you so much, Reed."

"I love you, too. Let's get you to the hospital and meet our son, okay?"

I let out a giggle and said, "Or daughter."

Reed shut the door, and I leaned my head back onto the back of the seat. I tried to take in good long breaths, but I swore I could almost feel another contraction coming on.

Oh no. This is too soon. I just had one!

I saw Layton pick up Gracie as Reed ran around the front of the truck and jumped in.

"Shit! I forgot my wallet." He jumped back out and ran into the house.

Layton opened the driver's door and smiled at me.

I smiled back and said, "What's up, cowboy?"

He let out a laugh and said, "I'm so happy for you, Courtney. I truly am. You're going to make a wonderful mother."

My smile faded slightly and then returned. "Do you know when the first time was that I really knew I liked you?"

Layton flashed me that damn smug smile that could melt any girl's panties. "When?"

"That first day I met you when you tried so hard to act like you weren't attracted to Whitley. I could see it in your eyes, and something told me that you were the one who was going to make my best friend happy."

Layton's smile spread wider on his face. "Yet, you still felt the need to threaten me on more than one occasion."

"Oh yeah, and it still holds true. You ever hurt her…I'll hurt you."

Layton laughed and said, "Courtney, you never cease to amaze me, you know that?"

Reed came running out of the house and yelled, "Get out of the way, Layton!"

Layton winked at me and said, "Good luck, Court. You're gonna do great. I'll have Whit call you, and we'll be there as soon as we can."

I winked back and said, "Just give her and Taylor a kiss from me. Don't come down there and sit and wait. Reed will call you—"

Reed jumped in the truck and said, "Yeah…we'll call. Got to go." He slammed the door shut and put the truck in drive, and then he practically ran over poor Layton.

I tried not to smile, but somehow, the calm man who had run into the house had come out a freaked-out man.

"Um…Reed, are you okay?" I asked as I reached for his hand.

He glanced at me quickly before looking back at the road. "We're having a baby. Do you realize that we…you and me…we're about to have a baby? I mean, this is not a lab puppy. This is a baby. A human baby!"

I bit down on my lip to hold in my laughter. "I thought I was going to be the one freaking out."

"I'm not freaking out. I'm not freaking out. Oh. My. God! Mr. Jenkins, could you drive *any* slower?"

I was going to have to apologize to our poor neighbor, Mr. Jenkins, for Reed almost running him off the road. I felt the contraction coming for real this time, and I grabbed and squeezed Reed's hand.

Somehow, me doing that calmed him down, and he said in a soft voice, "Breathe, baby…that's it. Just take deep breaths, and breathe through the contraction."

From that point on, until we got to the hospital, Reed was calm as a cucumber. Me, on the other hand—the closer we got, the more scared I got.

Reed pulled up to the ER and jumped out of his truck. He ran around to open my door. He helped me out of the truck and then into the ER.

A nurse came over with a wheelchair and smiled as she said, "Dad, you go park the car, and I'll take her over to labor and delivery. Did y'all preregister?"

Reed and I both said, "Yes," at the same time.

Before I knew it, I was in a room, and the contractions were coming faster and faster. Reed had asked the nurse when they would give me the epidural, and she said the anesthesiologist was on her way.

"Thank God," Reed said as he looked at me and smiled.

"Why are you thanking God? I'm the one in pain!" I said as another contraction swept over my body.

Reed leaned down and kissed me on the forehead. "I'm so sorry, Courtney. I wish I could take all the pain away from you. I'd do it in a heartbeat, angel. Seeing you in pain about brings me to my knees. When you hurt, I hurt. When you're happy, I'm happy. I just want you to be happy."

Oh. My. God. He is my husband. Mine. Who would have thought that Reed *Moore would be the one to swoon me more than any book boyfriend ever could?*

I thought back to that first night I'd met him. His cocky attitude and drop-me-to-my-knees smile of his had captured my heart from the first second I saw him. Months of denying our feelings for each other, hurting each other with words we didn't mean, and finally admitting our love for each other had brought us to this very second, and I wouldn't trade any of it.

"You make me feel so amazing," I said as I pulled him down toward me.

He slammed his lips against mine. I wasn't sure how long we'd been kissing before we heard a female voice clearing her throat.

Reed gave me that smile that drove me insane with lust. "I'd be lost without your love," he said as he brushed his thumb across my lower lip. "Completely and utterly lost."

"I love you," I whispered.

He leaned his forehead against mine and closed his eyes. "I love you, too, Courtney. I love you so damn much."

"One more push, Courtney, just one more," Dr. Miller said.

I thrashed my head back and forth. "I can't. I'm so tired. I can't push anymore," I said.

Reed kissed the back of my hand. I'd been pushing for almost three hours.

"Just cut the baby out. Clearly, he or she is stubborn, like the father."

Dr. Miller and Reed both chuckled.

"Courtney, I see the baby's head. One more good push, and you will get to meet your baby."

Reed moved to look, and the moment he let out a gasp and said, "Oh my God," I knew I had to give it one more try.

"Fine! Okay, but this is the last time I'm pushing. I just want to close my eyes and rest."

Dr. Miller gave me a smile and said, "Deal. On the next contraction, give me a good push."

They had taken me off the epidural, so I could feel my contractions and then push when I felt them. At this point, I was so tired that I didn't think I could even feel the pain.

I felt the contraction coming.

Dr. Miller said, "Okay, Courtney, you can do this."

I squeezed Reed's hand and took a deep breath as I started pushing.

Reed leaned over and said, "Come on, baby. I'm so damn proud of you. You can do this."

Somehow, I mustered up the strength to push with all my might. Then, I felt the baby coming out, and the moment she was out, I collapsed back onto the bed. I felt Reed's hot breath up against my ear.

He said, "Courtney…my God…you did it, angel. You did it. I'm so proud of you."

"Reed, Courtney, meet your son."

I looked up and saw Dr. Miller holding our baby in his hands.

He quickly looked at Reed and asked if he wanted to cut the umbilical cord, and Reed said, "Yes."

I watched as tears ran down Reed's face.

What must this be like for him?

I wondered if he'd ever thought about if his first child had been a boy or a girl. He'd never brought it up or talked about it since the day he'd asked me to marry him.

Our baby started crying, drawing me out of my daydream and back into the moment. The tears were streaming down my face as I took in our son's first moments. I smiled as I watched the nurse clean and wrap him in a blanket. The nurse walked over and placed him in my arms as Reed stood next to me.

"He's perfect. My God…he's breathtakingly beautiful," I whispered.

Reed gently ran the back of his fingers across our son's head. "Like his mother."

I glanced up at Reed and said, "And his father. You have your son, Reed. Are you happy?" I smiled up at him.

He wiped away a tear and stared into my eyes. For a few brief moments, we were lost in each other's gaze.

"I've never been so happy in my entire life. You've made every one of my dreams come true." He leaned down and kissed me as our baby made the sweetest sounds I'd ever heard. When he pulled back, he said, "I love you, Courtney."

I let a small sob escape before I looked back down at the baby and then back up at Reed. "I love you, too, Reed." I slowly pulled my gaze from the man I loved more than life itself and stared at the new man in my life. "Walker Nickolas Moore, are you ready for this?"

Reed let out a laugh.

I looked up and asked him, "Are you ready to hold him?"

Reed nodded his head frantically and held out his arms. He reached down and gently took our son into his arms. I watched as the two of them just stared at each other while Reed gently stroked Walker's face. Reed began walking around as he continued to carefully study Walker. He pulled the blanket back and looked at every single finger and repeated the same process with Walker's toes, and I let out a giggle. Most of the people in the room were beginning to leave now, and we were down to the doctor and one nurse. Then, Dr. Miller talked to Reed and me for a few brief minutes.

I peeked over at Reed and Walker, and I fell more in love with my husband as the seconds passed by.

"I'm so glad to finally meet you, sweet angel. Thank you for giving Mommy a pretty easy pregnancy. You're already a gentleman, I see."

Oh. My. God. Swoon the shit out of me.

"Oh, man…Walker, there are so many things I have planned for us. I'm going to teach you everything there is to know about football, baseball, and golf. Layton and I are going to teach you all about the cattle business and everything about horses. I can't wait to get you on a horse. You're going to know everything about the trees and plants—"

I rolled my eyes and said, "Oh God, no!"

Reed looked up at me and smiled as he winked. My heart dropped, and I realized that just seeing my husband standing there, holding our child and talking to him about all of his plans for the future, turned me the hell on.

I looked at the nurse and asked in a hushed voice, "How long do we have to wait to have sex?"

She giggled and said, "Six weeks."

"Six weeks!" I practically shouted.

Reed looked over at me and said, "Six weeks for what?"

"Nothing," I quickly said. *Shit.* I had to keep that bit of information away from Reed because if he heard that, he would be a stickler for the rules and not touch me for six weeks.

I quickly looked back at the nurse and mouthed, *Six weeks*?

She laughed again and said as she looked at Reed, "It's funny. Just seeing them hold our children, getting lost in that love they share, is a bit of a turn-on, isn't it?"

I looked at Reed and smiled. "I'll say. I'm going to have to be creative for the next six weeks."

When I looked back up at the nurse, we both began laughing. Reed was now sitting down, holding Walker, and still going on a mile a minute. I felt my eyelids fighting to stay open.

As I was drifting in and out of sleep, I heard Reed say, "I love you, my sweet baby boy."

I opened my eyes and saw Reed staring at me. He got up and placed Walker in his little bed, and then he walked up to me. He leaned down and gently kissed my lips.

"I could never love you more than I do in this very moment. You look so beautiful that you take my breath away. I promise you that I'm going to spend the rest of my life making you and Walker so happy. Thank you."

I tilted my head and smiled. "For what?"

Reed ran the back of his hand down the side of my face, and my whole body trembled.

"For making all my dreams come true. I dreamed of one day being able to say that I found the perfect love. That night when you first smiled at me, you were the dream I had waited so long for, and I thank God every day for you."

I tried to talk as I held back my tears. "Oh, Reed…"

He kissed me again, and I slid my hand around to the back of his neck. I held him in our kiss just a bit longer. When he finally pulled away, I looked into his eyes.

"Thank you, Reed. Thank you for your love, for always putting me first, and for taking such good care of me. Thank you for your never-ending knowledge of plants."

Reed let out a chuckle as I winked.

"But most of all, thank you for giving us the best love story there is. Ours is a beautiful, passionate, caring, and never-ending love."

I slid over and patted the bed. Reed crawled in and pulled me into his arms. I didn't think I could ever love him more than I did right now.

"I never thought I could love you more than I do right now, Courtney."

I sucked in a breath of air as I closed my eyes, and I just let the tears fall. "I feel the same, Reed. I love you."

He kissed the back of my head and whispered, "I love you, too, angel."

The sounds of Reed's steady breathing relaxed me even more as I drifted off to sleep. I fell into a deep sleep and dreamed of Reed chasing a little boy and a little girl around the backyard.

Finally, I had my happily ever after.

THIRTY-TWO

REED

I jumped out of the truck and quickly opened the back door, so I could help Courtney with the baby. I was a nervous wreck while driving home from the hospital, and Courtney had told me twice to please drive faster than forty miles per hour.

I smiled when I looked at our baby sleeping in the car seat. My phone beeped with a text message. I pulled it out and saw it was from Layton.

> *Layton: Are y'all home yet? How slow did you drive? I think I went forty all the way home, and Whit bitched the whole time.*
>
> *Reed: Ha! Same here, dude. Fucking scared as hell to drive with Walker in the car. Does it get better?*
>
> *Layton: No.*
>
> *Reed: Thanks for that. Are y'all coming over soon?*
>
> *Layton: Yep! Whit is feeding Taylor now, and we will be over soon. Wanted to let y'all get settled in. If Court's emotions are anything like Whit's, she will be crying and need some time.*
>
> *Reed: Talk about emotions. Did you know we have to wait six weeks to have sex? SIX WEEKS! Dude…I'm gonna die.*
>
> *Layton: Oh, trust me…you will find new ways to have fun.*

I smiled as I read Layton's last text. I looked up to see Courtney staring at me with one of those looks.

"Really? You're standing there, texting, while I'm waiting to get our son out of this truck and into the house?"

I let out a chuckle, and then I reached up and kissed her. "I have a surprise for you."

She grinned from ear to ear. "Oh yeah? I have one for you, too."

I wiggled my eyebrows up and down. "Is your surprise going to give you multiple orgasms?"

Her smile dropped, and the look in her eyes turned to lust. She slowly shook her head and said, "No. Hurry. He might sleep for another thirty minutes at least!"

She pushed me out of her way as she slowly got out of the truck. I knew she was sore as hell after delivering my eight-pounds-two-ounces baby boy. I helped her down and then grabbed the small suitcase.

"I'll take that. You get Walker, and don't trip with him."

I turned around and looked at her with a frown. "Great. I wasn't even thinking of tripping with him, Court. Now, I'm going to worry about tripping!"

Courtney smiled as she took a few steps back and then yelled, "Wait! Where is Gracie?"

I panicked for a second before I remembered Layton had said he brought her home. "Layton has her."

"Oh, thank God. I don't think I could deal with her right now. But when is he bringing her back?"

I shrugged and asked, "When do you want her back?"

She looked at me like I was crazy. "Tonight! I haven't seen my baby girl in a couple of days. I'm outnumbered with men. I need my girl. Plus, I want her and Walker to bond."

My mouth dropped open. "That dog is getting nowhere near my son."

She rolled her eyes and said, "I beg to differ, my dear. She gets to sniff Walker and learn his scent. He's a new pup to the pack."

"You just referred to our son as a dog. Do you realize that?"

Courtney laughed and said, "Come on, I want my multiple orgasms."

I felt my dick jump as I watched my beautiful wife walk away. I turned back to look at Walker sleeping in his car seat. The damn thing swallowed him up, and he looked so delicate.

"Please, dear God, don't ever let me drop him."

I reached over, unclipped the car seat, and gently took it out of the truck. I'd never walked so slow in my life as I made my way up the porch and through the front door. The bassinet was in our room, so I headed straight there, making sure I didn't trip over any dog toys.

When I walked into our room, Court was jumping up and down, silently clapping. "He's home! He's home!" she whispered.

I set the car seat down on the bed, and Walker made a noise. We both stood perfectly still until we were sure he was still asleep. Courtney reached in and unclasped the seat belt that I was pretty sure had been designed by a NASCAR driver. She reached in and gently scooped up Walker. She held him to her as she brought him over and put him in the bassinet. He never made a sound. I let out the breath I had been holding and smiled at Courtney as she looked back at me and gave me a thumbs-up.

She took a few steps back, and then she quickly turned and threw herself into my body. It wasn't long before we were stripping most of our clothes off of each other, and I was hovering over Courtney's body.

"Fuck, I wish I could make love to you right now," I said as I pushed my dick against her panties.

She moaned and arched her body up. "Reed…" she moaned as she began touching her breasts.

I wanted to kiss her breasts, but I knew better. I reached over and opened the side drawer. I pulled out the small, thin vibrator I had bought for her. I slid to the side of her and turned it on. I placed it on the outside of her panties. The moment she felt it, she sucked in a breath of air.

"Put it inside my panties…please, Reed."

I barely pulled her panties down and touched the vibrator to her clit. Within seconds, she was saying my name over and over again as she reached down and grabbed my dick, and then she began stroking it.

"Shit…Courtney…go faster," I whispered.

She did what I'd asked. I turned the vibrator up, and she began thrashing her head back and forth.

"Reed…I'm going to come again." She squeezed my dick harder and pumped her hand faster.

"Court…baby, I don't want to come all over our sheets."

She stopped moving her hand and let out a long moan. Watching her come was one of my favorite things. The way her skin flushed and the way she said my name as she came…

Shit, six weeks is too damn long.

Courtney was breathing hard as she was coming down from her orgasm. When she finally got her breathing under control, she said, "I'm not going to be able to wait six weeks. Fuck that."

I let out a laugh and stood up. I made my way into the bathroom. Courtney followed me and turned on the shower. She set the baby monitor down and gave me a sexier-than-hell smile.

"Your turn, Mr. Moore." She held out her hands as she walked backward into the shower.

Once we got in and got wet, she dropped to her knees and took me into her mouth.

"Ah…shit…that feels amazing, baby."

I ran my hands through her wet hair as I watched her take me in deeper. I dropped my head back and let out a moan as she let her teeth barely skim across my dick. She moved her hand up and began playing with my balls, and then she started to go faster and deeper each time. I felt it building and grabbed her hair.

"Court…baby, I'm gonna come, so if you don't want to, stop now, and I'll finish with my—"

She hummed against my dick, and that was my undoing.

"Holy fuck…" I said as I came hard and fast.

She never stopped moving the whole time. When she finally got every drop out of me, I leaned back against the shower, panting. I looked at her as she let the water run all over her face and in her mouth. She looked sexy as fuck as her hands moved all over her body. We had two showerheads, and one was a rain showerhead, so water was falling everywhere on her body. I pushed off the wall and grabbed her. I pulled her lips to mine and kissed her.

I moved my hand down and between her legs. "I don't want to hurt you, angel, so I'm only going to touch your clit."

"Yes…" she whispered.

I massaged her clit, building her into another orgasm. She grabbed my shoulders as she began moving against my hand. When she started calling out my name, I slowed down and bit down on her lower lip before kissing her again. She practically went limp in my arms, and I knew I had worn her out too much.

"Baby, I'm sorry."

She shook her head and looked at me as her beautiful blue eyes sparkled. "Three weeks. I'm only waiting three weeks."

I laughed and shook my head. "Come on, let's get dried off and see if you can nap before Walker wakes up."

Courtney fell fast asleep within about two minutes. I walked into the kitchen, and then I took out some chicken to throw on the grill and also pulled out some fresh veggies. Thank God Wesley had stopped by the store and stocked us up on some food. After peeking in on Walker and Court, both still asleep, I walked outside and started the grill. Then, I hit Layton's number on my cell.

"Welcome home, dude," Layton said as I heard Whitley yell the same thing in the background.

"Thanks! Hey, I'm starting up the grill, and Court and Walker have been taking a good nap, so y'all head on over anytime."

"Sounds good. Whit made dessert and a salad, so we'll head that way now."

I nodded my head and said, "Perfect. Court should be awake by the time y'all get here."

"Sounds good. See ya in a few," Layton said.

"See ya soon." I hit End and headed back into the house.

As I walked by the nursery, I saw the door was open. I knew I had shut it before we'd left, so I walked into the room and turned on the light. I looked around, and the picture frame hanging above the crib instantly caught my eye. I walked up to it and sucked in a breath of air. It was a giant frame filled with dry flowers. The closer I looked, I realized they were the flowers from the garden out back that I had been giving to Courtney during her pregnancy. I stumbled back and felt the tears building in my eyes.

"Do you like it?"

I spun around and saw Courtney standing in the doorway, holding Walker. Something happened in that moment, and I was so overcome with happiness that I had to grab on to the crib to hold myself up. I struggled to find words to talk. I nodded as she smiled bigger.

"I saved a flower or two from each bouquet and dried them out. I got the idea to frame them from Whit. I don't think you even realized what you were doing when you placed those flowers there each time."

"Wha-what did I do?" I said as my voice cracked.

"You showed me over and over again how you would never give up on me. You'd never give up on our love. You made me realize that this crazy ride we were on before we got to right here…in this very moment…was only preparing us for the future. It taught us that we wouldn't give up…ever. You pulled me out of the dark and brought me into the light. I wanted to show you that I feel the same way. I'll never give up on our love or us because our love is a true love and so rare, Reed. This love that we share together is worth the dark road it took to get here."

I choked out my sobs as I watched her walk over. She set Walker down in the crib, and then I pulled her into my arms and held her as tight as I could.

"I love you, Courtney. Thank you for letting me love you."

"Reed, I love you so much."

I pulled back and wiped her tears away with my thumbs. "No more dark roads and broken dreams, angel. Only sunlit roads and dreams coming true from this point on."

"Is that a promise?" Courtney said as she scrunched up her nose and smiled.

I kissed the tip of her nose and looked down at Walker before turning my eyes to hers. "That's a promise."

Five Years Later

"Ava Grace! Do not bite Gracie's ear," I said.

Reed, Walker, and Jase ran by, yelling, "Tackle, Uncle Layton!"

Whitley laughed as she walked up and gave Taylor and Ava each a cupcake. "I can't believe Walker and Taylor are five. Time has just flown by."

I smiled as I looked around and nodded. "And Ava and Jase are just turning four. It's unreal."

Whitley let out a laugh. "You know what's unreal is both pregnancies, we were just weeks apart from each other."

I giggled and nodded my head. "That's because you and Layton didn't wait your full six weeks!"

Whitley turned and looked at me, mouth hanging open. "Excuse me. You had Ava a week after I had Jase. Who didn't wait her full six weeks? I wouldn't doubt that y'all were having sex a few days after Walker was born."

"Pesh. I wish, but Reed did make up for it in so many different ways," I said as I wiggled my eyebrows up and down.

"Please. Layton wrote the book on how to make me feel good and—"

"Girls, please. After all these years, you would think you'd remember when y'all are in public and not to talk about your sex life," Mimi said as she walked by and scooped up Ava before heading toward the swings.

"Me, too, Aunt Mimi! I want to swing, too! I get to go first! It's my birthday, y'all!" Taylor yelled out as she took off after Mimi and Ava.

I sat down and let out a sigh. "Y'all still talking about another one?" I asked as I looked over at Whitley.

She shook her head. "No. I think Taylor and Jase are enough. I mean, how lucky are we that we had a girl and a boy? I love our little family, and I am perfectly content with it just how it is." She glanced over at me and gave my shoulder a push. "What about you?"

"Nope. Reed already has an appointment to get the old balls snipped."

"Yuck. I didn't need that visual," Whitley said as she made a gagging sound.

We sat there in silence as we watched our little world playing out in front of us. Reed, Layton, and Kevin were playing tag football with the boys while Mimi, Melanie, Jen, and Kate played with the girls on the swings.

I couldn't help but notice how Kevin and Jen kept looking at each other. They had been dating for the last two years, and Jen didn't know it, but Kevin was going to pop the question tonight. I smiled, thinking about it and how happy Jen would finally be. We all knew Mike was the love of her life, and Kevin had spent a few years letting guilt get in his way of pursuing his best friend's girl. But when Layton had told him that Mike would want Jen to be with someone he had trusted and loved like a brother, Kevin had finally given in and asked Jen out.

"Hey, Whit?" I asked as I watched Reed running after Walker.

"Yeah, Court?"

"Did you ever imagine your life could be this happy?" I asked.

Reed happened to look up, and his eyes caught mine. I sucked in a breath of air and placed my hands on my stomach. He still had the power to make me feel like a teenager in love.

"Nope, not until the first time Layton made love to me. I think I knew in that moment that everything was going to be okay."

I nodded as I smiled at Reed.

He gave me that crooked smile of his and then mouthed, *I love you.*

I bit down on my lip and mouthed it back.

"What about you?" she asked.

We both turned and looked at each other.

"I would have to say it was the same for me. I knew the first time Reed made love to me."

We smiled at each other, and then I let out a giggle.

"You know what just hit me? Layton and Reed both made love to us for the first time in a shower!"

We both started laughing like little girls who had just shared a naughty secret.

"There ya go. That explains it all!" Whitley said.

As the day went on, Reed and I had exchanged looks multiple times, and each time, I had to fight the urge to touch myself to release the buildup between my legs.

I was cutting the birthday cake when I felt him walk up behind me. He wrapped his arms around me and began kissing my neck.

"Mmm…that feels good," I whispered.

He bit my earlobe, and it felt like a jolt of electricity was running through my body.

"I know what would feel better."

I turned my head and looked at him. "What?"

Reed looked all around and then motioned with his head toward the trees.

"The trees? What about them?"

He turned my body until I was facing him. He took the knife out of my hand and set it on the table. The next thing I knew, we were sneaking away from everyone. With the way our property went downhill, we were out of sight in no time flat.

Reed pushed me up against a tree and lifted up my white dress.

"Oh my God, Reed, what are you doing?" I asked in a hushed voice.

Reed handed me his cowboy hat, and he began unbuttoning his pants. He pushed them down, exposing his hard dick. I licked my lips as I looked back up into his eyes.

"I promised to fuck my wife at least once a week, and it dawned on me earlier…it's been a few weeks since she's had a good, hard fuck."

I gave him a wicked smile, dropped his hat, and reached for my panties. I pulled them off as Reed's smile spread wider across his face.

"Well, who am I to stand in the way of a promise?"

The End

If you or anyone you know has suffered from abuse, please contact

http://www.rainn.org/

or call the National Sexual Assault Hotline

1-800-656-HOPE (4673)

"That's it, baby. Breathe in and out," Layton whispered into my ear as he brushed back my hair.

I smiled and tried to do what he'd said, but it hurt so much. "Layton, I just need this baby out of me—like, right now."

Layton chuckled and said, "I know, Whit. Baby, it won't be much longer now. I love you so much, and you amaze me."

I turned and looked into Layton's eyes, and I felt an almost immediate release of pain. I had been pushing for a while now, and I was pretty sure this baby had decided today was not the day to make a grand appearance.

"Whitley, if you can give me one more good push, I think that will do it," Dr. Johnson said.

I nodded my head and weakly said, "Okay."

Dr. Johnson smiled. "Ready? Give me a good push, Whitley."

I somehow mustered up all the energy I had while I squeezed the hell out of Layton's hand as I sat up some and pushed with all my might. Right when I was about to give up, I felt an instant relief.

I collapsed back onto the bed as I heard the sounds of our baby fill the air. I looked up and saw Layton crying, and I began crying. When I turned and looked at our beautiful baby girl in Dr. Johnson's hands, I really began crying. Everything sounded muffled as I heard the doctor tell Layton to cut the cord. Dr. Johnson handed my baby girl to a nurse, who quickly took her over to a table and began cleaning her up.

"Whitley," Layton whispered in my ear.

I slowly pulled my eyes from the baby and looked at Layton. The tears running down his face caused me to fall in love with him even more, if that were even possible.

Layton smiled at me, and his blue eyes sparkled as he said, "Baby, that was the most amazing thing I've ever seen. I'm so proud of you, and at the same time, I'm in complete awe of you. I love you so much, Whitley. Thank you for making me the happiest man on earth."

I couldn't even talk. I was so lost in the moment that the only thing I could do was let out a sob as I said, "Layton."

He smiled as he bent down and gently kissed my lips.

"Mr. and Mrs. Morris, your baby girl is very eager to meet y'all," the nurse said as she walked up and handed Taylor to Layton.

I would never be able to describe the look of love on Layton's face. I tried to take in every second of it, so I would never forget it.

Layton sucked in a breath and said, "Taylor Elizabeth Morris, I will forever love you and protect you from all things…including boys."

I let out a giggle as I watched Layton inspect each of her fingers and then her toes. My heart was beating so hard and loud in my chest that I was sure everyone could hear it.

"You, little girl, have made me the happiest daddy ever," Layton said as he gently rocked our baby in his arms.

Oh Lord…

I wasn't sure how this man could do it, but he just kept proving to me that I could fall in love with him more and more.

Layton looked up at me as a nurse began sitting me up. "Time for your mommy to hold you, pumpkin."

I reached my arms out, and the moment Layton placed our daughter into my arms, something happened. I wasn't sure what it was, but I felt a warm sensation spread through my whole body. Then, she looked into my eyes, and I tried desperately not to cry harder.

"Hi, baby girl. Oh, how I've longed to see your beautiful face."

Our daughter held my eyes captive, and I had never in my life felt so at peace and so happy. Nothing would ever top this moment for the rest of my life.

Layton leaned down and kissed Taylor on the forehead before kissing me on the lips. He pulled back some and said, "I've never seen two more beautiful women in my entire life. I will always protect both of you and love you with all my heart. I will never let you down, I promise you. I love you, Whitley."

A sob escaped my mouth. "Layton, I love you so much. You could never let us down—ever."

Layton sat down on the bed and gently began tracing his finger down the side of Taylor's face. She slowly started closing her eyes as she drifted off to sleep.

I smiled at Layton as I asked, "Are you ready for this ride?"

He smiled back and let out a little chuckle. "I've never been so ready in my life."

I let out a sigh as I crawled back into the hospital bed. I smiled and shook my head as I thought back to the look on poor Reed's face when

Layton had declared that if Reed and Courtney had a son, he would never be allowed near Taylor.

Layton had walked Reed and Courtney out, and I was taking advantage of the peace and quiet for a few minutes. I reached for my purse and began looking for my bag that had all my hair bands in it.

A white paper caught my eye, and I reached for it and slowly pulled it out.

The letter.

I closed my eyes and began to open it up. I had read it over a year ago, and Layton had never once asked me what the letter said. I slowly took a deep breath and began reading the letter from Layton's father again.

Whitley,

I will never forget the look in your eyes as I talked about the little town of Llano, Texas. With the questions you asked and the way you took in every single word I said, I just knew there was something special about you. I could never put my finger on it, but I had this desire to tell you about Texas.

I look back now and realize it had nothing to do with me and everything to do with fate and Layton's mother. She brought me into your world, so I could help lead you to Layton. I don't believe in coincidences, Whitley. I believe with all my heart that you and Layton are meant to be together...to save each other.

I see the way my son looks at you, just like I see the way you look at him. The love you share reminds me of a great love I once knew. It was a love so powerful that I had to catch my breath anytime she walked into a room. I did anything to make her happy... and when I couldn't take away her pain, it destroyed my entire world.

My dream, Whitley, is for you and Layton to share a wonderful and long life together. I pray you have a son or a daughter who will bring you happiness like Layton and Mike brought me.

I just have one request. I know I have no right to even ask, but I'm going to anyway. Whitley, love him with your whole heart and soul. Let him know that he can't always protect you even though he so desperately wants to and that it is okay that he can't always protect you. He needs to know that, Whitley. Remind him that pain always makes you stronger. Every single day, remind him that he was and is loved—oh, how his mother and I loved him.

I thank God every day that he brought you into Layton's life. He couldn't have picked a more beautiful woman, inside and out, to love my son.

Thank you, Whitley. Thank you for saving my son. Knowing that Layton is happy and so very loved, all because of you, means the world to me.

Sincerely,
Jack

I folded the letter back up and stuck it into my bag. I took a deep breath as I closed my eyes and thanked God for all the blessings in my life. I opened my eyes and glanced over at Taylor, who was sleeping. I carefully got out of bed and walked over to her.

I looked down at my little angel. "Taylor, your daddy means so very much to me. I can't wait for all the memories you two will make together. He is such an amazing man." I smiled and wiped the tear off my cheek.

"He will love you with his whole heart and do anything to protect you, just like he does with me. As the two main girls in his life, our job is to love him back." I let out a giggle. "He is so easy to love, Taylor. Oh, your daddy…I fell head over heels in love with him the first time he opened his mouth and talked to me. He has a way of doing that."

I dropped my head back some and looked up. I closed my eyes and whispered, "I promise you, I will love him with my heart and soul always."

Layton's arms wrapped around me, and I felt his hot breath on my neck. "I love you, Whitley."

I turned around, and when I saw the tear rolling down his face, I sucked in a breath of air. "Layton, you are my entire world. I love you more than anything. I need you to know something though."

The smile on his face slightly faded. "Is everything okay?"

I smiled and placed my hand on the side of his face as I nodded. "It's never been better." I looked down and then back into his eyes. "Layton, I know that you would do anything to protect Taylor and me, but I need you to know that you can't protect us from everything. Just always know that the only thing we ever need from you is your love. Your love will get us through anything, Layton."

He closed his eyes and slowly nodded his head. When he opened his eyes, they were filled with tears. "I never want to lose you, Whitley—ever."

I reached up and pulled his lips to mine. I kissed him and poured as much love into the kiss as I possibly could. When I pulled back, I smiled and said, "We are going to live a beautiful, long life together, Layton, but sometimes, we will have to experience pain. Just always remember, the pain will make us stronger, and we will learn to fight even harder."

Layton's eyes widened as he took a step back from me. "What did you just say?" he whispered.

"Um…that we are going to have a beautiful life together?"

He shook his head. "About the pain."

I took a deep breath and said, "Life isn't always going to be happy times, but it will make us stronger. The pain we experience in life will always make us stronger."

Layton's face turned white, and he took a few steps back before he hit the bed and sat down. He dropped his face into his hands, and I stood there, frozen. My heart was slamming in my chest, and I was trying to figure out what I had just said that caused him to react the way he had.

I walked up to him, and he quickly wrapped his arms around me and pulled me to him. I began pushing my fingers through his hair as I just let him hold me. After almost five minutes, he pulled back some and stood up. He placed his finger on my chin until my eyes met his.

"The day my mother died, she told Mike and me that we always needed to remember that our pain would always make us stronger…that the pain and hurt we encountered in life would teach us a lesson and make us stronger."

I sucked in a breath, and it finally hit me.

Remind him that pain always makes you stronger.

Layton's father had told me to remind Layton of what his mother had said to him.

"Layton…the letter," I whispered.

He looked at me as he tilted his head.

I attempted to clear my throat. "Your father's letter to me…he told me to remind you that pain would always make you stronger, and it just…it just…I know why he told me that now."

Layton brought me in closer to him, and we both just held each other.

He pulled back and smiled at me. "Are you ready?"

I tilted my head and looked at him. "Am I ready for what?"

He threw his head back and laughed as he glanced back at Taylor. Then, he looked back into my eyes. "This crazy ride we are about to be on."

I giggled and said, "I've never been more ready for anything in my life, cowboy."

Layton placed both of his hands on my face, and right before he kissed me, he whispered, "You're the love of my life. Thank you for reminding me and for loving me."

I smiled and said, "I'll always love you, Layton. Our love will never be broken."

LOOK FOR

Walker AND Taylor's

STORY...

BROKEN promises

January 2015

I watched as Walker and Jase said good-bye to their friends as the last people from the party filed out of the barn. When Walker turned and smiled at me, my heart stopped beating.

I need to stop this and stop it right away.

He's your best friend, Taylor. Nothing more.

I smiled back and looked over toward Ava and her best friend, Cindy. I slowly glanced back over at Walker and Jase.

Walker had been my best friend since I could remember. Our parents were best friends, so we were always together. Family vacations, birthdays, holidays—whatever it was, and our families did it together. Walker had vowed at age six that he would always protect Ava and me. We were his whole world, and no one would ever hurt his sisters.

The problem was, Ava was his sister, and I was the best friend…who had been in love with him since he declared that first promise.

Jase let out a laugh and looked at me. "How do you think it went?"

I shook my head and said, "If Mom and Dad find out that you threw Walker and me a going-away party in their barn, they are going to be pissed."

Jase and Ava both started laughing.

"Please. I've heard all the stories of Uncle Layton's pontoon parties. One little barn party is nothing," Ava said.

Jase looked at Ava and winked. "A girl after my own heart."

Ava gave Jase the finger and turned to head out of the barn. "Cindy and I are heading home, Tay. See you in a few," she called over her shoulder.

Jase watched Ava walk out of the barn, and then he turned and laughed. "Good thing I have a girlfriend." He walked up and shook Walker's hand, and then he reached down and kissed me on the cheek. "Love you, sis," he whispered.

"Watch it. Ava is still my baby sister, Jase," Walker said.

Jase let out a laugh and walked out of the barn but not before saying, "I threw the party. Y'all clean up."

I stood up and called out, "Jase Morris! You better get your ass back in here right now and help clean all this up!"

Walker shook his head. "Come on. By the time you talk him into coming to help, we can have the whole place cleaned up."

As Walker and I began cleaning up the empty cups and trash, we talked about college. Walker was going to Texas A&M and majoring in biological and agricultural engineering. I was going to Baylor University and getting my degree in education. My dream was to be an elementary school teacher right here in Llano.

"Are you still thinking of minoring in horticulture?" I asked as I threw the last empty cup away. I wiped my sticky hands on my pants.

Jase had promised no alcohol, but I was pretty sure that some people had snuck some in, and the evidence was all over my hands.

Walker let out a chuckle. "I'm not sure. I think I'll be too busy with my major, and my dad really doesn't want me pushing it."

I walked over and rinsed off my hands in the sink at the end of the barn. I made my way over to a bunch of hay bales. I flopped down and let out a laugh. "I think you probably know just as much as the teachers anyway with what all you've learned from your dad."

He nodded his head. "Yeah. My main goal is to help my dad and Layton out on the ranch. I'm itching to get into the racehorse world, but my damn dad won't even let me go to any more races."

I threw my head back and laughed. As I pulled my knees up to my chest, I looked at Walker and shook my head. "You don't think it has anything to do with the fact that he caught you getting people to place bets on the horses, do you?"

Walker gave me that smile that had been melting my heart for years as he sat down next to me. I'd learned to cover up how I really felt about him, but he still did things to the pit of my stomach.

"Tay, can I ask you something?"

I shrugged my shoulders and said, "Of course you can. You never have to ask that."

He looked away and out the barn door. "Why haven't you ever dated anyone for very long?"

His question totally caught me off guard, and I dropped my legs and sat up as I cleared my throat. "Um…I don't know. I want to be with that one person who…who, um…"

Walker was still staring off in the distance as he said, "Makes your heart stop beating when the person walks into a room?" he barely said.

I just stared at him. "Yes."

"I want the type of love my parents have," Walker said with a smile as he slowly turned and looked into my eyes.

"Yeah…me, too," I whispered as I looked away. "What about you? Never found that one girl who makes your heart stop?" I asked as I bumped his shoulder with mine.

When he reached down and took my hand, I sucked in a breath of air and tried to contain the crazy feeling zipping through my body. I looked at him, and as our eyes met, something happened. Something changed between us, and my heart was slamming in my chest.

Walker stood, pulled me up, and brought me closer to his body. When he placed his finger on my chin, his eyes landed on my lips, and I fought to hold in the moan I so desperately wanted to let out. He slowly leaned down and brushed his lips against mine, and we shared our first kiss. It was slow…yet full of passion. Our tongues danced together, and we both let out a moan as Walker pulled me against his body.

When he pulled his lips away, he whispered, "Promise me something."

I swallowed hard and whispered back, "Anything."

Walker looked into my eyes and smiled. "Wait for me, Taylor."

I smiled. "Okay."

"Say it, Taylor," Walker said.

I tried desperately to ignore the feeling of him pressing himself into me. "I promise you, Walker, I'll wait for you."

THANK YOU

I have to thank God first. If he hadn't blessed me with the gift of storytelling, none of this would even be possible.

Darrin Elliott—You truly inspire me in more ways than you know. Thank you for loving me like you do. Thank you for putting up with what you do, and thank you for supporting me as I chase this dream of mine. I love you forever and always.

Lauren Elliott—Can I just say the older you get, the more fun it is getting? You are truly your father's daughter, and if you only knew how many things you inspire me to write about, you would probably just keep your mouth shut! I love you, and I am so proud of you. I'm also glad you got your "smart math" from your father.

Heather Davenport—Again, I have to say it…I would be lost without you. Your friendship means so very much to me. Thank you most of all for being real with me and for not being afraid to tell me when a scene sucks. You truly do rock, girl! Love you lots!

Kristin Mayer—The other Special K! What would I do without you? You keep me sane. You let me bitch when I need to bitch, and you make me laugh until I almost pee my pants at least once a day. I'm so glad we are friends, and I'm so glad you sent me that Bullshit button…oh, and my Magic 8-Ball!

Molly McAdams—I hope you know how it kills me to go more than one week apart for our lunches. Your friendship means the world to me, and I would be lost without you. You make me laugh…you make me GASP…you make me say WTF…and you make my heart feel happy! #PeasAndCarrots

Gary Taylor—Thank you for your never-ending support. Thank you for your songs, too. You and I are like kindred souls when it comes to songs. Don't ever stop sending them because they almost always inspire a scene. Your friendship means the world to me, and I love you like a brother.

Kathy Bankard—My quote fairy and so much more! I know how busy you are, so I can't thank you enough for all that you do for me. Most importantly, thank you for your friendship. It means more to me than you know!

Jovana Shirley—How you put up with me and my silly grammatical mistakes that I seem to keep making book after book, I'll never know, but thank God you do! You are the queen of editing and formatting. You turn my babies into something so wonderful, and for that, I can never thank you enough.

Jemma Scarry—You are an amazing friend, and I could never thank you enough for dropping everything when I send you a book to beta read. Thank you for not being afraid to say something is off or needs to be reworked. Your little notes make me laugh, and you would totally kick ass as an editor…just saying! I can't wait to see your face in July! Love you, girl!

JoJo Belle—I really wish you would just move to Texas already! Thank you, JoJo, for being such a wonderful friend. Thank you for reading my books when I send them to you and for giving me your honest feedback. I love the notes you leave for me while you are reading. They totally make my day. You make me laugh, girl, and I cannot wait to see you in July. I'm tackle-hugging your ass!

Nikki Sievert— I'm so glad Kristin gave me your name! I know we just met but I can't thank you enough for beta reading for me!

My Street Team (Kelly's Most Wanted)—Thank you for everything you do for me! I can't even begin to say what it means to me that you would take time out of your own busy worlds to spread the word about these books. I hope that I can continue to write stories that you fall in love with, including cowboys who melt your heart!

My HIPPA Girls—Fifty of the most amazing women ever. Most of y'all were on my original street team, and the fact that you stick with me blows my mind. Thank you for letting me bounce ideas off of y'all…for letting me vent…and for just being amazing friends. I'd be lost without you girls!

My Wanted and Broken Discussion boards—What can I say? Y'all make me laugh, you make cry, and you make me want to be a better author and person every day. Thank you so much for your support. You will never know what it means to me.

To All My Readers and Friends—None of this would be possible if it wasn't for y'all. Thank you so much for your support. Thank you for letting me share the stories in my head with you. Here is to many more to come!

PLAYLIST

"Ask Me" by Amy Grant—Epilogue

"Kiss Me Now" by Katie Armiger—Reed and Courtney realize that they are going to spend three weeks together.

"The Simple Life" by Drake White—Reed shows Courtney his house.

"Walking on Air" by Katy Perry—Reed and Courtney dancing at the club in Austin.

"Mine Would Be You" by Blake Shelton—Reed kisses Courtney for the first time.

"Everything Has Changed" by Taylor Swift and Ed Sheeran—Reed and Courtney's relationship changes after they kiss for the first time.

"Oops! I Did It Again" by Britney Spears—Courtney dances in the kitchen while making tacos.

"Told You So" by Cassadee Pope—Courtney's brother tells her that Noah is with him in Texas.

"Don't Let Me Be Lonely" by The Band Perry—Reed waits for Courtney after he makes dinner.

"Cyclone" by Baby Bash—Courtney decides to show Reed how she really feels about him by dancing with him.

"We Were Us" by Keith Urban—Reed and Courtney drive down the country roads late at night.

"Doin' What She Likes" by Blake Shelton—Reed does all the things that Courtney likes.

"We Both Know" by Colbie Caillat and Gavin DeGraw—Reed and Courtney make love for the first time.

"I'm Movin' On" by Rascal Flatts—Courtney lets go of her pain and hurt after she tells Reed about Noah.

"Echo" by Jason Walker—Reed holds Courtney after she tells him about Noah.

"I Wanna Make You Close Your Eyes" by Dierks Bentley—Reed tells Courtney that he wants to love her forever.

"Better Than I Used to Be" by Tim McGraw—Reed tells Courtney about his past.

"Beneath Your Beautiful" by Shaun Reynolds—Reed and Courtney make love after Reed tells Courtney about his past.

"Adore You" by Miley Cyrus—Reed and Courtney make love after they get engaged.

"Mean to Me" by Brett Eldredge—Reed and Courtney dance at the pontoon party.

"Who I Am" by Chris Young—Reed and Courtney decide to get married in Lake Tahoe after making love in Reed's truck.

"Good Times" by Cassadee Pope—Reed, Courtney, Layton, and Whitley are in Lake Tahoe.

"Down" by Jason Walker—Courtney runs away from Reed when she thinks he has changed his mind about marrying her.

"Thank You for Loving Me" by Bon Jovi—Reed talks to Courtney before she tells Whitley about Noah.

"Lift Me Up" by Christina Aguilera—Courtney is afraid to tell Reed that she is pregnant.

"Come Away with Me" by Norah Jones—On the night before their wedding, Reed makes love to Courtney after finding out that she is pregnant.

"God Gave Me You" by Blake Shelton—Reed and Courtney get married.

"Slow Down" by Selena Gomez—Courtney dances with Reed at the club and tries to turn him on.

"Cyclone" by Baby Bash—Courtney and Reed dance at the club in Lake Tahoe.

"If" by Janet Jackson—Reed makes love to Courtney in the club.

"Her Man" by Gary Allan—Reed takes Courtney home and shows her the tree house that he built.

"Survivor" by Destiny's Child—Courtney is with Noah in the library.

"You Hear a Song" by Cassadee Pop—After Courtney's run-in with Noah, Reed tells her how beautiful she is and how much he loves her as she looks at her reflection in the hotel mirror.

"She Will Be Free" by Josh Abbott Band—Reed and Courtney together on Christmas morning.

"Little Moments" by Brad Paisley—Reed and Courtney bring home Walker.

"Not Giving Up" by Amy Grant—Courtney tells Reed how strong and true their love is after Reed finds the framed dried flowers.

[1]

CPSIA information can be obtained at www.ICGtesting.com
Printed in the USA
LVOW12s1939070514

384806LV00017B/876/P

9 780991 309658